I0779083

HENRY J. PARKS
THE DARK MATTER

BOOK THREE

KYLLINGMARK

This is the third book in a three part series by authors Jeremiah and Della Kyllingmark

ISBN 978-0-9861070-1-6

Cover Illustration Copyright © 2014 by TW Studios

Cover design by Troy Worden.

Editing by Mary Harrington, Lori Kyllingmark, and Annetta Kyllingmark

CHAPTER 1

Parks and Della had escaped Barron's exploding shell but his bike was badly damaged. The explosion left two large gashes in the seat and the front headlight was ripped completely off. Yet, other than that, it was operational. With a few kicks it revved to life as Parks helped Della on.

"You two take care of yourselves," Doctor Flint admonished.

"Don't worry," Parks replied. "She'll be just fine, I'll see to that. Just remember in about nine months I'll be back for you."

The crystal Parks had taped on in place of the headlamp lit up the road like it was midday, at least to Parks, but no one else could see anything coming down the road. Yet, he still played it safe by taking the side streets and alleys, being careful to avoid Management checkpoints. He slowed up only once when he came upon a roadblock. He coasted by, watching the Cadets sitting in their vehicles, straining to hear where the sound was coming from. They must have thought it was carrying in from some other road because they didn't bother to pull out and give chase. It took them nearly forty-five minutes to reach the huge lot of warehouses set along the far edge of the city. He pulled off the main road and then followed the familiar path which led him to the special warehouse. It was black inside but the crystal provided all the illumination he needed.

"Where are we?" Della asked in the blackness as Parks shut off the bike.

"On our way to the Island and safety, there is a secret entrance below the floor."

He reached behind a steel beam and hit the controls. Instantly the floor began to rise and light streamed out, momentarily blinding them, as it flooded the warehouse. Parks climbed back aboard and drove down the ramp leading to the underground tunnel. The ramp closed tightly behind him and overhead lights came on ahead of them as they traveled along. The tunnel led out of the city and under the wilderness for a great distance. Della had only heard stories of this construction marvel but had never actually seen it herself. She admired the great effort it must have taken to build, yet, as they drove along, she couldn't help think what lay ahead.

Not the Island, but their lives.

They were always on the run and hiding. Never being able to relax and enjoy what most people take for granted. They had to struggle just to survive. Then the little life within stirred reminding her of what was really important. She snuggled in tightly and held on as the miles melted under their wheels.

Parks was careful to avoid bumps or anything that might jar Della even a little and before long the giant blast door guarding the entrance to the Island appeared. He expected to see it open as he approached assuming, the Colonel had observed his coming from one of the many closed circuit cameras lining the tunnel, but to his surprise, it didn't.

"Hello!" Parks shouted as he got off the bike, his voice echoing down the massive tunnel behind them. "I don't get it. They should know we're here by now. The Colonel watches these monitors like a hawk."

Parks checked the heavy walk door next to the main blast door. It was as solid as any you might find, with seals and heavy steel bracing. A small key pad sat next to the door as Parks searched his mind for the code. The Colonel had given it to him once but that seemed like eons ago. Parks studied it for a few moments. The ten number keypad was alphanumeric so the numbers corresponded to letters.

"DILIGENCE," Parks said suddenly.

"What are you talking about, Henry?" Della asked.

"345443623." Parks responded as he typed the number in. "DILIGENCE is the code."

There was a faint sound of motors activating as the heavy pins holding the door released. A whoosh of warm air hit Parks' face as the seals around the door released. He helped Della off the bike and then pushed it into the cavernous entrance of the facility known as the Island. The area was well lit and extended nearly out of sight in multiple directions. But what struck him this time was the silence. Every time he had been here before there were always people milling about performing various needed functions. Today, the area was empty, and the electric people mover that ran throughout the facility sat motionless in the center of the massive room.

"What's going on around here?" Parks asked himself as he walked around checking corridors for signs of life. "I would have expected a welcoming committee by now."

He proceeded down the ramp towards a familiar area where they had first met the Colonel nearly a year ago. It held the central hub of activity on the upper section consisting of a large dining facility, many offices and some living quarters. He pulled up to the tall doors guarding the entrance and parked. However, they only found a vacant hall. Then, they headed for the elevators and descended to the Colonel's office on a lower floor, yet, strangely, the doors opened to yet another empty floor.

"Where do you think everybody is?" Della asked trying not to sound nervous as they checked room after room.

"I can't imagine," Parks answered as they walked back to the elevator. "There's another floor below us where they keep the elderly and infirmed. We can look there."

The door shut and the elevator moved quietly down and opened again.

"What's going on here?" Parks demanded.

Greg let out a scream as Parks grabbed him by the arm. He was hurrying down the hall and hadn't noticed the elevator open or Parks and Della come off.

"Mr. P-P-Parks." Greg said in relief. "I-I-I didn't see you."

"Where is everybody?" Parks asked again.

"They've g-g-gone on a m-m-mission."

"What mission? Where have they gone?"

"I d-d-don't know exactly b-b-but I'm glad you're here. I've started t-t-to w-w-worry about them. M-m-maybe you can come down to the Colonel's office w-with me."

Greg led the way down the long hall to the Colonel's office where a large bank of closed circuit screens flickered on the wall.

"So that's why the door wasn't open for us." Parks said. "You're having technical difficulties."

"That's w-what I've been working on." Greg replied. "There w-was a problem with the m-m-main generator and we had to move everyone below."

"What about this mission you were talking about?"

"About a m-m-month ago two women appeared from a s-s-side tunnel. They w-w-were obviously not from our city and they were in a bad way. T-t-they looked like they hadn't eaten in a w-w-while and m-m-must have walked for miles."

"How did they get here and why did they come?"

"T-t-they said they drove a machine until it r-r-ran out of fuel. T-t-then they walked hoping to find help. Apparently, their city had b-b-been destroyed and t-t-they were desperate."

"The Colonel always wanted to know where the tunnels went but how could he help them? The only car he had was the one Jim left."

"S-s-somebody has been dropping vehicles off l-l-like the wilderness is a junk yard or something. The C-c-colonel has b-b-been bringing them in. Good rigs, too. There were lots of big t-t-trucks and s-such."

"Well, I guess I know where those came from. Management has been taking them from county folks and now we know what they were doing with them."

"T-t-the Colonel picked the b-b-best ones and a bunch of gas cans. M-m-many people volunteered to g-g-go with him and help but I thought t-t-they would be back by now. I'm getting w-w-worried."

"Can you show me which tunnel they went in?"

"S-s-sure," Greg answered. "J-j-just follow me to the upper floor."

"Are you going to be ok here without me?" Parks asked Della tenderly. "I might be gone a while."

"You go," Della answered firmly, "I'll be fine."

Parks hugged her tightly and kissed her on the cheek before following Greg to the elevator. Once they landed on the top floor, Greg showed him which tunnel the Colonel entered. Whatever this facility had been in the past, one thing was sure it was connected to places unknown.

"I'll be back as soon as possible," Parks said after refueling his bike. "Keep an eye on Della for me would you?"

"Y-y-you can c-count on m-m-me, sir," Greg replied.

Parks shook Greg's hand firmly and then was off and down the tunnel. He was amazed that it worked identically like the other one. Lights came on leading the way as he zoomed along and then turned off behind him. The only difference he noted was the temperature. The tunnel to the city was always warm but this one seemed much colder. He traveled for hours passing numerous smaller side tunnels. He knew not to take any of those as it was obvious you couldn't get large vehicles down them. Parks kept the accelerator wide open and at some point was doing more than a hundred and thirty miles an hour. The painted lines on the pavement were close to becoming one solid white line as he flew along. Suddenly, after driving a considerable distance further, the lights overhead stopped coming on and his makeshift crystal headlamp took over. Parks slowed as he began to see evidence of rubble and broken concrete scattered across the road. Soon the tunnel became narrower with even greater signs of damage and destruction. Finally, he arrived at another blast door like the one at the opposite end only this one was a mass of bent and twisted steel. Whatever happened here was not good. There had been a serious explosion or worse, as there was little remaining of what should have been another Island.

Parks drove as best he could around piles of debris and wires hanging from the ceiling on the inside of Island two. He checked around momentarily until he was satisfied there were no people living down below, then drove up a large ramp, bringing him to the surface.

This area was different from the barren wilderness he was used to. Large trees and thick brush filled the landscape. Parks stopped his bike and spent a few minutes scouting around on foot. It was clear whoever had his friends must have followed the only road out, if it could be called a road. All he saw was a nearly overgrown path leading into some dark woods, but at least his reconnaissance produced some tire tracks. This had to be the way they went. The dirt road continued for several miles until it stopped at a locked gate leading onto a paved road. It took little effort for Parks to slice through the lock with one of his crystal blades, but determining which way to go from here was a different matter.

He had two choices, left or right.

This time he chose left just because as many times as he had tried to be right of late he was wrong. It was an arbitrary decision but so what. He had to go one way or the other anyway. He followed the road for several miles before the landscape changed to a scattering of burned out houses and destroyed farms. It was clear that a devastating battle had been waged here. Destruction was everywhere. Soon the countryside turned to more heavily populated areas and the beginning of what was left of a city. Parks cruised slowly along, observing crumbling structures and desolation.

Finally, he pulled up and stopped in front of what looked to have been one of the city's main buildings. He parked his bike and walked up the stairs toward the main entrance, stepping over blocks of broken cement and brick along the way. The heavy wooden doors guarding the entrance looked out of sorts as they were hanging at odd angles, barely on their hinges. Parks pushed them out of the way and entered. Inside was no different than outside with nearly everything once defining the structure broken and strewn about. Everything was in chaos. Table, chairs, desks, lamps, chandeliers, and every other form of civilization once adorning the building was either destroyed or nearly so. Parks approached the front of the large room and noted the presence of dark red stains. Blood was splattered everywhere. Something horrendous had happened here, but why? Why such devastation and who was responsible?

Then the hair on the back of his neck stood up as he suddenly felt he was not alone. Parks slid his hand around the handle of a crystal blade and, in one smooth motion, pulled it from its sheath. He spun around bringing it to bear on who ever dared challenge him.

But no one was there.

"Maybe I'm getting jumpy," he thought as he scanned the darkened room. Then he spotted a figure moving in the shadows. "Show yourself or else!" Parks demanded.

"I mean you no harm," a small voice came from behind the safety of some rubble.

Then a small, young woman, no more than fourteen years old, stepped into a shaft of light coming through a crack in the ceiling. She was obviously scared and hungry. Her clothes were torn and dirty. Parks immediately returned his blade to its sheath.

"I won't hurt you," Parks said gently. "You just startled me is all. Look, I have some dried fruit with me." He said reaching into his pocket. "You're welcome to it."

The young woman studied the fruit like a wild rabbit would a carrot on a string. Parks laid it down on the top of a broken piece of concrete and stepped a safe distance away. The young girl came slowly through the rubble and grabbed the fruit, quickly devouring it.

"You don't have to worry," Parks said encouragingly. "I have more."

He pulled another handful from his coat and reached out towards her. This time she took it from his hand, but he could tell she was uneasy.

"Thank you, thank you for your generosity," the young teenager said as she swallowed the last bite. "It's been more than a few days since I've eaten."

"What happened here?" Parks asked as he squatted down and looked into her eyes.

"Everybody's dead," she said flatly.

"Why is that?"

"They were killed," the girl replied, retreating to a safe distance.

"What's your name?" Parks asked trying to put the girl at ease.

"My name is Joanna," she replied sensing he wasn't going to hurt her. "I can tell you what happened if you want, but I will have to start from the beginning."

"Please do. I need to know."

"When I was little, my dad used to tell me and my sister stories, old stories of a time when our city was destroyed. He said the stories were a warning to always be on guard against the darkness. Guard against a time when people would become different and start hating each other until only chaos and death remained. Then, so the stories said, a strange darkness would cover the city and destroy it too. My dad was very adamant and would tell us the story at least once a year so we would remember."

"My father used to tell me and my sister similar stories when we were little. Are you saying this actually happened?"

"Yes, and it was worse than the stories described," the girl answered hesitantly as she looked up at Parks. "It seems like only yesterday when everything changed. It started small with scattered reports from some local farmers. They claimed a wild beast was attacking their animals. It didn't seem like that big a deal at first but quickly became more serious. Soon whole farms

10

were being destroyed and people were afraid to even go outside. Food shortages started and then it got really bad. The city elders tried to calm everyone and catch the animal responsible but they couldn't."

The girl was obviously distressed and Parks felt horrible for her but there was still more to tell.

"You will probably think I'm crazy," she continued taking a deep breath, "but it's time I told someone. The strange beast was only the beginning. You might say it started the fire, a fire of anger and fighting that just wouldn't stop no matter how hard the city fathers tried. It seemed like trust just evaporated and people didn't seem to care anymore. There were riots in the streets and death everywhere. My father took us to the hills and hid me and my sister in a cave. Then he went back to try and see what he could do to stop the senseless violence and return peace to the city. I stayed in the cave as long as I could with my sister but then decided to see if I could find dad. I was almost to the outskirts when this deep feeling of fear came over me."

"Did you see something that frightened you?"

"No, it was more of a feeling, but it came as the sky suddenly turned dark, like a storm or something was approaching, only there were no clouds. I just started running and running."

"Did you see anything else, like solders, like a red army?"

"I was afraid to look back," she continued, "but I could hear them coming. They were chanting and the ground was shaking."

"Were you able to find your father?"

"No, it was like he just disappeared and a lot of other people with him."

"I'm so sorry to hear that," Parks said quietly as they stepped outside. "Is there anyone you know of that did make it?"

"There are a few. They're trying to rebuild the city but I thought they would have given up by now."

"I think some friends of mine may have come to help them," Parks replied.

"If they have, you need to be careful," the girl answered. "Their leader was young when the city was attacked and if she has taken control anything is possible."

"How do I find them?" Parks asked, looking around at the

level of devastation.

"Just follow the main street until you reach a large pile of rubble then turn right," she replied. "I told you all this but I don't even know your name?"

"You may call me Parks," he replied as they continued down the steps. "Do you stay here all by yourself? What about your sister? What happened to her?"

"I don't think about that and I've found it's safer to be alone."

"Look, after I've found my friends I'll come back for you. You can't stay out here alone forever. That's no life for a young girl. The place we come from has plenty of resources and friendly people. You would be more than welcome."

"That's very kind of you. You know there is one story my dad used to tell that I did like." She said as she pulled a long chain off from around her neck. "It was about a day when I would meet a man. He would be very kind and helpful but would need this. I'm not sure if you're that man or not but I can't see why I should keep it any longer."

She took what appeared to be a key of sorts off the chain and handed it to Parks. He examined it closely and instantly could tell it was old and probably very valuable.

"I can't take this," Parks protested. "It belongs to your family. It's part of your heritage"

"The story says the man who stands before the door will need this key." The girl answered. "It was a mystery to my dad and I never understood it either but, with all we've been through, I can't see why you shouldn't have it. You've shown kindness and have a good heart. If you are this man, you will need the key."

Parks smiled at the girl as he slid the key into one of the pockets on the inside of his coat.

"One more thing," Parks asked as he got onto his bike, "when was your city attacked? These ruins look like they've been here awhile."

"It's been more than ten years now," the young teenager replied. "But it seems much longer. Time passes slowly here."

"Ten years!" Parks mused as he reached down and turned the key just as a gust of wind rose and blew dust into his eyes. "But how is that right?" he said as he wiped his eyes. "You're no more than fourteen. You would have to be at least twenty something." His vision cleared and he looked over to hear her answer but there was no one there. "What the heck!" Parks exclaimed as he hopped off his bike.

He spent a few moments checking around the empty ruins for signs of her but there were none. The wind picked up again and blew dust devils that danced across the courtyard. Confused, Parks climbed back on his bike after taking one more, long look around. Then he pulled the key she had given him out of his pocket to confirm he hadn't dreamt the whole thing before heading in the direction she had given. Whatever lay ahead, Parks was sure things were not as they appeared.

CHAPTER 2

Philip rolled down the dusty road in his truck towards where his brother had parked the motor home. It had been a long journey but at least they succeeded in saving Rich. As soon as Philip parked, Lori and James assisted Rich Lindberg into the motor home. He was only skin and bones due to being slowly starved to death at the Western Economic Development District for not answering Management's questions. Once they got him comfortable, Lori immediately fixed him some nourishment.

After eating and sleeping for a few hours, Rich sat up and they were relieved to see a gleam of life return to his eyes.

"I can't thank you enough," he said sincerely. "I was beginning to think I would never see the outside world again."

"What happened?" Philip asked. "How could anyone do such a thing to you? You're one of the most respected people in the city and the city's only real engineer."

"Management happened," Rich responded evenly. "They knew I was once head of the city fathers and began a campaign to get rid of me. It started innocently enough, one day I hired a new secretary. She was smart and attractive and seemed quite capable. But I soon became suspicious when I caught her going through my private files. They were in a locked cabinet but somehow she managed to make a copy of my key. Of course I fired her on the spot but that just seemed to ignite things. The next thing I knew I was being hauled into the Citadel on sexual harassment charges. She was crying and claiming I groped her and made suggestive remarks. The next thing I knew, more charges were being filed, as people I had never seen before began to accuse me of even worse crimes. Then they had me evaluated by a psychologist who determined I should be committed to the WEDD for my own good."

"That's crazy," James said. "People know you, they know you would never do such things."

"That's just it," Rich replied. "The people behind this are willing to go to any length to get what they want."

"What do you mean?" Lori asked.

"Look at the facts," he responded. "I was once head of the biggest company in the city, a company my father founded, based on his father's work. We go back generations even to the beginning, just like your families. And it seems we're the people they fear most because we hold the secrets to the future."

"Then why didn't they just kill you?" Philip asked, "why all the security and torment?"

"They want to know something that I wouldn't tell them," Rich said. "Philip, do you remember in Mr. Beatty's science class when we had to learn those ancient symbols? You were there too, James."

"Yeah, I remember getting extra homework," James lamented. "We had to stay after school while everyone else went home."

"I remember those," Philip replied. "They were like another language or something and they seemed like children had drawn them. I never did quite catch on except the one that looked like a large bird with two heads. It was supposed to indicate safety and protection."

"Exactly," he answered becoming more energized by the minute. "Those symbols actually hold a secret, the secret to the power our city runs on and an even greater secret my dad shared only with me. That secret is hidden in a place no one but me knows, and not all their torturing could get me to reveal it."

"So, what you're saying is, this special information is safe, for now," James said.

"It is, but I'm sure they won't rest until they have me back."

"Well, what do we do?" Lori asked as she took a seat next to James.

"I've been thinking about that," Rich replied. "Philip, do you still have connections to the city fathers?"

"I think so but I've heard they've all been "retired," so to speak," Philip answered. "I'm also sure they're keeping a low profile especially after your disappearance. It would be nearly impossible to locate them."

"There's something we can do about that," Rich said confidently. "I've a method of communication Management is not aware of. There's a hidden vault built into the floor of my office where I've hidden a special radio."

"What kind of radio?" Lori asked.

"It's an old school CB," Rich replied. "People gave those up years ago but I maintained a network of key people just in case. So, if the city fathers are still alive, we'll be able to reach them. If only there was a way to get over there."

"Hmm," Philip pondered as he leaned back into his seat. "You know, maybe there is a way."

"What are you saying?" James asked, glancing around nervously. "You're not putting me into another wheelchair."

"Relax," Philip assured him. "That's not what this situation requires but we are going to need a diversion. Here's what I have in mind…"

Philip went on to explain his plan. It was bold and dangerous and, after considerable convincing, even James was on board.

Their next move would begin after midnight.

"I can't believe they put us on patrol down here again," the young Cadet moaned as they pulled onto one of the downtown streets.

"No kidding, especially with Parks still on the loose," the cadet's partner replied. "We should be out looking for him, not driving around these old buildings. Sometimes I just don't get General Allison. There's about as much activity down here as there is in the kiddy park."

"Hey, what was that?" the cadet said as he slammed on his brakes and pulled to the side of the street.

"I'm on it," the other cadet shouted as he grabbed his Nullifier and jumped out of the truck.

He quickly took off running down the sidewalk towards an alley surrounded by tall buildings as his partner did a quick U-turn. Suddenly, a bright flash of light shot from the alley just as he got there. Without slowing, he turned the light on the end of his Nullifier and raced down the alley.

Unfortunately, there was no way the large SUV would fit but it made a good road block. The driver sat there watching as his partner's light bounced from side to side illuminating the brick walls. Then a second flash of light blinded him followed by a loud boom.

"What is happening?" the driver exclaimed.

16

He blinked several times and rubbed his eyes to work out the giant white spot as he groped for his Nullifier before stumbling out of the truck and heading down the alley. He had gone only about twenty yards when he tripped over his partner who was sprawled on the concrete.

"Are you alright?" the cadet asked as knelt by his side.

"I think so. My ears are ringing and I still can't see much, just give me a hand," he replied as he started to stand. "What just happened?"

"From what I can tell, someone rigged an explosive device of some type. You must have hit a trip wire or something."

They worked their way back to their truck and then made a call to report the situation. In the meantime, Rich was leading Philip around the back of his old office building.

"Do you think your diversion worked?" Rich asked.

"I hope so," Philip answered, "but we had best be quick about it. I'm sure this place will be crawling with Cadets in a few minutes. Hey, how are we going to get in? This place is locked up tight."

"I'm not an engineer for nothing," Rich replied as he stopped along the back of the building. "But I'm going to need your help. I don't have my full strength back yet."

Rich pushed a brick in with his left hand and then a second with his right as a section of the brick wall opened inward slightly. Philip pushed it open enough for the two men to slide in before it closed tight behindly them.

"This way," Rich said as he clicked on his flashlight.

The two men followed a narrow path between a false wall and the exterior of the building before arriving at a tall metal ladder. Rich climbed to the top of the three story building and exited onto a narrow landing as Philip followed and then waited on the top rung.

"Good, it's empty," Rich said as he slid back a narrow panel and looked into the room.

He pulled a metal lever and the wall slid open revealing Rich's old office.

"We had best be quick," Philip said quietly. "There may be security on this floor."

"Help me move this," Rich said as he went to one end of

Lucy Lane's desk, "someone put a desk in my way."

The desk was large and heavy and it took both men working together on one end to move it enough to get at the vault. Rich squatted on the hardwood floor and pushed on one corner of a board which, in turn, lifted another. A few more carefully placed moves and a panel on the floor raised up revealing a safe with a combination dial. Rich opened it to reveal a stack of crisp twenty dollar bills, a pistol, some envelopes stuffed with papers, and a large hand held CB.

"Open the bag," Rich said as he began to pull everything out of the safe.

He stuffed the large canvas bag Philip had full before tucking the pistol into his waist band and slinging the radio around his neck.

"Come on, let's get out of here," Rich said quietly as he closed up the safe and slid back the floor boards.

Philip grabbed the corner of Lucy's desk while Rich took the other. Unfortunately, Rich was still weak from the months of malnutrition and lost his grip just as they nearly had the desk back in place. It dropped with a loud thud on the hardwood floor. The two men froze as the sound echoed through the room and out into the adjacent hall.

"I think someone heard us," Rich whispered.

There wasn't time to move the desk any further as the sound of keys could be heard in the lock. They quickly ducked behind the wall and barely managed to shut the secret panel when the door opened and a janitor flipped on the lights. Rich watched through the eye slit cut neatly into a picture frame as the man began checking the room. He looked behind the door and under the desk before shaking his head and turning off the lights. The two men breathed a sigh of relief as the janitor shut and locked the door.

"Man that was close!" Philip exclaimed as they exited the building the way they entered. "I thought we were goners there for a moment."

"We're not home free yet," Rich warned. "We still have to get across the street and into the park without getting caught."

They stayed in the shadows and worked their way between the buildings. Meanwhile, James was waiting in the municipal park down the street behind a maintenance shed. The streetlights littering both sides of the street meant crossing could expose them if their timing wasn't perfect. Philip had hoped Parks' flash bang explosives he took from the barn would keep any Management patrols busy long enough for them to make their escape but now he wasn't as sure.

"Come on," Philip said as he started across the street with Rich tightly on his heels.

They were only halfway across when a set of lights appeared several blocks away. In Rich's weakened state, he stumbled but Philip caught him before he fell. Philip was sure they were spotted as he helped Rich the rest of the way. All they could do was duck behind a large Oak tree as the headlights slowed to a stop.

"They've got us for sure now," Rich said. "Look, you run for the truck while I distract them. I'll just slow you down anyway. Here, take the bag and the radio." Rich continued as he pulled the pistol from his belt. "Go man, go!"

But Philip wasn't about to leave his friend even though the situation was dire. Just then a familiar voice spoke.

"Come on fellas," James said. "I can't park in the street all night. We need to get going."

"James, you big lug," Philip exclaimed as he helped Rich to the truck. "I thought I told you to wait for us in the park."

"Yeah, yeah, whatever," James responded as he turned down a side street. "I was getting bored so I thought I would park where I could see you two come out. Man those explosives you set were quite the thing. I bet they could be heard for miles. I even saw the flash from behind the maintenance shed."

"Check that out," Rich observed as they drove along one of the side streets overlooking the main road. "Looks like Management's sending out the cavalry. That place will be swarming in a few minutes."

They watched as a stream of emergency lights converged from all directions on the alley.

"Hey, turn off the lights," Philip ordered. "We don't need to draw attention to ourselves."

Fortunately, the moonlit sky was enough to allow James to make it back to the motor home safely without the use of headlights. Lori was anxiously waiting when they pulled in but a few minutes of explanation was all it took for her to feel better and it wasn't long before they were settled into their beds.

It had been an exhausting night.

"Hey, what was all the excitement about last night?" Lucy asked her assistant as she exited the elevator.

"Just some kids playing with fireworks from what I hear," the young man replied. "They blew up a garbage can or something a couple of blocks down the street. They're launching an investigation but you know how those things go, just a lot of showboating now."

Lucy unlocked her office and threw her briefcase onto the floor before settling into her chair. She was about to pick up her phone when she felt something wasn't right.

"Come in here," Lucy barked into her intercom. "Who moved my desk?" She demanded as her assistant arrived.

"I don't know," he replied, "probably janitorial. They clean at night and must have needed to move it."

"They never have before," Lucy said as she got up and walked around to the front. "See, there're marks where the legs have been since the day I moved in. They always wax around it but never moved it. And, what's this." She said bending down to examine the corner of a piece of paper sticking between the floor boards.

Lucy tugged on the paper and out slid a twenty dollar bill.

"That's one way to make money," her assistant joked, "but, how did it get in there?"

"That's a very good question and I'm going to find out right now," Lucy said as she returned to her phone. "General, I need a crew sent up to my office as soon as possible. I believe the incident down here last night may not have had anything to do with juveniles. In fact, we may have a situation here."

Lucy sat back in her chair as she pondered the twenty dollar bill she was holding. Obviously, this was no coincidence. Rich escaped the WEDD and now his old office had been compromised. Something was going on and she was going to get to the bottom of it.

That same morning, Rich was up early and starting to look a little more like his old self. A few of Lori's good home cooked meals had done wonders. He was sitting on the bench outside when Philip found him talking to someone on the CB radio.

"What's going on?" Philip asked.

"Management's watching," Rich replied. "Do you remember Jerry Jefferies?"

"You mean "JJ" the wealthy diamond mine owner?" Philip asked.

"The same," Rich answered as he turned off the CB and set it on the table. "JJ is the only city father who successfully resisted since the day they got here in spite of the fact Management has done everything possible to take over his business. However, with his private militia, he's been able to keep them at bay. In addition, when the city surrendered, JJ was able to work out a deal with them. He agreed to give Management half of his holdings and control of his part of the city in exchange for allowing him to keep his diamond mine and mining operations. I guess they must have been in a reasoning mood back then because he got away with it. However, that doesn't mean they haven't done everything in their power to stop him since. Yet, JJ's a tough old bird but now he says things are different. According to his sources, Management is preparing for something much bigger. They're about to move on the city and he doesn't think even his defenses will hold up for long."

"What does 'move on the city' mean?" Philip asked feeling desperation beginning to set in.

"I think we're talking about 'round two'" Rich responded. "The first time we surrendered and negotiated but it looks like all we bought was time. This can only mean whatever they came looking for must be within their grasp."

"What? I thought they got what they wanted," James said. "They took over the city didn't they?"

"I wish it was that simple," Rich replied. "No, I'm afraid they came for something more. If you remember the line from the old story,"

'Darkness sweeps over the land and takes with it the light of man.'

"I never really understood that phrase until I was visited one day in that place you guys pulled me out of by one of the board of directors. It was strange, a strange encounter, to say the least, because he only asked questions about my family heritage and why my ancestors rebuilt the city. I told him a few things from the ancient stories but he seemed most interested in what drove them and how they found the strength and determination for such a task. I said there's always hope in the human heart for a better future. Then he did the weirdest thing. He just looked at me for a moment in an odd sort of way, smiled and then laughed the most hideous laugh I've ever heard. I can honestly say I've never felt a presence like that before. It was as if all the light in the room was sucked out."

CHAPTER 3

Dave was fuming as he followed the long sidewalk to his house. Parks had escaped again and knowing now he was the one he needed to focus on was of little use. He entered his library where his hapless servant was still bound and gagged.

"You weren't much help," Dave said as he picked the large man off the floor with one hand. "Normally, I would fire you or worse, dispose of you."

The man's eyes were wide open and bulging as sweat began to form on his brow. He knew Dave the President could be quite ruthless but he had never faced him when he was angry. The man's feet dangled above the floor as Dave considered his options. Then he gently set the man down as something caught his eye.

"What's this?" Dave asked as he lifted one of his overturned bookcases and steadied it against the wall.

He moved a pile of books off a glowing red crystal blade.

"Isn't this interesting," he said as he picked up the blade. "Parks must have dropped it in the struggle. I've never seen anything quite so lovely in my life. Maybe my encounter with Parks wasn't a waste of time after all."

Dave admired his reflection in the brightly glowing blade and stood there transfixed for a few moments. Then he began feeling a power surging through his body as he turned towards his servant who was leaning against a bookcase trying to work free of his bonds. As Dave moved closer to him, the man stopped struggling and his eyes filled with fear. He swallowed hard as Dave held the blade to his throat.

"I had considered granting leniency for your failure," Dave said with a sneer. "But, as you well know, there's no room for weakness in our business."

With that statement, Dave reached up and removed the gag from his mouth.

"You know I've always served you faithfully, sir," the man pleaded in a deep voice. "Parks jumped me when I went out to wash your limousine. He took my suit off and tied me up. There was nothing I could do to stop him."

"Yeah, yeah, yeah, excuses, excuses," Dave said as he

spun around the room admiring the red blade. "But, what worries me most," Dave continued, "is you know about this crystal. The Board provided you as my personal security guard and that makes me wonder. Are you really loyal to me or are you more loyal to the Board?"

"I always considered those to be one and the same thing," the man replied.

"Well, they're not," Dave snapped.

"Sir, I have a family and you know I'll do whatever you say. My loyalty is with you and you alone."

Dave looked up into the big man's face with a smile but the blade had already done its work. Still, to Dave's amazement, the man didn't fall dead as expected rather he just slowly dissipated in a wisp of black smoke.

"What!" Dave exclaimed. "I should have known the Board would put a spy in my midst. That means they've been watching my every move and, if they don't already know, they'll soon find out about this thing and Parks. But, then again," Dave pondered, "maybe that isn't such a bad thing. They're after one thing and only one, they must have the Gifts. Well, at least without him they won't be tracking me for a while, so I can do a little more searching on my own. The next time we have a board meeting, won't they be surprised when I show up with this blade."

Dave was angry and felt betrayed but he was equally determined to get out in front and do whatever it took to secure the Gifts for himself. Yet, that was not going to be an easy task. As of yet, no one really knew exactly what they were or where to find them. But he was certain Parks had at least one if not more and he was equally confident Parks didn't know what he had. Dave would have to play this smart if he was to succeed. That's when he decided to make another visit to the Mystic.

"Come in," the old woman said as Dave knocked on the black painted door. "I've been expecting you," she continued as she sat in a creaking rocking chair next to a stone fireplace.

"I've come for more information," Dave said as his eyes adjusted to the dim candlelight. "What have you got for me now?"

"Twenty five dollars please," the Mystic said as she opened an old carved wood box sitting next to her on a small white marble table.

"Skip that," Dave replied as he sat down. "What I have for you is worth way more than a few paltry dollars if you can tell me what I want to know."

"More of these?" the woman asked as she pulled the small red crystal Dave gave her on his last visit from the box.

"Yes, more of those," Dave answered impatiently.

The old woman shut the box and leaned back in her rocking chair. Even though the summer skies were blue and the temperatures in the mid-eighties, the house felt cold, in spite of the crackling fire that, once in a while, threw sparks into the room. The flames danced on Dave's face as he studied the woman closely. She sat silently for a while with her eyes closed and her hands tucked under her chin. Dave was becoming increasingly agitated and about to explode when the woman spoke.

"You want to know where the Gifts are and who has them, or at least some of them. I watched you when you left here last and you suspect someone. You think Parks has them and you want to know how to find him. Why is that so important to you?"

"You're right," Dave replied. "It is Parks. But don't ask me stupid questions. What's important to me, and to you, is that I find him. Can you help me with that or not?"

"I can, to a point," the woman replied. "Parks has been seeking something but it's not the Gifts that you are so concerned with and maybe that's the very reason he's been able to find them. They're hidden in places no one would suspect. Some are out in the open but you would never think to look there. Others have been placed in hiding by people who feared and respected their power. I can see many things but I cannot tell you where to look."

"Then you're of no value," Dave said as his face twisted with anger.

"Don't be so sure," the old woman replied. "There are other things I can tell you, things that may lead you to him."

Dave swallowed his anger for a moment as he crossed his legs and leaned back. He was not one for patience but he had come this far and would give 'The Mystic' a few more moments before deciding her fate.

"You see, Mr. Henry J. Parks is an anomaly, of sorts, not

your ordinary soul," she continued unaware or unafraid of the danger she was in. "All people live with emotions, some good, some bad, but mostly just average. But, Mr. Parks is different somehow. His emotions are linked to his seeking, which makes him hard to read and find. I must also warn you that finding him may not be so profitable for you."

"Let me be the judge of that," Dave snapped. "Can you tell me where he's at or not?"

"Yes and no," the woman replied.

"Well, what is it, yes or no?" Dave continued become increasingly agitated and impatient.

"You'll find him where you don't expect him to be," the woman said slowly, "because he's driven by something, something I've not seen before. He wants to know how certain things 'work' if you will and is seeking information. But he's not so unlike you in that regard. Yet, the only thing I see is a place. It's isolated there and he feels safe."

"Is it his parent's house? Barron burned it to the ground but he might have gone back there anyway."

"It's not his parent's house nor is it in the city," the woman replied. "I see it connected to other places through tunnels reaching in all directions."

"That's it?" Dave nearly exploded. "That's what you see, tunnels? Come on, you've got to do better than that."

"That's all I see," the woman replied as she began slowly rocking.

Dave sat there for a few moments, staring into the fire.

"Ok," he said finally. "But I expect you to keep looking for me. The Gifts are my main focus and I'll be returning here again for more information. You find me something I can use and there'll be more of these in your future."

Dave pulled a leather bag from his coat, opened the drawstring, and poured a small pile of bright red crystals on the table.

"Just be aware," the old lady said as Dave was about to leave. "What you're intending may lead to an unexpected end, an end you won't like. I suggest you forget Parks and focus on other things before you turn to mist."

Dave gave the old lady a sneer before exiting to his car. He could care less of the woman's dark prediction. His goals were clear and he was focused. If things were going to turn out badly for anyone, it was going to be Parks. Of that, he was certain.

However, the more immediate problem he faced was the Board. He was now sure they'd been monitoring his movements, but that was ok since they couldn't know what he was thinking. He would continue to work behind the scenes until he got the break he needed. And, maybe the weird "tunnel" vision the old woman had meant something after all. All he needed to do was keep the pressure on and that's when he decided to make an unexpected move.

"Mr. President!" General Allison said as she nearly jumped out of her chair. "I didn't know you were coming."

"Relax, General," Dave said. "I just came to talk. I need some information. You remember the kid you captured, the one that escaped. What more can you tell me about him. Is there anything that wasn't in your report?"

"I believe I pretty much covered it all. He seemed ordinary enough, except when he suddenly changed into this super powered guy and ripped the place apart."

"Maybe you missed something," Dave pressed, "just a small detail. Think hard about it."

"Well, I was about to plant a crystal in his chest." General Allison continued. "Dad said it was the one thing no one can resist. The red crystals take over their body and then their minds but before I could slip it into the tube he broke free."

"Are you sure that's all?" Dave asked intently.

"All except the color."

"The color?"

"Yeah, he turned bright blue," General Allison replied, "as he smashed through the door and disappeared. It was like he was on fire or something."

"Interesting, come by my office later this week. I want to go over a few new things with you."

Dave left General Allison and headed to his car, his mind burning.

"Blast it all, this isn't going to be as easy as I hoped," Dave thought to himself. "Parks has been distributing his crystals to these young people, very smart of him, indeed. Well, maybe I have to go back to the playbook and start over. Get out the map and start positioning the Testers. Yeah, that's it, I'll put the pressure on where Parks will feel it the most and then see what happens."

Dave smiled broadly as he turned into the main complex. The old woman's warnings seemed less worrisome as he walked briskly to his office.

CHAPTER 4

The guys went with Joshua to his Parents' home to spend the night. His house was large and ornate as his father was the general manager for the city's largest construction company. Josh's mom welcomed them with hugs and a warm 'hello.' Her first concern was to make sure they were fed. She was well prepared with several large pizzas sitting on the kitchen counter.

"You boys dig in," Joshua's mom said encouragingly. "I'll have your beds turned down in a few minutes."

"What's been going on?" His dad asked. "You guys look worried."

"We don't know too much," David replied. "But what we do know is there are Testers running around out there and Management is up to something. We're contacting as many people as we can letting them know to pass the word. It's time to bear arms and be ready."

"I was afraid it was coming to that," Josh's dad said soberly. "The Management people I deal with seem very nervous of late and they've cancelled several projects for no good reason. I've been cautiously asking around but nobody's talking. Now I know why."

"Your rooms are ready," His mom said brightly as she came back into the kitchen.

"Thanks Mom. We'll talk more about this in the morning, Dad."

They thanked Joshua's parents and headed to their respective rooms. Once they finished brushing their teeth, they all gathered in the large recreational room next to the pool. They needed some time to unwind and digest everything they'd been through. To get things going, David challenged Normand to a game of table tennis drawing everyone's attention except Josh, who had climbed to the 'crow's nest,' as he liked to call it. It was an observatory his father built above the house. It was surrounded by glass on every side.

The sky was clear, except for a few light clouds, as he looked through the large telescope at the stars. He quickly became bored and started scanning the city instead.

"Guys, GUYS!" Joshua nearly shouted. "You need to see

this.”

“What’s going on?” David asked as he joined him.

“Take a look over there,” Josh said anxiously.

“I don’t see anything,” David responded as he put his eye to the lens.

“Look over by where the section of wall was replaced by a gate.”

“All I see is blackness,” David answered. “What am I supposed to be seeing?” Just then the thin cloud momentarily dimming the moonlight, moved out of the way and David gasped. “Those look like Testers.”

“Testers,” Normand said as he joined his friends. “What are you saying?”

“See for yourself,” David replied as he stepped away. “The gate is open and they’re flooding in.”

Everyone took a turn watching as compact red warriors flowed into the lower region. This was the first place the Testers broke through the wall and the city was defenseless to stop them. If it hadn’t been for the city father’s quick surrender, all would have been destroyed. Since then, Management built a gate in the broken wall and now that’s where they were entering.

“What are we going to do?” Isaac asked anxiously. “Those guys are killers and now they’re inside the city.”

“We’ve got to warn the people somehow,” Troy said. “I know what we can do. We’ll get in touch with Jim. He can broadcast a warning or something.”

“We can’t do that,” David replied. “We don’t know where he is. All we know is we’re to meet him tomorrow night at the school, remember? He could be hiding anywhere and we have no way to contact him.”

“Well, we’ve got to do something,” Isaac said. “David, your parents are safely out of the city but my mom and dad live near where they’re assembling. I’m going down and try to get them out before it’s too late.”

“He’s right,” Normand said. “My parents live closer this way but it looks like they have enough Testers to do just about anything. They’ll march through the city in no time.”

“Ok, I’ve got an idea,” David said as he got out of his night shirt and put his clothes back on. “There’s a warehouse down there with an escape tunnel under it. If we can get your families in without being spotted, we can get them out of the city and to safety."

"What about everybody else?" Troy asked. "What happens to them?"

"I don't know," David answered, "all we can do is get people out the best we can. If there's someone you want to come along, go get them now. Just be careful about it. If we draw attention to ourselves and get caught, no one will be going anywhere."

They knew David was right. It was nearly three AM as they climbed into Normand's truck. Josh woke his parents and explained the situation before they left.

"I'm stopping by Kenzie's apartment to warn the girls," Normand said as he pulled onto the street.

The night was clear and the city streets deserted as they made their way along. There wasn't much to talk about as a heavy feeling of despair settled over their minds. This was like a dream, no nightmare, from the past. Bringing Testers in could only mean disaster. They'd traveled only several dozen blocks when a set of headlights settled in behind them.

"Who's following us?" Josh asked anxiously as he tried to see past the bright lights.

"I can't tell," Normand replied. "Maybe it's someone coming home late."

"No such luck!" David exclaimed as the truck behind them turned on flashing lights.

It was clearly a security vehicle.

"What should I do?" Normand asked.

"Unless you think you can outrun him," David replied, "you're going to have to pull over."

Normand thought about it for a few seconds and then put on his signal light and pulled to the curb.

"You guys sit tight and let me do the talking," Normand said as he rolled down his window.

Several Cadets got out of their vehicle and approached the truck. One came around to Normand's window while the other stood at the back.

"Identification cards," the Cadet commanded.

"Sure," Normand responded as they all passed their cards to Normand who handed them over.

"What are you guys doing out so late tonight?" the Cadet continued as he looked over their identification. The other Cadet was walking around the truck shining his flashlight on their faces as they sat perfectly still and stared straight ahead.

"We were at a party," Normand answered calmly.

"Where was this party?" the Cadet continued, momentarily blinding Normand with his flashlight.

"It was at a friend's house," Normand lied as he covered his eyes with his hand.

The Cadet looked up at his partner who had finished examining the boys through the side windows and repositioned himself at the rear of the truck.

"Please hand me the keys and step out of the vehicle," the Cadet commanded as he took a step back.

"What's the problem?" Normand protested.

"I need you to step out of the vehicle," the Cadet said more forcefully as he put his hand on his Nullifier.

"Fine," Normand said flatly as he shot a worried look at David. "But I would like to know what this's all about," he continued as he handed off his keys and opened his door. "We haven't been drinking or anything."

"The rest of you need to get out as well and join your friend," the Cadet said as his partner waived Normand over to the front of their SUV.

The guys piled out and did as instructed. Then Normand watched in horror as the Cadet began searching his truck. He knew it wouldn't take long for him to find the crystal blade he kept tucked under his seat. He was getting more nervous by the second and had to do something.

"Hey!" Normand exclaimed, stepping out of line. "My parents are well known around here. I can get you guys in a lot of trouble for…"

Normand's sentence was cut short as the Cadet watching them hit him in the stomach with the butt end of his Nullifier.

He doubled over and hit the pavement with a thud. Without even thinking, Josh clubbed the Cadet in the chest with his forearm, knocking him against the tailgate, and away from Normand. He was about to help Normand to his feet when a bright flash of light blinded them all. The source of the blast was the business end of a Nullifier resting on the top of Normand's truck and aimed directly at Joshua. The Cadet searching the truck had seen his partner hit through the rear window and had stepped up on the running board. The blast sent Josh flying through the air and into the grassy ditch nearby. David reacted first by pulling a crystal blade from a pocket inside his coat and threw it with deadly accuracy. It hit the Cadet that shot Josh squarely in the chest. The blade entered to the handle without even cutting the Cadet's uniform or breaking his skin. But, inside his body, the blade had done its work, severing the artery to his heart. He fell backwards off the truck and onto the blacktop as his partner attempted to wheel around with his Nullifier. But Isaac was quicker and ripped the weapon from his hand and, in one smooth move, spun around and crushed his skull with the butt end.

Troy and Burke dove into the ditch to rescue Josh but the blast from the Nullifier had gone completely through his chest leaving a hole the size of a softball and he wasn't moving. There was no blood, only the stench of cauterized flesh.

"Josh! Josh! Can you hear me?" Troy shouted as he knelt beside him in the wet grass.

But Joshua didn't respond or move. He just stared blankly at the star lit sky.

"They killed him," Burke said numbly as he looked into Troy's eyes. "They really killed him."

Burke held Josh's head then slipped his arms under his shoulders as Troy grabbed his legs. They gently lifted him out of the ditch. They were quickly joined by their friends, who helped lay him on the bed of Normand's truck. They were in a state of shock as they stood there silently staring at him as if they expected him to sit up and say something.

"We've got to get out of here," Isaac said finally, breaking the silence. "Somebody is surely coming. I heard one of those guys talking on his radio and reporting us."

"Wait a minute!" David exclaimed as he stooped down to examine the man Isaac killed. "I know this guy."

"I didn't mean to kill him," Isaac said as he knelt next to David. "But I had to stop him. I think he would have killed us all with that weapon of his."

"I know," David said reassuringly. "I didn't mean to kill his partner either. It just happened. We were only protecting each other."

"You said you knew him. Who is he?" Isaac asked.

"He's a guy I knew from school. He was a few years behind me but his sister was in my class." David answered as they rolled his body out from under Normand's truck where he had fallen.

"He was our second baseman," Troy said from behind. "We played all through school. He must have recognized me. Why didn't he say something?"

"It's what Parks warned me about," David replied earnestly. "He said the BOJ order was not the same anymore and that they were training Cadets to be killers. Now we have firsthand experience and its cost the lives of three people."

"Are you going to be ok?" Troy asked David. "Do you think you'll get crystal sickness like I did when I killed those Testers?"

"I don't know," David replied more concerned about the situation than the risk to himself. "We must to do something about this fast. We can't just leave their bodies on the road and we have to get Joshua out of here, to his family."

They turned off the flashing lights from the Management vehicle and pulled it off the road before putting the two Cadets inside. They left them propped up with seat belts holding them in place and hoping no one would find them for a while. Then they wrapped Joshua in a blanket Normand had stashed under one of his seats and headed towards Dr. Flint's place. It was the only logical option. The Testers would just have to wait. However, deep feelings of sadness welled up inside each young man as they drove away. Joshua had been a close friend, no, a brother, to them and losing him was beyond anything they could have imagined.

Normand was taking it the hardest, second guessing his decision to pull over instead of trying to outrun them. They may have had a better chance if he had and Joshua might still be alive. But the circumstances were what they were and there was no way to change anything now. No, what was most apparent was the danger they faced from people who should have been their friends, people who now seemed to have changed, changed into ruthless killers. Were the old stories of hatred and death really just stories or were they beginning to see the past repeat itself and the ancient story come alive?

CHAPTER 5

"You're really starting to like this 'cloak-n-dagger' stuff aren't you?" Philip asked as they rounded a sharp bend heading back into the city.

"That's not the word I had in mind," James replied with a half-smile. "More like 'survival' if you really want to know. Since I met up with you, I've been interned in the Western Economic Development District for a week, pushed around in wheelchairs, chased by who knows who, and had to save your butt at least twice."

"Whoa there big fella. I seem to remember saving you from that nasty place. Not to mention, I'm the one who drove us out of there without getting caught, remember."

James was about to reply when Rich interrupted.

"You're going to need to take the next right," Rich instructed. "According to JJ's instructions, we have to go around the old warehouse district and then follow the road towards Grace Mountain."

"That's over by where my old farm used to be," Philip replied. "But I don't remember any meeting places around there. It's all trees, rocks, and a steep climb on foot."

"JJ said to follow the road until it becomes gravel and then for another three miles until you come to a grove of giant cedar trees," Rich continued. "He said it will all be clear at that point."

Philip knew this area well and couldn't help remembering the fateful day he led Henry and Kirsten up the mountain in search of what he thought was a bear. Little did he know his son was going to be attacked and nearly killed by the Zender. The thought of something so horrible happening still plagued him even after all these years. In fact, this would be the first time since the episode he had set foot on the mountain.

"There's a good spot," Rich said as they pulled into the cedar grove.

"Now what," James asked as they piled out under a bright star filled sky.

"I really don't know," Rich replied. "All JJ said was to find the large cedar grove and everything would make sense."

James lumbered around the back of the truck while Rich and Philip tried to make sense out of JJ's instructions. They stood there for a moment before deciding to take off in different directions to see if they could find something. They had only gone a hundred yards or so when they heard James yell.

"Hey, guys! There's a path back here."

Rich and Philip joined him behind a large tree where a narrow path entered into the brush.

"Looks more like a deer trail than anything," Philip said as he focused his flashlight.

"It won't hurt to see where it goes," James said as he pushed back a tree limb and started in.

Philip made his way past James and took the lead through the dense underbrush, working his way up the mountain.

"I wish I had known we were going to be hiking," Philip said, "I would have worn my boots."

After fighting their way at least a mile in, the trail finally dead ended at a large boulder near the base of a sheer rock face.

"I give up," James said as he sat on a nearby log. "We claw our way through the brush in the dark, to end up here. You must have taken a wrong turn or there's another tree somewhere else."

"Wait a minute," Rich said as he examined the rock. "Do you guys see what I see?"

They focused on the spot on the ground where Rich was training his flashlight.

"I see what you mean," Philip replied.

"What? What do you see?" James asked anxiously.

"I'll show you," Rich said as he handed James his flashlight.

Rich felt around the side of the boulder and then there was a click. Suddenly, the boulder swung around and opened to a well-lit cave.

"That rock is perfectly balanced," Philip said as he followed Rich into the cave. "Whoever designed that must have understood physics."

Once the three men were inside, the rock swung shut, sealing them in. They followed the narrow cave as it wound through the mountain. It went up for quite a distance before leveling off. They no longer needed their flashlights as they were in what appeared to be an old mine shaft that was well lit by electric bulbs strung on a thin wire. Finally, the shaft opened into a large cavernous room filled with people they immediately recognized.

"Well, I thought you'd never make it," JJ said as he got up from his chair.

"This is quite the place you have here," Rich replied as he glanced up at the high ceiling. "And I really like your front door."

"This was once my family's most productive diamond mine," JJ replied. "When I was a boy, I helped my father and grandfather chisel diamonds out of the rocks. They even designed the mine with some specialties like that rock door you came through. You may know, I was always wary of those scary stories we were taught. They seemed a little too convincing to just be stories. So, once I got old enough and inherited the mine I expanded it by adding some additional storage which really came in handy when Management took over. I was able to put nearly all my raw diamonds in here and a lot of other important things too, including quite an arsenal as you'll soon see, but plenty of time for that later. You must recognize everyone here."

Indeed the men did recognize the city fathers and went around shaking hands before getting down to business.

"Thank you all for coming," Rich said as he took a seat around a large wooden table.

"It's good to see you again," Tim said. "We've heard stories of some bad things. Are you doing ok?"

"Well, I spent more than a few days under their loving care," Rich replied. "They were looking for information but didn't get any from me. But that's not why we're here. We came to discuss something you may already be aware of. Testers have been spotted near the city walls."

"You can't be serious," JJ replied, "I haven't heard anything like that. Testers, are you sure?"

"Yes and I'm more than serious," Rich continued. "Management is preparing for something and I'm sure it's not going to be good."

"My son thinks they may already be euthanizing people and my brother, here, says they're enticing people in from the county," Philip said. "Could it be they're stopping resistance before it starts by eliminating as many people as possible? It's a scary thought."

"I've heard something about that," Tim interjected. Tim was an old time lawyer who worked with HOT News and Jim Banner for years. "Just rumors, mind you but what if you're right? This could signal even worse things to come. Hey, is it true your son singlehandedly wiped out the Citadel. Last I heard he was working with Management."

"That's a long story," Philip replied. "Let's just say, his eyes have been opened and he's doing everything he can to make the city safe again, but he needs our help."

"We want to help but all we have to go on right now are rumors," Tim continued. "What we need is hard evidence to mount a public resistance."

"Rumors or not," JJ interjected, "we have to be prepared for the worst. That's why I was so glad to hear your voice again, Rich. I knew with you around we would have a chance of driving Management out."

"Thank you for hearing us," Philip replied. "You've proved coming here was the right move. You see, our first order of business was to meet with you remaining members of the city fathers and then, with your help, formulate a plan to free the city. We have some ideas and believe we should start by arming citizens as much as possible. You know Management confiscated all firearms when they arrived but I hid some and so did a lot of other people. Moreover, if you have stockpiled weapons, we could really get this thing going. I can begin pulling people together right away."

"It would help if you could provide us a list of names," JJ said sincerely, "That way we could bring the weapons to them discreetly. I have delivery vans that would work perfectly for the job."

Philip provided the names of main resistance leaders he knew of, as did Rich. James was the only one that held back, even though JJ tried to talk him into telling. James just insisted the people he knew lived in the county and were already well armed. They wouldn't need any help.

"Before you men go," JJ said as he raised up on his cane, "let me show you around a little more. I think you'll like what you see.”

They followed JJ through a maze of corridors, passing rooms filled with automatic weapons and munitions. Finally, they came upon a large, well furnished, section of the cave.

“This is very nice,” James commented. “It looks more like an apartment. Do you stay down here often?”

“I used to,” JJ replied, “but not so much anymore.”

“Thank you for showing us around,” Rich replied, “but we should really be going. There’s lots of work to do now.”

While they were distracted, JJ slipped back to the main entrance and, without warning, reached up and pulled a handle. Suddenly, a heavy steel gate lowered from the ceiling and locked into a slot on the floor.

“What are you doing!?” Rich demanded as he pounded on the gate.

“I’m sorry men,” JJ said as he was joined by the remaining city fathers. “Things aren’t as simple as you might think. You see Management found out about our little club. They intercepted a message sent by Jim Banner, the weatherman, and cornered us with it. We had to make a deal and agree none of us would help the resistance. Look, I have grandchildren at stake. We can’t fight these guys.”

“You coward,” Philip exclaimed. “I’ve got family too and my wife is dead because of them. If we don’t stop them they’re not going to quit until they’ve killed us all. Your agreement means nothing to these hard hearted animals. Come on man, let us out.”

“Sorry, but we have to go,” JJ said as he turned reluctantly. “The place you’re in has everything you need. There’s plenty of water and food and it’s quite comfortable. I’ll come back and check on you in a few days. Take care, my friends.”

Philip, James and Rich shouted and cursed as the city fathers disappeared behind another special boulder that pivoted into place behind the heavy steel bars. The realization they were trapped quickly settled in.

“The whole world is turned upside down,” James lamented as he plopped down on a couch. “Our friends become our enemies and the people we’re supposed to be able to trust the most only let us down. Worse, Lori is expecting us back and you know how worried she gets. But the way that blasted JJ makes it sound the whole world will be gone by the time we get out of here."

"And we couldn't have been more stupid," Philip agreed. "We just gave them the names of some of the most important resisters in the city. Who knows what's going to happen to them now, and it's our fault."

"It might seem hopeless," Rich replied, "but that's how I felt before you guys showed up and saved me from being starved to death. Everything looked bleak until you arrived. Now we need to do the same for our family and friends. Come on guys, let's put our minds together and come up with an escape plan."

The men gathered on the sofa for a while discussing plan after plan but they all seemed to end with a solid rock wall and a heavy steel gate.

Finally, James changed the conversation and started talking about the mine itself.

"Hey," he said, "it's our twenty fifth anniversary next week. Wouldn't it be nice to break into JJ's diamond stash and take a few? Lori could have quite the bling."

"Like that's going to happen," Rich replied. "I bet he has those protected with armed guards."

"Wait a minute. Do you guys want to hear a funny story?" Philip asked suddenly.

"I'm not in much of a humorous mood," James replied, "but go ahead if you have to."

"It's not that kind of funny," Philip replied. "I just remembered, Henry told me a story that just might help us."

"What kind of story?" Rich asked as he leaned forward.

"He told me of something he found when he was a teenager. That something is what he credited with saving his life when he was attacked in the cave on this very mountain."

"Ok, ok, you got my attention," James said eagerly. "What is it, man? Don't keep us waiting."

"It may not seem like much but Henry swears by it," Philip replied as he pulled a bright blue stone out of his pocket.

"That's very pretty," Rich said as he examined it closely. "But just how is this going to help us."

"I'm really not sure," Philip replied, "just that Henry said no rock walls could hold him prisoner as long as he had this crystal or one like it."

"Did he tell you how this thing works?" Rich asked.

"Sort of, he said to hold the crystal tightly in your hand then you can move through solid rock, and whoever is connected to you can too. That's it. That's all I know."

"I guess it's better than standing around doing nothing," James said.

"So what do we do next?" Rich said excitedly.

"Henry said to concentrate on the crystal," Philip replied as held it against the rock wall for a few moments unsure of what to expect. "He also said never separate from the one holding the crystal. I guess we'll find out if my son's secret works."

"Is anything happening yet?" James asked anxiously as he was in line behind Rich and couldn't see what Philip was doing.

"Nothing yet," Philip replied. "No, wait, something's happening. The wall is changing."

His speech was cut short as the solid rock wall began to glow bright orange and turned translucent like thick syrup. Philip reached for the stone face and his hand passed into the rock.

"Come on men!" Philip commanded as he stepped into the rock. "Just stay focused and don't let go."

Philip disappeared into the rock face followed by Rich and then James. James had a hold of Rich's shirttail while Rich was holding Philip's arm as they walked slowly through stone. The bright glow from the crystal illumined Philip's path as they worked their way along. Philip was hopeful he was headed towards another mine shaft since he couldn't see far in the crystal light. He was afraid of going through the metal bars and boulder in case JJ had placed a guard outside.

Meanwhile, James became fascinated by the experience and began looking around as they moved through the rock. Then something caught his eye as he passed by.

"So JJ's got all the diamonds out of here, eh," James said as he saw the largest diamond ever. It was about the size of a softball and, even in its raw form, sparkled brightly from the glow of the blue crystal. "Won't that just be the best anniversary present ever?" he continued as he reached out and plucked the diamond from the rock like picking an apple off a tree. But, in the process, he let Rich's shirttail slip through his fingers. James slowed, thinking the other two had heard him, as he examined the diamond more closely but they continued moving unaware he had let go and sounds don't pass through rock.

"This isn't going to fit on Lori's finger but I bet I could get it cut up and made into the most beautiful necklace of all time."

James' attention returned to following his brother through the solid rock but he quickly realized his mistake as the granite around him began to solidify. He pushed with all his six foot nine might but the light from the crystal Philip was holding quickly faded from sight.

"We're out!" Philip exclaimed as he stepped into one of the side tunnels.

"That was awesome!" Rich agreed as he joined him.

They stood there for a few moments deciding which direction to take and then Phillip's heart jumped into his throat.

"Where's James?!"

"He was right behind me!" Rich exclaimed as they examined the rock wall they had just come through.

"I'm going in after him," Philip said as he held the crystal against the wall.

"It's too late," Rich moaned as he grabbed Philip by the arm. "He's inside solid rock and you would have no idea where. We were walking all over the place. There's no path back to your brother."

"No!" Philip shouted as he pounded on the wall. "You can't be gone you big dope. I need you! I need you." Philip said as he leaned into the rock wall.

Rich took Philip by the shoulders and gently led him down the mine shaft towards where they first came in. The large boulder swung out of the way and they found Philip's truck parked right where he left it.

"What am I going to tell Lori?" Philip lamented as he leaned both hands on the hood of his truck.

"I don't know," Rich replied, "a loss like this is beyond words. I'm not sure fighting Management is worth it. Maybe we should quit and make a break for it instead. Who knows what next great tragedy lies ahead!"

"No," Philip replied firmly, lifting his head and gritting his teeth. "They started this fight but we're going to finish it."

They climbed into the truck and headed down Grace

Mountain. There were no words to describe the sorrow they were feeling, but the deep determination etched into their faces told the real story.

CHAPTER 6

Parks pulled away from the strange encounter with the mysterious young girl, heading in the direction she recommended. He drove around piles of rubble while morbidly admiring the total devastation.

"This looks like Tester handiwork to me," Parks thought as he passed one building that seemed destroyed from the inside out. Large gashes in the stone, apparently made by hard steel blades, testified to their destructive ability.

Parks had gone nearly a mile when he decided it would be best to take a less noisy approach and go the rest of the way on foot. There was no telling what he might be up against. He pulled over behind a collapsed building and shoved the motorcycle under a large slab of concrete. After following what resembled a road for another half mile or so he started hearing the sound of a loud female voice and some activity. He climbed over a ridge and there, below, were his friends from the Island, busily clearing away the entrance to a large building. Overlooking them were machine gun nests set into the side of the hill. They were manned by soldiers in heavy body armor, while a blonde woman, standing on the back of a flatbed truck with a bullhorn, shouted instructions.

Then he spotted the Colonel who was busy filling wheelbarrows with debris but there was no way to get his attention.

"Everyone's focused on the workers," Parks thought as he moved behind the ridge, "but their gun stations are poorly laid out. If I were to take them out one by one from the top down they couldn't lay down any cross fire with those heavy machine guns. They can only shoot downward. But that doesn't mean they couldn't put up a fight with small arms fire. I'll just have to chance it."

Parks was no novice at being unseen. He chose the one at the very top first, which fortunately, was manned only by a single soldier. He was positioned on a large piece of broken concrete and sitting behind a machine gun overlooking the activity below. Parks would have to climb down the ridge, littered with debris, without disturbing anything, or things would get interesting fast. He made his way quietly along the ridge moving steadily in the direction of the first soldier on his list. Fortunately, the heavy body armor included a helmet providing little peripheral vision. Parks positioned himself and then dropped silently the final ten feet behind the soldier. The man didn't move as he drew his crystal blade. All he needed to do was grab the man by the neck as he sank the blade deep into his back.

Parks slowly crept up behind him but stopped as he noticed something that seemed curiously out of place. The hands resting on the gun were not those of a rugged soldier. The fingers were slender and the nails painted a dark blue. Parks slid his blade back into his belt before grabbing the soldier by the shoulders and slamming what turned out to be a young woman to the concrete. He held his hand tightly over her mouth as her helmet fell off and out poured long blonde hair. The young girl's eyes were wide with fear as Parks held her down. She appeared to be in her early twenties and the suit she had on was stuffed with paper and cloth to make her look big. In reality, she could barely move. Parks pulled some of the stuffing out and used it to make a gag and then to tie her arms and feet. He then positioned her back into her chair and tied her to it. She struggled slightly but to no avail. Then Parks looked more closely at the other soldiers manning similar guns and realized they were all the same, young women hiding behind body armor.

Parks methodically worked his way through each nest, sometimes subduing two at a time but with equal results. He finished the final one at the bottom of the ridge and then carefully surveyed the last obstacle. The woman at the bullhorn had an automatic weapon hanging from her side and Parks had to assume she knew how to use it. But she was focused on the workers and didn't notice as he climbed onto the truck behind her. The Colonel spotted Parks from where he was and stood up. He was about to shout when Parks put a boot into her back sending her sprawling to the hard ground below. He was on her in a second, planting a foot on the gun as he pulled her to her feet with one hand.

"It's safe now," Parks shouted to the stunned crowd.

"They can't hurt you. Quit what you're doing and come on over."

"Parks," the Colonel lamented as he ran up, "What are you doing? They don't have us captured. We're here voluntarily. We're helping these people."

"Huh?" Parks said with a confused look still holding the woman by the scruff of her neck.

"Put me down," she said indignantly.

"I don't get it," Parks said as he dropped the young lady.

"They came to us looking for help," the Colonel replied. "They want to get into this building but they can't on their own. There are no men left to help them and they're not strong enough so we agreed."

"But what's with all the fake security?" Parks asked curiously.

"There're some who live out there," the young woman said as she pointed towards a distant forest. "They come here and try to overcome us and they would hurt us if they knew we are weak so we set this ruse up. They believe there are men among us and that we are powerful and can capture other people but I guess that's over."

"Hey, I'm sorry for kicking you like that," Parks said sheepishly, "and you had best send somebody up to free your friends."

The Colonel waived to several men who scrambled up the hill and cut them loose.

"My name is Abigail," the young woman began, "I'm the oldest and the leader here. It's been over fifteen years since we lost our families and homes. My father was one of the city elders and did his best to save us. I was little then but can still remember his face and how he tried to protect me and my twin sister. We all heard the ancient stories and everyone thought they were only legends. But they weren't. They were real. That's when an unstoppable animal began attacking our livestock and then our people. Some tried to kill it but it just kept coming and coming."

"This all sounds too familiar," the Colonel interrupted, "but we have work to do. Parks, we've dug our way into the building and were just clearing a larger opening when you interrupted. Maybe you'd like to come inside and see what we've found."

Parks and Abigail followed the Colonel as he led the way

to a small opening where they had to get down on their bellies and slide beneath a broken pillar. The Colonel led the way with his flashlight and, after about ten feet of crawling, they slid down the pile where they were greeted by a cavernous building.

"This was once the main meeting place for the city," the Colonel explained.

"That's correct," Abigail replied. "I remember my father coming here as head of the city elders."

"What did you want to show me?" Parks asked.

"It's in here," the Colonel said as he led the way down a long hall and through a set of broken doors. The room was large and scattered about with debris but, in the center, stood a marble platform. "I examined this closely," the Colonel continued, "and it revealed a secret of sorts."

The Colonel pushed the platform slightly revealing a hidden compartment underneath.

"To be honest, the first time I saw this was when I tripped over a chunk of concrete and fell into it," the Colonel said. "That's really how I found this."

The compartment was packed with scrolls that appeared very old.

"My father told us stories just like the ones written in here," Abigail replied as she rolled open one. "He was responsible for passing on this information to our people but we didn't know where they were kept. That was a closely guarded secret passed on from elder to elder. They may have been lost to us if the Colonel hadn't found them. Anyway, the stories contained in here were just that, until 'THEY' came and then the stories became all too real."

"They, who are they?" Parks asked, becoming increasingly curious.

"All I can remember is a darkness you could feel and then the arrival of these vicious short red creatures."

"Testers," Parks exclaimed.

"Exactly," the Colonel said. "I've read through a number of these and the stories are hauntingly similar to the ones I've heard from you. Is it possible what is happening at our city happens to other cities too?"

"We weren't even aware of this city or any other until now," Parks replied, "but it appears we're not alone and it also seems we share a common fate.”

“I kind of wish you hadn’t said that,” the Colonel said. “I’ve been reading, like I said, and there’s more to this story than just Testers. They warn about something called the ‘End of All Light.’ They don’t explain it much but, from what I can tell, it sucks the life out of everything and leaves only blackness behind.”

“I felt just what you’re describing,” Abigail said slowly. “The last image I have is this dark cloud coming in from the wasteland and covering our city.”

“How old were you?” Parks asked.

“I think maybe thirteen. My mother had taken me to a safe place prepared for us in the nearby hills. Dad and my twin sister were to join us but never did. It took a long time but we finally accepted they must have perished when the city went down. It was hard and a sad time but my mom kept us safe with other refugees for a long time. When we finally came out this is what we found, total devastation and no survivors. Mom did a good job of caring for me until she passed. I think the strain of everything was too much for her.”

“What happened to all the men?” Parks asked.

“There are some left but not the kind you want around. Like I said before, we have to maintain an image of power and strength or they’ll come down and attack us. Even so, sometimes at night we hear them rummaging through our work sites. So far they’ve been too afraid to try and break into where we stay. We live in a fortified building, up the street, that wasn’t completely destroyed. We had them convinced there are men here with weapons. That is until you came. But it probably doesn’t matter anyway. Our food is running out and there’s no way for us to rebuild or safely forage for more food. That’s why we decided to make the journey, in hopes of finding someone out there, someone who would help us.”

“Who among us would be willing to stay around and help these young ladies?” the Colonel asked after they crawled back outside. “They’re asking for our help to get them started rebuilding this place.”

Hands shot up everywhere as many young men and women volunteered to stay.

“We’ll send supplies and whatever other resources they

may require and I'll come back here myself in a month or so to see how you're making out." The Colonel said as he climbed into one of the trucks. "Until then, keep your hopes high and always remember the future is your friend."

"As are you," Abigail said with a smile.

"Hey," Parks said as she walked with him to his bike. "There was a young teenager I met in the other part of the city when I first came in. She told me about you and directed me here. Who's she?"

"What teenager?" Abigail asked. "The only women I know are here with us. It's not safe anywhere else."

"That's strange but she gave me this," Parks continued as he held out the golden key. "I don't understand why she wanted me to have it."

"My, oh my," Abigail cried out as she stumbled back. "I haven't seen that in years."

"You recognize it?" Parks asked.

"It belonged to my grandmother but I thought it was lost. The last time I saw it my sister was holding it, just before we were separated. I never thought I would see it again. How did you get it?"

"The girl said her name was Joanna. She gave it to me."

"That just can't be possible!" Abigail exclaimed. "My sister's name was Joanna but she should be much older than a teenager. I'm twenty four."

"I don't know what to say," Parks said as he let out a low whistle. "I just know I met someone over there who gave me this."

"Then you keep the key," Abigail said. "If that was my sister you met and she wanted you to have this, I do too. In the meantime, we'll stay focused on our work here."

Parks hugged her as the people choosing to return to the Island began climbing aboard trucks and buses. It would be a long ride back and Parks was kind of glad he didn't have anyone to talk with as he pulled his bike out of hiding. He slowed for a moment as he approached where he last saw the young teenager. He was tempted to stop and look for her when a cold wind blew across his face and the hair on the back of his neck stood up. He hit the accelerator and headed for the tunnel returning him to the Island. He had his fill of adventure and strange encounters for one day. But little did he know how events were changing and what awaited his return.

CHAPTER 7

"Hello Mrs. Green," David said softly as Joshua's mom opened their front door, "may we come in?"

"Why certainly," Mrs. Green replied. "Josh isn't home right now but you're welcome to wait."

"Um, is Mr. Green here too?" David asked quietly.

"He's just out in the garage," she replied. "He bought Josh a car for his twenty-fifth birthday next week. It's a surprise and his dad's been working on it for over two months. It's been tough keeping Josh out of the garage. All he has left is to paint it 'candy apple' red. Joshua's going to be so surprised. You know, his dad and I were getting old when Josh came along but we've done our best to give him direction and a good start in life. He's grown up to be so responsible and all. It really makes a person proud."

Mrs. Green went through the kitchen and into the garage to fetch Joshua's father while David gave Normand a squeeze on the shoulder. Normand was doing his best to hold his emotions in check but there was no easy way to break the news.

Mr. Green came in wiping his greasy hands on a rag. The Greens were a loving couple and quite wealthy. They were also part of the secret resistance which is why Della chose them to take Josh. She knew they would take care of him and also help him understand the struggle the city was up against. They loved him as if he was their own son and Joshua felt equally the same.

"You fellas look mighty serious," Mr. Green said as he leaned back against the counter. "Josh told us about the Testers he spotted. I was hoping to get his car running before we had to leave. It's tough to just drop everything and go but we will if we have to. Is everything ok?"

"We couldn't be sorrier," David began slowly. "After we left here last night we were pulled over by a Cadet patrol. I guess they're out in force now. Well, everything seemed ok at first but then one of the Cadets got pushy and Josh stepped in. None of us expected what happened next. One of them shot Josh in the chest with a Nullifier and killed him."

Mr. Green went into momentary shock as Mrs. Green buried her face in her hands and instantly began weeping.

Normand and David did their best to console them and Mrs. Green hung onto her husband's neck for a long time. When they were finally able to leave, Mr. Green said he would come around to Dr. Flints place and make arrangements to collect Joshua.

"I can't believe this is happening," David replied quietly as Mr. Green walked them to the door. "Josh was a great friend. He deserved better."

"You know," Mr. Green responded, "we survived the original attack and, now that Joshua is gone, I think my wife will agree we can do more here than in hiding or on the run. We're not a vindictive sort but something has to be done. You guys go on and do whatever's in your hearts. I'll make the necessary arrangements with Dr. Flint. Just remember, if you need anything, don't hesitate to let us know."

"The world is upside down," Normand said as they left. "Our classmates, no, maybe even old friends are now murderers and fiends. I hate it but I'm starting to think maybe Troy has the right idea. Why not just start killing the bastards and get it over with."

"I know how you feel," David replied. "My parents were nearly taken out, not very long ago as was I. But we need clear heads. If we start acting foolish, now, who knows what's going to happen. Joshua's death will not be in vain if we stay focused. The first thing we have to do is get as many of those we care about to safety. Then we can focus on Management."

Normand reluctantly agreed as they made their way across town. It was certain the bodies of the two Cadets had been discovered so they were especially careful to avoid any main roads. Management would be searching for their killers and wouldn't make the same mistake twice. Any contact would likely lead to more deadly violence.

"I can't believe you haven't gotten crystal sickness from using your blade the way you did," Troy said as David stepped into Dr. Flint's house, "I went down right away."

"I had nothing against those guys I just reacted to the situation. It's only if your motives are wrong."

52

"Well it's obvious the Testers aren't our only enemy," Troy continued. "Now it seems the Cadets have joined against us and they're just as ruthless."

"How do we get people out before it's too late?" Burke asked.

"There's a way," David replied. "Parks found it years ago but we have to keep it secret. If information should get out, we're going to lose our advantage. We just need to go and start picking people up who need to get to safety."

"What about Kirsten and Kenzie?" Burke asked. "We haven't heard from them yet."

"I say we stay on course and meet at the school as we decided before." David replied. "There's no evidence the Testers are moving, and we don't know how many there are. But, we may be able to get ahead of the situation if we hurry."

The guys agreed and piled into their vehicles to head for the rendezvous at the school. They split up as usual, taking different routes to their meeting place, only this time they parked behind the building under some trees, just to make doubly sure they weren't spotted. They were the first ones there and David led the way into the auditorium. This time there was no basketball play, they just sat quietly on the bleachers and waited.

After about an hour, everyone else had arrived. David took the lead and explained what had happened to Joshua. Troy had to calm Kenzie down as she was ready to mount up and attack right then. Kirsten and Rita felt the same anger and pain ripping though their hearts. They were equally tempted to go after Management but they controlled their emotions and recognized what was really happening.

The urgency at hand was the safety of the people.

"We need to get as many as we can out of here, as quickly as possible," David said. "Management has their Cadets heavily armed and, even worse, the Testers are moving about and we're not sure where. I suggest we split up in separate vehicles and meet at a second rendezvous point. I think some of us should consider getting to the Island and safety."

"We're not going anywhere," Kirsten replied, thinking David was referring to her. "The city's going to need security and we're it. We were entrusted with these crystal blades and we've trained for just such a moment. You have your lists. Follow them but be careful not to kill without cause. Capture should always be your first goal. Only use lethal force as a last resort."

"I get it," David said, "But some of us still have family we may want to get out of harm's way and some are too old or weak to fight. I can get them out and then come back to join you."

"I don't like it," Kirsten said. "As soon as we begin evacuations where do we stop? Every one of us has someone we want to protect but need I remind you, your adopted parents knew the risk when they took you in. They were the original resisters and have protected you all these years from being drawn into Management's clutches. They could have run at any time but didn't. They raised you knowing a day like this would come. But I will agree you can take those who are weak and infirmed, but make sure you ask them first. I have a feeling even the weakest among us wouldn't want to miss this fight."

"You might be right," Jim replied. "We ran out of the city ourselves not too long ago and had to come back. Even in the county there was no relief. They pursued us and would have killed us if it weren't for Kenzie. Management's looking for movement and anyone caught would be captured and possibly killed. I suggest we try to reconnect with the city fathers. One of them gave me a radio that operates on a special frequency and, if I can get word to them, we'll have a better chance."

"It's agreed then," Kirsten said. "We'll rally those we know are ready and capable but wait for Jim's word. It's a good plan and I know it'll work."

Their agreed upon plan was once things began to happen each of them would rally to the resistance leaders scattered throughout the city. From there the resistance would start by taking over the various power centers in the city and capturing Management Leaders. If they could cut off the head, the rest of the organization would fall. At least that was their belief. Unfortunately, none had considered the BOJ Order being against them.

That was an unexpected problem.

"Kirsten's right, I know," David said to Burke as he pulled out. "But you and some of the other guys have family here. I say we have time to make a quick trip out and come right back. What's it going to hurt? Management isn't moving on the city yet and it'll take all of six hours to make the round trip. Nobody's going to miss us in that short of time."

"I don't know," Burke replied reluctantly. "Kirsten seemed awfully certain about that. I hate to go against anything she says."

"I don't like to either," David argued, "but think about it. Will you be able to fight knowing your parents are in harm's way? Besides, maybe we can hook up with Parks while we're at it. I believe he's there right now and we're going to need him, right?"

Burke thought about it for a while before reluctantly agreeing. They would pick up his van and get Normand to bring his work truck. They could carry at least fourteen people between them and that would take care of all close relatives. Normand felt just as reluctant when David told him, but he did like the idea of getting at least some people to safety. In an hour, they'd picked up everyone they could and were gathered just outside the warehouse door.

"From here on," David said, "you are going to see something very few people know about. But trust me. In a few hours, you'll be somewhere safe, I promise."

David opened the large warehouse door and then closed it as the two vehicles pulled in. He then directed them to the entrance and opened the secret door in the floor. Normand and Burke pulled down into the cavernous tunnel that led from the city, through the wilderness, and to the Island. David climbed in the front with Normand after hitting the switch, concealing their escape route. In a few moments, they were flying through the tunnel, with lights sensing their presence coming on in front, lighting the way as usual.

"This is amazing," Normand exclaimed. "How did you know about this?"

"Parks showed me and it's how I brought my mom and dad to safety." David answered. "I haven't seen them since so I'm looking forward to this, even if we can't stay but a minute."

"Who built this thing and why?" Normand asked.

"Parks said it was some military thing built years ago," David replied. "Apparently, there's a network of tunnels stretching all over the place, designed to move people and equipment around. From what I gather, it was set up to protect us from invaders but something obviously went wrong and we don't know what that something was. There's a man called "the Colonel" who was part of the military effort, but even he doesn't know what happened."

They'd been traveling for a quite some time when signs along the way began warning them to slow down. Before long, they pulled up to the large reinforced blast doors and David was about to get out when they began to open on their own. The two vehicles pulled into the cavernous underground facility known as the Island.

"Hello," came the friendly greeting and wave as Dr. Larson came walking towards them. "What are you guys doing out here?"

"We've come with some disturbing news and some people who need a safe place," David said as he was flanked by Normand and Burke. Everyone else was piling out and stretching from the long drive. "I need to speak with Parks right away."

"Parks isn't here at the moment," Dr. Larson replied. "Come on down below with me and I'll explain what's going on."

By then, Greg had arrived with one of the large people movers. He had recognized David through one of the many cameras stationed along the way and had opened the door and alerted Dr. Larson. People were full of questions, and amazed at what they were seeing, but now was not the time for a tour as David climbed on and sat next to Dr. Larson. The ride below was all the time he had to explain recent events. It seemed David felt he was constantly telling someone what had happened to Joshua and the impending crisis in the city, and it wasn't getting any easier.

Dr. Larson was as saddened as much as anyone, but this was no time for emotion. That would have to be saved for later.

"We expect Parks back anytime," she explained. "He went to locate the Colonel and take care of some people in need. Greg will help everyone get settled in," Dr. Larson continued. "In the meantime, you boys are welcome to wait until Parks gets here, I'm just not sure how long that might be."

"We can't wait very long," David replied. "I just want to let Parks know what we're doing. Kirsten is leading the resistance and intends to capture Management's key personnel and hold them hostage. She believes that will break their spirit and organization. However, we have to be ready as things are likely to become very ugly very fast and we need as much help as we can get."

"That's very concerning!" Dr. Larson exclaimed. "I didn't realize things were degrading so quickly. I'll let Parks know the moment I see him."

"Where are mom and dad?" David asked as he looked about.

"They went with the rescue group. It sounds like there may be another city, similar to ours, that suffered total destruction. They're just trying to help."

"Another city," Normand exclaimed. "We never heard that before but I guess it's logical. We probably would have eventually found each other if we weren't always focused on rebuilding and protecting our own."

David was happy to hear his parents were ok and that they had volunteered to help. He knew how much his mom and dad loved to be involved in community events. This would be right up their alley.

They hung around long enough to eat but the situation in the city was pressing on the young men. They made some quick goodbyes before entering the tunnel for the return trip. It was a gutsy move to bring people to the Island, but they were glad they had. Not only were the people who were important to them safe, but they learned there was another city. They even started thinking that if there was one other city, maybe there could be even more. It was a good feeling knowing they were not alone.

CHAPTER 8

"The Board is meeting tonight," Dave's secretary said as she entered his office. "Are you going to be available?"

"Tell them I might be a little late," Dave responded curtly. "I'll also need to start interviewing for another personal assistant. Put in a call to Barron and see if he has any Cadets that would work."

"Is there something I should know?" she asked intently.

"No, just follow my instructions."

Dave leaned back and stared out the window as she closed the door and left. He was buried in thought as he considered the Mystic's words. "So Parks is hiding somewhere with tunnels reaching in all directions." Dave mused as he got up and stood at his window. "Hmm, could be the wilderness. I've heard there are caves and a lot of trails. Not to mention, he spent his youth out there and knows the area better than any. He'll likely be hard to find so what I need is to get him to reveal himself."

Dave sat back down and picked up the phone.

"Barron," Dave barked, "I want you to begin a sweep of the wilderness starting from the South end of the city. Parks is out there and I want him found."

"Begging your pardon sir," Barron replied, "but do you know how much area you're talking about? I don't have enough resources to do something like that."

"Fine," Dave snapped. "Then tell me what progress you're making in locating Parks. I need that guy fast."

"My plan is in motion and I expect results soon."

"You had better get something very soon," Dave fumed as he slammed the phone down. "I can't believe that guy. One minute he's promising action and the next he wants me to wait."

Dave was disgusted as he pulled a cloth from his briefcase, set it on his desk and then carefully unwrapped the red crystal blade Parks had left behind. It was as beautiful as ever and Dave admired his own reflection as he held the blade up in the light. He instantly felt better and even smiled to himself.

But then the room began to melt away as Dave's mind was drawn through the blade to another place and time.

"What are we going to do," a distraught woman asked as she came running up. "They're everywhere, overrunning the city."

"You'll have to get to one of the shelters," Dave replied. "There's nothing I can do for you, woman." He said as he pushed her away.

He made his way through smoldering debris and across an open field heading for the bunker. He dodged his way along, staying low and out of sight, before arriving at the heavy steel door.

"Come in! Come in!" an old grey headed man said as he pushed the door open.

Dave stepped into a dimly lit room while the man closed and locked the door behind him. A group of distinguished men were huddled over a map spread out on a table.

"They've completely destroyed the East side," one of the men lamented as he put a large X across an area on the map with a red felt pen. "At this rate, the city will be rubble in less than a week."

"You've seen them," another man stated as Dave began examining the map. "What are our choices? What can we do?"

"We've some armaments in reserve," Dave replied. "However, from what I've seen, they're largely ineffective. Their armor appears to be quite strong. Yesterday, I saw ten of them take a direct hit from a rocket and it barely slowed them down. It's like they feel it coming and then group together forming into a singular object. As powerful as the blast was, it only dislodged and destroyed a few of them. We really don't have the power to stop them. There're just too many."

"Well, what are we going to do?" the men nearly shouted in unison. "We have to get our people to safety somehow, before it's too late."

"Oh, I wouldn't say that," Dave replied as he stepped back from the table. "You see, I managed to arrange a meeting with their leaders yesterday."

"You did?" one of the older men asked. "What were they like, what did they say?"

"They said we don't seem to have what they're looking

for," Dave replied. "But they do have something to offer. Anyone willing to come over to their side will be spared and given opportunity to follow them to the next site."

"That's downright crazy," one of the leaders said as he stepped under the dim light bulb hanging from the ceiling. "Surrender to them, to this? Our goal should be to get as many out of the city as quickly as possible. That shouldn't take more than a day or two. I say we hold our defensive positions and then hit them with everything we've got."

A collective chorus of "you're right" and "we'll beat them back" rang through the concrete structure.

"That's what I told them you would say," Dave said as he stepped further back. "But you know, they offered quite a good deal and I thought you might at least be interested in knowing the details."

"Have you lost your mind, Dave?" one of the men asked. "You can't bargain with death and win."

"Oh, I've already done that," he said as he turned and walked towards the door, "and I think I came out the winner."

With that word, he spun around and pulled an automatic weapon from under his coat.

"It's too bad you didn't choose the winning side with me."

Dave shook his head as he stepped outside. The roar from the muzzle left a ringing in his ears. He stood there for a moment listening to the sounds of chaos as Testers tore through the city. Panic and fear followed by death was everywhere but Dave felt quite peaceful. Then, suddenly, a group of Testers came running towards him, their blades flashing in the morning light. He prepared himself for the worst but, to his amazement, they ran past as if he wasn't even there.

"Now that's more like it," he said with a smile.

Dave felt quite smug as he stepped over countless bodies torn and ripped by the Testers. He was heading for the tent where he had last met with the six leaders of the invasion force. But then unexpectedly his attention turned towards a small boy sitting on a curb throwing what appeared to be a large shiny marble into the air and catching it over and over again. At that very moment, a troop of Testers were coming down the street seeking anything that moved and their attention was instantly drawn to the boy.

Yet, he seemed oblivious to the impending doom and Dave just folded his arms to watch them do their work. They lumbered ever closer and closer raising their blades above their heads and Dave found himself genuinely enjoying the event.

"Why doesn't the kid run?" he mused. "He's probably just too stupid like the rest of these losers."

The Testers were almost upon him when the boy suddenly jumped to his feet and threw the marble at the lead Tester. It passed through the first and then boomeranged around and through the rest of them before returning to the boy's hand. The Testers wobbled for a moment then stumbled forward before collapsing into a pile of dead red.

Dave gasped at the sight, frozen in his boots. Then the little boy turned, looked deep into Dave's eyes and the next thing Dave knew, he was running and screaming in fear.

Instantly, Dave's mind returned to his office.

"I remember that day quite well but there was no little boy stopping Testers," he nearly yelled as he dropped the blade onto his desk and pushed himself away in disgust. "What does this mean? Am I supposed to believe some kid is more powerful than us? Well, that's ridiculous," Dave assured himself. "Management is the most powerful force there is and this can only be some weird thing."

Still, he no longer felt quite as good as he carefully wrapped the blade and returned it to his briefcase.

"I'm going to find Barron and make sure he knows what I expect," Dave fumed as he pulled out of his parking spot. "I'm not waiting for anything, including him."

He took the road around the backside of the city where the old warehouses stood. He had instructed Barron to bring the Testers into the city through the rear gate and position them for duty. Dave spotted Barron walking down a field to where the Testers were lined up and pulled his truck off the main road. He roared up behind him and rolled down his window.

"What's going on, Boss?" Barron asked as Dave pulled to a stop.

"I want you to take a group of these out into the wilderness. You might not be able to canvas the whole area but we can at least go on a little hunting exercise."

"You think we can hunt Parks with these things?" Barron

asked.

"You're going to find out where Parks is hiding," Dave commanded. "I don't have to explain myself to you. Besides, I have reason to believe he's out there and you're just the man for the job."

"Look, I'd like nothing better than to find him," Barron replied, "but you must know it may end up being just a waste of time. But if that's what you want, I'll get started right away."

"Good!" Dave said sharply as he drove off, "and don't come back without him."

Barron didn't like the veiled threat but he knew his duty.

Dave, on the other hand, was starting to feel better again. Even though he missed the board meeting, he was sure they would have nothing to say once he explained what he was doing. He was passing one of the warehouses when something caught his eye.

"You know, I don't usually care what happens down here but today I'm going to catch me some trespassers." He said as he pulled into a large graveled area.

He watched as two vehicles entered one of the warehouses. He got out and snuck around the side looking for a back way in but the doors were boarded up and there were no windows. So, instead, he came around front to the only functioning door.

"This is going to be like shooting fish in a barrel," Dave snickered as he pulled back the door and slid inside.

The only light in the building came through holes in the walls, mostly illuminating floating dust. It took a few moments for his eyes to adjust. Then he began scanning the cavernous warehouse for its unauthorized guests.

"What the," Dave exclaimed as he walked through the building. "This place is empty and there's nowhere to hide. Where could they have gone?"

Confused, he pushed the large sliding door all the way open to allow in more light and then began examining the dust covered concrete floor. Sure enough, he hadn't imagined it. There were tire tracks. He followed them across the building to the far wall.

"How did they do it?" Dave mumbled as he examined the wall.

The dusty floor revealed some tennis shoe imprints that didn't go anywhere and the tire tracks ended at the edge of a large concrete slab.

"I don't get it," Dave said as he closely examined the area. "They should be right here but they're not."

He continued following the shoe tracks which seemed to head towards one of the building pillars. Then he noticed an area about chest high on the side of the column where years of dust had been wiped off. Dave reached around the column until he felt something. He flipped what seemed to be a switch and instantly the sound of large motors and gears broke the silence of the warehouse as the concrete slab behind him began to rise from the floor. In a matter of seconds, it was tilted up and a ramp appeared leading underground.

"Ho, ho," Dave exclaimed excitedly as he walked slowly down the ramp. "So this is where they went but where does it go?"

He stood at the bottom looking down a long partially lighted tunnel for a good long time. It was becoming more apparent this was a significant find. He walked back into the warehouse, flipped the switch, and lowered the slab again.

"Whoever those people were and wherever this thing goes deserves a closer look," Dave thought as he slid the large warehouse door shut and got back into his rig. "The Mystic mentioned a tunnel and here it is. This is getting better by the minute but I wouldn't want the chickens to fly the coop before the fox can get them."

Dave was brimming with excitement as he pulled onto the street. This day was turning into one of his best ever.

CHAPTER 9

"Hello, hello." Jim said into the large hand held CB radio. "Do you read me?"

Kirsten provided him a secret code if he managed to get a response but Jim had been trying for nearly an hour with no results. He and Rita left the elementary school and drove back to the house Jim's lawyer friend, Tim, had provided to pick up some additional supplies but frustration was beginning to set in. They needed to join up with the larger resistance movement which Kirsten indicated could already be mobilizing. He set the radio on the kitchen table for a moment as he thought how different his two cousins were. Kirsten was the strength behind the resistance having given her life to its success and the training of the young people Parks saved. She was smart and worked hard to keep their identities safe. Parks, on the other hand, went public and joined Management believing his BOJ Order would eventually change them from inside. Kill them with kindness, so to speak.

But that hadn't worked out so well.

"Jim, Jim!" Rita said as she hurried into the living room with the radio. "I think someone's responding."

Jim grabbed the radio as he took the paper Kirsten gave him out of his shirt pocket.

"This is R. O. D." A crackly voice said again. "Are you there, over?"

"Location 3, time F as in friend." Jim read off the paper.

There was a long pause and Jim thought for a second he'd lost him.

"Could you repeat the location?" The voice asked.

"Location 3," Jim repeated.

"Are you sure?"

"Yes, that's it."

"I read you loud and clear. R. O. D. out." The voice said.

"Who do you think that was?" Rita asked.

"We're about to find out." Jim replied as a bead of sweat rolled off his forehead. "Come on, let's load the car and get going.”

“Where’s Location 3?” Rita asked as she got behind the wheel.

“Do you know where the old cannery is?”

“Yes, on the far side of the city in the warehouse division.”

“Well, that’s where we’re going.”

“That place is nearly abandoned.” Rita said. “Most businesses left after the takeover. It was too costly to repair all the damage.”

The cannery was one of those businesses. Large rusting steel structures loomed in the distance as they approached. The old cannery was a maze of conveyors and overgrown roads leading to long since idled machinery.

“Why aren’t we driving in?” Rita asked as Jim motioned for her to pull off the road a good half mile before the entrance and shut off the car.

“One thing I’ve learned is to never take anything for granted,” Jim replied as he stepped out. “We’re plenty early so let’s do some walking around and figure out the lay of the place.”

Jim and Rita crossed a deep ditch and then squeezed through a broken section in the long chain link fence that surrounded the cannery. Rita nearly jumped when they startled a few pigeons nesting in the frame of a building and instinctively grabbed Jim’s arm. He squeezed her hand affectionately as they continued on.

The sun was slipping down and throwing long shadows across their path as they approached what seemed the logical meeting place. A single low structure set in the center of the cannery that was once the administration building. Then the hair on the back of Jim’s neck stood up as he pulled Rita into the shadows.

“What is it?” Rita asked anxiously.

“I don’t know,” Jim replied. “Maybe I’m getting paranoid but this just doesn’t feel right. I know these guys are all secretive and such but why meet here. If no one knows your identity it would seem just as good to meet somewhere normal. If someone spotted them here it would look really suspicious. Maybe this place is abandoned but people do still travel this road. It would take only one suspicious person to see a light on in this place and they're all toast."

"I get what you're saying but now what? Do we leave?"

"Not yet," Jim answered. "My watch says quarter of five and they won't be expecting us until six. See that window on the top of this building?" Jim said as he pointed up. "I bet there's a stairway to it and it overlooks this entire area. Why don't we see if we can get up there?"

Jim led the way through the darkened building being mindful not to make any noise with Rita tight on his heels. The smell of old machinery and grease was everywhere and before long they were on the stairs. Rita wore rubber soled shoes but Jim had on a pair with leather soles and he struggled to keep quiet as they climbed. Fortunately, no one was around to hear him and they reached the top without incident. It wasn't the best place to wait as the building was cold and they had come dressed in summer attire but the view was great as it overlooked not only the old cannery but also the South end of the city. Jim cleaned off a metal beam with his shirt sleeve so he and Rita could sit while they waited. They had a very quiet conversation going until they were interrupted by the sound of an approaching vehicle. In a few moments, a large black car pulled up next to the administration building below.

"That's Tim," Jim said excitedly under his breath. "I guess I was wrong about this."

He was about to let out a loud whistle when it caught in his throat. The driver's door opened and out stepped a man Jim instantly recognized.

"Oh crap!" Jim said as he pulled Rita out of the window. "That's Barron."

The rest of the doors opened and out poured Cadets armed with Nullifiers.

"You didn't find him at the house?" Tim said. "I had that place bugged so that's how I knew they were home. Are you sure you had the right address?"

"I'm sure," Barron growled, "but we'll get him when he arrives. In the meantime, I'll position these guys where they can block any escape, not that he will escape mind you." Barron glanced up at the tall building just as Jim ducked back into the shadows. "Are you sure there's no one else around this place?" Barron asked.

"I would think not," Tim responded. "This is about as remote as you get."

Barron kept looking intently at the opening high above, straining to see if someone was there while Jim began sweating profusely. There was only one way out of here, down the same set of stairs Barron would use to catch them.

"What's the matter?" Tim asked as he joined Barron looking up at the building.

"I thought I saw movement in that opening," Barron replied.

He was about to dispatch a Cadet to check it out when, suddenly, a white dove flew across the sky and landed in the opening. It was quickly joined by two more that walked back and forth cooing. Jim and Rita were frozen in the darkness but the doves were oblivious to their presence. They stayed a few moments, and then flew off just as suddenly as they came.

"Stupid birds," Barron snapped as his attention returned to the task at hand. "You two take up positions along the entrance," Barron commanded. "Once they drive past you, wait until they've pulled up to the building and Tim greets them before moving in. I don't want them to make a break for it in their vehicle. Go on, get going. We have maybe a half hour before they arrive."

Jim's mind was racing as Barron followed Tim into the building below while the Cadets did as instructed.

"We have to get out of here, fast," Jim said to Rita. "The car is hidden but not that well if someone really wants to look."

Jim took off his shoes and they made their way quietly down the steel stairs. He slipped them back on at the bottom and they worked their way through the building. The building was dark and Jim hit his head twice on low hanging pipes before making it to a rear door that was stuck halfway open.

They squeezed out and waited for the Cadets to take their positions along the main entrance before snaking their way through the maze of buildings to the hole in the fence where they came in. They were back in their car and, before they knew it, heading away from certain capture.

"I thought Tim was one of us," Rita said anxiously.

"I know. I did too," Jim responded. "But he's not and that means this whole thing is screwy. If one of the city fathers is compromised then we have to assume they all are and that means we can't trust anyone."

"What are you going to do?"

"We have to stop anyone else from meeting down here," Jim said as he pulled off at the intersection.

"But we're sitting ducks!" Rita exclaimed. "You can't park out in the open like this."

"We have to," Jim replied earnestly. "We don't know how many resisters may be coming, or who that was we were speaking with, but they will surely be driving into a trap. If Tim knew what Location 3 meant, he likely knows what time "F" means too. You stay in the car and keep the motor running."

Jim got out and walked to the far edge of the road where he could see anyone approaching. It wasn't but a few minutes before a large white four door pickup turned onto the cannery road. Jim stepped into the middle of the street forcing the truck to stop.

"Hey buddy," Jim said as he approached the window and a large middle aged man with a grey beard. The rest of the truck was full of quite serious looking people. "This may sound a bit strange but I made a call earlier today on a CB radio inviting certain people to a meeting just down the road."

Jim swallowed hard as the man's eyes narrowed but didn't say a word.

"Anyway, if you happen to know anything about that, there's a group of unfriendly people waiting at Location 3 and I would suggest you turn around and leave."

The man looked hard at him and then glanced over at Rita's ashen face.

"That's pretty gutsy of you to stop us," the man said. "I could be anybody you know."

"I get that," Jim said, suddenly feeling like making a break for the car. "I just felt it was important enough to take the chance."

"Well, thank you for that," the man said as a broad smile broke over his face. "I'm the one you talked to. You two go on and get out of here. I'll take care of everything from here."

Relieved, Jim did exactly that and in a moment they were heading away.

"That worked out well," Rita said, relieved. "Where are

we going next?"

"Well, we certainly can't go back to the safe house. You heard what Tim said, they have the place bugged. They've been listening to everything we've been saying. Man, this is bad. We're going to need to find everyone we can and let them know what's happening. This is becoming more impossible all the time."

Jim decided to go to the only place he was sure hadn't been compromised, Dr. Flint's office. They had never mentioned it in conversation so he was sure Management didn't know. They would check in there first before setting out on a search.

Meanwhile, Philip and Rich were arriving at James and Lori's motor home.

"Hi," Lori said cheerfully as she stood on the top step with the door open. "I wasn't sure when you would be back so I made a stew in the crock pot. It's should be done…hey, where's James?"

"You need to sit down," Philip said as he climbed into the motor home and the small living quarters. "We've something to tell you."

Lori could feel the anguish in Philip's voice as she slid down onto the couch.

"I'm very sorry," Philip said slowly.

"No! No! It can't be true!" Lori exploded. "Tell me he's ok. Please Philip, tell me he's going to be ok." She said as she grabbed him by the arm.

Philip and Rich did their best to console Lori as the day dragged past but there was no consoling possible. Just as Philip felt when he lost Pearl, now he watched his sister-in-law suffering through unimaginable grief. Even worse, Philip shared her grief having just lost his only brother. It was a long and painful night yet somehow, they finally managed to fall asleep but it was more due to pure exhaustion than anything else.

"Huh, what," Philip said as he blinked his eyes open. The morning sun was pouring in through the thin curtains as he sat up on the narrow couch. He paused for a moment and then heard someone bang a second time on the aluminum door a few feet from his head.

Both Rich and Lori were still sleeping as Philip reached over and opened the curtain to see who was outside. But, whoever it was, had moved out of sight. Philip slipped on his shoes and reached under the couch for a wooden baseball bat James had kept there in case of intruders. He cautiously opened the door, with the bat ready for duty. The gravel crunched under his feet as he moved as quietly as possible, prepared to meet the unknown adversary. He crept around the front of the motor home with the bat held high and then saw the back of a large man apparently trying to peek into the windows. Philip was about to land a crushing blow to the back of his head when the man quickly spun around.

"You guys sleep like rocks," James said flatly, grabbing the head of the bat. "Hey, what were you planning on doing with this thing?"

"James!" Philip nearly shouted as he dropped the bat. "How, what, where…"

"You only need 'who' and 'when' and you have the makings of a story." James quipped. "How about we go inside? I'm plenty tired and cold."

"You old goat," Philip said as he gave his brother a big hug. "I can't believe it's really you. Come on, we've got to wake everyone up."

Lori nearly flew off the bed over the driver's compartment when she heard James' voice. She kissed him then punched him in the chest while Rich slapped him on the arm and it was sheer madness as everyone wanted answers all at once.

"Let's all sit down," Philip said. "What happened to you? You were right behind us and then you were gone. We thought for sure you were dead. How did you get out of that rock wall?"

"Well, first of all," James began, "I want you to know how mad I was that you guys took off without me. Do you know how far it is from Grace Mountain to here? My feet are killing me."

"Yeah, yeah," Philip said impatiently. "Enough with the complaining the last time we saw you we were walking into solid rock. How did you get out?"

"Oh that," James replied, enjoying the spotlight for a moment. "Well, you said to hold onto Rich but while we were passing through the rock, I spotted the biggest diamond I'd ever seen and I couldn't hold him and grab the diamond at the same time so I guess I let go. I thought I could just grab it quickly but you guys disappeared. I probably would still be in that rock, like you all thought, if it wasn't for this," James said as he pulled the huge diamond from his pocket and held it up. "From what I can figure out, the diamond absorbed enough energy from that blue crystal of yours, enough to get me out of there. But, what I couldn't tell was which way you went after I came out into one of the mine shafts. I hollered but no one answered. You guys were already gone."

Philip leaned back and took a long appreciative look at his brother. They had moved apart years before with Philip farming in the city and James with his orchard in the county. They had not seen much of each other over the years, but right then it seemed like they had never been separated.

"One other thing," James said as he stretched out his hand to Lori, "The reason I stopped, was to get this for you."

"I've never needed jewelry," Lori replied as she took the huge diamond from his hand. "I've only ever needed you. But, seeing as you nearly got yourself killed getting it for me it seems only fitting I take it. But just you remember this one thing, if you ever do anything like this again, you'll have wished you had gotten stuck in that old stone wall."

The motor home rocked with laughter for a good long while as sadness and pain were quickly forgotten and things seemed good again. But they knew things were not right. Some of the city fathers must have made a deal and that didn't sit well with anyone. They were beginning to realize their enemies were not just Management but people they once considered friends and that was truly frightening.

CHAPTER 10

Parks led the way through the tunnel and back to the Island. Greg had fixed the technical troubles and was watching the monitors closely, keeping a sharp lookout for their return. He ran for Della the moment he saw Parks pass the outer camera. She was waiting when the doors opened and Parks rode in, followed by the Colonel and the rest of the people who had decided to return.

"Hi honey," Parks said as he hopped off his motorcycle. "Am I ever glad to see you!"

"It's good to have you safely back," Della replied. "Is everything ok?"

"There's quite a story to tell," Park answered, "but it's all good. We learned there are other people like us who have endured great loss and also believe some of those running our city may even be responsible for their sorrows. Some people chose to stay behind and help them out. It was a very generous thing to do."

"Mr. P-P-Parks! Mr. P-P-Parks." Greg said anxiously as he came running up.

"Hi Greg," Parks replied. "What's going on? Take a second and catch your breath. What's so important?"

"Something is not r-r-right." Greg replied. "I-I-I tried to tell David, b-b-but he was in too big of a h-h-hurry to leave."

"What's not right?" Parks asked as he read the concern on Greg's face.

"I d-don't know exactly," Greg answered. "T-t-there is a sensor on the other end of the tunnel w-w-where you open the d-d-door and come d-down, s-s-see." Greg said as he handed a printout to Parks. "That's where the d-d-door opened the first time." He continued pointing at the printout. "B-b-but then twenty minutes later the d-d-door opened a second time. I-I-I asked David if he c-c-came through twice but he said n-n-no. I don't get it."

"Hmm," Parks said as he looked it over closely, "there's no way this could be a mistake and you're thinking some unknown person opened the door after David shut it, right?"

"T-t-that's what I said to David b-b-but he left anyway," Greg said.

"There's even more," Della said as Parks tried to grasp the full implications of what Greg said. "There have been other significant happenings since you left."

Della went on to tell him of Joshua's death and the appearance of the Testers. Parks was struck hard by what happened to Josh, as a deep cloud of anger began to settle over his mind.

"I think you had best prepare for the worst," Parks said to the Colonel. "If the escape tunnel has been compromised, it'll be only a matter of time before Management will be coming."

"Don't worry about us. We can take care of ourselves," the Colonel said as he walked Parks to his motorcycle. "But, you're the one who had best be careful. I have a feeling you're already in grave danger."

Parks glanced over at Della whose face was covered with concern as the Colonel quickly realized his mistake, but it was too late.

"I'll be fine," Parks reassured Della. "You stay here where it's safe and don't worry. I'll be back soon and this will all be behind us."

Della was not reassured yet she had no choice but to keep her chin up. She kissed Parks affectionately and didn't want to stop holding him, but she had to let him go. If they were to have a future for the child she was carrying, Parks was going to have to stop Management. Della and the Colonel stood side by side as Parks roared through the blast doors and into the tunnel heading for the City. The doors shut tightly behind him and the lights came on as before, as he disappeared out of sight. Parks would have a good long ride to plan his next move. Eventually, signs began to appear alerting Parks to the fast approaching end of the tunnel but he pulled up well short and parked his bike under one of the many strategically placed escape ladders.

"This one should be about a hundred and fifty feet or so from the exit and just outside the warehouse." Parks thought as he began climbing the steel cage ladder.

He turned the round handle releasing the locks and then pushed hard with his shoulder. It opened with a whoosh of air, dust and sand. Parks emerged into the bright light of the day and quickly closed the lid behind him. It was cleverly disguised as a steel marker indicating an underground power line with warnings not to dig. He carefully scouted the perimeter of the warehouse looking for suspicious activity and was not disappointed.

"That's a Management vehicle if I ever saw one," Parks thought as he came around. "Looks like they're inside but I'm going to need their wheels. It's time to check things out."

Parks slid behind the large door and into the relative darkness of the warehouse. He stayed low and worked quietly along the perimeter of the walls straining to see who was there. Then he spotted two Cadets sitting on overturned buckets left from some long since completed project discussing personal matters and oblivious to Parks as he slowly and silently crept up behind them. They were covered with body armor and each one had a Nullifier sitting on his lap. Obviously they were there to guard the once secret entrance to the Island and nab anyone who came out. Parks slid the crystal blade from the belt around his waist as he got within a mere ten feet of them. He squatted tight to the ground for a few seconds, coiling his body, before leaping. He hit one just under the back of his helmet with the handle of his blade and the other with his forearm. The Cadet he hit with the blade slumped to the ground while the other bounced off a steel column, sending a shower of dust down.

Before the Cadet could recover, Parks was on him ripping his Nullifier away and then slamming his head into the steel column. The helmet took some of the impact before it split in two. The Cadet's eyes glazed over but remained wide open as Parks held him off his feet with one hand and brought his crystal blade to bear on his throat.

"I'll gut you like a pig if don't answer my question right," Parks threatened. "Where are the people who came through here earlier?"

"They're not here," the Cadet gasped.

"I know they're not here, dummy," Parks said as he raised his blade to where the Cadet could get a closer look at it. "Where've they been taken?"

"They didn't tell me," The Cadet replied. "Look, I'm not lying. I belong to the BOJ Order."

"The BOJ Order," Parks replied incredulously. "You're

not much more than twenty years old. What would you know of the Order?"

"I just turned twenty one and they promoted me," the Cadet choked. "The badge on my uniform is my proof."

Parks couldn't help laughing as he looked the hapless young man over. Then he realized the insidiousness of Management's work. They were enlisting Cadets with the promise of easy advancement, advancement that really meant nothing. Parks personally trained Cadets into the Order but it took years of hard work and an undying commitment to excellence. There had never been anyone, including himself, who achieved such honor at such a young age. But Management managed to reduce the Order to name only and now was using it to build a ruthless band of killers with the authority and mystique of the Order behind them.

Parks was disgusted at the thought.

"Here's what's going to happen," Parks said as he slowly lowered the Cadet to the floor. "You're going to give me the keys to your ride outside and then you and your sleeping friend over there are going to wait patiently until I return for you. I know you carry several sets of handcuffs so let's get you two comfortable."

Parks stripped them of their keys and made sure they had no weapons before attaching them to one of the large steel building columns. Then he climbed into the black SUV and pulled out with only one thought in mind, he had to find David, Normand, and Burke before it was too late. He figured they would likely take them to the Citadel even if it was mostly destroyed. Parks had few choices and none of them felt good at the moment. He could try and bluff his way in wearing the uniform he took off one of the Cadets or try and attack the facility a second time.

Then he had an idea. If they brought the boys back to the Citadel there would be a record of it in the guard shack at the entrance. Harry required copious record keeping, so this would be the most likely place to begin. Problem was, the shack was manned by a heavily armed guard behind bulletproof glass and concrete. Worse, the guard could see in all directions so sneaking up was out of the question.

"I guess the best approach is the direct one," Parks said to himself as he parked the SUV in a dense grove of trees. "It's quarter to four so I'll wait until shift change at four that way they'll know something happened to the guys I left in the warehouse. While they're off searching, I can get all the information I need."

Sure enough, a bunch of SUV's left in a hurry from the Citadel and, once he was certain they were gone, he pulled the cap he had taken off one of the men over his face and made his approach. He had one of their shirts on but it was too small and he had already ripped the back and arms out. If he had to get out for any reason, the guard would spot him immediately. So, he lowered the seat down and back as far as it would go hoping the tinted windows would hide his identity long enough as he slowly drove towards the main entrance. He stopped and waited as the guard checked the number on the truck he was driving before coming out with clipboard in hand.

"You guys are late," the guard said as walked up to the window. Parks kept his head behind the center post where the guard couldn't see his face. "What kept you? We just sent a patrol out to find you guys," the guard continued as he hopped onto the running board to get a signature on his clipboard.

Parks reached out, grabbed the guard by his collar and yanked his head into the top of the door. The impact splattered blood across the side of the truck and onto the steering wheel. Then he pulled his unconscious body in through the window and shoved him into the passenger seat while he looked over the information on the clipboard.

"No one's been in with any prisoners," Parks lamented as he reviewed the day's activity. "That means they must be holding them somewhere else, but where?"

He turned around, left and, after about a half mile, reached over, opened the passenger door, and deposited the guard in a ditch. He was flying blind now and it didn't make him happy. Management must have moved some of their operations since he attacked the Citadel and he needed to find someone who might know where. The only person he could think of was Aaron. If he didn't already know something he would likely be able to find out.

Aaron lived in a condo in an upscale part of the city where a Management vehicle would not draw attention. Most of the people who lived in those neighborhoods worked for

Management in some capacity or another. But he couldn't afford to allow the stolen rig he was driving to be identified or seen in front of Aaron's place. That would be a problem, so he parked at the end of a local playground under a large tree.

He imagined young mothers and grandparents watching children playing on swings and climbing things built for their amusement. Parks sat for a few minutes enjoying the scene in his mind before realizing how barren the place had become. There were no happy people just windswept dusty fields. It was an eerie lonely place and clear evidence of the underlying fear permeating their city.

He took off the hat and shirt and threw them on the front seat before locking up the truck. Then he wrapped his coat and blades and stuffed them inside his back pack. He was worried how out of place he might appear in his leather pants and shirt. He certainly didn't look anything like a local. But he had to get into Aaron's condo without drawing attention to himself. There were sidewalks along both sides of the streets and they were as empty as the playground. That helped but didn't guarantee someone couldn't come out or drive by so he decided on a different approach. The houses were built close together, some less than ten feet apart. The house on the end had a tall brick chimney that extended well above the roof line. All he had to do was get over the tall wooden privacy fence that surrounded the yard, run across about fifty feet of lawn, climb the chimney guarded by windows on both sides, then cross about twenty roofs to Aaron's place all without being spotted.

"That's why I make the big bucks," Parks laughed to himself as he waited behind a bush for a car to pass before racing across the street, through a grassy area with a fire plug in the middle and easily jumping the fence.

He dropped silently, checking for dogs or children but fortunately there were neither. He began the climb and was about half way up when he passed the dining room window. Pausing for a moment, he noticed several open suitcases on the dining room table. A woman came in with a young boy, about eight years old tight on her heels. Parks swung out of sight as he clung with his fingernails to the bricks.

"Mom, why do we have to leave?" the little boy asked. "I like it here and my friends are close."

"Don't worry honey," the woman said. "Your friends are leaving too."

Just then, the father came in and hustled the boy off to his room.

"Why are we leaving?" the woman asked with a frown.

"We have to," the man said gently. "The rumors I've been hearing at the office for months aren't just rumors anymore. My boss called several of us into his office and told us we had best come up with a safe place to be for a while. He said he was told by his boss, resisters were preparing to attack the city and grab anyone they could get their hands on to use as hostages. So, I took two weeks of vacation and told him we were going camping. Now come on, we need to get out of here."

Parks waited until they left the room before finishing his climb to the roof.

"Always about the resisters," Parks lamented. "Management has these people so brainwashed they'll think the Testers coming at them are resisters in disguise. I just can't believe it. People are so stupid."

Parks leapt from roof to roof making sure not to be seen or heard but it wasn't easy in the bright afternoon sun and more than once he had to hide on one side or the other of a roof so as not to be spotted. Finally, he arrived at Aaron's condo and dropped to a small balcony graced by two glass doors. Fortunately, they weren't locked and he was able to slip inside. Aaron wasn't home so he proceeded to make himself comfortable while waiting. He raided the fridge but all he got for his efforts was some left over pizza and diet soda. It wasn't long before Parks heard the key in the lock and slipped into the shadows in case Aaron wasn't alone.

"Hi Aaron," Parks said.

"Aieeh," Aaron nearly screamed. "Parks, what the heck are you doing here? You nearly scared me to death."

"Sorry about that but I had to reach you and I didn't know any other way. Look, we need to go over some things quickly. Have a seat and we'll talk."

Aaron slid into a chair across from Parks at the small kitchen counter.

"Were you able to make it back into the Citadel ok?" Parks asked.

"Yes, you made so much chaos the day you knocked the building down no one noticed me join the crowd. Since then, they've stopped bringing people in from the county and I've been reassigned to the Manager's security team. Harry's gone, as you well know, and General Allison has taken over for him but I haven't seen Barron for a while. The other creepy guy, Mr. Grey, who acts more like a secret service agent than an administrator, is involved in some kind of investigation. I'm not sure exactly what. They gave me the job of analyzing the Citadel's remaining assets to determine if we could fend off another attack, should one come. It makes it possible for me to get some information but they're staying very tight lipped."

"Do you know if Management has another operational facility?"

"Actually, from my review of the books, it looks like they have several. Why do you want to know? Are you thinking of taking another one out?"

"Maybe," Parks replied before filling Aaron in on the recent events.

"Man, if they've got David, Normand, and Burke," Aaron said anxiously, "they're going to hurt them to get the answers they want. We need to get them out right now."

"That's the reason I'm here," Parks replied calmly. "But I must know where to look. Can you tell me where those other facilities are?"

"I've never been to any of them or seen their addresses on any paperwork," Aaron replied glumly. "But I overheard Mr. Grey talking on the phone right before I left today and he said something about the prize being at the port. It seemed rather unusual because he's never on the phone but he sure left in a hurry. He was going somewhere important."

"Where's this 'port' he mentioned." Parks pressed.

"Like I said," Aaron replied, "I don't know. But the port could mean a couple of things. There are some docks down by the East River or it could mean one of the transport terminals on the North end where Management takes in supplies. Both places have lots of activity from what I've seen on some of the reports that have crossed my desk, but I couldn't tell you which one or which building. There are literally tons of buildings in both places."

"It's not much to go on but it's better than nothing. Can you give me a lift out of here?"

"Sure, I'm parked in the garage so no one will see you get in. You can lie on the back seat and cover up with a blanket."

"One more thing, I'll need you to do what you can to gather as much information as possible," Parks said as they got into Aaron's car. "You've got the crystal I gave you. Use it to contact me. Just know there has been some weird interference with the crystals of late and I haven't been able to contact David so I can't guarantee it'll work, but try anyway."

Aaron drove to a safe place and let Parks out, but neither of them had much to say as they parted. They could both feel the knot in their gut tightening, knowing their friends were likely fighting for their lives, and there was nothing they could do about it---*yet*.

CHAPTER 11

"Now we can have that meeting!" Dave assured himself as he approached the board room. "The Board may have felt shunned when I didn't come last night, but this will more than make up for it."

Dave confidently pushed the door open and stepped into the room where six ordinary looking men sat at a long table intently looking as Dave strolled in and took his seat.

"Let's not waste anyone's time," Dave began. "You expected a report on the Gifts and the resisters. I've got both and they're quite good. First, the resisters have revealed themselves," Dave continued looking from member to member, "and I've discovered one of their best kept secrets. They apparently have a hideout somewhere in the wilderness and they're able to access it through a series of underground tunnels. I've caught three of the traitors already and they're currently undergoing interrogation. Soon we'll know the extent of their operations and what abilities they may or may not have. Once we are confident of their condition, I see a total takeover and the permanent ruin of their efforts to resist. Better yet, Parks will be taken with them as he's involved up to his eyeballs."

Dave pushed back from the table with a big smile plastered across his face but, to his chagrin, they just stared at him emotionlessly.

"Hey, I thought you would be excited to hear the news," Dave said, becoming irritated. "This is a major step forward in our complete control of the city."

"You mentioned 'Gifts,'" Number six said flatly. "What do you have for us?"

"Only this," Dave said as he opened his briefcase and set a cloth on the table.

The six got up and gathered around intently interested as he slowly unwrapped the red crystal blade.

"I took this off Parks," Dave exclaimed gleefully. "It must have great significance or he wouldn't have it. What do you say now?"

"We say you're a fool," Number Three replied as he returned to his seat. "You've found nothing but a very old blade left here from the first time we came to this sorry place. We offered someone, like you, something he could hold onto and use but he couldn't handle it. He said it gave him only visions and nightmares so he buried it where no one could find it until now, that is. It's worthless to us."

"Well, now that I have it, what should I do with it?" Dave asked, feeling more than a little deflated.

"Do what you want," Number Five replied. "Its power will help you but remember the last one who used it couldn't handle it and destroyed himself. Is that all you have?"

"For now," Dave said as he rolled the blade back up and got up to leave. "But I'll find those Gifts soon, just you wait and see."

"We grow tired of waiting," Number One replied. "We've already given you much time but you return with nothing. It's time we began working more closely with you. This man called Parks," Number One continued, "must be dealt with differently. We've felt his power growing but that doesn't concern us. What does concern us is that he influences people's emotions. That's what cannot be allowed to continue. People cannot feel they have anyone to help them or anyone who does not obey. The frustration and fear that comes from despair is required. We expect you to get us the Gifts but not take your focus off Parks. He must be dealt with."

Dave stopped and gave the six the hardest look he could muster but they simply returned to their seats with the same placid look they always had. They waited for Dave to exit before speaking.

"Why do we continue waiting?" Number Five asked.

"Be patient, my brother," Number Four responded. "Let him do what he can. We'll start the process when he has the Gifts for us."

"I'm not sure he can get them," Number Five said. "He seems less powerful than we first thought. Bringing that old blade here was a good example. How can we trust he will do any better now?"

"Ah, but that's the point," Number Six said. "He brought

the blade because he thought it was important to us. That's evidence enough of his loyalty so I say we give him a little more time. See if he can get the Gifts and that one called Parks. If he does, we shall reward him. If he doesn't…"

The six men began laughing in unison as they got up and slowly filed out the back door.

Dave was excited as he returned to his office for some last minute business. Even though he was caught flatfooted with the red crystal blade, he could feel the Board's support growing. They had to know how valuable he really was. After all, he found the tunnel and captured some key resisters.

"Hello," Dave said as he made a quick call, "anything yet? No, well keep working. They won't hold out forever."

Meanwhile, George Marshal, the man who saved Bruce Clawson and now a foremen down at the Central Power Processor unit was just finishing up for the day. He worked for Bruce and was promoted into Bruce's position after he 'died.'

George was a good employee and smart enough to keep his opinions to himself but he worried he might have been promoted for other reasons. He felt his superiors wanted to keep an eye on him. After all, he was close to Bruce at one time. But it didn't really matter as George did his best to keep his nose out of trouble and stay focused on his work.

It was late in the day as George was making his final rounds. He stopped by each control room to review the day shifts reports and check the stability of the system. Things seemed normal as he reviewed printouts and talked briefly with his team leaders. It had been a long day and he felt especially tired. He was ready to call it a day.

Then he suddenly remembered there was a late shipment of needed raw materials and his off-loaders had already hit the showers. He jumped on his scooter, headed to the outer area to take care of it himself, and arrived just as the truck was pulling up to the loading dock.

"Running a little late today?" George asked as he greeted the driver and started examining his load.

"Yeah, there was some issue at the main gate. The guard went home or something without telling anyone. They had to send someone out with keys just to let me in. Sure is weird how that building collapsed and all. Did you ever hear what happened?"

"They tell me it was an earthquake," George answered, satisfied the paperwork was in order. "But who knows? You would think a quake that big would have damaged more than just one building."

George climbed onto one of the transporters and began removing large containers and stacking them in the cavernous warehouse. It took him a little over fifteen minutes to clear the truck and get the driver ready to go. He signed for the goods and mounted his scooter to head back to the office when he realized he hadn't pulled the packing slips off the containers.

"I'd probably forget my own head today if it wasn't attached," George lamented as he weaved through the warehouse ripping slips off containers as he zoomed past.

Then something caught his eye. A light was coming from the old abandoned office on the other side of the rail tracks. It was the one place he made off limits to his crew. He worried they might sneak out there and play cards or sleep when nobody was watching. If they were caught by anyone but him, he would be in big trouble too.

"I can't believe they'd try that," George fumed as he squealed the tires on his scooter. "Well, at least it's not my crew. They're gone for the day. But I'm going to chew some serious butt and there may even be some pink slips before this is over."

George parked his scooter inside the warehouse and walked the rest of the way. He was steaming mad as he prepared to burst in on whomever had nerve enough to defy his order. But, then he heard voices he didn't recognize coming from inside. He slowly rose up and peeked through the only window. George managed to catch the gasp in his throat before it could make its way out. He immediately recognized the man in the dark suit. He was the guy that broke into his apartment and beat him senseless. It was a moment that was unforgettable as George recalled the small, medium built man in the dark suit knocking him around. Then he began breaking his fingers before shoving a small red glowing crystal into his chest.

That was something George could never forget.

Now, inside were three young men in various stages of distress and the same small man determined to add to their suffering. George's first instinct was to bust in but he quickly remembered how powerful this guy is. He would have no chance yet he had to do something.

Then he had an idea.

George crept back to his scooter and took off for the plant. If those three guys were going to have a chance, he needed help. The evening crew was just beginning operations as he came wheeling around. He'd worked with most of the men on every shift and knew who was good in a fight. First, he found a large bucket loader and then began making the rounds.

"Me, climb in there," one of the men protested. "It's against safety regulations. You know that."

"You grab a wrench, a hammer or whatever you can," George shouted from the cab, "and get your butt in here or I'll climb down there and kick it in."

There were no more protests as George filled the bucket with large, somewhat confused, men. He only stopped long enough to tell them there was going to be a fight. He said someone had broken into the plant and security couldn't be counted on. It was up to them to save their plant and their jobs. It was a lie but he had the men's attention and more than a few of them were looking forward to breaking some heads and on company time to boot. George stopped the bucket loader and let the men out on the edge of the tracks. He told them to follow his lead but be ready for anything. He said these guys were tough and they would be in for the fight of their lives.

"Open up in there!" George shouted as he tried the office door.

It was locked but, in a few moments, he heard the lock turn and out stepped Mr. Grey pulling the door tightly behind him.

"You men get out of here," he commanded, looking the crowd over through his dark glasses. "This is Management business and you're trespassing."

"You're the one trespassing," George replied angrily. "This is company property. If you don't want any trouble, you can leave now."

Mr. Grey looked at George and then at the group of large men carrying wrenches and lengths of pipe, and they didn't seem moved by his assertions.

"I am telling you to leave, NOW!" Mr. Grey said, raising

his voice an octave or two, "you don't belong here."

Then Mr. Grey made a fundamental error. He shoved George off the office wooden steps into the arms of his workers and that was all it took. George responded with a quick uppercut that caught Mr. Grey on the point of his chin. The crowd stood in stunned surprise as the small man just readjusted his glasses. The shot from George should have dropped him but it didn't. In fact, it didn't even faze him as he picked George up by his shirt and threw him onto the railroad tracks. Then a roar went up from the men as they attacked. They hit the little man with everything they had as he waded into them but nothing could slow him down. He deflected a blow from a steel pipe with one arm while taking a shot from a pipe wrench on the back of his head, without so much as a flinch. George saw his opportunity while the fight was underway to get inside and try to free the young men. He opened the office door and was instantly sickened by the sight.

Each man was stripped to only his underwear and tied tight in heavy steel chairs. The smaller man on the far end was slumped against his bonds and his head was hanging off to one side with a steady drip of blood from his mouth that was pooling on the floor. The other two were beaten badly and only semiconscious as George flipped open his knife to cut them free.

"Cut my ropes first," Normand pleaded as he watched through the open door.

Mr. Grey was gaining the upper hand over his attackers.

George did as requested and reached behind Normand to cut the rope securing his hands but, before he could cut his feet free, Normand lunged for a small table with their belongings on it. He grabbed for his ring as he landed face down on the wooden floor. The table and everything on it crashed upon him as he slid the ring on and pointed it in Mr. Grey's direction. A bright blue light momentarily blinded everyone but, when their eyes readjusted, Mr. Grey was gone and only the telltale wisp of smoke remained before a gust of wind blew it away.

"We've got to get out of here fast," Normand insisted as several men came in to help. They moved the table off of him and helped him up as George cut the ropes off his feet. "He'll be back with help."

"We've got to get you guys to the hospital fast," George said as he cut David free.

David stumbled to his feet and nearly fell over. Thankfully one of the men grabbed him before he could. Just like Normand, his face was a bloody mess and both eyes were nearly swollen shut.

"Give me a hand here," George commanded to one of his men as he addressed Burke.

"Is he conscious?" Normand asked as the men supported Burke by the shoulders as George cut his bonds.

"I'm afraid not," George replied quietly. "I think he's dead."

Those words filled the room with unimaginable sorrow yet there was nothing anyone could do as the men carried Burke's lifeless body across the railroad tracks towards the power plant. Both David and Normand refused help as they limped behind their fallen friend. They weren't going to the hospital either so George agreed to take them anywhere they wanted. He had a large station wagon which today served as both rescue vehicle and hearse.

CHAPTER 12

Kenzie and Kirsten left the meeting at the school with heavy hearts. The thought of Joshua dead at the hands of people they grew up with and once trusted was too much to bear.

"I can't believe he's gone," Kenzie groaned, "he was always such a good friend."

"I know," Kirsten said sadly, "but we have to make his sacrifice count. Josh was doing more than his duty, he was protecting his friends. That needs to be honored and remembered."

Kenzie agreed. She and Josh were best friends but Kirsten cared just as much.

"One other thing," Kirsten said quietly, "if it's ok with you, I'd like to stay a few more days."

"I think that would be great. I don't feel like being alone right now anyway."

The drive back to Kenzie's apartment was uneventful and there was little conversation. Once they got there, they both busied themselves making food. It was getting late when they finished eating and were about to call it a night and head to their respective bedrooms when Kirsten suddenly froze.

"I've got it!" She exclaimed.

"What? What do you have?" Kenzie asked as she straightened up.

"Everyone is terrified of Management, right?" Kirsten asked.

"Pretty much," Kenzie replied. "They've all the power and are running the city."

"But what if they're as afraid, or even more so than us?"

"What would make you say that? Look at what they've done and how they're bringing in Testers. Maybe to destroy the city, like they tried once before."

"That's my point exactly," Kirsten said excitedly. "They couldn't destroy the city then even with the Testers. What if they're actually the ones afraid of losing? What if they really don't know what to do? The ancient story tells of the fearsome beast and a darkness that covers the land that always ends in total devastation of the city, right? That's why it's such a scary story. So, if we believe the story is true and a warning to future generations, why is the city still here when the forces that are supposed to destroy it are also here?"

"Oh, I get it now," Kenzie replied. "You're saying the city should be in ruins, destroyed years ago. But the story never mentions it surviving for even a short time. The Zender initiates the chaos that ultimately results in destruction. But that didn't happen."

"Exactly," Kirsten exclaimed. "According to what I've heard, the thousand years are up and yet we're still here. Somehow they're bogged down and maybe can't get away from us anymore than we've been able to escape them. Maybe we're seeing the writing of a new story, one that could end completely different and maybe that's what they're afraid of. So, now, in their desperation, they're trying to recreate the terror and fear that came with their arrival. And I'm sure that means we can expect more bad things. But what if that doesn't work?"

Kenzie leaned back with her hands behind her head as she considered the thought.

"Think about it. Doesn't that explain a lot of things?" Kirsten continued. "I think they came, as they have in the past, if you believe the story, to take what they wanted and leave. No one had ever put up a winning fight. They just destroyed and left, so tricking them into staying by surrendering was, by all accounts, a brilliant move. They couldn't terrorize the people and destroy the city like they had before instead they had to stay and try to run the show. That's not what they're good at, obviously. So now they're becoming increasingly desperate."

"I like it," Kenzie said, "But what good does knowing that do us?"

"It only helps us if we can find out why they're still here and what they need. If we can do that, maybe we can end this thing forever."

It was an interesting idea for sure but continuing this line of thought would have to wait as both women were exhausted, mostly from the emotional stress of the day. There was a bedroom on each end of Kenzie's apartment, separated by the kitchen and living room. Kirsten had the one off the living room and settled in for the night. But her mind was not ready to rest as she continued to meditate on recent events. After several hours, she finally fell asleep.

"You two are such a big help to me," Pearl said encouragingly as Kirsten and Henry followed her into the greenhouse. "Today we're going to plant some radishes and string beans. You get the wheel barrow and fill it with compost," she said to Henry, "while your sister and I get the beds ready."

Kirsten loved helping her mom work. She dug in with a shovel while her mom took a rake. After some vigorous effort, they were ready for Henry to dump in the first barrel of compost. They continued working it into the soil while Henry went for another load. Soon they were ready to plant but Henry always got bored at this part of the process and wandered off to explore more interesting things in the large greenhouse. Things like the small birds that flittered from rafter to rafter. They had nested in one and he was careful not to disturb it as he watched the mother bringing food to her young. Kirsten, on the other hand, stayed right with Pearl until they were finished.

"That looks really good," Kirsten said as she wiped the sweat off her brow with the back of her dirty glove.

"It really does," Pearl agreed. "And you know there's something even more important planted here, something that could really help you."

"Help me?" Kirsten asked somewhat confused. "Help me how?"

"Help you with your understanding," Pearl replied as she turned towards her young daughter. "But to make it work you're going to have to wake up. You have to wake up now. WAKE UP, KIRSTEN, WAKE UP!"

Kirsten took a gasp of air as she bolted upright in bed then slowly relaxed back into her pillow. She had been dreaming but it felt so real and she could still hear her mother's voice in her head. It almost felt like she was in the room.

Suddenly, she heard voices coming from outside and a knock on the door.

"Who could be here at this time of night?" Kirsten thought as she swung her feet out of bed and grabbed her robe.

She was almost to the door when she realized someone

was already in the apartment.

"We understand you have dealings with this woman." A gruff voice said as she cracked the bedroom door.

She could see a large Cadet standing in the doorway with a picture in his hand. Kenzie took the photo and looked it over sleepily and then handed it back.

"Sorry, don't recognize her." Kenzie said with a yawn. "Who is she and why do you think she's here?"

"She's wanted for questioning," The Cadet snapped, "and her name is Kirsten Parks, as if you didn't know."

Kirsten swallowed hard as a second Cadet pushed past the first into the apartment.

"Wait just a minute!" Kenzie protested as she put her hand on the second Cadet's chest. "You can't break in here without permission."

"We can do anything we want," the Cadet said as he shoved her hand away. "You answer the questions or you'll find yourself somewhere you don't want to be, or maybe you do?" the Cadet continued with a smug smile as he grabbed Kenzie by the arm and pulled her tight to his chest.

Kenzie's right knee landed in the appropriate place as the Cadet's face turned several shades of red before dropping to his knees. Kirsten was about to come to Kenzie's aid when the first Cadet spoke again.

"You deserved that," he said to his partner. "Now get up!" the Cadet continued returning his attention to Kenzie. "I don't want to make this more difficult for you than it already is but we have to search your apartment. You can take your complaint to our manager in the morning if you wish but, as soon as my partner has recovered, we'll begin."

"I'm fine," the Cadet said straightening his back and glaring at Kenzie.

Kirsten quietly closed the door as she considered her options. The apartment was small and it would only take them a few moments to get to her room. Fortunately, it was on the ground floor so she opened the window and quietly slipped out. Other voices were coming from the front which meant there were more. She closed the window just as the bedroom door opened and the light came on. Kirsten slipped behind some bushes at a neighbor's apartment and watched.

"What's this all about?" the Cadet Kenzie kneed demanded.

"My niece spent a couple of nights here a while back," Kenzie replied calmly, "and I haven't got around to picking the room up, as if it's any of your business."

"It's all my business," the Cadet growled. "You're lying. I can see it in your face."

Kenzie held her ground and looked hard into the man's eyes without flinching.

"The apartment's empty," the first Cadet said as he burst into the bedroom. "We'll be going, for now. However, if you see that woman, you'll let us know, right?"

"Like I told you the first time," Kenzie replied as she followed them to the door. "I don't know her."

Kenzie slammed the door behind them and bolted it. They quickly gathered with two more on the sidewalk.

"We came up empty," one of them said. "We checked around the entire building and there wasn't anyone."

"She knows something," the injured Cadet said bitterly. "I just feel it. Why don't you let me go back in and find out? I can get her to talk or at least have fun trying."

"You had your chance," the senior Cadet replied. "If she knows something, we'll deal with her later. Right now we have a few more places to check and then we'll come back if we need to."

The men piled into their two SUVs and headed out of the apartment complex. Kenzie was watching from behind the living room curtain with the lights off as they left. Once she was certain they were gone, she headed into Kirsten's room.

"Kirsten, Kirsten," she whispered anxiously as she slowly moved into the dark room.

Then she heard tapping on the window. She quickly opened it and helped Kirsten back into the room.

"Are you ok?" Kenzie asked as she shut the window.

"I'm fine," Kirsten replied, "but those guys mean business. I'd better get out of here right away. I overheard them say they're coming back and I can't be here when they do. Anyway, I can't believe you clobbered that guy. That was a gutsy move."

"Oh him, nah," Kenzie replied. "I recognized him from

school. Anyway, it was just a reflex from my training days. But I really don't like you having to leave. Where are you going to go? Your apartment can't be safe if they came here looking for you."

"I'm not going to say just in case they might be listening somehow," Kirsten answered. "Besides, I need to follow up on a lead of my own. I received some unexpected direction tonight."

Kirsten got dressed, said goodbye, and quietly slipped around the back of Kenzie's apartment. The night air was cool but felt refreshing as she pondered the dream.

"There must be a reason I dreamt about the old greenhouse," she thought. "It seemed as real as actually being there."

She was indeed "waking up" as she began crossing streets and running down darkened alleys. Things seemed as crazy as ever but now it was up to her to find some long awaited answers and, if she was right about Management, she had no time to spare.

CHAPTER 13

Jim pulled into Dr. Flint's driveway wondering how long it would be until Management found out about this place too. Everywhere else they had been was compromised in one way or another so it would be foolish to think they would fare any better here and that really worried Jim. He felt like they were slowly being marginalized and methodically pushed into a tighter and tighter corner. But they had no choice as he parked behind the main house in the servant's quarters. They needed some time to figure out their next move.

"I hope everyone's ok," Rita said as Jim rang the doorbell.

"I know what you mean," Jim replied gently, "this isn't the way I thought things were going to work but it is what it is."

"No kidding," Rita retorted. "All we've done is to go from one dangerous event to the next."

It took a couple more rings before Dr. Flint let them in. The look on his face answered many questions. Management may not have discovered what was going on here yet but their handiwork was evident. Joshua's body was still lying in one of the rooms waiting for the memorial services his parents had arranged. They made up a believable story about a tragic horse riding accident and the good Doctor certified the death certificate. That seemed to satisfy any curiosity for the moment but had done little to sooth the pain.

"I never thought it would come to this," Dr. Flint said as he led them into his living quarters, "I'm a physician not a fighter. However, I can't allow this to continue without doing something."

"What are you thinking?" Jim asked as he stood next to the couch.

"Follow me and I'll show you," Dr. Flint said as he slid open a panel in his living room wall and put a key into the deadbolt hidden inside.

A muffled click signaled the release of a lock behind the

wall and a narrow door popped opened. Dr. Flint hit the light switch as a set of stairs descending underground appeared. Rita and Jim followed him as they made their way down the circular steel stairs to a small room built under the house.

"You're the only two people, other than my late wife and myself, to have ever stepped foot down here since we bought this place," Dr. Flint confessed. "We discovered this room quite by chance years ago and were confused at first to why it's even here. Then, after checking it over carefully, we discovered its special purpose."

Dr. Flint felt under a bench set against the wall and pushed a button. There was a low humming sound as a section of the wall moved out. He pushed the wall the rest of the way open and went in.

"Well, I'll be!" Jim exclaimed. "There're weapons of all sorts in here and some of them could be antiques," he continued as he examined a bow strapped with what appeared to be animal hide.

"My wife and I believed this was once a weapons depot of some sort," Dr. Flint explained. "People must have used this spot to hide their stuff but, eventually, someone built this room and then a house over it and the secret panel we came through. Anyway, you can see there're plenty of weapons to choose from including those automatic rifles. They may be old but they still work. I keep them oiled and clean. It's my only real hobby since my wife passed and I'm not sure why, really, I don't even like guns that much."

Jim and Rita examined the wide assortment of weapons. There were enough here to outfit a small army with guns, knives, swords, bows, arrows, and specialized throwing weapons. There were even boxes of grenades and land mines stacked on shelves in the back.

"I'll get the bag from the car," Jim said eagerly as he headed for the stairs. "These will definitely help level the playing field."

He quickly returned and they proceeded to fill the bag with most everything he could carry while Rita and Dr. Flint strapped guns across their shoulders and carried boxes of ammunition to the car. Two trips later, the trunk was full yet they had barely made a dent in the weapon stash.

"We're going to be rather conspicuous in this inconspicuous car Tim provided," Jim said as he started it up. "If you don't mind, we're going to need to do a little visual modification."

"You'll find everything you need in the garage," the doctor said as he went back in the house.

True enough, Jim found some orange metal spray paint cans on a shelf. It wasn't a great paint job, by any means, but at least it wasn't black anymore. They stayed with the doctor the remainder of the day to allow the paint to dry before taking their leave. Jim had figured out where to go next and now was the time.

"You drive," Jim said as he got into the passenger seat with several large caliber handguns on his lap and an automatic rifle snuggled in at his feet.

"If someone pulls us over," Rita said, "I want you to stay put. I'll jump out and meet them at the back. I don't want you using those things unless we have no other choice."

"I don't want to use these at all," Jim replied. "My goal is far bigger but we have to be ready for anything, like it or not."

Jim directed Rita around the suburbs of the city being mindful to avoid the major interchanges. They would have less of a chance being spotted that way. Soon they arrived at one of the many housing developments and then a small cul-de-sac. She pulled up to the curb and shut off the motor.

"I won't need any of these yet," Jim said as he laid them on the back seat and covered them with the blanket. "Just make sure the doors are locked."

Rita joined him on the sidewalk as they approached an older house. Jim rang the bell, but at first no one answered. They were about to leave when the door slowly opened and an arm shot out pulling him inside. Rita quickly followed not sure what was happening.

"What's going on?" Jim asked straining to see as his eyes had yet to adjust to the dim light.

He jerked his arm away and was ready for anything.

"Sorry about that, but it's good to see you," Chris said. He was once Jim's senior assistant at HOT News and a friend as well.

All the curtains were closed tightly and the house had a

musty smell about it as Jim relaxed and returned the greeting.

"It seems like forever since we last saw you," Karen, Chris's wife added with a slight smile. "You're looking good."

They all recognized Rita and moved into the living room and sat down but Chris seemed anxious and somewhat agitated.

"Why are you here?" Chris asked bluntly as his wife left the room to get some coffee.

"So much has happened," Jim started, "that I don't know where to begin but I guess the best place is where we left off last. I told you then to take care of your family until we could meet again and it looks like you're doing just that."

"I'm doing my best," Chris replied quickly. "I finally got a call from one of the electronic supply companies I put a resume' into and they offered me a job. I'm working swing shifts mostly."

"Well that's great," Jim continued, trying to be upbeat. "But I've got bigger news for you."

"Here we go," Karen interrupted as she put a pot of coffee and a small plate of cookies on the table.

"What news?" Chris asked, becoming increasingly agitated. "Last time you had news, I lost my job and nearly everything else."

"It's ok, Chris," Karen said as she put her hand on his shoulder. "Jim's only here to help. I'm sorry," she continued, "we've been under a lot of stress lately."

"I understand," Jim went on, "and maybe we shouldn't have come. It seems I've gotten you into something way more dangerous than I realized."

"What do you mean?" Chris asked as he shot a nervous glance to his wife.

"I believe it's possible you got that call from your current employer because Management wants to keep tabs on you." Jim said flatly. Karen's eyes opened wide and she gasped as Jim continued. "Anyone connected to me is under suspicion. Management has become increasingly paranoid and may think you're part of a plot or something, I don't know. My question is, do you want to be involved or not?"

"Involved how, with what?" Chris asked.

"A group of us are working together," Jim replied calmly, "but we need more. It's dangerous but we have to do something before it's too late."

"Maybe it's already too late," Chris replied as he shot a worried glance at his wife. "Tell him about our new neighbors."

"New neighbors?" Jim said curiously.

"Well, things seemed normal enough at first," Karen replied, somewhat reluctantly. "Chris got his new job and then the next day *they* moved into the vacant house across the street. It may be a coincidence that the husband just happens to work at the same place with Chris. But then there's the wife. She's the nosiest person I've ever seen. I can't even go outside to get the mail without her coming over. We do our best to avoid them but it's nearly impossible. At times, we feel like prisoners in our own home."

"Yeah, and being the new guy on the job I didn't know what to expect so it was nice having a friend, at first." Chris said nervously. "But now I can hardly go to the bathroom without him being right there. And, you know what's really weird, I hardly ever see him do any work."

"You think they might be watching you?" Rita asked as she went to the front window. "It looks like they're home. I see a car in their driveway that wasn't there when we came."

"They went out earlier," Karen said as she joined her, "but I have a sneaking suspicion they'll be coming over any minute to find out whose car that is parked out front."

"Then we had best be going," Jim said as he got off the couch. "But you didn't answer the question," Jim continued as he looked hard into Chris's eyes. "Are you in or not?"

Chris shot a nervous glance to his wife who just shrugged her shoulders. They were both up against it.

"You can count on me," Chris said finally. "What do you want me to do?"

"Get Danny and Ray and meet us down at the old Elementary School tonight at ten." Jim replied. "If you think you can still trust them."

"We'll be there," Chris said feeling a sudden surge of confidence.

Jim shook his hand and Rita gave Karen a hug before heading for their car. They had almost made it when a loud voice sent shivers up their spines.

"Howdy neighbors."

A tall lanky man was strolling across the road with a thin woman tight at his side. Chris and Karen could only stand and watch helplessly.

"I don't believe we've had the pleasure," the man said, approaching with an outstretched hand. "I'm Rick."

Jim was about to open the car door but hesitated at the man's gregarious attitude.

"Nice to meet you," Jim replied, shaking the man's hand. "Well, we've got to be going."

Jim reached for the door handle as the man leaned over the hood of his car.

"Interesting paint job you've got there," Rick said. "Did you get that done at a local garage?"

"Yeah, some kids had a real charge at my expense," Jim lied. "They painted graffiti all over the car and I had to cover it up. It was really offensive."

"Real sorry to hear that," Rick said as he ran his hand over the fender. "You know, I've a real good friend that does painting out of his home. Why don't you give me your name and address and I'll have him call you."

"That's really kind of you," Jim said, doing his best not to be rude. "But I already have it scheduled, maybe next time. Well, nice meeting you," Jim said as he attempted to leave for the second time.

"We can really save you some money here." Rick insisted, ignoring Jim's statement. "Our friend is really, really good. Isn't that right, dear?"

"Oh, you're so right," his wife agreed as she joined her husband's banter. "Seems the people who owned the house before us had no idea how to match colors but he came over and really made it pop. He can paint anything. You must come over and see."

"Uh, maybe some other time," Jim said as he opened the door and shot an annoyed glance at Rita. "We really have to get going."

He climbed in and shut the door while Rick and his wife continued examining the paint. Rita started the car as Jim reluctantly rolled down the window.

"Really nice meeting you folks," Rick said, leaning on the roof of the car. "Hey, you guys hiding a body in the back seat or something?" He said jokingly as he spotted the blanket covering the weapons.

"Just keeping the dust off my guitar," Jim retorted as Rita dropped the car into gear and began pulling away from the curb.

"I'm a musician, too," Rick pursued but Rita was already in the middle of a U turn and even squealed the tires slightly as they left. The two 'neighbors' watched intently as they left and Jim was sure they were memorizing the license plate.

"That settles it!" Jim exclaimed as Rita began the standard evasive route through the city. "These people are everywhere. We'd better move quickly if we're going to have any chance. Management seems to be figuring all this out and, with the city fathers on their side, we're totally unsupported. Don't go that way," Jim said as Rita was about to turn for the abandoned Elementary School. "I need to go uptown and get some things."

"Is that really necessary?" Rita asked. "I'm pretty rattled at the moment and driving around town isn't doing my stomach any good."

"It really is," Jim insisted. "I'm sorry, but we have to do this."

Fortunately, Jim was able to quickly complete his business and get them out of the city without incident. But he was sure his hair was beginning to turn grey. Rita drove them back to the Elementary School and they hid the car as best they could. It would be a tense wait for Chris and the other two men but they found some ways to pass the time. A deck of cards helped and before long it was dark.

Jim's watch showed ten fifteen.

"Do you think something happened to them?" Rita asked nervously.

"They'll be here," Jim replied. "They have to be."

He had no sooner spoken when two sets of headlights appeared at the school entrance. The lights approached and then went off as they parked. Both Jim and Rita trained their automatic rifles on the walkway coming from the parking lot. They could hear footsteps approaching and, at the last possible moment, Jim hit a powerful flashlight. Chris let out a surprised yelp as the men covered their eyes.

"Hi guys," Jim said relieved as he pointed the flashlight at the ground. "It's really good to see you.

"You scared me half to death!" Chris exclaimed.

"Sorry about that," Jim replied. "Hi Danny," Jim said as he shook his hand. "Where's Ray? Is he coming?"

"I couldn't find Ray," Chris answered. "He wasn't at home when I went by to pick him up."

"Come on in," Jim said as he opened the door to the auditorium, "and I'll explain." Jim set the flashlight on one of the bleachers where it cast eerie shadows on the hardwood floor as Jim began. "We're going back to HOT News and broadcast a segment that's going to turn Management on its head."

"HOT News," Danny exclaimed. "That place is gutted and it's watched like a hawk. There's nothing for us over there."

"So I've been told." Jim replied calmly. "But that's not going to stop us. I went uptown today and picked up some needed equipment. Yeah its older stuff and not the best but it'll work. We're going inside HOT News for one final broadcast."

"That's crazy," Chris said. "Even if the equipment works, Management would be on us before we got started. We've been in there several times trying to get our personal things out and have to be careful no one sees our flashlights. They'd come a running if they did. How can we do a broadcast under those conditions?"

"Leave that to me," Jim replied confidently. "You get a hold of Ray and then the three of you meet me at HOT News in two nights. I've got a lot of equipment but please bring anything you think might be helpful. I might have forgotten something. We're going to get one shot at this and we'd better make it good. What do you think? Are you guys in or not?"

The two men looked at each other and then slowly nodded yes. Jim explained a few more things before they parted. Jim and Rita watched as their headlights disappeared into the blackness before settling into the car for a less than comfortable night's sleep. Jim took the front seat with a large pistol nestled within easy reach on the dash while Rita had the rear seat. It would be a long cold night but Jim didn't care. He was finally seeing clearly. A few more nights and this deal would be over. Then people would finally have a chance to see what's really going on. It's all going to be better soon, he assured himself.

CHAPTER 14

Aaron dropped Parks off along one of the streets bordering the East River. He quickly hopped an eight foot high chain link fence dropping in behind some old dry docked fishing boats sitting on blocks. The dock area was surrounded by dilapidated buildings with only a few that might show signs of life. Management had shut down access to the river for everyone except those trusted few they had favor upon. There was a time when this was a bustling area full of sports fishermen and weekend boaters. Now it was nearly empty as Parks wove his way along looking for clues to the disappearance of David, Normand, and Burke. He just couldn't understand why they weren't responding to the crystals he had given them. They should have been able to hear his thoughts just as Aaron had.

Parks was careful to stay in the shadows as he checked building after building. He was beginning to think the place was deserted as he approached the mile long boardwalk snaking along the edge of the East River. A cool wind blowing in from the North sent a shiver up his spine as he passed row after row of empty floating moorage docks. Then, in the distance, he saw what appeared to be a small garbage scow. It was pulled up to a loading dock behind the only well maintained warehouse he had seen. Lights illuminating the area spilled onto the river, dancing across the shallow white caps.

"It's pretty late to be loading garbage," Parks thought as he got off the boardwalk and began circling around the warehouse.

He came around the front and was relieved to see there wasn't any security to deal with. He checked the door and found it unlocked, which made entry simple. The front section of the building was filled with offices all of which were dark and appeared empty except a rear one by a door apparently leading to the main part of the building. The door was half open as Parks quietly came down the hall listening for voices. He slowly peeked around the corner where he could see a chair behind a large desk. Relieved there was no one there, Parks cracked the door separating the offices from the main building. It opened to a walkway marked with yellow striping surrounded by boxes and crates of different sizes. They would make for adequate cover as he moved deeper into the large warehouse. Suddenly, a set of voices approached as Parks quickly found cover behind a stack of crates.

"It has to be done tonight," a voice barked as two men passed through the door to the offices. "There can be no excuses. I want them off and the boat back before dawn."

Parks strained to hear more as the door closed but that was all he got. He stayed still for a few moments to ensure the two men were not coming right back out. Satisfied he could come out of hiding, he continued following the painted path until it opened into the full warehouse with storage racks filled to the ceiling and the sound of a forklift moving between the building and the garbage scow. More voices carried through the building as Parks moved stealthily between large racks filled with motors and boat propellers until he could get a look at what was going on. He found an opening between two boxes that gave him a view of three men apparently building large wooden crates of some sort. Parks moved closer to get a better look and slid between two rows of racks. But before he could see what they were doing, the skipper returned.

"Finish those up fast," the large man said as he strolled past, towards the dock. "We leave in twenty minutes."

There was no time to waste if Parks wanted to know what was going on. He quietly moved around boxes and old crates stuffed with rusting gear and made his way outside to the dock. The skipper had gone to the bridge and started the engines as the deck hands busily secured the cargo. Parks found a place to hide between the mysterious boxes and watched as the remaining ones were loaded. In a few moments, the skipper leaned over the rail and hollered to cast off.

The boat roared out onto the river heading in the direction of the wilderness. Parks watched as miles of river banks passed in the moonlit night. After what seemed like forever the steady vibration and roar of the large engine began to subside as a dock he had never seen before appeared in the distance. He dropped off the side of the boat and hung by one of the ropes used to tie up as the boat slowed and then gently bumped against the row of rubber tires hanging against the pier.

"Tie 'er up boys," the skipper shouted. "This is the last load."

Parks silently lowered himself down and then swam underwater before surfacing behind some reeds under the pier. He waited until they offloaded the boat and its lights disappeared up the river before climbing onto the wooden dock.

"What in the world is going on here?" Parks asked himself as he walked into a storage area surrounded by high barbed wire.

The boxes the men offloaded were lined up and apparently awaiting removal, but by who? A back gate showed tire tracks from some large vehicles and a big forklift sat waiting for duty. Curiosity was getting the best of him as he grabbed a corner of one of the containers and pulled. After a few attempts, some of the screws gave way and half the top splintered open just wide enough to get a look inside.

"What the heck!" Parks exclaimed, sliding one of his crystal blades inside like a flashlight. "Now there are two smaller boxes inside and shiny red to boot. Why would you put boxes inside more boxes? Just doesn't make sense."

He was about to rip the rest of the crate apart when he heard a faint hum in the distance. Hopping on top of a crate, Parks looked out over the wilderness where he could see a row of lights bobbing in the distance and heading his way. He quickly found a spot next to the dock where he could see and not be seen and, before long, three large transport trucks arrived. Men piled out and immediately started loading the crates. Parks considered stopping them but realized these were just young Cadets and he didn't want any of them hurt without good reason. They finished loading and then departed the way they had come. He was tempted to follow them when, instead, he decided to go back to the warehouse for answers.

"What would Management be doing way out here?" Parks wondered as he began running along the bank of the river towards the warehouse. "I've been that way before but it only leads into the wilderness and there are no facilities there. In fact, there is nothing out there except..." Parks paused for a moment as he looked back at the lights disappearing in the distance. "No,

104

it couldn't be the Island. No one knows about that."

His mind continued searching for answers as he jumped numerous drainage ditches and waded some shallow streams before returning to the warehouse. Yet, the answers he was seeking seemed illusive. As he crept alongside the warehouse, he was relieved to find the workers hadn't all left. He could hear voices coming from inside and estimated there to be at no more than ten of them. There was no need for stealth mode this time as he required answers and fast.

"Hello! Hello!" Parks yelled as he strolled through the wide overhead door into the bright insides of the building, "anybody home?"

A group of men quickly appeared, coming from every direction and surrounding Parks.

"This is private property and you're trespassing," one of the men declared. "You need to leave now."

"Hey, I recognize that guy," another man said. "He's the one the bosses have been looking for. His picture was on the news last night."

"Better get the skipper," the first man said.

In a few moments a large bearded man with a long scar running down his right cheek appeared.

"What do you want here?" the man asked in a cold voice. "You had best get going before I call in the authorities."

"Just a minute," Parks said calmly. "What's this all about? I don't understand what you're doing here."

"And there's no reason you should," the skipper answered as he nodded to several men who picked up two by fours and short pipes. "You were warned. Now if memory serves me right, there's a reward for you."

The men quickly tightened around Parks as the skipper folded his hands and smiled. Only it wasn't Parks that hit the floor. It was his men in one fashion or another. He had one of his crystal blades tucked up his sleeve and it dropped neatly into his hand as the attack began. The motion was effortless as he spun through the men dispatching some permanently, others only into unconsciousness, and a few more moaning in agony as his blade removed more than just the weapon they were holding. When Parks was finished, he calmly walked up to the skipper whose eyes were wide open with fear and amazement. He reached into his pocket for his gun but it was too late as Parks slid his blade under the skipper's throat.

"What do you want?" the skipper asked as Parks took his gun and tossed it aside.

"Some questions answered. You're going to tell me all about what's going on here. What was in those crates you hauled tonight and where are they going?"

"I don't know anything," the skipper said as he shrunk back from Parks' blade.

"Oh, I think you do," Parks replied, lowering his blade slightly. "We can do this the easy way or the hard way."

Without turning from the skipper, Parks elbowed one of the men in the face who had recovered enough to pick up a pipe and was about to hit him in the back of the head. The man crumpled on the floor as Parks grabbed the skipper by the arm and marched him into the office.

"This is how it's going to go," Parks said in a quiet voice as he threw the skipper into his chair. "You are going to tell me what I want to know or I'm going to begin cutting your fingers off one at a time. And, when I run out of those, I am going to start in on your face. That scar of yours won't look so lonely when I'm finished."

"But I'm telling you the truth," the skipper protested. "I don't know anything."

Parks could feel the anger growing as he stared hard into the skipper's eyes. This man was like all the others, taking and hurting without caring. But Parks was not about to let him continue as he held the man's hand down on the desk and waved his blade in the air.

"Pinkie first, Parks said with a smile as his blade sliced through the wooden table, mere inches from the skipper's finger.

"Ok, ok!" the skipper exclaimed. "I'll tell you everything. Just please don't hurt me."

Parks released the skipper's hand and straddled a chair as he listened to his story.

"They offered me money to crate and haul these heavy red boxes, see," the skipper began.

"They, who are they?" Parks interjected.

"I don't know their names," the skipper replied. "They always paid me in cash. But they were like those guys in the suits, you know, the Management types. Anyway, they came in with a proposition. I package and deliver them out there. That was the deal and that's all I know."

"Where do the red boxes come from?" Parks pressed.

"They didn't tell me but they're kind of weird," the skipper replied suddenly feeling even more uncomfortable as he noticed Parks' eyes glow a dark red. "They have a panel on one side that blinks. Anyway, I got nervous about them. Thought they could be bombs or something so I had the guys that delivered them followed. They drove back to some prison looking sort of place. I think it's that Citadel or something. Anyway, my chief mate stayed around for a while watching as people were brought into a building but they never came out. He really thought it was strange that they took the vehicles they came in and loaded them in trucks. Look, none of it makes any sense. We just do what we're told and keep our noses clean."

"Alright," Parks replied getting up as the anger surging through his chest began to abate, "I'm going to check out what you told me. In the meantime, I suggest you get those men of yours some medical attention. They're going to need it. But if you think you should report this, think again. I'll come back and take those fingers and maybe even more."

"Hey, I'm no Management lover," the skipper said anxiously as Parks' eyes glowed brighter. "We're just running a business here."

Parks turned to leave and that moment of distraction was all the skipper needed. He slipped open his desk drawer and pulled out a long knife he used for gutting fish. He jumped across the desk intending to stab Parks in the back but Parks was too quick as he deflected the blow and delivered one of his own, a crystal blade in the skipper's chest. The skipper staggered back into his chair with a confused look on his face.

"You, you knew I would try something," he gasped. "What, no blood?" The skipper said as he looked down at his shirt.

But his head didn't come back up. It just sank into his chest and rolled off to one side as his body relaxed in a bizarre sort of way. Yet, Parks felt no remorse. He figured the guy was just another one of Management's faithful's. But he was disappointed as he closed the office door and headed out of the building. He had no more information on David, Normand, or Burke's location than when he came.

But he had learned one thing Management's propaganda was working, instilling hatred for him and, maybe the resistance itself. He saw that in the eyes of the skipper and his crew. This would make trusting anybody a dangerous thing. Taking that bit of information, Parks took off for the next logical place to look, the transport terminals. They were on the other side of the city and traveling during the day would be especially dangerous. Yet, the dark feeling in his gut was tearing at him and seemed to be growing more powerful than ever. It was troubling that his emotions were turning cold.

CHAPTER 15

"This whole affair is turning crazier by the minute," Philip said as he stepped out of his brother's motor home and put one foot on the picnic table. "Management seems to know our every move. I don't know what more we can do to put the brakes on what they're doing. It seems impossible."

"Not completely impossible," Rich replied as he sat at the end of the picnic table and gazed out over the river. "I have something here that may help." He continued as he opened the knapsack he filled when they raided his old office. Out poured a pile of crisp twenty dollar bills, two guns, some envelopes stuffed with papers, and a large CB.

"What good is that going to do us?" Philip asked.

"Well, the guns works," Rich said as he handed it to James, "and money always comes in handy. However, I do agree this radio is no good." Rich continued as he set if off to one side. "But what is most valuable has yet to be revealed. I know it's in here somewhere." Rich continued as he took envelope after envelope and dumped them on the picnic table. He sifted through the pile while James and Philip just looked at each other and shrugged their shoulders. "Aha!" Rich exclaimed as he pulled out a strange looking key from the pile of papers. "Now we're in business."

"What's the key for?" James asked.

"It's not just any key," Rich replied, "and what it opens will astound you."

"What are we talking about here?" Philip asked, suddenly becoming interested.

"It's part of our family legacy, our shared history if you would," Rich began. "My family, like yours, has been in the city for eons. Well, my father passed down the same stories your fathers did scaring us so we wouldn't forget them even when we got older. Then, when he felt I was old enough, he showed me something he had invented. It was a small shiny metal box with only a slot for this key. Then he told me never to open it unless things were desperate.”

“Man, curiosity would have killed me,” James said as he examined the key.

“I know,” Rich continued. “But I trusted my father and, if he told me to do something, I did it.”

“What do you think’s in it?” Philip asked.

“I don’t know,” Rich replied. “Dad just said what’s in there appears ordinary but isn’t and will only help if all hope is lost. I tried to open it once when the invasion came. I thought certainly this was as desperate a time as there ever was but the key wouldn’t turn, it wouldn’t open.”

“Maybe it’s broken or doesn’t work,” James said.

“I thought something like that myself at the time and even started questioning if my dad was the brilliant inventor I thought he was. Why would he give me something that didn’t work? However, since then, I’ve had time to reflect and now wonder if we weren’t in as hopeless a situation as we thought back then. There’s no doubt that was a rough time but the surrender fixed that, at least for a season. Now these new thoughts keep coming to me. Thoughts about the stories and how different this is from what we were told. I’m beginning to think we might be writing something new. A new story, so to speak but we’re going to need all the help we can get because, from what I’ve seen, there isn’t a lot of time left.”

“So, let’s go get it and see what we have,” Philip said. “I can’t see how we could get into much more trouble than we are in now. The thing should open right up if what you’re saying is true.”

“That could be a bit of a problem,” Rich replied. “You guys know I designed the power generation plant, right.”

“Yes and it’s a great thing, why?” Philip asked.

“Well, before I lost my position, I added a special storage vault for the cube Dad gave me, underneath the main generator. I had a feeling I might need it someday but didn’t want it getting lost or stolen so I built a special place for it inside the concrete wall in the service room that can only be accessed by a hidden control pad.”

“Yeesh,” James sneered.

“Well, I was running the show at the time,” Rich replied defensively. “How was I to know this was going to happen? I just

110

thought it would be safest there."

"And so it has been," Philip said. "You put it in a place no one would ever find, but now we have to go get it, right?"

"Who in the world do you guys think we are?" James asked. "We run around like crazy burglars or something breaking in here, breaking in there. Now you want us to break into the Citadel, sneak past layer after layer of security, then enter the main generation unit, climb under it and find a hidden box. Oh, and if I forgot to mention it, we have to get out again all without being caught. If you haven't noticed, we're just two old farmers and an engineer. Have you gone completely mad?"

"Come on brother," Philip encouraged. "What's life without a little adventure? Look, we've already proven we can do tough things, why not try for the impossible."

"Not to mention we have a farm and life out there in the county but here we are hiding," Lori interjected. "I don't like the risk and wish we could leave these things for someone else to do but we can't. We can't go on living like this. It's time to finish this thing and get out of here for good. Get back to the life we all once knew and loved."

"Alright, I'm in," James said reluctantly after looking at his wife for a good long time.

"Just promise me one thing," Lori continued as she stepped in front of James. "You'll bring him back safe and sound. Ok?"

"You have my word," Philip replied.

Lori smiled as confidently as possible and then turned and gave her husband a solid hug. The three men sat at the picnic table and begin formulating their plan. Everything they'd done prior seemed minuscule by comparison to this job. They'd be going straight into the lion's den and they knew it. But they felt whatever Rich's father put in that box must hold the secret to something important, something vital, and it was worth the risk.

"Tell me one more time how we're getting in there," James asked still feeling somewhat skeptical.

"We're going to watch shift changes and see which of the workers take the city bus," Philip replied. "Then I'm going to need you to board the bus to steal an ID off one of them. Once you have the ID, Rich will duplicate it and make us each name tags. With the ID, we can join in with the crowd of workers on one of the shifts, probably night shift, and we're in. That way we avoid security. Rich will lead the way as he knows the place better than anyone."

"Why do all three of us have to go in?" James asked. "I could be the getaway man like before and wait for you guys in the car."

"Like we said," Philip replied, trying not to sound annoyed, "if Rich gets into trouble, we're going to have to be there for him. You'll be packing one of these guns and I'll have the other. Come on, James, you know it'll work. We just have to get ready and then do our thing."

James wasn't as confident as his brother but went along with the plan anyway. The employee entrance to the power generation plant was separate from the main entrance to the Citadel and was guarded only by a turnstile with cameras and a card reader. They let James out on a street corner where the bus made its stop and then parked in the lot across the street where they could watch the employees come out. Three thirty on the nose, people began filing out of the building. Some of them had rides waiting while others came across the street and got into their respective vehicles. But there were a few others who waited for the bus.

James got on with them and watched from the back as three men and a woman took their seats. Two men sat together and chatted quietly as the bus moved along. The woman came back and took a seat behind him while the other man sat near the front. James noticed the man sitting at the front was carrying a metal lunch box with his identity tag attached to the handle by a plastic strap. He watched as several stops came and went but the man sat silently looking out the window. Finally, James noticed the man pick up his coat, the lunch box and a paper he tucked under his arm. He stood up grabbing the overhead bar as the bus slowed. James got up and worked his way to the front and stood behind the man. The bus stopped and the door opened. The man stepped off but, as he did, James stepped off with him pushing him against the bus door before it had completely opened and nearly knocking him down.

"I'm sorry," James said as the man's lunchbox bounced on the sidewalk.

"Why don't you watch where you're going?" the man

said gruffly as James picked up his lunch box and handed it to him. "Well, I guess there's no real harm done," the man said in a softer tone as James' six foot nine, three hundred pound form towered over him.

"Sorry man," James said with a smile as he turned and quickly headed up the street.

The bus roared past as James walked around the corner to where Philip and Rich were waiting. He opened the door and hopped in as Philip took off.

"Did you get it?" Rich asked anxiously, leaning over the front seat.

"Easy as pie," James said proudly as he pulled the ID out of his pocket and handed it to Rich.

"This is even better than I hoped," Rich said as he examined the ID.

"What do you mean?" Philip asked as he glanced over at Rich.

"It's a maintenance ID," Rich replied. "That means we can get in and not worry about supervision. You see, maintenance works without supervision at night and on the weekends. However, they only run a skeleton crew so we have to come up with a reason why three additional maintenance men are showing up for work. Anyway there's no time to worry about that yet. Let's go to that printing place uptown and do a little creative work."

Rich was good at taking the ID apart, duplicating it, and substituting pictures they took in a small photo booth inside the printing shop. They purchased a few plastic sleeves and slid the ID's in before paying for the printing and leaving. They had half of what they needed. Their next stop was at a work wear store where they purchased clothing consistent with company safety requirements. Their final purchases were three orange hardhats and some safety glasses at a local hardware store.

"Now at least we look the part," James said, "but that still doesn't get us in. No one is going to know us and, at our age, we certainly won't pass for new hires."

"Maybe that's to our advantage," Rich said thoughtfully. "We just have to bluff our way in claiming to be a special maintenance crew brought in to examine the Pulsator."

"What's that?" James asked.

"It's the heart of my contribution to the family business," Rich replied. "I discovered a way to store wasted energy making the generation facility twice as efficient. However, no one but me really understands how it works and I have a way of making it "act up" so to speak. The panic will be immediate so we'll have to time this right, before they can make any calls. I figure we'll have about ten minutes at the most to get inside the facility and get what we came for."

Rich had taken one other thing from his office when they had broke in. It was a small control pad with three buttons on it, red, blue, and green.

"What's that for?" James asked as Rich pulled the controller from his pocket.

"You know," Rich replied thoughtfully, "an engineer shouldn't be afraid to reveal technical secrets but I was. I built the Pulsator with an internal control that would allow me to make it do anything including shut down completely. I think we can use this to make life tough on the night maintenance crew."

The three men stayed in the parking lot across from the Citadel until well after midnight. The only illumination came from the lights high on top of the building and those surrounding the turnstile. Rich pushed a combination of the three buttons on the controller as they crossed the street. By the time they made the turnstile, the lights were diming and brightening as power surged through the system. They ran their cards through the reader and headed inside. Alarms were already sounding and lights flashing as they entered through the walk door. Panicked workers were running in all directions as they quickly located the maintenance office.

"We need to reset the Pulsator," Rich said to a maintenance man with a phone in one hand and a phone book in the other.

"Who, who are you?" the man asked, startled by their sudden appearance.

"We're your best friends," Rich said boldly as he walked toward the desk. "We're part of a specially trained maintenance team and we're here to fix the situation."

"How did you get here so quickly?" The man asked suspiciously but seeming more than a little relieved at their presence.

"Just like the fire department," James replied. "The alarm rings and we have less than ten minutes to be on-site."

"Well, come on," the maintenance man said, overcoming his suspicions as he shot up from the desk. "Let's get you in."

He led the way through the building and to a large metal door at the base of the central unit. The four men entered and began a long climb down several sets of metal stairs. The system was moving and shaking the building so hard it sent dust cascading down from the rafters and choking the air as they headed towards their destination.

The Pulsator sat in the center of a large underground room with mammoth pipes coming down from the units above, and vent pipes leading out. It had a specialized control panel designed by Rich with symbols only he understood. It was the one piece of information Management hoped to get out of him when they were starving him at the EDD.

"It's going to take us some time," Rich said to the maintenance man as he slipped under the panel and began pulling a cover off. James and Philip followed his lead and began doing similar things. "You can go back to your rounds. We should have this fixed in about a half hour."

The maintenance man looked around at the three men not sure what to do when the Pulsator shuddered again knocking a piece of loose concrete off the wall that nearly hit him. He didn't waste any more time getting up the stairs and out the door.

"The panel's this way," Rich said hopping up off the floor after the man was out of sight.

They rounded a corner and followed a narrow walkway behind the Pulsator. Rich felt along the concrete wall and pushed on a square panel which moved back, revealing the hidden storage area. Rich pulled out the metal box they had come for and put it in a large bag James had brought along.

"We'd best get out of here fast," James said nervously as Rich sealed up the secret safe.

"You're right," Philip replied. "No doubt the maintenance man must have made a call to someone by now."

Rich pushed the buttons on his controller and the Pulsator slowly stopped vibrating and before long was running smoothly again. He shoved the controller into his pocket as they hustled up the metal stairs to the doorway. But as soon as they got out they were intercepted by the maintenance man and his partner.

"We got it fixed," Rich said as they began walking towards the exit. "You should be just fine now."

"I'll need you to help me with my report," the man insisted. "Come on in the office for a minute so we can get this done."

The three men hesitated for a moment and then reluctantly followed the two men to the office. They seemed friendly enough. However, once they got in the office, the maintenance man they had first met didn't seem very interested in reporting anything and did his best to talk about everything and anything in general.

"We really must be going," Rich said after a few moments. "Where's that report you needed signed?"

"Oh, the report," the man replied, as he shot a nervous glance at this partner. "Uh, you'll have to wait here while I go get it. I forgot it in my electric cart."

The man got up from his desk but, instead of leaving, he pulled a gun from his pocket.

"I don't know who you fellas are but I know you're not who you say you are. We have no external maintenance crew and I have the highest maintenance security clearance there is." He continued as he ripped Rich's badge from his shirt pocket. "I checked the scanner and you're not the man the system says should be here. You guys just sit tight while we wait for security to arrive."

James was sitting next to the other maintenance worker who was about to pull a gun from his pocket but, before he could, James grabbed him by the arm and threw him into his partner. He was on the two men in a second and with only two blows from his massive fists rendered them both unconscious.

The three men made a break for it heading across the facility to the exit door and then the turnstile. They could see flashing lights coming from the direction of the Citadel and knew they had only a few seconds. They tried their card in the turnstile but it didn't respond. Management shut it down when they realized something was wrong. Then Rich pulled the controller from his pocket and pushed a new combination. The surrounding lights went instantly bright, nearly blinding them, before they began blowing in a cascade of sparks. Within seconds, the entire area was engulfed in darkness.

"That should do it," Rich said as he pushed through the now powerless turnstile.

In a few moments, they were racing down the street in Philip's truck with the lights off.

"I can't believe we did it again!" James exclaimed.

"Believe it," Rich replied as he returned the Pulsator to normal the second time. "But, now the real work begins."

"Come on, open it!" James exclaimed as Philip drove them back to the motor home. "I'm dying to see what's in there."

"You and your curiosity," Rich replied. "We need to be rested and prepared for whatever this is. It can wait until morning."

Lori was relieved to see them return but didn't let anyone know. What they were doing required bravery from all and she was not about to show fear for any reason. They settled in for what would likely be another restless night's sleep.

CHAPTER 16

Kirsten worked her way across the city from Kenzie's apartment heading for the greenhouse. It was located below the city on the West side, hidden deep in the outer area of the city, an area not many people were aware of. But, getting there would be no easy feat. She couldn't take her car as she was sure Management would be looking for it so she went on foot, towards the outer area. It was an undeveloped section of the city filled with small valleys, streams, and rugged terrain. She was an expert hiker and able to create paths where most people would have seen only barriers. It was a long laborious trek but she was up for it. Night turned to day as she made her way along, still hearing her mother's voice in her head.

Hours passed as Kirsten was careful to stay out of sight. It was late afternoon when the wall came into view and, then, the doors. They were tall, outfitted with large metal hinges, held together with thick steel strapping, and would have looked at home guarding some old castle.

"I don't think even Parks knew about this little trick," Kirsten thought as she examined the large keyhole located between the two wooden doors. She rotated the metal escutcheon around the keyhole to the left half way and then back past center, before returning it to where it started. Kirsten pushed and the door creaked open in protest. "Mom always called that the "guest latch." Kirsten thought proudly to herself as she followed the narrow path, overgrown with brambles and bushes, leading up a small hill. "It's there for those who don't have a key but belong in here anyway."

Soon, the dark glass structure came into sight. It was old and covered with moss and the glass doors were a deep eerie dark green. Kirsten pushed them open and entered into the cold damp building. She waited for a moment till her eyes adjusted to the dim light. It hadn't been cared for in years and there were plenty of wild looking plants popping out of containers and growing out of control. Her heart fell a little at the sight, remembering how much time and effort they had spent keeping this place in pristine condition.

"Mom loved growing herbs, medicinal plants, and food here and so did I," Kirsten thought as she wandered through the building, sampling fruit from plants still producing their goodness, but it had been a long time since they had anyone to share with. She was hungry after her long trek and found it satisfying as she ate from the long ignored bounty. She was thirsty too and remembered a source of fresh water that flowed out of the rock face behind the building. It was directed through a series of pipes that poured into troughs, feeding plants throughout the building. She cupped her hands under the open spigot and drank.

Just then, Kirsten heard a noise.

She gasped as standing in the darkened entrance was the outline of a tall hulking figure. All she could make out was two burning red eyes as she reached for the handle of the crystal blade she kept in a sash around her waist. She was trapped and her only way of escape was through the approaching figure. But then the man stepped into a stream of light flowing through one of the roof panels.

"Parks!" Kirsten exclaimed. "You nearly scared me to death. What are you doing here?"

"Sorry about that," he said as he hugged his sister. "I noticed the main door open down below and came in to check. I haven't been in here in a very long time," He continued as he scanned the inside of the building.

"Yeah, we spent a lot of time here when we were kids," Kirsten said. "Mom and I were working while you found places to hide outside."

"Oh, right," Parks replied jovially, "and who was the one doing all the heavy lifting? ME, while you stayed close to mom pretending to help."

Kirsten looked at her brother and then started laughing. It felt good to be together again.

"What brings you way out here?" Kirsten asked as they walked outside. She wondered about the color of his eyes but chalked it up to a lighting effect.

"I'm looking for David, Normand and Burke. Have you seen them anywhere?

"Not for a few days or so." Kirsten replied. "Is there a problem?"

"I don't know. I can't seem to get any of them to respond and I'm feeling a sense of trouble. It has me concerned."

"Why come way out here? I would think you would find them in the city somewhere."

"I've had to use this route more of late. Being an outlaw has its challenges you know. Right now I'm heading towards the transport terminals and had better get moving. I have a lead that indicates they're by a dock of some sort. But what are you doing out here?"

"I'm not sure how to answer that," Kirsten said as they reached the wall. "There's something in the greenhouse I need to find. It's important."

"What is it?" Parks asked.

"I wish I knew," Kirsten answered. "I just know it's in there and I have to find it."

"You're going to search for something but you don't know what you're looking for," Parks replied, raising his eyebrows. "That certainly sounds like me all over. But why here?"

"Ok, you're probably going to think I'm crazy," Kirsten replied reluctantly, "Mom told me to come here."

"Mom told you?" Parks said, surprised.

"I thought you would think I was crazy but I had this incredibly vivid dream, Parks. Mom told me to come here and that it would make sense when I did."

"Does it make sense?"

"Not really, at least not yet, but meeting you here seems more than a coincidence. What are the odds?"

"I hope you find what you're looking for," Parks replied. "I'm searching too, and I feel like we're getting closer to figuring out what's really going on. Where can I find you?"

"The best place to look for me would be Dr. Flint's place. Some of us are using it as a central rendezvous and you can leave a message there if nothing else."

"Ok, we'll connect in a few days," Parks said as he opened the door to leave. "You take care of yourself and stay safe."

Kirsten said goodbye as she shut the door. Parks took off

on a steady jog. She slowly walked back up the path and entered the darkened greenhouse half wondering what she was doing.

"Mom, why did you bring me here?" Kirsten asked in frustration. "I don't get it. What do you want me to see?"

She leaned against one of the many concrete raised beds and folded her arms. She could search the place if she only knew what she was looking for. Finally, not knowing what else to do, she slowly walked through the building looking for anything that might be something. Then she started thinking about the many times they were here together and trying to remember if anything seemed out of the ordinary.

"You like the way it shines, don't you?" she remembered her mother saying when Kirsten was little and held the golden locket her mother wore around her neck. "One day it'll be yours and show you the secret place."

"A secret place," Kirsten said as she took the locket off from around her neck. "I never understood what she meant by that."

Kirsten flipped the locket open and inside was a picture of her parents the day they got married. Out of curiosity, she reached in with a fingernail and gently removed the picture. Underneath was a small diagram etched on the inside of the locket. Kirsten took it outside into the sunlight where she could get a better look. The diagram did indeed look like the greenhouse but in the center was the symbol of a six sided star.

She walked back in with the locket still open and started examining the building more closely. She looked and looked before her gaze fell upon the tip of a triangle carved into the floor at the base of one of the raised beds. Kirsten knelt down and brushed years of dust and dirt away. In a few moments, the full image of a six point star appeared. She was getting more excited now as the star appeared to be in the middle of a floor tile. She quickly looked around and found an old pointed shovel and a hand trowel. Working feverously, she chipped away at the tile and, after ten minutes or so, the edge began to break loose. A few seconds later, she was able to pry it out of the floor. Underneath was a small black leather pouch cinched at the top with a velvet ribbon. She undid the ribbon and out dropped an unusually shaped medallion into the palm of her hand.

"This is old," Kirsten said as she examined it closely,

"and I wonder what the strange symbols mean. Mom must have felt this was very important or she wouldn't have gone to all this trouble but what do I do with it?"

She went outside into the light again to examine the medallion. It was about three inches in diameter, a quarter inch thick, and looked like a cookie somebody had taken a bite out of. On one side was a third of a six pointed star image and on the other what looked like flames. She put it back into the pouch and then her pocket before opening the locket to return her parent's picture. It was then she noticed something else inside the locket she hadn't seen before. She strained to make out a faint image behind the star in the locket.

"Hmm," Kirsten said thoughtfully as she held the locket in the bright light of the sun, "that looks like a diagram of a much larger piece."

Then it dawned on her as she pulled the medallion out. Inside the "bite" was a small grove which seemed to correspond to a thin decorative rim around the perimeter of the locket.

"You don't think?" Kirsten said as she lined up the locket with the grove on the medallion and then there was a slight click as it locked into place. "Well, I would never have suspected that. But it looks like there's room for two more like Mom's medallion but where would I find those?"

Kirsten attempted to take the unusual object apart so she could put the locket back around her neck but there didn't seem to be a release and she didn't want to force them apart and maybe ruin it so she carefully flipped it over and began feeling the back. After a few moments, she felt a small lever and moved it thinking that must be the release. But, instead of separating the two objects, it opened a hidden compartment.

Inside was a very small golden dial with a line of what appeared to be diamonds across the center ending in a tiny blue stone.

"I wonder what this is for," Kirsten puzzled. Then, as she moved around to get a better look she noticed the dial didn't move with the locket. "If I didn't know better," Kirsten thought, "I would say this is a compass except it doesn't point north." Then she had an inspired idea, "what if this thing points towards the nearest of the remaining two pieces? It's as believable a thought as any but it seems to be pointing towards the city which presents a bit of a problem. Management is likely on the prowl for me so how am I going to follow this thing in that direction?"

Kirsten sat down on an old log bench built years before by her father as she considered all options.

"Alright," Kirsten exclaimed. "I'm not doing any good here so my next choice is really no choice at all, I have to find those other two pieces. Why? Who knows, except Mom said I was a fourth generation daughter which must mean something." Kirsten sat for a few moments more contemplating the situation carefully. "So this is what I've decided a fourth generation daughter should do, not stop until I have completed whatever it is I should complete. I only wish I knew what that was."

Kirsten got up and put the object in the pocket of her sweatshirt as she walked towards the heavy wooden doors. She stood in the opening looking back up the path she had followed so many times before but didn't feel sadness or loss. Instead, she realized her mother had hidden something just for her. Something that might help find a hidden truth that could help them all. The thought injected a new feeling of hope, removing the one long since crushed under Management's cruel attitude. That hope would prove more powerful than even she could know.

CHAPTER 17

"Do you think they'll come?" Rita asked with a worried tone in her voice as Jim extinguished the small fire he made to keep them warm.

"They'll come," Jim said confidently. "But you can stay at Flint's place. You'll be safe there."

"You know my answer," Rita said adamantly as she got in behind the steering wheel. "Whatever we do, we do together and I'm not letting you out of my sight."

Jim couldn't help but be worried. What he had in mind would bring Management like bees to honey. But he also knew Rita was committed. That was a good feeling he never wanted to lose. So, in spite of his concerns, he hopped into the passenger seat as they made their way to HOT News.

The building was dark and felt dead. Nothing like when it was the most vibrant place in the city. The many broadcasts Jim made, the people he worked with, the fans, all created such a powerful energy and being Jim the Weatherman really suited him. But then came the day he met Greg and that all changed. Since then, his life had been one unfolding nightmare after another.

Jim's mind reset to the present. He looked over at Rita and smiled. They were going to make a difference, he was sure of it.

Rita pulled around behind and parked tight to the building and away from the lone parking lot light. They sat quietly watching for a while before Jim spotted a set of lights coming down the road. Whoever it was turned into HOT News and immediately shut them off. Rita and Jim watched as the car drove past, relieved to see it was Chris. Rita flashed the lights twice and Chris pulled up next to them. Jim was happy to see Ray and Danny were with him as he was going to need all the help he could get.

"What's the plan?" Chris asked anxiously.

"We'll need to get this equipment inside," Jim said. "I

have a generator we can use to power up. Once we get set up, we can activate the antenna and do a quick check. This is going to require some time and fancy wiring so I'm very happy you guys came. There's no way I could have done this on my own."

They backed up to the rear entrance and offloaded the equipment. Being exposed in the light was giving Jim heartburn, but they had no choice. Rita helped with the flashlight as the men went to the heart of HOT News' production studios. They chose the least trashed one and began straightening up before they could set up. It was a pain with only flashlights but, in about an hour, they had the place ready to go. Jim quickly explained his plan.

"I have the original recordings I made last year." Jim said as the men gathered around. "But I'm not sure they're enough. We've learned about a deeper and more sinister plot than any of us could have imagined. There are Testers inside the city right now."

"Testers? Here?" Danny gasped. "Then we need to quit what we're doing and get out, now."

"And just where would we go?" Jim replied. "Yeah, that's right, there's nowhere to hide. Management has a choke hold on the city and, even if a few of us could escape, what would happen to everyone else? Are we really ok with only saving ourselves? Could we live with that?"

"Maybe," Ray replied. "I'm no hero and neither are these guys. I watched those things kill two of my cousins. I was trapped and would have endured a similar fate if the city hadn't surrendered when it did. They were coming down my driveway and only 20 feet away when they stopped."

"I get it," Jim interjected. "We were all there and we were all scared. But there's no surrender option this time. We have to find a way to stop them."

"And you think broadcasting is going to accomplish that?" Danny asked. "Are you crazy?"

"Come on guys," Chris said. "Let's listen to what Jim has in mind. If what he's saying is true, we're dead anyway."

Jim looked around at his friends illumined only by the flashlight Rita was holding.

"We're going to go live," Jim said confidently. "HOT News still has the most powerful antenna in the city so what I have in mind will explode into everyone's morning show. I know Management was able to endure my broadcast last year and make me into the bad guy. But there's been a shift since people are feeling the losses. So, when I come back, they'll see Management for what they really are. It'll become a rallying cry for the resistance and, maybe then, we'll have half a chance. Look, it's the only shot we have. Just know there are others in the city risking everything, too. We're not alone in this."

The fear Jim sensed in the men seemed to dissipate for a moment but then things turned ugly.

"Ok, I've heard enough," Ray said as he pulled a gun from his waistband. "Everybody stay where I can see you."

"What are you doing?" Chris asked angrily as he took a step in Ray's direction.

"Don't do it," Ray said as he waved the gun around menacingly. "I only came along to see what Jim was up to. Now I see he's as crazy as ever and resisting Management is as wild as it gets. You really think doing a show is going to stop anything? Not a chance. Management will be all over you before you can even push play. Come on, let's go down and talk to them."

"What made you sell out?" Jim asked without moving. "You were a good friend. Why are you doing this?"

"Friend, FRIEND?" Ray shouted angrily. "You sold us out when you broadcasted the first time. We were thrown out of work and shunned and would have been homeless in less than four months if it wasn't for some Management friends I have. They offered me a job at one of their studios and I took it. All I had to do was agree to obey their directives and report any suspicious activity. I think you'll find most of the people in this city doing exactly the same thing."

"I'm really sorry for all your pain," Jim said sincerely. "I know my first broadcast may have been a little aggressive but someone had to do something. People, our people, were dying. Look Management doesn't care about you. They never have. If you can't see that, you must be blind."

"Blind or not," Ray replied, "get going. I'm not going to be a part of this and will probably get a big reward for turning the four of you in. I also want the names of the other people you mentioned. The more you tell me the easier it'll be on you."

They stepped into the dark hallway and were halfway

down when, suddenly, it plunged into darkness as Rita shut off her flashlight. Ray began shouting, commanding the light be turned back on, and then started shooting wildly. But the muzzle flashes only served to give his location away as another flash came from the side. Rita turned the flashlight back on and Ray was lying on his back with a sizable hole in his chest. His eyes were rolled back and he was obviously dead. Jim had kept one of the forty five caliber handguns in his coat pocket just in case they were interrupted by Management. He never thought he would need to use it on a friend.

"Are you ok?" Rita asked as she stood up. She dropped to the floor instinctively to avoided being shot.

"I'm ok," Jim replied.

But Danny wasn't as fortunate. He was hit in the head with one of Ray's wild shots.

"It's not your fault," Chris said as he put his hand on Jim's shoulder. "Fear and chaos has changed us all. Ray was a good guy at one time he just couldn't take the pressure but you can't blame yourself for that. We all make choices and he made his, but Danny deserved better. Now what do we do?"

"I don't know." Jim replied sadly. "Every time we try and do something to stop the madness we get more of it. I would never have involved you if I knew this would happen. We better just get out of here. Someone has likely heard the shots."

"No," Chris said. "We're not going, not just yet. Maybe Ray gave in but Danny didn't and neither have I. It's going to take longer but I still think we can put the equipment together and do what we came to do."

"But what if Ray contacted Management about us?" Rita asked nervously.

"He couldn't have," Chris replied. "I never told either one of them what we were doing or where we were going. He could have guessed but I didn't mention your name either. No, I think we're safe for now. Come on let's see what we can do."

They put the two men's bodies into a side office and returned to the studio where they spent the next four hours hooking up the equipment. Fortunately, even though the original equipment had been removed, the wiring was still there making it possible to hook everything to a central control panel. Even the antenna was attached. The last thing to do was hook up the generator they had brought. Jim put it into an adjacent room facing the rear parking lot and opened a window. The noise from the generator would carry but he had to ventilate the exhaust. He started it and returned to the studio once all the electrical cords were plugged in.

"Testing, testing," Chris said as he took his place in the control room. "I'm getting a little feedback probably coming from the generator. Its power isn't 'clean' so, it is, what it is."

"It's nearly six," Jim said as Rita helped him with his lapel mike. "Most people will be up getting ready for work or school so this is the only opportunity we have. Did you get that booster hooked up ok, Chris?"

"It is and should give the antenna quite a kick," Chris answered. "The signal will blast the Management stations right off the air and put you in. But you're going to have less than ten minutes. The booster will overheat and blow if I push it any harder."

The generator couldn't produce enough power to run the lights so Rita set up the three flashlights she had brought along. The light washed Jim out a bit and gave him a ghostly look when Chris checked the monitors. But Jim felt it added to the effect and gave him a more dynamic appearance.

"This is Jim the Weatherman broadcasting live from HOT News," Jim began as Chris hit the switch. "Yes, I said HOT News. Gather around and listen closely my friends to what I have to say. You are about to be shocked but I can assure you this is real. Over the last ten years, Management has used fear and intimidation to control and turn us against each other. Not only that, but they have been busy collecting information on each of us, and intend to use it against us. Our city has been seized, but there is something even more terrifying. They have secretly positioned Testers on the South end. Testers are again inside our city and we can only guess what dark purpose they'll serve. Most of us lost someone at their hands and now they're back. I urge you to pack up what you can: provisions, weapons, your family, and prepare for the worst. Some of you listening may already have a plan. Implement it now and trust only those closest to you. There are traitors among us. Just be aware you cannot leave the city. All routes are guarded and attempted escape will only mean capture. Gather whatever weapons and provisions you may have and join up with others who are willing to fight. It's time for all good citizens to choose sides. Your future depends on your decision. May the ROD assist you! This is Jim Banner signing off."

"Did it go?" Jim asked as he walked off stage.

"I can't tell for sure," Chris replied. "The equipment worked. That's all I know."

"Time to go," Rita said as the windows began to glow from the early morning light. "I'm sure they're coming our way right now."

Jim and Chris didn't need any encouragement as they began racing for the exit with Rita leading the way. There was no time to say any goodbyes as they jumped into their respective vehicles. In a few seconds they were racing down the road in separate directions.

"What happens next?" Rita asked as she turned down a side street.

"I don't know," Jim replied solemnly. "I just hope we survive this. Management is holding all the cards."

They returned safely to the elementary school where they hid the car and went inside. It was dark and cold as Jim unlocked the administration office they were using. He then went to the maintenance room where the backup generator was located. He had been using the generator sparingly to conserve whatever fuel was left from when the school shut down. He started it and then hustled back to watch the early morning news on a small TV someone had left behind.

"You've got to see this," Rita said as Jim came through the door. "It went through alright but they're calling it a terrorist broadcast."

"No one's going to believe that," Jim said as he sat down. "Turn it up. I've got to hear this."

"This morning, you may have seen a very strange interruption in your broadcasting," a young smiling blonde woman said. "Our sources indicate this was accomplished through an attack on one of our stations. Information is just now coming in. It looks like this person, who identified himself as Jim, and an unknown number of conspirators broke in and killed an entire morning crew of fifteen workers. Video of the incident is just coming in. Let's cut to Barry. Barry, what do you have for us?”

"Thank you, Michele," the man said as they began panning a Management broadcast station. "If you have young children near the TV, you may want to take them out of the room. The scenes we're about to show are very graphic."

The camera continued running as images of emergency workers pulling what appeared to be dead people from the building filled the screen. There was blood, death, and destruction everywhere.

"Management is on site assessing the situation," Barry continued as the camera cut back to him. "But, from what we're being told, the death toll could go up, back to you Michele."

"This is just another example of the type of people we have been investigating," she continued as the camera cut to the studio. "The death toll continues to mount and is added to the two hundred and twenty three people who perished when the Citadel was destroyed by Henry J. Parks, the suspected ring leader of the terrorist group known only as the ROD. There is also the mysterious disappearance of the head of the Citadel and City security, Harry Allison. This video surfaced just this week. Parents please take your young children from the room before we run this graphic video."

A sceen appeared on the screen with several hooded figures and a man resembling Harry tied to a post. The video stops just as several men take aim and apparently shoot him.

"Oh no," Rita gasped.

"We normally don't like showing this kind of behavior," the woman continued, "but Management felt it was necessary to reveal how sick these people really are. Then there were the two Cadets found only three days ago murdered in their car. Please be assured Management is doing all they can to find the people responsible for these heinous crimes and bring them to justice but we need your help. If you have any information on the whereabouts of any of these people, please call the number on the bottom of your screen. However, do not approach them on your own. They are considered armed and deadly."

"I've seen all I can take," Jim said as he turned off the TV.

"What does it mean?" Rita asked. "Harry wasn't killed and we didn't kill those people."

130

"It's a set up," Jim replied glumly. "Now we're the bad guys. We're the terrorists not them. They must have suspected I would try a rebroadcast and had those videos ready just in case."

"Bastards," Rita exclaimed. "But at least you did something. You told people the truth and maybe some will make it out. Some will understand and those that don't, well, they have chosen to believe the lie. There's nothing you could do for them anyway."

"Maybe you're right," Jim said as he sat back and looked out the window at the empty parking lot. He felt sick. what else could go wrong?

It wasn't going to take long to find out.

CHAPTER 18

"You guys going to be ok?" George asked as they drove towards Flint's office.

"Never," David answered angrily. "I'll never forget or forgive them for what they've done. It was as if he didn't even care if he got answers or not. He just wanted to keep punching us and beating us until he beat Burke to death. I'll never forget that."

"We should have told him what he wanted to know," Normand said through clenched teeth. "Then, maybe, Burke would still be alive."

"He would never have let us live," David snapped. "That's not what they do. Always remember that. We can't change anything that they've done but we can do something about what we're doing. They wanted this and now they're going to get it."

George pulled in behind Dr. Flint who just happened to be returning from the city with some needed supplies.

"You boys get into my office right away," The doctor said as he quickly evaluated their condition. "I'll be right in to help you."

"Uh, doc," George said cautiously as he took some packages out of the trunk of the doctor's car. "There's one more in the back but I'm afraid he's dead."

The doctor immediately went to George's station wagon and climbed in. He began examining Burke who was lying motionless.

"This boy's not dead!" Dr. Flint nearly shouted.

"But, but I felt for breathing," George protested. "He wasn't breathing."

"Just barely breathing," Dr. Flint said as he climbed out. "Grab the gurney in the hall and hurry!"

George did as instructed and, in a few minutes, they were wheeling Burke down the hall and into a room. Both David and Normand saw them race by and followed.

"Is he going to be ok?" David asked intently as he

watched the doctor put in an IV.

"How did this happen?" Dr. Flint asked, ignoring David's question as he checked Burke's eyes.

"We were attacked," Normand replied.

"We must get him to the hospital," the doctor said as he set down his stethoscope. "He has a severe concussion and possibly bleeding on the brain. They'll have to do an MRI to be sure. He also appears to have several broken ribs and other contusions. I won't know the full extent of his injuries until I get the MRI results."

"We can't go back to that hospital," David protested, "the guys that attacked us are likely watching it. They'll kill him if they know he's there."

"I'll take care of that," the doctor replied. "As far as anyone knows, he's my worker and fell off the roof."

Dr. Flint did exactly that but, before he left for the hospital, he patched up David and Normand as best he could. Their injuries were painful but relatively minor compared to Burke with some bruised ribs and plenty of cuts and bruises. George helped Dr. Flint get Burke loaded but didn't ride along. He had no idea what was going on and wanted to stay behind to get some answers of his own. George returned to the house and the two young men, as the doctor sped off.

"You're Bruce's kid, right?" George asked David.

"I am," David replied.

"I knew it," George continued. "Hey, I'm really sorry about what happened. I liked your dad a lot."

David hesitated for a moment before continuing.

"Dad's ok, we faked his death to keep Management from killing him."

"You did what?" George exclaimed. "I went to his funeral and was one of the pall bearers. I just can't believe it. Well, that's about the best news I've had in a very long time. How did you do it and where is he?"

"It's plenty complicated," David answered. "Just know he's safe. What we need to do is figure out our next move, whatever that is."

"Your next move is to stay right here," George said firmly. "The doctor told me to make sure you two didn't go anywhere. You need to recover. That was quite a beating you took."

"I suppose you're right," David responded. "But staying here is not an option. There are things to do."

George looked at him with a hard look hoping to intimidate both of them into doing what the doctor wanted but quickly realized that wasn't going to work. Instead he told them he had the keys to his truck in his pocket and they weren't strong enough to take them from him, at least not yet.

Meanwhile Management was not sitting still.

"What are you doing here?" Dave asked as he met Mr. Grey coming from the direction of the board room. "You're supposed to be interrogating the prisoners."

But Mr. Grey just continued walking past Dave ignoring him and his question.

"Now wait just a minute," Dave said angrily as he grabbed him by the shoulder and spun him around.

"What do you want?" Mr. Grey asked coldly.

"Last time I spoke with you, you were supposed to be taking care of business. Well, what happened? What did you find out?"

"Nothing happened. They were freed and have been taken to places unknown. I've been instructed to forget them. The Board doesn't consider them important at the moment."

"What can be more important than knowing where those tunnels go?"

"You'll have to find out for yourself," Mr. Grey snapped as he turned and headed down the hall again.

Dave stood there wondering what had changed but then realized this could be for the best. Mr. Grey answered to the Board and it was clear he couldn't be trusted. Barron, on the other hand, was eager to get ahead and destroy Parks. That was an advantage he could depend on.

"I want you to get out to the warehouse." Dave said into his phone. "Gather some of the Testers. As many as you can get in a transport truck and see where that thing goes…What do you want?" Dave snapped as he covered the receiver with his hand.

"Sorry sir," Aaron said as he stepped into Dave's office. "I have these papers for you to sign."

"Just leave them on my desk," Dave replied. Aaron did as instructed and Dave returned to his call. "Like I was saying, I'll meet you at the equipment yard. We'll pick up two transport trucks and load them with Testers. We must find out what this tunnel thing is all about."

Dave was convinced the answers were waiting for him wherever that strange tunnel went. It had to be the hiding place of Parks. Why else couldn't he get a handle on his location? And the board was obviously losing patience so the pressure was mounting but if he could get just one Gift, that would keep the Board satisfied, until he found another. That could only mean one thing, finding Parks was key.

He hustled out to meet Barron.

Meanwhile Aaron was returning to his office. He overheard enough of Dave's conversation to know Parks was in trouble and he must let him know. He shared an office with three other coworkers separated only by six foot tall cubical barriers. He made his way into his cubical. It wasn't quite lunch time yet but he had to get the information out somehow. Parks' life likely depended on it. He sat with his back to the opening and pulled the blue crystal hanging on a chain around his neck. He held it tightly in his hand and concentrated. It was something he had never done before and had no idea if it would even work.

"Parks, Parks," Aaron thought as he lowered his head and leaned over his desk. "They know about the Island and they're coming for you."

"Aaron," Parks replied in his mind as he stopped just outside the transportation terminal. "Who's coming?"

"Barron and Testers is what I heard," Aaron continued. "They're loading up transport trucks now."

"Thanks Aaron," Parks said, "and keep safe. Bad things are coming."

"Do you have a minute?" A thin voice said abruptly.

Aaron's head snapped up as he slid the crystal into his pocket. He spun around to see Mr. Grey standing in the cubical entry.

"Yes sir," Aaron replied quickly trying to disguise his fear. "What can I do for you?"

"You're the analyst, correct?"

"Yes, that's correct,"

"Good," Mr. Grey said eagerly. "I need you to do a computer search for me using the word 'backspin.' Sort your findings by name and address. This is priority one. Stop everything else you're doing and bring the report to my office as soon as it's done."

"Backspin," Aaron said as he breathed a long sigh of relief after Mr. Grey left. "Whatever is that?"

Aaron was connected to the most powerful computer system in the city. In fact, he had helped design software capable of reading all electronic communications regardless of their type. He thought it was to protect the city but had since realized what a powerful tool he'd put into the hands of those likely aiming to do the hurting. He began writing the query and then sent it into the vast storehouse of information located on servers throughout the city. He then sat back and waited as the cursor on his screen blinked brightly.

Then <REPORT READY> came on the screen.

Aaron was more than a little surprised his query actually produced something. He sent the report to his printer and soon it was spitting out paper.

"Amazing," Aaron thought as he began thumbing through the stack. "The word 'backspin' seems to come up in the strangest context. Check out this phone conversation between what seems to be two elderly women."

"I'm going to the quilting meeting tonight. It should be backspin."

"That's what I was hoping. See you there."

Aaron continued reading and continued finding references to this innocuous term in email, texts, and phone messages, but what did it mean? He had no choice but to deliver his findings, so he headed over to Mr. Grey's office several doors down the hall. He knocked and then entered. Mr. Grey was standing at the window looking outside.

"Your report, sir," Aaron said as he laid it on his desk and then turned to leave.

"Please sit," Mr. Grey said as he turned and returned to his chair.

"I've a lot of work to do," Aaron protested as he hesitated at the door.

"It can wait," Mr. Grey continued waving Aaron to the chair. "What I have to say is much more important."

Aaron reluctantly slid into the chair as Mr. Grey took his

report and began to scan it.

"You're confused," Mr. Grey said as he stopped reading for a moment and looked up at Aaron through his dark glasses, "I can tell that sort of thing. I think you may also be a little afraid. But, not to worry, I've been watching you and checked your file. You come from a good family, have a strong educational background, and, most importantly, have served with zero marks on your record. You were also in charge of our county 'rewards' program. I see you're ambitious and have the qualities we are looking to advance. I realize you're not a military man but, then, neither am I. I serve at the Board's desire and you shall too if you're interested. Let me show you something that might help you decide."

Mr. Grey got up and led Aaron into the next room where a large map hung on the wall. Aaron suppressed a gasp as he suddenly realized this was the map Isaac told him about.

"As you can tell," Mr. Grey continued, "this is a map of the city, divided into four quadrants. Until now, we've been struggling to understand the most effective way of eliminating resistance in the city. You provided the key today and will be rewarded."

"I really don't understand," Aaron said hesitantly.

"The word, 'backspin,' that you searched for me," Mr. Grey continued, "was provided by one of the people from the county I personally 'interviewed.' It seems the resistance uses this code word in random communications to set up meetings and share information. While it may not be completely clear how it works, that doesn't matter now. You've provided a list of every time it has ever been used. Now you'll go back on-line and research who those people are. Find out where they live and what they do. I could tell by glancing through your report that many numbers are blocked and e-mails coded. Your job will be to get their names as quickly as possible."

Aaron's heart sunk at the thought he had betrayed the resistance without realizing it. He provided Management a huge advantage that could crush them forever.

"One last thing before you go," Mr. Grey said encouragingly, "do a good job and I can see you taking over this department very shortly. It will include a sizable raise and put you on the advancement ladder. Management will need some new blood as the city completes its cycle."

Aaron's mind was burning as he returned to his cubical. What did Mr. Grey mean about the city completing its cycle? That made no sense. Then there was the map with the red dots. Could those be Testers? If they were, Mr. Grey made a crucial error as Aaron had snapped some pictures with his phone when Mr. Grey was distracted. He just needed to get this information out to Parks right away. Maybe this fight had a chance after all.

Aaron quickly packed up his laptop and left the building. On his way across the parking lot, he glanced back at the building and noticed Mr. Grey watching and smiling at him from his window. He threw back a wave and didn't think much about it at first but then his stomach churned as he drove off. It wasn't like Mr. Grey to smile about anything. Maybe this wasn't going to be as easy as he thought.

CHAPTER 19

Parks squatted behind a large bush, and looked through the chain-link fence into the transportation terminal. It was the only other loading dock he could think of, and where he hoped to find David, Normand, and Burke. He was determined to rescue them, but he couldn't ignore Aaron's communication. If they knew about the Island, no one would be safe, especially Della.

But he was on the north end of the city, and the wilderness was at the south end. It would take more than a day just to reach the warehouses without transportation. Then he had to get out of the city and across the wilderness, and try to beat Management there. He sat there quietly for a few minutes, considering his options.

"I love you, honey!" he said in his heart, "but I've got to help these guys. I'm coming for you as quick as I can."

He took his crystal blade, and sliced through the fencing. The transportation terminal was filled with large trucks and container vans lined up against massive storage warehouses. It was where all goods were processed and distributed to the retail outlets throughout the city.

He was careful to avoid detection as he moved towards the docks. He was a little confused, as he had expected a lot of activity. This was the supply heart of the city, and usually bustling. For some reason, nearly all the trucks were parked and empty today.

He hopped onto the large concrete loading dock, and walked between the vans and the closed overhead doors. As he came around a stack of pallets and some large empty cardboard boxes, he noticed one of the doors open and the sound of a distant forklift.

Parks slid inside the door and behind some crates, and watched as a forklift buzzed past with a load. The driver went into the container van and then came back into the warehouse for more. He returned with one more load and then stopped on the dock and proceeded to lock up the van.

"Hi buddy," Parks said as he walked up behind the rather large man. "How's it going?"

"What?" the startled man said as he jumped around with a pipe he was using to close the van doors. "What're you doing here? This place is restricted. You need to get out of here."

"Not much going on around here," Parks said, ignoring the man's bluster. "I thought this place would be much busier."

"Well, we haven't been getting deliveries from the county for a while," the man replied, relaxing just a little. "We're pretty much just emptying out warehouses."

"Why do you think that is?" Parks asked as he walked to the edge of the dock.

"Look, mister," the man replied. "You need to leave, or I'll have to call security."

"Do you know who I am?" Parks asked as he turned to face the big man with the pipe.

"No. Should I?" The man asked, narrowing his eyes as he sized him up.

"I'm Henry J. Parks."

"Huh," the man said as he froze for a moment. "You're Parks. Man, I'm sorry. I didn't recognize you. What are you doing way out here?"

"I'm looking for my friends. I was told they were being held where there were some docks. I've been at the docks on the East river, and now I'm here. These are the only other docks I know of."

"I wish I could help you," the man said as he leaned against his forklift. "This place has been dead for weeks, and I can assure you there's nobody here but me."

"I can't believe it!" Parks said, clenching his fists. "This was my last hope for those guys, and now I've wasted valuable time. There's no way I can get across town and into the wilderness in time."

"Hey," the man said brightly, "you need to get somewhere fast? I have something that will help. Come on, and take a look at this.”

The man led the way into the warehouse, and deep into the back where some large crates were being unpacked.

“I’m supposed to have this ready for delivery tomorrow,” the man said as they came around a corner. “Some Management goomer named Barns or Barrens or something ordered this thing.”

“Barron?” Parks asked.

“Yeah, that’s the guy. I’ll just have to say someone broke in when I was busy, and took the dang thing.”

“I can’t thank you enough,” Parks said.

He checked over the small, bright-blue fiberglass dune buggy. “This thing has one heck of a motor. What was Barron planning to do with it, fly?”

“Don’t know, but you’re welcome to it,” the man said.

He grabbed a five-gallon can of gas, and started pouring it in.

“I never did like those Management types. They are always getting on me for one thing or the other. Now they’re pushing to get this place emptied out, but they ain’t saying what people are supposed to do when there’s no more food. I haven’t seen a thing come down that road for nearly two weeks now. Things are going to get mighty rough real soon.”

“You don’t know the half of it,” Parks said as he squeezed in behind the wheel. “Look, you seem like a good guy. I can tell you there is going to be some serious trouble coming very soon, and you need to do whatever you can to protect yourself and your family.”

“What kind of trouble?” the man asked with a puzzled look.

“The kind like when our city surrendered. I can’t say more, but thanks for your help.”

Parks shook the man’s hand, and fired up the dune buggy. It roared to life, and he took off in a cloud of dust through the warehouse door, down the long ramp leading off the loading dock, and into the cool night air.

He stopped at the locked gate just long enough to slice it

open with his crystal blade, and then he was gone. The small vehicle was fast and powerful as he began powering through the city streets. He didn't bother taking side roads this time, as he couldn't afford even a minute's delay. Several Management vehicles spotted him and began pursuit, but they were no match for the little buggy, and Parks easily left them in the dust. But he couldn't stop them from radioing ahead, and setting up road blocks.

He caught air as he came over a long rise that descended towards three large SUVs, blocking his approach to the city wall. They were sitting sideways in the road, with cadets sheltered behind them, holding Nullifiers.

He wedged his backpack against the throttle, and climbed into the passenger seat. He was going through them, one way or the other.

The cadets were shocked at the sight of Parks careening towards them. The two crystal blades he had drawn from the sash around his waist glistened in their headlights.

He steered the dune buggy with his left knee, and managed to keep it pointed directly down the center of the road. The cadets started firing their Nullifiers, and the first three shots narrowly missed, passing into a wooded area behind him, blasting large trees apart, and starting several fires. Parks believed he could deflect the blasts, but really hoped his visage would cause the cadets to panic, and miss. He was sadly mistaken as the next blast hit him squarely in the chest.

The bright explosion should have disintegrated both Parks and the dune buggy, but it didn't. Instead, it enveloped him in a light so bright, the cadets were momentarily blinded. The blast reformed in front of him for an instant, then returned with equal fury towards the cadets.

A hole slightly larger than the dune buggy formed, as both the unfortunate cadets and part of their vehicles instantly vaporized. Parks dropped behind the steering wheel as he drove through what remained, and slid to a stop.

The rear of one SUV was gone, and the front half of the other as he walked back to the smoldering situation. One of the cadets, not directly in the way of the blast, lay dying with nearly half his body gone. He didn't look much more than eighteen.

Parks knelt down, and put his hand under his head.

"I wish there was something I could do," he said tenderly.

"You're Parks, aren't you?" the young man said with a gasp.

"Yes, I am."

"We were told you were nothing but a weakling and a traitor," the man said.

He reached up with his remaining arm, ripped the badge off his coat, and threw it in the dirt.

"Don't think too badly of us, Mr. Parks," he said weakly. "Now I see the truth..."

What was left of the young man's body relaxed, and his eyes glazed over. Parks laid his head gently on the blacktop. There was a time he had led the Order with a vision for a future filled with respect and honor only now the slimy fruit of Management's despicable doings was ripening and it disgusted him.

"Why am I still here?" Parks asked himself as he stood and began walking back to the dune buggy. "Those blasts should have done as much or more to me.

Then he looked down at a neat round, burnt hole in his shirt. Behind it hung the unusually-shaped golden medallion Julie had given him the day he left the Ancients. He didn't know how it worked, but it had just saved his life.

Parks climbed back in the idling dune buggy, and took off in the direction of the wilderness. He had no idea how much of a head start he had, so every second counted. It would be safer to drive to the far gate, which was only guarded by video cameras, but that also meant he was going to lose at least another two hours.

Then he had an idea.

There was a ridge to the north with an extended overhang. He and Kirsten used to sit up there as kids, and watch the sun set. Maybe his little gift from Barron had enough spunk to make the jump.

It was a risky, all-or-nothing move, but he was desperate. For all he knew, he was too late anyway. He pulled off the road, and took down a section of barbed wire fence that led to a wide open field with a hill at the top. He drove up the hill, chasing a few snipe as he approached the edge of the overhang. It was fenced to keep cattle from accidentally falling fifty feet to a rocky grave.

"That's a little farther than I remembered," Parks said as he hopped the fence, and looked over the edge.

The wall below and the road running next to it were actually cut through the hill. The engineers had felt it advantageous to continue on a direct line when they built the wall rather than going over or around the steep hill. The half on the opposite side was lower than where Parks was standing, but nearly two hundred feet separated them.

One large flat rock sat just behind the fence, and Parks eyed it carefully. He noticed a pile of old cedar fence posts partially overgrown with blackberries. Parks sliced them away with his crystal blade, and began piling the posts in front of the rock.

"I don't know if I would call that a ramp," he said as he stood back from his creation, "but it's going to have to do."

He took one more long look, and ran a quick calculation in his mind. He drove the dune buggy a hundred yards or so into the field, and lined it up to his makeshift ramp. He would need to get up to full speed if he had any chance of clearing the gap.

The large balloon tires tore into the grass, and the powerful machine pinned him into the seat. Aiming across the field, he kept the buggy focused on the ramp, and in a matter of seconds, he was sailing through the air. He looked over the side just enough to see the dark outline of the road and wall below, but his attention quickly returned to the rapidly-approaching hill.

He cleared the edge of the hill by a little more than six feet. The buggy bounced high on its tires, and Parks would have been ejected if it weren't for the harness holding him in. It bounced sideways, flipped over several times, and came to a rest in a cloud of dirt and dust.

The roll cage and heavy frame protected both Parks and the rig from any real damage. Only one of the front fiberglass fenders was cracked from the impact. Parks sat for a moment, regaining his bearings. Then he hit the starter, and the motor roared to life again. He floored it, and took off for the Island, laughing to himself on how upset Barron would be if he knew the gift he had bought for himself was about to be his undoing.

CHAPTER 20

Kirsten left the greenhouse, and began the long trek back to the city. The strange medallion she had found indicated there were additional components like the locket her mother had given her. They were somewhere in the direction of the city, and she felt compelled to find them, despite the risk.

She crossed ditches, and went through bushes and woods, always careful not to be seen. That became more difficult as she approached the edge of the city. Apartment houses and businesses rose into view, making it more and more unlikely she could remain hidden. She dashed across a street, and into an alley. Her plan was to find some mode of transportation that could get her where she needed to go without being seen and she was not disappointed as she rounded a corner and found a delivery van idling in the street.

"Here you go, ma'am," said a young man, handing several small packages to a rather harried-looking woman. He hopped back behind the wheel, and took off for his next delivery.

He crossed several intersections, and drove down a narrow, bricked alley lined with service doors. The driver checked his paperwork, and reached for the handle of the heavy metal door separating him from his packages. The only way in was with the key he kept on a strap attached to his wrist.

Before he could turn the key, the door slid open.

"Come in!" Kirsten exclaimed.

She ripped the door open, and pulled him in by the collar, throwing him to the back of the van. A pile of boxes cascaded down on him, and he crumpled to the floor.

"Sorry about that," she said, and put out her hand to help him up.

"What do you want?" the man asked, refusing her hand.

"Look, I'm not here to hurt you," she said softly. "I need a ride."

"Where do you want to go?" the man asked, pulling

himself up using the shelving on the side of his van. "I have a job to do you know," he said as he started putting the fallen packages back in place. People are going to come looking for me if I don't get them delivered on time."

"I have no problem helping you finish your route," Kirsten said, as she noticed an extra shirt hanging on the end of the rack. "I can't tell you where I'm going yet, but someday you'll be glad you helped me. I promise I'll have you back to your depot before quitting time."

The short, muscular young man looked at the slightly-built woman standing between him and the exit to his van. He considered taking her down for just a moment, but then felt an overwhelming need to help her, even though he knew it could cost him his job.

"Alright. If you help me finish, I'll give you a lift where you want to go," he said after a few seconds. Put on this extra shirt, take this package, and follow me."

They wove their way through the city, stopping at businesses and homes, delivering packages. Kirsten was careful not to let the driver out of her sight, just in case, but he was quite willing to use her help, and even flirted with her a little as the day wore on. The moment of truth finally came after they delivered the last package.

"So where are we going?" he asked enthusiastically as he jumped behind the wheel.

She pulled out the medallion, and opened the back.

"Sort of that way," she said, pointing in the direction of the river.

"You mean you're not sure where we're going?" the man asked incredulously.

"Just drive," she commanded.

He pulled the brake, and the truck lurched forward. They moved steadily through the streets, guessing which turns to take. Eventually, they came to the outskirts of the city, and she asked him to pull into a graveled parking area.

"Thanks for the ride."

She opened the door, and stepped out.

"But there's nothing out here," he protested. suddenly feeling concerned leaving a pretty girl alone on a lonely road.

"I'll be ok," she replied as she turned and walked out onto the road. "I know you didn't have to help me, Kent, but I'm glad you did. Hopefully I can return the favor someday."

Kent rubbed his chin for a moment, then reluctantly pulled out of the lot, and headed for his depot. He watched in his rear-view mirror as she disappeared behind a curve in the road. This had been one of the most confusing days of his career, and it would probably be best to forget all about it.

Kirsten was wearing her hooded sweatshirt, and she put the hood on as she began a steady jog down the road. The needle pointed southeast, but that would take her across rough fields dotted with ponds and bogs. Her best bet was to stay on the road, and take whichever side roads led in the general direction she wanted to go. It was a long run, but she was up for it.

She was alone until dusk, when a jeep roared past. She glanced over her shoulder, and saw the brake lights come on as it made a U-turn behind her. In a few moments, it pulled up alongside.

"Hey, beautiful," a man said through his open window. "Where are you going?"

Kirsten ignored him, and continued jogging. She noticed there appeared to be more men inside, and they were all crowded against the driver's side to get a better look.

The driver pulled ahead a short distance, and cut her off.

"Hey, we just need to know where you're going," he said.

He jumped out, and was quickly joined by two other men.

Kirsten slowed to a stop. Two of the men approached her from the front, and the other circled around behind.

"We need some identification," the man said in what he probably thought was a soothing tone. "It seems odd that someone like you would be jogging out here after dusk."

"You guys are cadets," Kirsten said, noticing the badge on the man's shirt, and their polished black shoes. Then she recognized him as the cadet who had threatened Kenzie the night they searched her apartment.

"Yeah, we belong to the Order," the guy replied. "So you know you're safe with us."

Without warning, the man grabbed her from behind. Another tried to get a hold of her legs. She kicked him in the chin, and he dropped like a sack of potatoes. She broke the grip of the guy holding her, and flipped him over her head into the driver. They fell in a heap, and she was on them in an instant. She punched the one who had grabbed her, and knocked him out.

"Hey, we meant no harm," the driver pleaded as Kirsten was about to deliver a similar fate to him. "We were just doing our jobs."

"Well, maybe you should focus more on your job than on harassing innocent people," Kirsten said curtly.

She pulled him to his feet with one hand.

"So, you're the BOJ boys I've heard about, going about attacking helpless females. You make the Order stink with your actions." She pushed him, and he fell back onto the road. "Take off your shoes, and the ones on your sleeping friends."

The man looked at her for a moment as he scrambled to his feet, unsure if he was going to obey or not. She punched him in the stomach so hard he doubled over. Once he got his breath back and could stand again, he quickly started taking shoes off before she could hit him again.

She threw them into a bog running alongside the road, and watched as they slowly sank out of sight. By now, the other two were struggling to their feet, and standing unsteadily before the diminutive woman.

"You tough guys," she said, climbing into their jeep, "should really enjoy this. I take your ride, and you walk back to town in your stocking feet. Just remember how lucky you are. If I ever see any of you again, you won't be able to walk anywhere, ever."

She roared off, leaving them in a cloud of dust.

The direction finder took her down a road traveling parallel to the river, passing old homes and farms.

"Where are you taking me?" Kirsten said to herself as mile after mile passed. "There aren't even any houses out this far."

She was beginning to think it was nothing but a futile search when the gravel road ended, and turned off into a wide parking area next to the river. As she did, the jeep's headlights illumined the shape of a large motor home.

She parked, and looked down at the direction finder, which was pointed right at the vehicle. There was a truck parked outside, and she was sure someone was peering out from behind the curtains. She pulled up next to the truck, and got out.

"Hello in there," she said as she walked around to the door.

The door opened, and a bright flashlight blinded her for a moment. She tensed, covered her eyes with her arm, and slid her hand around the handle of the crystal blade concealed inside her sweatshirt.

"Kirsten," came the warm greeting. "How did you find us way out here?"

"Dad," she exclaimed, relieved it was her father.

She gave him a big hug, and saw her aunt and uncle smiling behind him.

"Wow! I would never have expected to find you guys."

"Come in," Aunt Lori said after giving her a hug. "You look tired and hungry. Let's see what I can find for you."

"Mr. Lindberg?" Kirsten said as she recognized Rich. "I haven't seen you in years."

"What about me," her Uncle James said, grabbing her around the shoulders.

"Oh, it's good to see some friendly faces again," she said as she sat down on the narrow couch. "How long have you been staying out here?"

"Longer than we planned to," Philip replied. "But with the house gone, it's been the safest place to hide. But what about you? How did you know where to find us?"

"I didn't," Kirsten answered. "I know you might think I'm crazy or something, but this led me here."

She pulled out the medallion with her mother's locket attached to it.

"I found this in the old greenhouse, and mom's locket just snapped in here. Then I discovered this pointer on the back, and followed it all the way here. Look, it's spinning like a top. I must be in the right place."

"Can I look at that?" Aunt Lori asked. "You're definitely in the right place," she said as Kirsten handed her the locket. "This is very old, and I only saw your mom wear it once, a long time ago. How did you find this?"

"Mom gave it to me the day she died."

"We come from original families that date back many years, maybe thousands," Lori said. "Each generation was told the story with very specific details none of us understood. One of those details describes an amulet with great power. It held a secret that would protect us from something called the 'Dark Matter.' But the amulet was divided up into four pieces long ago to protect it from those who wanted to destroy it. Who was given the pieces was kept secret yet the story said a time would come when it would have to be reassembled but only a fourth generation daughter would know how. You have already put two parts together. Kirsten, you must be that daughter."

Lori looked at James, who nodded. She reached around the front of the cab, and pulled a box out from under the seat. She handed the box to Kirsten, who opened it.

"These are nearly identical," Kirsten said, holding it up. There was an etching of what appeared to be a book on the back.

"What do you think they mean?"

"I don't know," Lori said. "But now you have three of four pieces. Why not see if that one fits."

Kirsten held the locket up, aligned the second medallion, and slid it on. It clicked into place alongside the first one, forming four points of a six-sided star. She passed it around the room, and when it came to her dad, he held it up in the light streaming through one of the motor home windows.

"The ancient stories are coming to pass," he said. "First Henry and the Zender, and now you with this. What can it all mean?"

No one knew what it meant, But they all knew something

powerful was happening. Kirsten felt something stir inside. She felt her mother's confidence, and realized she wasn't alone. She believed she was on the right path, even though more questions than answers remained.

CHAPTER 21

"I can't leave it like this," Jim said, slamming his fist on the counter. "There's got to be something we can do."

"There's nothing anyone can do."

Rita slid her arm around his shoulders.

"Come on, Jim, we need to get out of the city."

"No, I'm not running," he said through clenched teeth. "I'm going to tear this thing apart, and I think I know just where to go. But I want to get you out first."

He looked hard into her eyes.

"We've been through this before," Rita replied, "I'm not leaving you."

"But this is different. What I'm thinking is not just dangerous. It's a suicide mission."

"And what do you call everything we've done lately? Suicide missions are all we've done. Come on, Jim, I mean it. We've got to run to survive."

"Run? Run where, Rita? No, we have to stop them. You know it, and I know it. But I have to do this alone this time. You need to trust me. I love you, and Flint's place is the best place for you right now."

"I do trust you," Rita said.

She looked long and hard into his eyes, knowing she was going to have to let him go. She grabbed him by the neck, held him for a moment, then kissed him tenderly on the cheek. "Maybe I can be of some help to the doctor," Rita said with a sigh. "There could be casualties."

"That's my girl!" Jim exclaimed. "I love you."

"I love you more," she said as they headed out the door.

The drive to Dr. Flint's was fraught with anxiety. It was hard to know who might see them and turn them in after Management's broadcast. Worse, they could be spotted by a cadet patrol. Fortunately, they made it safely, and he stashed the car behind the house. David answered the door.

"You look like crap," Jim said as he entered. "What happened to you?"

"Remember Mr. Grey? Well, let's just say he didn't get the answers he wanted," David said.

He led the way into the doctor's living room where Normand was watching Management's coverage of Jim's efforts on TV.

"Quite a broadcast," Normand said as he stood up to greet them. "You're a really bad person from what they say. How did you do all those things anyway?"

"Seems we're all terrorists," Jim replied, "but how about we give them something to really worry about."

"What are you saying?" David asked.

"They made one mistake in their broadcast. They showed the missing head of the Citadel, Harry Allison, getting shot by some supposed radical resisters, when I know for a fact Parks has removed him from the city, and he's safely stored at what we like to call the "Island." All I need to do is bring him back alive, and 'presto' they're shown to be the liars we know they are."

"You can't bring Harry back," David said. "Management would kill you before you even got close to broadcasting, and they would have to kill Harry too. Once a guy's dead, he's dead."

"I haven't worked all the details out yet," Jim replied, ignoring Rita's worried look, "but seeing you boys gives me a great idea. We go to the Island together, and bring him back with us. Let's put our heads together, and figure this thing out. I know I can do it with your help"

"They're getting more powerful by the minute," Normand said. "You just have to look at us to know that, but I'm ready to do whatever it takes."

"I am too," David said, "but we should think this through a little more first. It's no easy task to get to and from the Island. You may not know this, but we were caught coming from there, and Management may have destroyed the tunnel, or be guarding it. Worse, they may have used it to reach the Island themselves, which could be really bad."

"No, I didn't know that." Jim replied grimly. "But Parks and I found the Island the first time through the wilderness. We can do that again. And if what you are saying is true, they may need our help if Management has found them."

"How do you propose to get out of the city?" Normand asked. "There are walls and gates you have to cross before you can even get to the wilderness."

"Dr. Flint has that covered," Jim said.

He led the way through the secret entrance, down the stairs, and to the room concealed in the wall.

"Wow!" Normand and David nearly exclaimed in unison.

"This is unbelievable" David continued as he ran his eyes down the rows and rows of weapons.

"All the firepower needed to blast our way out of the city is right here. I say we load up the car, and get with it. Who knows? Maybe a good explosion or two will get their minds off the Island."

David and Normand were quite willing to help, and equally eager to do whatever it took to stop Management. They had had enough of sitting around, especially after George had left. At least now they had something to do, and a chance to get even. It wasn't long before the car was loaded, and they were ready.

"I'll be back soon," Jim reassured Rita. "We're getting close to the end of this deal, and with a live Harry revealed, I know we can expose the truth. Just keep low while I'm gone. Testers are nothing to fool with, and they're here in the city somewhere."

Jim started the car, and drove out headed in the direction of the southeast gate. The drive was filled with the uncomfortable feeling that Management was somehow watching their every move.

When they got to the gate, it was standing open.

"What the heck!" Jim exclaimed.

He pulled over a safe distance from the gate. "That thing's always shut. Why would it be open?"

"They brought the Testers in through there," David said.

"Maybe they don't think they'll need a gate anymore."

The simplicity of David's reply chilled them. Testers meant death and destruction, and with their being stationed a mile or so towards the city, they had effectively cut off escape.

But they had driven to this point without seeing any Testers, or other Management types. It felt like a trap, but the gate was open, and only a quarter mile of road stood between them and the wilderness.

"I don't like it," Normand said. "It doesn't make sense to me. They've left an open escape route."

"No they haven't!" David shouted. "Look at that."

They all stared in disbelief as a flood of red began pouring over a distant ridge, headed towards the open gate.

"Testers," Jim gulped, "thousands of them. They're bringing in reinforcements."

"I don't think a TV broadcast is going to stop those things," Normand said numbly.

Jim quickly assessed their situation. Everything inside him wanted to go back and grab Rita, and head for places unknown. But he couldn't do it. He had to make a play, and get to the Island somehow. They had maybe forty-five minutes before even more Testers would be flooding into the city.

"Here's what we're going to do," he said calmly.

He hopped out of the car, and opened the trunk. "We have a dozen anti-tank, anti-personnel, anti-everything mines. David, you and Normand are going to place them under soft sand or behind bushes as I drive along. This radio transmitter will detonate them one at a time or all at once. But first, I need to get that gate shut, and the best way is to "blind" whoever is watching."

Jim pulled a rifle with a high-powered scope from the back, and took aim at the first camera. It exploded in a shower of plastic and glass. The second one fared no better."

"Nice shooting!" David exclaimed as Jim floored it for the gate.

"Yeah, target shooting has always been my strong point."

"You'd better be a crack driver, too," Normand said. "The

gate is closing."

But Jim already had the powerful car flying down the slight incline. The gate, made from heavy steel, could withstand a direct hit from just about anything you could throw at it, so if he didn't have it timed right, they would be little more than bug splatter. Jim's knuckles turned white as he aimed for the rapidly-closing opening.

Miraculously, the car shot through the narrowing opening, losing only the side view mirrors, and ripping the rear bumper off as they emerged into the wilderness.

"Couldn't you have timed that a little closer?" Normand asked, prying his hands off the back of the seat.

"I'm going to stop every hundred yards or so," Jim said, ignoring Normand's comment, "then one of you jump out and set a mine."

Jim ripped along, stopping only long enough for Normand and David to set the mines. They buried the final three mines along the front of the gate, where Jim expected the Testers would pile up, waiting for it to open.

When it was done, they flew along the wall, and slid to a stop in a shallow drainage ditch. The three men crawled to the edge, where they could watch the stream of Testers flowing over the final ridge.

"I hope this works," David whispered.

"It'll work," Jim replied quietly. "I just want them to group together before we light them up."

They waited and watched as the Testers acted predictably, lining up in front of the gate in tightly packed rows of at least a hundred each.

"I haven't seen this many in one place since the city was attacked year ago," Jim said as the last of the Testers arrived, "but this should slow them down a bit."

He pushed the main button on the remote. Nothing happened. He pushed it again, but it still didn't work.

"Let me see," Normand whispered, pulling out a small jackknife. "Sometimes you have to move the batteries around a little if they've been sitting for a while. Ok, try it again."

He handed it back to Jim.

This time it worked. The blast was even larger than expected, sending rocks and large pieces of sod raining down. They ran to the car, dove in, and took off. Debris thundered down on the roof as they drove away.

"We might have been a little too close," he said as he stopped a safe distance away.

They all got out to view their handiwork.

"But I think they were even closer," he said with a laugh.

The mushroom cloud rising from the blast zone included a dark cloud that swirled up with it. They expected to see considerable carnage and pieces of Testers splattered about but there were none.

"I guess we vaporized them," Jim said enthusiastically. "That should put a significant crimp in Management's plan. Now, let's get on with our next stop."

Before Jim could pull away, a frightening thought hit Normand.

"Wait a minute," he said. "I hope I'm wrong, but I think I've seen this before. Look, the wind is blowing southwest, but that cloud is moving northeast into the city. See, it's holding together, and heading somewhere on its own."

"What are you saying?" David asked.

"I've personally destroyed that little dark-suited Management thug with the dark glasses three times," Normand replied. "Each time he vaporizes, but somehow he comes back. I thought at first he had a twin brother or something, but now I know it's the same guy. We haven't killed those Testers; we've just sent them somewhere else. I'm afraid they'll be back."

The truth of Normand's statement shuddered through Jim's mind. Was Management really that powerful? Was there no way to stop them? Jim pointed the car in the direction of the Island, and forced himself to concentrate on the task at hand.

So much was at stake, and it was impossible to know if anything they were doing would actually work. Jim forced himself to think of what could be. He imagined a new day when he and Rita could enjoy a life together. That was the only thought keeping him going.

CHAPTER 22

Dave had intended to send Barron and a small team of Testers into the wilderness to search for Parks, but changed his mind when he discovered the tunnel hidden inside the warehouse. Even though Mr. Grey hadn't gotten any useful information out of David, Normand, or Burke, he was sure the tunnel would lead him to Parks's secret hiding place. All he needed to do was load up trucks with Testers and weapons, and drive.

"Are you sure you want to come along?" Barron asked as Dave met him in the equipment yard. "It could be dangerous."

"I want to see Parks's face when I shove this through his chest," Dave said as he showed Barron the red crystal blade slung around his waist.

"That's really something!" Barron exclaimed. "Where did you get this thing?"

"I took it off of Parks," Dave replied. "The next time he sees it will be his last."

Barron held the blade for a moment, feeling a surge of strength run up his arm and into his chest. He hadn't been the same since his last run-in with Parks, but holding the red crystal somehow made him feel new again. It had energy unlike anything he had felt before.

"We'd better be going," Barron said as he reluctantly handed the blade back. "We still have to load up."

Dave hopped into one of the large personnel carriers, and Barron took another. They would drive to where the Testers were grouped, and then on to the warehouse and the mysterious tunnel. His thoughts began to drift off to his meeting earlier in the day with the mystic.

"What can you tell me?" he asked impatiently as the old woman pulled a hood over her head, and focused on the table.

Her face was barely visible as she closed her eyes, and began mumbling in a strange language. It was the second time he had been in her 'inner' room, and he was no less annoyed. The dark room, candles, and trance did nothing for him. But he had learned the mystic was right about a great many things, so he waited, reluctantly.

"The gifts are being assembled in the city," the old woman said in a wispy voice. "People don't know yet what they possess, but they are beginning to suspect they have something special. It is only a matter of time before it becomes clear to them."

"Can you tell me what they are and where they are?"

"It's hidden from me," she replied. "I can only say the people gathering them are from the 'before' families."

"Before, before what?"

"Before the city was first destroyed," the mystic responded. "You're chasing one of them. The man called Parks. But I must warn you, this will not go well for you."

"Look harder!" Dave demanded, ignoring her warning. "Tell me about the gifts."

"I cannot," she said, taking off her hood. "They're hidden from me as I said."

"You can, and you will." Dave said.

He pulled the red crystal blade from a sheath around his waist, and pointed it at her throat. "Look harder."

The old woman looked at his angry face, and the sharp end of the blade for a moment. Reluctantly, she pulled her hood back up, and re-focused on the glassy table. She began mumbling again in the same strange language as Dave watched. Suddenly, the center of the small table began to glow brightly, and turned into what appeared to be liquid.

"Near water is one," the woman gasped.

"Water, what water? Look harder you fool," Dave insisted. "Don't stop now."

"A place where there are boats," the woman strained as the intensity of the light streaming from the table increased.

She was about to speak again when the table flashed, blinding Dave for a moment. When his eyes readjusted to the dim candlelight, there in the middle of the room was her table, smoldering, and broken in half.

"I told you not to force me!" the old woman said angrily. "The door has closed to the other side, and I can't get back there now."

"That's ok," Dave said calmly as he stood up to leave. "And since you can't 'see' anymore, you are really of no use to me."

The crimson blade flashed in the flicker of the candles as Dave drove it through her heart. She sat there, unmoving, as he pulled the blade out. It didn't leave a mark on her dress, or produce any blood. Her body slumped forward, and her head hit her chest before she crumpled to the floor.

Dave exited through the heavy velvet curtains into her front room, kicking an oil lamp over as he passed by. By the time he was in his truck, the flames were flickering behind the windows as they caught the curtains on fire.

"That stupid woman thought she could frighten me," Dave thought as he drove through town. "Well, she was crazy, yeah. Crazy dead. Parks isn't so tough. Last time he confronted me, I sent him running like a child. This time I'll save him the running, and take his life."

Dave was laughing as he pulled in where the Testers were grouped. Barron was right behind, and in a few minutes, they had their trucks full. Dave took the lead to the warehouse, and before long they were driving down the tunnel, headed for the Island.

He was impressed with the massive effort it must have taken to build such a thing, and how successful the builders had been to keep it secret for so long. The lights came on in front and off in back as the two large trucks rumbled along. Hours passed before Dave became aware of the small cameras concealed along the walls.

"They know we're coming," he said over the truck radio to Barron.

"Yeah, and so what," Barron growled. "It won't save them from me."

"But we don't know how many there are, or what firepower they may have," Dave replied. "We should be ready for anything."

"Doesn't matter," Barron replied. "The Testers will handle the light work. I just want a shot at Parks."

"You'll have to wait your turn," Dave quipped.

Soon, signs began to appear along the sides of the tunnel, instructing them to slow. In a few moments, the looming blast door approached.

"I know you can see us," Dave hollered.

He climbed down from his truck, and stood in front of the door.

"We can do this the hard way or the easy way. You decide. If I have to blast through this door, I'll kill everyone on the other side. You open it, and I'll only kill those who resist. Everyone else can come with me to the safety of the city. I'll give you five minutes to decide."

"But we've already decided," a voice said from a speaker above the doors. "I'm going to open the doors for you, but I suggest you turn around and leave."

"Hah!" Dave said as the doors began to move.

He hopped back into the truck, and drove into the vast underground facility. It was well-lit and empty, except for one lone figure standing in the center.

Parks.

Dave stopped some fifty feet back and hit his air brakes as Barron stopped alongside.

"Surrendering isn't going to save you," Dave said as he climbed out and addressed Parks. "I'm going to kill you, tie you on the hood of my truck, and parade your dead body through the city. It will be a sight to behold, and a lesson never forgotten."

"Hi, Barron," Parks said, ignoring Dave's comments.

Barron was staying back by his truck.

"Looks like you're moving around ok again."

"Yeah, the doc did a good job fixing me up after you pounded me." Barron replied coldly.

"Who said anything about surrendering?" Parks asked as he turned his attention to Dave. "I think you'll wish you'd stayed behind."

"We'll see about that," Dave said as he pulled the red

crystal blade out. "Seems like you lost this in my house, but I came to return it to you. Barron, why don't you release our friends? Parks needs a quick lesson in humility."

Barron went behind Dave's truck, and opened the door releasing the twenty Testers packed inside. He didn't open his own truck. They came around and lined up in front of Dave, awaiting direction. Barron returned to the relative safety of his truck's fender to watch.

The Testers drew wicked looking sharp weapons as they grouped into attack formation. They began moving steadily towards Parks, who just stood calmly, watching their approach. Then he pulled two blue crystal blades, and with one in each hand, started running towards the Testers.

The Testers drew tightly together, with spears, axes, and swords all pointed at the approaching Parks. The twenty Testers had become a singular killing organism. They were ready when Parks met them ,slashing and stabbing furiously. Parks sliced his way through, and in only a few moments, left a pile of dead red Testers. They quickly dissolved into a dark mist, swirled about, and exited through an exhaust fan in the ceiling.

"You were mentioning surrender," Parks said, holding his blades at his side. "I suggest you do just that, and lay down your weapons. I'll see to it you're not hurt."

"Barron," Dave commanded, "you take him down."

"I'm sorry," Barron replied, "I didn't think to bring my Eliminator."

"Then I guess it's just you and me." Parks said. "Why not lay down your blade, and get it over with?"

"Hah," the President sneered. "I'll not be so easy on you this time as I was before. You still owe me for the mess you made in my house. I'll deal with you later," he growled, glancing towards Barron, who just shrugged his shoulders.

Dave raised his red crystal blade, and rushed Parks. His first blow came at Parks's head, but was stopped with one blade. A shower of purple sparks cascaded across the floor from the contact of the two blades. Dave's eyes were burning as he tried time and again to cut Parks, but he was blocked on every strike.

164

Parks saw an opening, and hit Dave in the ribs with the handle of his blade. Dave flew backwards, sprawling onto the floor, and skidded to a stop in front of Barron's truck. The red crystal blade flew from his hand, and landed at Barron's feet.

"You'll not get away this time!" Dave said.

He struggled to his feet, holding his side, and reached inside his coat for a pistol-sized Nullifier. "This will end you for good."

Before he could pull the trigger, his eyes opened wide, and his mouth dropped. He looked down at the pointed end of the red crystal blade sticking through the center of his chest.

"I'll be the one who kills Parks," Barron whispered into Dave's ear before pulling the blade out. "When I'm good and ready."

Dave stumbled forward and turned, mouthing a silent 'why?'

Barron shrugged.

"I think it's time for a new President anyway, don't you?"

Dave fell face-first onto the hard concrete, and died.

"You can keep the truck," Barron said as he quickly climbed into his. "I'll take these Testers back with me, but we'll meet again, Henry J. Parks, and, when we do, you'll meet a worse fate than that idiot. I'll settle our score for good!"

Before Parks could react, Barron wheeled the truck around, and tore down the tunnel for the city.

Just then, Della raced out of the shadows, followed by the colonel, and a large group of heavily-armed men.

"Are you crazy?!" Della exclaimed as Parks gathered her into his arms. "The colonel wouldn't let any of us out to help you. He said you made him swear to let you handle this on your own. I can't believe you sometimes."

"I know," Parks replied as he squeezed her, "but I couldn't let anything happen to you. I have to face these challenges alone. I've been running for too long, and the longer I run, the stronger the energy gets. The time has come, Della, for me to face everything."

Several men removed Dave's body, and put it into the

back of the truck.

Suddenly, the large section of roof where the ramp to the wilderness was began rising.

"We've got company." the colonel said, listening to his ear piece.

The group of men quickly readied their weapons for the next unknown threat.

"Whoa, there," the colonel exclaimed. "Lower your weapons. I said company, not enemies."

A beat-up, poorly-painted orange car came flying down the ramp, and screeched to a stop. Out popped Jim, David, and Normand.

"Management is coming!" Jim exclaimed excitedly. "We've got to get ready to fight. They have Testers, and who knows what else."

Parks, Della and the colonel couldn't help releasing a good laugh to Jim's utter confusion. They finally explained what had just happened. The three men breathed a huge sigh of relief before sharing their own disturbing experiences.

"I've been looking for you." Parks said to David and Normand. "Are you guys ok?"

"A little sore, but otherwise we're fine."

"And Burke?"

"He's recuperating under Dr. Flint's care." Normand replied.

"Do you believe it matters the President is dead?" the colonel interrupted as they walked into his underground office. "This might be the break we've been hoping for."

"It's hard to tell," Parks answered thoughtfully. "I'm not sure the President had that much to do with anything. He may be just one of many pawns but not the head. No, Management is more than him or those like him. Management is something else altogether."

"What are you saying?" David asked.

"It's hard to explain," Parks replied. "It's something I've felt, like a bad dream you can't wake up from. I've come to believe it's an intelligent energy that feeds off our darkest emotions. I know this sounds crazy, but I can feel it in me now, clawing at my mind, and working to make me angry and hateful. It's all I can do sometimes just to keep myself under control.

"I worry I won't be able to resist its pull forever, and I might do something I'll regret for the rest of my life."

The group stood there, stunned at Parks's sudden revelation. No one knew what to say or how to respond, so the conversation turned back to more immediate concerns.

"I want to bring Harry back to the city," Jim announced.

"Why would you do a thing like that?" the colonel asked. "He's one of our most dangerous prisoners. We keep him safely locked away in a high-security cell."

"Management claims we've killed him," Jim answered. "They even have a video of him being shot by a firing squad of resisters. If I were to get him in front of a camera and show everyone he's still alive, it would destroy their credibility."

"That's a tall order," the colonel said, sinking into his seat. "What do you think, Parks?"

"I think it's worth a try. Jim has the help of some very competent men here," he said, glancing at David and Normand. "If anyone could make it happen, they could."

"What about you?" Della asked after the meeting was over. "Do you really have to do this thing without me?"

"I'm not without you," Parks replied tenderly. "You're the most important thing I have. You're what I hold onto when it gets dark inside. But I must do this for us.

I realize people don't get it, and you probably don't either, but you have to understand. I've been infected. You've seen it; I know you have. And this thing in me is growing stronger every day. If I don't figure out how to destroy it, it will destroy me. Don't ask me how, but I believe defeating it is the key to understanding the Dark Matter, even if we really don't know what that is.

It's all confusing, but I believe this is all connected to Management in some way. They're at the center of everything. Look, you'll be safe here, and I don't want to worry about you. No one's coming back this way after today's events."

Della held him for a long time. It had been a rugged ordeal, but it wasn't over yet. She felt a small kick inside her belly, and looked up at Parks tenderly. She smiled, kissed him on the cheek, and headed for her doctor duties, caring for the sick and infirm. Parks watched her leave, and as he did, he felt a resurgence of determination. In that moment, he knew everything would turn out alright.

CHAPTER 23

Aaron was busy formulating a plan as he drove to his apartment. Mr. Grey had revealed the map Burke must have seen that day through the portal. It had to be the one Isaac had asked about. Aaron had secretly taken a picture of it with his phone when Mr. Grey turned away, and now he knew where the Testers were positioned, and how Management planned to search for resisters. But he felt terrible about giving Mr. Grey the report on those using the code word 'backspin.' That one mistake could spell doom for countless people.

"I must find Kirsten," he thought as he pulled into his apartment. "She would know what to do, but I don't know where to start looking."

He entered his apartment, and grabbed a quick bite to eat before getting dressed to go out. He figured his best bet would be to drop by Kenzie's apartment, and see if she knew anything.

"Aaron?" Kenzie said, somewhat surprised as she answered the door. "What are you doing here?"

"I need to talk with Kirsten," Aaron replied. "Is she here?"

"Let's not talk out here."

She pulled him in, and shut the door. "Why are you here, and what do you want with Kirsten?"

"Look, I realize you might not think the best of me," Aaron replied quietly, "But you have to know that's all in the past. I'm working with Parks, and need to get some vital information to the ROD as soon as possible. Can you help?"

"Well," Kenzie began reluctantly, "Kirsten had to escape from here several nights ago after Management came looking for her. I don't know where she went. She wouldn't say. And I haven't seen anyone else either. I'm worried they might be watching my apartment, and if they are, they know you're here."

"I didn't see anyone outside," Aaron said, trying to sound confident. "I think we're safe for now, but I can't wait with this information. Where do you think I should go?"

"I think I know where we can start," Kenzie said, grabbing her jacket. "You drive, and I'll navigate."

Kenzie directed Aaron to Normand's apartment. It was a long shot, but she was hoping the guys would be there. It was getting dark as they pulled up, and she was sure she saw a curtain move.

"It's me," Kenzie whispered as she quietly rapped on the door.

"Come in, quick," Isaac said.

Aaron followed Kenzie into the darkened apartment. The shades were pulled, and Isaac was holding a flashlight at the floor to keep the light from being spotted.

"Hey Aaron," Troy said. "I haven't seen you for a long time."

"I know," Aaron replied. "I've been out of touch with everybody."

"Aaron's got some vital information," Kenzie interrupted. "Does anyone know where Kirsten is?"

"We haven't seen her," Isaac responded. "In fact, we haven't seen anybody. Troy and I have been hiding out here, and are prepared to move fast if we have to. I guess you don't know any more than we do. What do you have for Kirsten?"

"Information on the map Burke saw," Aaron replied as he called up the picture on his phone. "This is where Management has positioned the Testers. Mr. Grey said they're planning to sweep through these quadrants, looking for people who have used the code word 'backspin.' They believe they're resisters. Do you guys know anything about that?"

"Yeah," Troy replied, "it was set up by David to mask communications between resisters. The word could be inserted into a normal conversation, followed by another phrase depending on what was being communicated. Everything after the word was meant to direct people to the next meeting place or whatever. They also used it to confirm the person they were talking to was in the resistance. If the person seemed confused by the injection of the word, they knew they were not 'one of us'."

"Well, Management caught onto it somehow," Aaron said. "Now they're just waiting for me to run a query, and report all their names and addresses."

"You can't do that!" Kenzie exclaimed. "People will be killed."

"I have no intention of doing that," Aaron retorted, "but I can only hold them off for so long with phony reports. It won't be long before they catch on, and then, well I suppose I'm toast. But in the meantime, people need to get organized and prepared fast."

"They're better prepared than you might think," Troy said. "Kirsten has been working towards building a city-wide emergency alert system. All she has to do is give the word, and well-armed resisters will take to the streets. They have detailed plans for every Management control center, including the Citadel, or what's left of it."

"But what about the Testers?" Aaron asked. "Those guys are not easy to take down."

"Oh yeah, Testers," Troy said. "I've dealt with them before. If they got loose in the city, it would be horrible. Let me have a look at that map again," he said, taking Aaron's phone. "You say the points on the map are where they are currently holding groups of Testers?"

"That's what I understand," Aaron replied. "Mr. Grey is waiting for my analysis, and then he's going to send the Testers into attack mode."

"Then that means they're spread around!" Troy exclaimed. "Management has made a fatal error. From what I know, Testers work best if they're together en masse. It's like they feed off of each other, making themselves increasingly powerful. Dividing them up gives us opportunity. If we hit them in smaller groups, we could destroy them before they had a chance to attack."

"I'm not so sure," Isaac said. "It depends on how many are in each location. We could pick one that was chock-full of them."

"They'll be split evenly," Troy said. "See on the map how the lines are drawn. The city has been divided up into four equal quadrants, and the Testers must be divided accordingly, I just know it. Management would release them from the outside in, and they would meet in the middle after destroying everything in their path. That way, nobody escapes."

It was a horrible statement but rang with a deep sense of truth as they tried to grapple with the thought.

"We had better start looking for Kirsten and Parks," Kenzie said. "We'll need their help."

"No we won't," Troy said confidently. "We can make this happen on our own. All we need is to gather as many resisters as we can, and then pick off the Testers before they can get started. The map shows where they're being held, and I know those areas. We just pick them off one at a time."

"Come on, Troy," Kenzie protested. "You remember what happened last time you fought them. You nearly lost your arm not to mention your life."

"I know," Troy said, "but I've learned a lot since then, and I'm not angry the way I was. Look, you go find Kirsten and Parks, and bring them here. In the meantime, we'll start organizing, while Aaron delays Management. We won't move on the Testers until you get back. Agreed?"

Kenzie looked hard at Troy, and nodded. The sky was darkening as the four of them piled into Aaron's car. Troy had already decided which quadrant to focus on. It was the area he had grown up in, and the one the Testers had come to when his parents were taken. He still knew people in that region, and who the resistance leaders were. Aaron dropped Isaac and Troy before returning Kenzie to her apartment.

"What's your next move?" Aaron asked as he walked Kenzie to her door.

"I'm going to run up to Dr. Flint's place. I know they've been using that as a central meeting place. It's remote, and the doctor doesn't seem to draw suspicion. I just hope someone will be there, or know where I can look next. What about you?"

"I guess I just go into work tomorrow and start slowing things down," Aaron said. "I have access to the main servers, so a few well-placed 'bugs' should keep things interesting for a while.

172

Nobody's getting any addresses out of me for quite some time."

"Be careful," Kenzie said as she squeezed Aaron's arm.

Aaron returned to his apartment, and a very restless night's sleep. He didn't like the idea of Troy's proceeding on his own, and hoped Kenzie would find Parks in time. But that wasn't what bothered him most. He could still see Mr. Grey's smiling face in the window.

"Good morning!" Aaron said brightly as the guard at the main gate approached his car.

"You're a little early aren't you?" the least friendly of all the guards said as he checked his badge.

No matter how perfect everything was, this guy had a knack for making him feel uncomfortable.

"Just catching up on things," Aaron replied with a half-smile.

"What things?" the guard pressed, watching Aaron's reaction closely.

"Quarterly reports mostly," Aaron replied, doing his best not to seem nervous or angry. He knew the guards had no idea what he did, but they were trained to be suspicious, and this guy was the best one at it.

"Oh," the guard said as he handed Aaron's badge back. "Well, get it done. We like efficiency around here."

The guard waved him through, and returned to the guard shack, where he put his feet up on the desk, and resumed reading the morning paper.

Aaron went straight to his office, and his plan. It was the second day he had managed to avoid Mr. Grey and providing any details on the locations of suspected resisters. That morning, however, his luck ran out.

"Do you have a minute?" Mr. Grey asked rhetorically as he stepped into Aaron's cubicle.

"Sure," he replied cheerfully, and followed Mr. Grey to his office.

"Please have a seat," the small man in the crisp dark suit said. "I understand you're working on the problem we spoke of the other day."

"Yes I am," Aaron replied quickly, trying not to appear nervous. but so far, I haven't been able to sync up my queries with the specific matrix. I expect to work through the individual anomalies preventing successful matching soon."

Aaron threw every distracting technical jargon he could at Mr. Grey in hopes of delaying Management's deployment of the Testers as long as possible. He had to give Troy and Isaac as much time as he could, and hope that Parks would arrive before it was too late.

"Hmm," Mr. Grey said thoughtfully.

He leaned back in his seat, and looked at Aaron through his dark glasses.

"That sounds interesting, but it's not the main reason I asked you in this morning. There's someone here who wants a word with you."

Aaron spun around in his seat as Mr. Grey's door opened, and in walked General Ivy Allison.

"General!" he exclaimed. "How good to see you again."

"Thank you," the general replied.

She strode over to a chair, and sat down.

"It's nice to see you too."

"Let's forgo the formalities," Mr. Grey said, "and get to the business at hand. I've discussed your assignment with General Allison, and she has some questions for you."

"It is my understanding you're looking for resisters who have used the code word 'backspin', correct?" the general said.

It wasn't really a question.

"Right," Aaron affirmed. "Mr. Grey brought it to my attention a few days ago. I was able to pull up certain 'tags' that should lead to the actual names of the individuals in question. That's where I am right now."

"Interesting."

She got up, and walked over to the window, looking out for a moment before continuing.

"By the way, who was that you went to see last night?"

"Um, I'm not sure what you mean," he said.

A bead of cold sweat ran down his cheek.

"The apartment across town you went to. Who were you meeting with?"

She spun around, facing him.

"I went over to see an old girlfriend," he lied. "Is that a problem?"

"Why were there no lights on in the apartment?"

General Allison stared at him, and he resisted the urge to shrink away.

"There were lights," he said uneasily. "She just had the curtains closed. Hey, what is this? Are you following me?"

"Your old girlfriend is under suspicion for collaborating with resisters," the general snapped. "We've had a watch on her apartment for some time, and were surprised when you dropped in. How do you explain leaving, and then going over to the other apartment with those two men?"

"She wanted to visit her brother, so I volunteered to drive, and he had a friend over," Aaron replied. "I hadn't met either one of them before. Anyway, I suggested we go out to a local pub for some food and drinks, but they didn't feel like it, so I took her home after hanging for awhile. Why would you think she's part of the resistance? I've known her a long time, and she comes from a good family. I can't see her getting involved in anything wrong."

"We know a lot of things, and I think you should be more careful whom you hang out with." General Allison leaned forward, her eyes narrowed.

"We'll let this one go, but let's see some movement on your task."

Aaron quietly shut the door behind him, and returned to his desk.

"What do you think?" the general asked.

"I think he's lying," Mr. Grey replied.

"You may be right. Keep an eye on him, and see what he does next. If he's in with them, we may be able to use that to our advantage."

Meanwhile, Aaron pulled up to his computer with a heavy heart. He knew he hadn't been very convincing. If he didn't produce a list of names soon, he would be exposed. Then an idea struck him. Maybe he still had a card or two left to play.

CHAPTER 24

Parks spent the remainder of the day and night with Della, and left early, right before sunrise. He didn't sleep much, but instead spent most of the time watching her sleep. She was beginning to show slightly, and he couldn't help imagining how different their lives would be once the baby was born.

It was a nice thought, but then his mind turned dark again. Management was aware of this place, and it wasn't safe anymore. He had little choice but to take the fight to them.

There would be no escaping.

He had instructed Jim, David, and Normand not to return to the city, but Jim had refused. He had to return for Rita's sake so Parks had recommended avoid the tunnel. Barron may have set traps with explosives, or most likely, had Testers waiting at the other end.

He climbed into the large transporter left by Dave, and headed up and out of the Island into the wilderness. He decided to try a new course, and not deal with the city walls, or any tunnels. This time, he was going to come in a completely different way with the help of his unique truck.

He was quite familiar with the machine he was driving. Many times while leading the BOJ Order, he would bring cadets down to the river in a truck just like this one. It was amphibious; designed for water rescue training, and other similar missions.

He decided his best course was to drive across the wilderness to the east river. There was a wide section that made the perfect entry point, about five miles from the city. It took him the better part of the morning to make the long drive across the barren landscape, but the six-wheeled truck was built for just such travel.

Parks pointed the nose into the river, and switched on the two large propellers under the rear of the transporter. They churned the water as the powerful motor pushed the large vehicle upstream, leaving a wide wake behind. The hum of the engine gave him time to think.

"Why was Dave so intent on getting me himself?" he mused. "He could have sent any of his lackeys but came only with Barron and some Testers. It just doesn't add up. Unless," he suddenly realized, "he was under pressure. He seemed very anxious to get information from me about the gifts. That would mean the gifts are still hidden if he was looking for them. Maybe I should pay more attention to finding them myself. If only I knew what I was looking for."

His attention returned to the work at hand as he approached his destination. There were a few places along this part of the river where boaters once launched. He slowed, and moved from the middle of the river to the edge, where he would hopefully spot the old concrete boat ramp. But the blackberry vines were growing wild, disguising its presence, and the river was at its summer low, making the banks too high to climb. Then he spotted the landmark he had been looking for; a tall cedar tree.

The tree was the center-piece of a long-abandoned riverside park where children had once played. It had a long rope swing, with an old tire tied to the end. They would swing out, and drop into a large eddy, where the current was slight.

He spun the truck around, and lined it up with the ramp. He could feel the tires gripping the submerged ramp as he flipped off the propellers. The massive truck rose out of the water, and he downshifted as he ripped through the heavy blackberry vines. Suddenly, a group of people came scrambling out of a large motor home in a panic, and piled into a pickup truck.

"Wait! Wait!" he yelled.

He opened the truck door, leaned out, and waved.

"Stop, that looks like Parks!" Kirsten exclaimed.

Philip looked in his rear-view mirror. He turned around, and pulled up in front of the massive bumper.

"Sorry to scare you with this thing," Parks said, hugging his family, "but I had no other way of getting here."

"I wouldn't say scared. You just surprised us is all," Kirsten replied defensively.

"What are you doing with this thing?" Philip asked.

"It's a long story, Dad. Hi, everyone, it's great to see you. Mr. Lindberg, you're here too?"

"You have to tell us everything," his uncle said as they gathered around the picnic table under the warm sun. "I'm dying to hear."

Parks took his time explaining recent events before turning his attention to Rich.

"I never anticipated seeing you," he said. "You can be of great assistance. I need to talk with the city fathers regarding Management. You're still the head, right?"

"I'm afraid not," Rich replied sadly. "Management has put tremendous pressure on everyone, and it looks like they caved. We tried to engage them, and nearly didn't make it back alive."

"Sorry to hear that. I had hoped to coordinate with them, but I guess not," Parks said. "Anyway, I have things I must do, and need to be going. It's so good to see everyone's ok. It's quite the load off my mind."

"Where are you going?" Kirsten asked.

Parks looked at the concerned faces sitting around him.

"Management is looking for the gifts, but they haven't found them yet," he said. "They're becoming increasingly desperate, but I have a plan to stop them."

"All by yourself?" Aunt Lori asked anxiously.

"Yes, I have to do this alone," he replied calmly.

"What's that thing glowing under your shirt?" Kirsten asked suddenly.

"Glowing thing," Parks asked, somewhat confused as he looked down at his chest. "I wasn't aware…"

He pulled the chain hung around his neck with the unusually-shaped object dangling from the end. It was the same object responsible for saving his life when he had been blasted by a Nullifier.

"No way," Kirsten exclaimed. "That's the missing piece."

"Missing piece of what?" Parks asked as Kirsten jumped up, and ran into the motor home.

"This is what I'm talking about."

She brought out a wooden box, and placed it on the table.

"What do you make of this?"

She pulled the strangely-shaped medallion with four points of a star on the front, and grabbed the one Parks was holding. His had the remaining two points on the front, and an image of a sword on the back. It was still glowing as she joined it to the medallion. It fit perfectly.

The moment it was complete, the medallion began to glow ever brighter, and became too hot to hold. Kirsten dropped it onto the wooden table. They all watched in amazement as it slowly burned into the top of the table while it welded itself into a singular object. The smoke cleared as the object slowly cooled.

Parks picked up the end of the chain, revealing a perfect, six-sided star on one side, and three distinct images on the other.

"What do you suppose it is?" Uncle James asked.

"I'm not really sure," he said, "but I can tell you one thing. The fragment I had protected me from certain death. It's hard to say what the entire thing can do."

"It's called the Shield of Theos," Aunt Lori said unexpectedly.

She sat next to Parks on the bench.

"My mother told me about it when I was a child. She said it was made by four craftsmen long, long ago. They discovered the design in an ancient book which told them what materials to use, and how to make it. The four craftsmen were brothers, well-skilled in their trades, and very old. The first was a miner who found the materials, the second an alchemist who blended the raw materials, the third a carver who created the molds, and the fourth a jeweler who finished the work, and made the engravings.

That night when the final piece was completed, the four met in the workshop to celebrate their achievement. The final step was to coat the pieces with a strange mixture of chemicals specified in the book. The alchemist brother finished his work and coated them. While they waited for it to cool, and before they could assemble it, a strange thing happened.

One of the brothers heard a noise outside, and went to the door to check. He was about to open it when a powerful animal burst through. It was large and hairy, with a triangular head, and had three claws on each foot. It tore through the men, killing them."

"Another great story you never told me," James lamented.

"Each of the four brothers had a granddaughter or great granddaughter," Lori continued, ignoring his interruption. "The girls were young, athletic, and brave, having been taught to hunt, and to protect the village they shared.

"Hearing the noise, the young women grabbed their weapons, and ran to the workshop to attack the large animal. At first it appeared the beast would kill them as well, but there was something about the spirit in which those girls fought. They were fearless, and though the animal was ferocious, it could not stand before their effort. It ran off into the darkness."

Lori paused. It looked to Jim as though she were reliving the moment, even though it had happened long before she was born.

"Three of the brothers were dead, and the fourth was barely alive. His granddaughter rushed to his side to see if she could help, but there was nothing she could do. Before the old man died, he looked tenderly into her eyes, and gave her this admonishment.

"You, and those with you tonight," he said, gathering his strength as he looked upon the four young women, "are our legacy. We are the first generation, and you the third and fourth. What my brothers and I have made shall be your inheritance, to be passed down from mother to daughter, generation to generation. Each of you must take a part of what we have created until the final generation, when only one daughter remains. Then it shall be hers, and she will know what to do."

"That's my mother's story," Lori concluded. "I've carried my piece and kept it, and my cousins must have done the same for all these many generations. Until today, I didn't know Pearl and I were related, and also whoever gave Parks the final piece. It appears that you are the final daughter as I have no daughters, and my unknown cousin must not have one either."

"Then I guess this is yours."

Parks handed the amulet to his sister.

"What do you think it means?" she asked.

"That's something we're going to have to figure out."

He got up from the table.

"I'm heading into the city. There's much work to do, and little time."

"I'm coming with you," Kirsten asserted. "Whatever happens next, we're going to be there together, just like that day in the cave."

She was referring to that fateful day when Parks and her dad had chased what they thought was a bear into the cave on Grace Mountain.

"It's dangerous out there alone," Philip said to his two kids. "I would rather we think of a way to work together as a team."

"I think Philip is right," Rich interjected. "Working together is always the better solution."

"Working together to do what?" Parks snapped. "From what I've seen, there's nothing any of you can do to help, no offense intended. No, I would feel much better knowing you're safe, and I would appreciate your staying right here until I can find an answer to this. That goes for you too, Kirsten."

"You're dreaming," Kirsten said quietly. "There's no way I'm staying here."

Parks wasn't happy, but he couldn't stop Kirsten if she wanted to do something. He was about to get back into the transporter when Rich spoke up.

"We went to a lot of trouble to get this," he said, lifting a shiny cube from a bag sitting next to him.

Parks was immediately interested.

"That looks cool. What is it?"

"My dad told me to open this only if all hope seemed lost," Rich replied. "Do you think all hope is lost?"

"Hmm," Parks hesitated at first, but answered confidently. "Of course there's hope. I'm still breathing and fighting."

"We feel that too," Rich said. "But sitting out here while you do our fighting for us means we have to hope in you, not ourselves. That's not how I was raised, and I don't think the rest of us here were either.

Also, your dad, uncle, and I went and retrieved this with all the odds against us. Honestly, I don't even know how to open it, or what it does. But I do know this: I'm not about to find out, at least not yet. So you need to come down off your high horse, and realize we're in this together, like it or not. You can go off on whatever mission you're on, but just know we're doing things too, with or without you."

Parks looked at his family.

"You're right. I'm sorry," he said finally.

He put his foot up on the picnic table bench, and folded his hands.

"I'm used to being on my own, and there are some things only I can do, but how about we coordinate our efforts. From what I understand, Management is about to move on the city, and they had captured David, Normand and Burke. I was looking for them before I had to make an emergency run to the Island.

"David and Normand showed up with Jim, and they said Burke is ok. But they also said there are Testers positioned in the city, and I expect them to move soon."

"Wow!" Rich replied as he rubbed his chin. "That's a tall order for one man. Tell you what, why don't you and your sister focus on the gifts while we see what we can do about the Testers. I still have some contacts in the city, and a few ideas. Your dad and uncle will be all the help I need. Let me have your cell phone."

Parks handed it over. Rich took out his pocket knife with screwdriver and other attachments, and went to work on the phone. In a few minutes he handed it back.

"I just changed the frequency," he said. "Now it will work with the base station here in the motor home. Your phone doesn't have enough power to send but it can receive, so whoever gets back here will be able to tell the others what's going on. This will be communication central."

Parks was about to take off with Kirsten when he turned back to Rich.

"Oh, by the way, why don't you put that cube thing away for now? Whatever it is, I don't think we need it, do you?"

"I think you might be right," Rich said as he returned it to the bag. But then he smiled and said, "If I didn't know better, I would say it's working already."

Parks and Kirsten took off down the long miles of graveled road. They had several hours of driving to catch up, and solidify their plan. There was much to do, and no time to waste.

CHAPTER 25

Barron made it back to the warehouse, and left the twenty Testers he had taken with him to the Island. He gave them specific orders to not allow anyone in or out of the tunnel without his permission. Then he took off for the Citadel, and an impromptu board meeting. This was his great opportunity to get what he had always wanted; a position of authority and power. He reached over, and put his hand on the red crystal blade lying on the seat beside him.

It felt warm, and brightened slightly at his touch.

Construction crews were busily removing busted concrete and twisted steel from the pile that was once the Citadel as Barron entered. He felt a certain sense of awe at Parks's accomplishment as he drove slowly past, but his attention quickly returned to the matter at hand.

"I'm here to see the board," he announced as he strolled off the elevator.

"Mr. Barron," the tall lady seated behind the desk said as she ran her black polished nails down the appointment calendar. "I don't see your name on the list today."

"Then put it there," he retorted gruffly. "This is an emergency, and the board will want to hear what I have to say."

She hesitated for a moment as she looked up into his dark eyes, then reached for the phone. She turned her back, and spoke softly into the phone so he couldn't hear.

"The board will see you," she said as she returned the phone to the receiver. "Just follow the corridor…"

She continued talking, but Barron was already strolling down the hall. He knew where the board room was, and would waste no time. This was sure to be a turning point. The long walk on polished marble floors past opulent furnishings, priceless paintings, and bronze sculptures led him to the plain wooden door with a single brass identification plate next to it that read "Board Room."

He pushed open the door, and strolled in.

"Have a seat, Mr. Barron," Number Six said. "We hear you bring good tidings."

"Not completely," Barron replied.

He stood behind the chair reserved for the president.

"Dave Castle and I followed a lead that led us to a far outpost of resisters where we encountered the renegade Parks. He killed the president in an ambush," he lied. "After a huge battle, where I was hopelessly outnumbered, mind you, I managed to escape with my life to bring you this news."

"Hmm," Number One mused as he looked Barron over. "I see you have removed the red crystal from your chest. The one we exchanged for the one Parks put there."

"Yeah, so what," Barron replied, feeling instantly uncomfortable. "I didn't like the way it made me feel, but I don't know what that has to do with anything."

"It has everything to do with it!" Number Five shot back. "The red crystals help keep things in balance, and hold our position here. We 'gave' you one to ensure your compliance, but you have rejected our 'gift.' Now you come with significant news, and expect us to trust you."

"Maybe this will help," Barron replied.

He pulled the red crystal blade from a scabbard strapped to his waist.

The room lit up brightly from the eerie red glow as Barron held the blade above his head. In one smooth motion, he sliced through the president's chair. It fell in two pieces, and he kicked them to the side as he stepped to the table. The outline of his body glowed as he laid the red crystal blade on the table before the board.

"I want my due!" he demanded.

He slammed both hands down, and leaned in towards the six. "I've been faithful to Management since the beginning, and have fought to preserve your power and position in the face of everything Parks and his resister friends have done. Make me president, and you'll see this city bow forever to your will. I'm the one that can both find the gifts you're seeking and destroy

Parks."

The six looked intently at Barron for a moment, and then back and forth at each other. Finally, Number Six replied.

"You are indeed powerful," he acknowledged, "and we will need a replacement. However, your purpose is not yet fulfilled. Mr. Grey will serve with you as co-president until the matter is fully resolved. Then we will decide who remains, and in what capacity. Until then, it is your duty to gather all the gifts, and bring them before us. But be clear on this point: failure is not an option."

Barron was elated as he walked down the hall, and turned into Dave's old office. He plopped into the plush leather chair, and put his feet on the massive desk.

"I don't mind sharing for now," he mused as he leaned back. "Mr. Grey can be of some help, so let's just get this ball rolling."

He reached out, picked up the phone, and, in a matter of moments, Mr. Grey was in his office.

Elsewhere in the city, Aaron was trying to get things of his own moving.

"We need to meet, right now," he said as he risked a quick cell call to Kenzie.

"Where?" Kenzie asked.

"At the school," he replied quietly, and hung up.

Aaron was sure he was under suspicion, but he had to chance it. He'd seen the map with the quadrants outlined on it, and had overheard Mr. Grey talking with General Allison. He saw the general go into Mr. Grey's office, and decided to see if he could find out something. Fortunately it was lunch time, and the floor was empty.

He decided to stay behind, and install a virus he had created to destroy all records related to the 'backspin' investigation he was supposed to be working on. Then he saw the general, and crept up to the office door.

"We can't wait for Aaron's report," the general was saying to Mr. Grey. "I have it on good authority the resistance is planning a move two days from today. We need to deploy the

Testers tonight, and begin a quadrant sweep tomorrow to beat their efforts.

"We'll start at quadrant four on the south end of the city by the warehouse district first. They'll cut off any attempt to escape into the wilderness, and once they've pushed through neighborhoods and businesses to the outer edge of the city center, we'll hit from the remaining sides equally."

"What are the instructions for the Testers?" Mr. Grey asked.

"The Testers will be divided into ten groups of fifty each, with an interrogator going with them," the General replied. "The interrogators will use these red crystals I received from the board to find the gifts, and the people who have them. Then the Testers will take care of those people."

Mr. Grey laughed, but Aaron felt sick to his stomach as he returned to his desk. There was no point in finishing the virus install now. Instead, he left a voice message on General Allison's phone, saying he wasn't feeling good, and needed to take the rest of the day off. He headed straight to the elementary school, being careful to make sure he wasn't followed. Kenzie was waiting for him as he pulled in, and hid his car behind the auditorium.

"What's so important?" Kenzie asked immediately.

"Management is moving on the city tomorrow," he said. "They'll be starting from the south end in the warehouse district. We need to get everyone together, and do something fast."

"How are we supposed to do that?" Kenzie asked. "I haven't seen anyone lately, and I don't know where they're hiding."

"We'll use Kirsten's method with the crystals," Aaron said. "I've been able to contact Parks that way. Maybe we can get through to him as well."

"I've been trying that," Kenzie replied. "But for some reason, nothing happens. It's like we're being blocked or something."

Aaron pulled the blue crystal from around his neck and concentrated, but after several minutes, he relaxed.

"You're right," he conceded. "I don't understand, but it's

not working. Troy said he was going to focus on the area he grew up in which is along Vista Drive in the suburbs on the west side of the city. The Testers are not focused there, so maybe we can find him."

Kenzie got into Aaron's car, and they made their way to Troy's old neighborhood. Aaron guessed correctly that Troy would have searched for the Testers, and not finding any, would have taken up a position where he could watch for their arrival. He and Isaac were sparring with their blades on a long-deserted baseball field on a hill overlooking the area when Aaron arrived.

"What are you guys doing up here?" Troy asked as he and Isaac ran up.

"The Testers are not coming this way first," Aaron said. "I've seen the map, and overheard Management's plan. We have maybe twelve hours before they attack on the south end of town."

"I'll follow you guys!" Troy exclaimed as he turned towards his car.

"Wait, wait!" Kenzie shouted. "We're going to need more help. What about David, Normand, and Burke? We must find them, and Kirsten too."

"There's no telling where they might be," Troy replied. "I've been trying to contact them for days. For some reason my crystal isn't working."

"We've had the same problem," Kenzie said. "It's like there's some kind of interference or something. But how could that be? No one but us knows about the power of the crystals Parks gave us, do they?"

Anxious glances were exchanged as they suddenly realized that an unknown force could be affecting their crystals.

Isaac broke the silence.

"Hey, guys, what the heck is that?"

He had walked to the edge of the parking lot, and was pointing in the direction of the warehouses. The others joined him quickly, and they stood there together for a moment, watching a small dark cloud slowly form.

"What do you think it is?" Aaron asked anxiously.

"It's the beginning," Kenzie said solemnly. "I've seen a

cloud like that before, and it has something to do with the Testers."

"Then we had better get moving," Troy replied. "The Testers have to be stopped, and we're the only ones available."

"I still don't like it," Kenzie cautioned. "There are only four of us, and we don't know how many there are of them."

"I agree," Troy replied, "but we can do this. I know we can. The things we've been through and the training we've received make us more than capable to stop a few Testers."

"But we don't know what we're up against," Kenzie protested.

"We'll do this smart," Troy insisted. "Kirsten taught us to keep out of sight, and attack when they least expect it. No one knows we're coming, so we couldn't have a greater element of surprise."

"Well, if you're all convinced," Kenzie said as she looked around at her friends. "I guess I can't let you go without me."

"Great! Let's do this," Troy said, and he took off for his truck.

They drove across the city, taking evasive actions to make sure they were not followed or spotted. Strangely, the majority of the streets were empty, and there was little traffic. It was as if the city itself was sensing danger, and people were hiding inside. Troy kept his eyes on the small dark cloud, and soon discovered it was not directly over the warehouses, but floating over a shallow, dried-out drainage pond.

The pond was surrounded by small trees, and overgrown with clumps of tall grass and scrub brush. They parked their cars along the road, and walked cautiously up the graveled driveway, past several concrete buildings housing pumps and other equipment. They crawled through the grass to the edge, and caught glimpses of red.

"This is even better than I hoped," Troy said quietly. "They're mingled in the grass down there, which means we can approach without being spotted. We'll just begin taking them out one by one."

"I say we work in teams of two," Aaron whispered.

"We'll split up, but stay in sight of each other, so if anything goes wrong, we can quickly regroup. Kenzie and I will take the left, and you and Isaac take the right."

Each one pulled out a crystal blade, and began quietly working their way towards the middle of the large pond. They agreed to each locate a Tester, and simultaneously rise up behind it, and sever its head before it could move. Then they would continue on to the next, and so on until they had killed them all. Aaron raised his hand as they all took positions behind the red creatures barely visible in the tall grass. He gave the signal, and all four warriors rose from the grass, and dealt a deadly blow.

"What the," Kenzie exclaimed as she turned to Aaron, who was holding a shiny red sheet.

"These aren't real," Troy said.

He ran forward, knocking over cardboard cutouts with red plastic hanging on them.

"It's a trap!" Isaac shouted.

But it was too late. A large group of cadets came out of hiding along the ridge of the pond above them, each one brandishing a Nullifier.

"I wouldn't do anything foolish if I were you," General Allison shouted, "unless you want to be blown apart. Put down your weapons, and raise your hands."

The group looked back and forth at each other for a moment. Troy was about to rush the heavily-armed cadets, but Isaac grabbed him by the arm.

"Don't do it, man. It's suicide."

Reluctantly, the four warriors dropped their crystal blades, and raised their hands. A group of cadets came down the side of the pond, and put handcuffs on them before gathering their weapons, and leading them up the side slope to the waiting General.

"Well, who do we have here?" General Allison asked as she looked them over. "I see our faithful analyst and his girlfriend. Then of course, there's the young man I was talking to a while back who managed to bust his way out of the Citadel," she continued as she walked past Isaac. "This other fine-looking young man I haven't met yet, but I imagine we'll have plenty of time to get to know one another. Tell you what," she said. "Why don't the four of you save us all a lot of trouble, and tell me who you're with, and where I can find the rest of the resistance."

"Hmm, not going to talk?" she continued as she stood in front of the small group. "Well, no worries. I would hate to disappoint Mr. Grey. He does love chatting with young people like you."

She waved her hand, and the cadets shoved them into the back of a transport truck hidden behind some trees. The flap over the rear of the truck closed, and several heavily-armed cadets climbed in to take up guard positions. The large truck bounced down the gravel road, and out onto the street. Without saying it, they all knew their next stop could be their last.

CHAPTER 26

"I still believe my idea will work," Jim said as he walked with David and Normand towards the colonel's office. "We grab that Harry fella, and take him with us back to the city. Then we take over the main Management broadcasting center, and put him on the air. People will have to admit Management faked the whole execution thing just to make the resistance look evil. I tell you, one more broadcast will change everything."

"That seems to be it with you," David replied flatly. "You think broadcasting the truth is going to set us all free. Well, I'm not sure people want to know the truth anymore. They're more satisfied living a lie."

"It's easy to be cynical," Jim responded, "I've felt that myself. But the lives of the people we care about may depend on what we do next."

They arrived at the colonel's office, and Jim went about explaining his plan. The colonel listened intently before responding.

"I see no reason to keep Harry here," he said. "Our medical staff has put him back together, so he's at least functional. However, we keep him locked up in our detainment area. Parks said he's a very dangerous man, and not to be trusted. Are you sure you want to take the chance?"

"We have little choice," Jim said, glancing at David. "For all we know, it may already be too late, but we have to keep trying."

"I agree with Jim," Normand said boldly. "Parks has shown the courage to go back and do what he can. Why shouldn't we find equal courage, and do something no one else can?"

"It's not about being afraid," David countered, "it's about making the right move. How do we know if we can even do all the things Jim suggests? Management is likely to be on guard like never before."

David leaned back, and looked at the three men before

continuing.

"Alright. I agree we have to do this. You can count me in."

"That's the spirit!" Jim exclaimed.

The colonel made a call, and within a half hour, Harry was being loaded into Jim's car. He was shackled with both hand and ankle cuffs, and there was a heavy cable connecting the two. They were taking no chances.

"What's your next step?" Jim asked as he slid in behind the wheel.

"Parks and I have agreed on a plan," the colonel answered. "He'll contact me with instructions when the time comes. In the meantime, we're preparing for what could be the final battle, and I have a feeling we're approaching the 'all or nothing' moment."

Jim felt all of that as he rolled up, and out of the Island. He took Parks's advice to stay out of the tunnel, but that didn't mean he had a better way of getting back into the city. Blowing up the Testers along the southeastern gate likely meant they would have to find another way in.

The city was protected by a tall wall, designed mostly to maintain separation from the wilderness; it also served as a formidable defense to anyone with hostile intent. But Jim had an idea that was sure to work. At least, he hoped it would.

"What exactly do you hope to get from bringing me back to the city?" Harry asked from the back seat. "The way I see it, you and your friends will be dead before long, unless, of course, you would like to make a deal. I might be able to save you if you're willing to cooperate."

"Hah!" Jim snapped. "You save us? You can't even save yourself. You don't know this, but your 'friends' in Management have already killed you off, and there's no way they're going to allow you to rise from the dead. If they catch us, they'll kill you all over again, only this time for real."

"You don't know what you're saying," Harry protested. "I'm the head of the Citadel, and a respected Management leader. I decide who lives and who dies."

"That ship has long since sailed," Jim replied.

He approached the final ridge where he could get a good look at the gate, and the large craters left from when they had blown up the Testers.

"What do you think, fellas?"

"It doesn't appear to be manned," David said. "I thought they would have cadets stationed out here by now."

"Maybe they don't care," Normand replied. "I mean, who would want to come back in after blowing up the place to escape?"

"Yeah, maybe," Jim answered thoughtfully, "but I wouldn't be too sure. They could be hiding in that distant tree line, just hoping we'll come back."

"Well, we can't stop now," David asserted. "I say the best approach is the direct one. We have some explosives we haven't used yet, so I say we come back in with style. The gate is shut, but all we have to do is open it enough to drive through, and we're there."

"That'll take some fancy driving," Normand said. "The piles of debris from those blasts are huge, and there are rocks strewn everywhere."

"If you guys can sneak down there and set the charges," Jim said, "I'll see to it we get through."

David and Normand unloaded the last of the explosives they had taken from Dr. Flint, and carried them down a long slope towards the gate. The force of the explosions that had destroyed the Testers had left large craters, which now served to hide their advancement.

They dove from hole to hole, constantly checking back with Jim. If Jim waved his arms, they were to race back to his location as fast as possible. But no one saw them as they reached the final hole, with only thirty feet separating them from the gate.

"Look up there," Normand whispered. "The cameras are still down. That means they can't see us. Maybe this is a better break than we thought."

They set the explosives at the bottom of the huge gate, and next to the large latch that held it shut. The thought was the gate was too heavy and fortified to be destroyed, but with enough explosives, the latch could be blown open, and the gate forced back on its track enough for them to drive through.

Normand and David raced up the slope, and slid in alongside Jim,

"Ok, we're set to go," David said.

"Here's the deal," Jim said. "We're going to have to blow that thing, and get through in one smooth move, because if they are waiting up there for us, we'll only have a few seconds before they hit us. We'll be sitting ducks."

"How close are you thinking of getting?" David asked. "We put enough explosives in there to make quite a bang."

"We're about to find out," Jim said as he punched the gas pedal.

A cloud of dust flew from behind the orange car as he raced down the slope, swerving around large rocks, upended shrubs, and over mounds of sand. Jim held the detonator in one hand, with his finger on the button. The car went airborne several times, but he had to wait for just the right moment. If he blew it too soon, they could be trapped. Blow it too late, and they would be killed. Harry curled up between David and Normand, who were grabbing onto anything they could find. Jim roared up next to the wall, and the fast-approaching gate. Beads of sweat formed on his brow as he held the detonator, and pushed the button.

The blast wave met them in midair just as Jim came over the top of a large mound of sand. The nose of the car went up momentarily before slamming down hard. They couldn't tell if it was blind luck or perfect timing as chunks of rock and cement ricocheted off the underside of the car. They bounced twice, sending hubcaps spinning into the distance, but Jim's hands were glued to the wheel as he hit the brakes hard, and spun the car towards the gate. Problem was, a cloud of dust obscured their approach, but this was no time for second guessing. If the gate wasn't open, they would crash into it, and die. All he could do was aim for what he hoped was the opening.

"Yee ha," Normand shouted as they shot through the wall onto the access road.

Their plan had worked. The gate was open, and they were through.

"We're not out of the fire yet," Jim said.

He raced towards a seldom-used side road buried among massive cedar trees.

"If I can get us in there, we can ditch the car, and make a run for it if we have to."

The fast-moving car ate up the remaining pavement before the road changed to gravel. To their surprise, there were no waiting Testers or cadets. Jim drove several miles before he slowed, and turned into an abandoned driveway protected by a row of trees.

"I can't believe it worked," Jim said as he peeled his hands off the steering wheel.

"You can't believe it?" David said incredulously. "It was your idea!"

"What do you make of all this?" Normand said.

He got out, and stretched for a moment. "No Management response. Do you think we took them by surprise?"

"It appears so," David answered, joining Normand. "But does that give us an advantage? We have to assume there will be a massive search underway soon."

The words were no sooner spoken when several Management vehicles roared past, their lights flashing.

"They can't know much," Jim said confidently. "The video cameras were down, and other than our skid marks, there is no evidence of who or what just happened. I think they'll be scratching their heads for a while, which means we still have a chance."

"You have no chance," Harry growled from the back seat. "You may think you've won something, but all you've really done is get caught in the spider's web. My offer still stands. Surrender, and I'll see to it that you're treated fairly."

"Treated fairly?" Jim snapped. "You mean like those poor souls you bused into the wilderness to die of starvation, or freeze to death? You don't know the meaning of fair. If I were you, I would keep my mouth shut before I stuff a rag in it."

"Where do we start?" David asked as Jim pulled onto the road.

"First, we reload at the doctor's place." Jim replied. "Then we see if we can hook up with anyone else who might be able to help."

Rita was relieved to see Jim, and ran outside to meet him. They embraced for a long moment before heading back inside.

"How's Burke doing?" Normand asked as they met the doctor in the hallway.

"There doesn't seem to be any permanent damage," Dr. Flint replied. "I'm planning on keeping him another night at the hospital, and then I'll bring him back here tomorrow morning. No one has been suspicious or concerned, but anything over a three day stay requires additional reporting. I would rather not have to answer any unnecessary questions."

"We can't thank you enough," David said. "If it wasn't for you, Burke wouldn't have made it."

"I hope you don't mind, doctor," Jim interjected, "but we need to get more 'supplies' from your basement."

"You're welcome to whatever you need. Is there any reason for me to be concerned?"

"I'm afraid there is."

Jim followed Dr. Flint through the secret panel in his living room, and down the narrow, twisting stairs to the hidden room below.

"Testers have been spotted inside the city walls. We believe Management is about to do something terrible, and you should prepare yourself."

"My wife and I lived here almost all our lives," the doctor replied, "and, since she passed two years ago this very week, I've been rattling around in here. It's just not been the same without her, but it makes me feel good knowing I'm in the fight again. You know, I never really did understand the surrender. I always thought we could have beat them, but that wasn't my call."

"Hey, that car of yours is pretty conspicuous," he continued. "I have an old Stargazer in the back garage that would do the job, and it's fully charged. Why not take it instead?"

There was no argument with that idea. David and Normand made several trips to the underground armory. They loaded the rear of the doctor's station wagon with every imaginable weapon or explosive they could find, but it barely made a dent in the doctor's arsenal. After some food and a quick explanation of Harry's presence, they were ready to move on.

"We'll be back here tomorrow evening to see how Burke's doing," David said.

"If all goes as planned," Jim cautioned. "We have a lot to do in the next twenty four hours."

Jim's slight pessimistic slip didn't go unnoticed, but they all understood that what they were planning could blow up in their faces as powerfully as the explosives they were carrying. Rita squeezed Jim's hand confidently as he smiled weakly back.

CHAPTER 27

"We can't sit around here any longer." Rich said as they watched Kirsten and Parks drive away. "I want to get downtown, and see our old friend Tim."

"Tim!" Philip exclaimed. "He was with the ones who locked us in the cave. What are you thinking?"

"Yeah, he got under your skin, no doubt," Rich replied. "But I know him, and he's one guy who can play both sides of the net, if you know what I mean."

"A true lawyer," James interjected.

"Exactly," Rich said. "The way I see it, he thinks we're still trapped in JJ's cave, and there's no reason to go back and check on us. I think he'll be plenty surprised to see our smiling faces when we drop in, and pay him a little visit."

Rich's sly smile indicated he had a plan, and that was good enough for Philip and James.

Lori agreed to stay behind, and monitor transmissions. They had a CB radio in their motor home, and Rich had refitted it, making it possible to pick up Management communications, even on their secure line. In addition, she could transmit any information she might get to them on a frequency Management wasn't aware of, or if they were, didn't monitor.

"You guys keep an eye on my hubby," Lori insisted as they loaded into Philip's truck. "I don't want any more trouble from him."

Philip and Rich agreed with a chuckle, but her point was well taken. What they were embarking on was dangerous for all of them. Philip put the truck in gear, and drove the long, dusty road until it finally transitioned to blacktop. They were sure it was safe this time to take the shortest route downtown, as no one would be looking for a pickup truck and three old farmers. They were wrong, however, and soon found themselves approaching a road block.

"We can't outrun them in this thing," Philip said as he

slowed to a stop behind three other vehicles waiting in line. "I guess we just have to see what they want."

"Where are you heading?" the young, heavily-armed cadet asked as his partner circled to the back of the truck.

"Into the city to pick up some supplies," Philip replied calmly.

"What kind of supplies?" the cadet pressed as he looked over their identification.

"Grain for the calves," Philip answered quietly.

"And it takes all three of you to do that?" the cadet asked as he looked across at Rich and James. "Hmm, you're both Parks it says here, and the other is a Lindberg. How do you know each other?"

Philip tried to formulate an answer in his mind. It was becoming obvious these men were not about to let them pass without satisfactory answers, and he couldn't think of a single one. The cadet ran his finger down a list on a clipboard, apparently expecting to find their names there. In the moment when they were distracted, Rich reached down between his knees, pulled out the glistening cube from his backpack, and got out of the truck.

"Get back in the car," the cadet standing at the right rear fender commanded.

"I just thought you guys might like to see this," Rich replied as he put the cube on the top of the truck. "It's very valuable."

Rich turned the key, and pushed a hidden button which opened the top. He buried his face in his coat as he allowed the cube to open slightly. The two cadets were taken by surprise. Instantly, a bright light shot out, catching the two cadets squarely in the eyes. Rich closed the cube, and climbed back in the truck.

"Let's go," he said as the cadet calmly returned their identification papers to Philip.

"Uh, what," Philip said with a dumbfounded look.

"Go!" Rich insisted. "Put the truck in drive, and go."

Philip looked over at the cadet standing next to his truck, and then back at Rich. He put his truck in gear and pulled away, expecting to be stopped with a blast from a Nullifier, but the two cadets didn't move.

"I don't get it," Philip said finally as he maneuvered around the road block.

"Well, I guess you deserve to know what just happened," Rich replied. "I suppose I should have told you, I do know what the invention my father made does. You see, my father was both a psychologist and a scientist. He became interested in how the human brain handles certain inputs. One day when we were hiking together up Grace Mountain, we came across a small cave entrance, and went inside to investigate."

"Yeah, I've been in one of them myself," Philip said.

"So you've said," Rich continued. "Anyway, we didn't go too deep before Dad noticed a glow coming from a side cave. He made me stay behind, and went to investigate on his own. A few minutes later, he came out with a rather blank look on his face. I asked him what he had found, but he didn't reply at first. After a few minutes, he began talking about the cave as if we had just come in. I asked him again what he had found, and he didn't even remember going in there.

Curiosity got the better of both of us, only this time Dad went in with his hat pulled down over his eyes, and his hood up. He came back the second time with what he called the "rock of forgetfulness", because if you looked at it, you would momentarily lose track of time, and forget whatever it was you were just doing.

He used to use it in his practice to help people get momentary relief from their hard lives, but when some people had lengthy lapses in memory, he decided to seal it in this lead-lined box. When he gave it to me, it was with the understanding it should never be used unless a circumstance arose where something drastic was required."

"What are we doing out here?" James quizzed from the back seat.

Rich and Philip broke out laughing as they realized James must have caught a reflection from the stone in the side view mirror.

"I just don't get you guys sometimes," James quipped.

"Don't let it bother you," Philip replied. "We're on a mission, so sit back and relax. We'll be there soon."

Philip drove straight through town to the financial business sector where Tim's office was located. Rich was interested in learning what had caused the city fathers to sell out. Philip parked in a nearby alley, and the three men headed for his office.

"Is your husband in?" Rich asked as he greeted Shirley, Tim's wife. Rich had gone to college with her and Tim, and had been the best man at their wedding.

"Rich!" Shirley exclaimed as she came around the desk to give him a hug. "It's been a long time since I last saw you. What have you been doing?"

"It's a long story," Rich said as he returned the hug. "We're here to see your husband. Is he in?"

"He is," she replied as she stepped behind her desk. "Let me ring him for you."

"That won't be necessary," Rich said as he stepped towards Tim's office. "He's expecting us."

Rich opened the door, with James and Philip tight on his heels. Tim was busy digging through some papers, and didn't notice them at first. The three men had already gathered around his desk before he realized they were there.

"Whaatttt," Tim stuttered as he dropped the folder he was holding onto the floor. "What are you doing here?"

"I thought you might be surprised to see us," Rich said.

He sat down in one of the lush leather chairs reserved for clients.

"My friends and I are not in a gracious mood. We need answers, Tim."

James was a gentle giant of a man, but when he put his mind to it, his six foot nine frame could be quite intimidating.

"Look," Tim said nervously, "it's not what you think. We locked you guys up there for your own safety."

"Don't BS me!" Rich said, slamming his fist on the table. "We came to you for help, and found you had sold us out."

"We never sold out," Tim countered as he steadied himself. "Management came to us after the city surrendered with a proposition. We join them, or face certain death."

"Yeah, I heard the same thing, but you didn't see me joining up," Rich snapped.

"I know. We all knew," Tim said. "The problem was there was no opportunity there, and it was only a matter of time anyway. They wanted complete power over everybody and everything. We felt they would be fair, and people would be ok, but then things began to change. We knew there was something really wrong even before Jim Banner ran that piece on the East Economic Diversity District. People were coming by my office, complaining about their loved ones disappearing."

"Dying is more like it," Rich interjected.

"That's what worried us most. I tried to get answers for them, but was told in no uncertain terms to keep my nose out. That's when we realized the mistake we had made. So we formed our secret organization, and began to plan to take Management down from the inside."

"Are you expecting us to believe you're working against Management?" Philip snapped.

"I realize you're afraid to trust me, but it's all true. The reason JJ trapped you was because you're on Management's most-wanted list, and letting you run around the city would only draw attention to our efforts, and possibly get you killed. Just coming here today may have jeopardized our work."

"Yeah, what exactly is your work?" asked a voice from behind the three men. It was Jim the Weatherman. "From what I've seen, your work is to get us all captured. We barely escaped that supposed 'safe' house you set us up in."

"Like I told you when you were here last, Jim," Tim replied defensively, "someone hacked our e-mail account. But what I didn't tell you is several of Management's head people came by, asking questions. I had to give them something. I told them you had come here with a crazy idea about broadcasting again, and that I had given you a car, and a place to stay. I told them what you were planning, and they bit."

"It seems more like you were saving your own hide," Jim said bitterly. "You nearly cost us our lives, and have kept the truth from being told."

"You can believe what you want, but I'm telling you, we are poised, and ready to take down Management from the inside."

"Ok, you've told a very tall tale," Rich spoke up. "But assuming you're telling the truth, answer this one thing for me. How do you plan to 'dispose' of Management?"

"Now that's the right question," Tim replied. "Management is divided into what they call 'responsibility' centers. That means every department, whether security, transportation, energy or whatever, has a central control. They do everything through their Managers, so take those guys out, and the whole system begins to collapse. No one will be able to make a decision anymore. Then the people we have on the ground will each take out their subordinates and assume control."

"You know," Jim said thoughtfully, "I think I believe you, but you don't have all the facts. Management is already positioning to attack with the help of the Testers. There's no way you're going to surprise anybody. I, on the other hand, could provide quite the climax to the story."

"What are you suggesting, Jim?" Rich asked as their attention turned to him.

"I have Harry Allison tied up in the back of my car." Jim replied.

"But Harry was killed!" Tim exclaimed. "We all saw it on television."

"Exactly. Management created the illusion of death to fortify their position that all resisters are evil. Everything they produced was aimed at perverting the minds of the people. I want to turn that around with a strong injection of truth. If you can help me get control of the Central Broadcast Station, I know I can send a message that cannot be denied, and a living, breathing Harry is the ultimate proof."

The room went silent for a moment as they grasped the depth of Jim's statement. Then Rich spoke up.

"We can give you the help you need. My plan was to pull

together certain significant families and begin to prepare for the coming Tester invasion, but if what Tim says is true, he's already got them ready."

"We did once share the same contacts," Tim confirmed.

"So we'll join with you," Rich continued, "if that's agreeable to all."

James and Philip nodded their approval.

"Great!" Jim exclaimed. "I've been to the station before, and know how to get in with the least amount of resistance. Rita, David, and Normand are with me, and they're guarding Harry so nothing funny happens. I have plenty of firepower, but if things go as planned, we won't need it."

"I'm really sorry for not handling this better," Tim said as he stood up. "You're my friends, but I guess sometimes it's hard to know how to do the right thing. I'll talk with the city fathers, and we'll be ready to do whatever it takes."

"You don't have much time," Jim said as he started for the door. "I'm broadcasting at six this evening."

"We know where every Manager lives, and their underlings," Tim assured them. "We'll dispatch our operatives to their locations, starting right now. Once you've secured the station, call me here at my office."

The men took their leave of Tim, feeling more confident than ever. Tim might be a lawyer, but he was no liar. They also realized the city father's good intentions were misconstrued by the circumstances that surrounded them all. Sometimes what's real and true is not as it appears. That was a lesson they all were about to learn in a big way.

CHAPTER 28

"Pull over here, brother," Kirsten said. "We need to talk before we go any further."

"What's on your mind?" Parks asked as he parked the large transport truck in a graveled access road.

"Everything," Kirsten replied. "It seems to me all we've been doing is 'beating the air,' fighting an invisible enemy as it were. I've helped organize and train good people, but for what? To fight what may turn out to be our neighbors, or the local grocer. What's this all about really?"

Parks leaned back, and took a long, loving look at his sister. His respect for her and all she had accomplished was profound, and she was right. They did need to talk, and it was long overdue.

"I've asked myself that very question a thousand times," Parks replied, "and the answer is always the same. I'm not sure. Every time I think I've got it figured out, something changes. First it was Barron, then Harry, now Dave. But they don't seem to know any more than we do. We all seem to be players in some larger game."

"I get that feeling too," Kirsten replied, "but at least now we're thinking. Let's see what we have. First, we know Management had a plan to destroy the city, right? But they couldn't because we surrendered. So then they had to dominate.

"But there's more to this than just control. Think about it, Parks. They had the perfect chance to destroy us, but they didn't, or couldn't. Why not? Then there is this insidious need to find these things called the "Gifts." They're even willing to kill to get them. Why? We don't even know what they are, and from what I hear, they don't either.

"Then there's this "Dark Matter" stuff. What's that? Something really bad that could destroy us, and it may already be here."

"That's the gist of it," Parks replied, "but how does

knowing that help us?"

"Hang on, I'm not through yet," Kirsten continued. "Maybe we're smarter than we give ourselves credit for. We know Management is preparing for a new fight, or worse, a destruction of some kind. The Testers are plenty evidence of that.

We also know Management hasn't been able to activate their plan, whatever that is, yet. Why? Well, from what you've just told me, and what I've learned, it has to be centered on those mysterious gifts. What do we know about them?"

"Well, anytime I've heard gifts being referenced, it's been about them being hidden, and no one knowing exactly what they are. Legend says they're things you wouldn't think were special because they appear ordinary."

"Have you ever seen anything like that?" Kirsten asked intently.

"Something ordinary but powerful, well, not really..." Parks replied, but then it struck him. "Wait a minute. There are some things we can't, explain. Do you remember when we were in that cave as kids? I was trapped alone in the room with the Zender, and you lowered the silver cord we found when we were helping mom in the greenhouse."

"Yes, and then you came out in spite of that huge bolder in the way."

"Right. It gave me the power to move through solid rock, and I've used it since, with the same results."

"Do you still have it?"

"Of course."

He lifted his shirt, unwound it from around his waist, and set it on the seat between them. "What else do you think we might have?"

"What about the meteor you found?" Kirsten said. "The crystals are ordinary in appearance, but we both know what they can do."

"You're right," Parks said as he placed a blade on the seat. "And then there's the amulet we pieced together. Just a section of it saved me from getting blasted by a Nullifier."

Kirsten pulled it from her bag, and put it on the seat with

the other two pieces.

"What else can we think of?" Kirsten asked, getting more excited by the minute.

"Well, we know it has to seem ordinary," Parks replied thoughtfully. "I have no idea what that would even look like. Or do I?"

He reached for the bag he had stowed under the seat, and put it in his lap. He unzipped a section, and pulled out the old worn book with the parchment stuffed inside.

"This book has caused me more grief than I can ever say," he said, "but it has also unlocked mysteries, and has power I can't explain. I won't even open the parchment. The last time I did, I started hallucinating. Oh, and then there's this."

He pulled the Magnifier from the bottom of the bag.

"You'll have to see this for yourself sometime. It's intense."

"Wow!" Kirsten exclaimed as she laid the pieces out on the seat between them. "These are a strange group alright, but I can't say they're anything other than ordinary: A book, a piece of old paper, simple necklace, cool-looking blades, a heavy amulet, and a round object that opens. Sure they're unique if you know how to use them, but just looking at them, you could easily pass them over without a second thought. Maybe that's how they've remained hidden all these years."

"You're saying these are the gifts? Come on, Kirsten. They're things of legend. You believe that's what this pile of stuff sitting on the seat is?"

"Why not?" Kirsten asked. "You said yourself each one of these has a special power. Remember the old rhyme. "Six Gifts there are, and yet one more."

"Right, I remember. 'The seventh stands before the door. He enters through to times before, and then emerges the eighth, who knows. So what? It's just a nursery rhyme?"

"What if it's not? What if there are two more? We'll need to find those too."

"We're making some huge assumptions here, but I guess this makes as much sense as anything. And if what you're saying is true, we definitely can't allow them to fall into Management's hands."

"Agreed," Kirsten replied, "and you're the best one to keep them. Why don't you take them, and if you have to, find a place to hide them."

Parks agreed. He stuffed the items into his bag, and returned the blade to the sash around his waist. The sun was just passing center, headed towards afternoon as he pulled out onto the main road. Kirsten suggested they drop by a local consignment store, and pick up clothes they could use for a disguise.

But before they could go there, he had to do something about the huge vehicle they were in. The best idea was to hide the truck where he could get it later if needed. But in the meantime, they needed to find another, less obvious means of transportation, and he knew just where to go.

"Hi, Joel," Parks said as he slung out of the truck. "I was hoping to find you home."

"What are you doing here with that thing?" Joel asked in amazement as he hopped off the porch.

"I have it on loan," Parks quipped. "Any chance we could leave it here somewhere for a while?"

"You can't be serious," Joel responded. "Management could come screaming in here any minute."

"I know, I'll get it out of here," Parks replied. "But I need a less conspicuous set of wheels. Could I borrow your station wagon for a bit?"

"That's not a problem," Joel answered. "Darla was allotted a new car, so she doesn't use it anymore. Why don't you follow me to the gravel pit? We're pulling out of the north end, so there's plenty of room on the south side to hide this thing."

Joel quickly threw a quart of oil in the old station wagon before leading the way to the pit. He opened a back gate that led behind some large piles of gravel. Fortunately, the pit was only a few miles from Joel and Darla's house, and before long, they had him home again.

"Thanks, man!" Parks said as he was about to pull out.

"I don't know what you're planning," he replied as he leaned on the car and glanced over at Kirsten, "but be careful. These guys aren't fooling."

"You and Darla need to be careful. In fact, it's time to get a plan together," Kirsten replied seriously. "Things are about to get ugly, and you had better be prepared to flee or fight. None of us are safe anymore."

The fear in Joel's eyes reflected Kirsten's words as they pulled away. Shortly, with the help of Kirsten's directions, they were downtown and pulling into the consignment store.

"You wait in the car," Kirsten said as she opened the door. "I'll find you something to wear."

Parks had backed into one of the spaces in the rear of the parking lot facing the street so he could watch traffic. Even in Joel's old beater he didn't feel safe. He had taken Management by surprise several times already, but not without taking huge risks. The sun was just peeking around the corner of the building, but had yet to find him as he reached into his bag, and pulled out the old book.

"A gift," he mused as he held it tightly in his hand.

He opened it, and began reading while he waited. The book had seemed impossible to understand at times, but today was different. He found himself drawn into a series of allegories as he read.

"Darkness covered the land," the old book said, "and the minds of the people were blinded. Then a man appeared, drenched in sweat from his struggle against the dark matter. A man filled with good intentions, but crippled by fear of what he might become if he let down his guard for even a moment. The darkness pressed in upon him from all sides, and a voice of comfort rose into his mind, encouraging him to let go, and embrace the darkness.

The pain became more severe as he looked around at people wandering about in darkness, unable to see. Faceless people, yet somehow, he knew them. Then they suddenly turned as one, pointing long, bony accusing fingers at him. They began to speak, calling him every vile and wicked name, chiding him for untold failures and evil doing. All he felt was emptiness as the sky above him went black.”

“Are you ok?” Kirsten asked anxiously as she shook Parks.

“What?” Parks asked groggily, blinking his eyes open.

“What happened to you? You were mumbling something strange. Were you dreaming?”

“I wasn’t napping,” Parks said. “It’s this book again. I just started reading, and the next thing I knew I was somewhere else, seeing and feeling things I can’t even describe.”

“Well, I found a few things that should help us,” Kirsten said, opening the bag full of old clothes. “We just need a place to change into them, and then we can move about a little less conspicuously.”

“Come on, sis,” Parks lamented. “You want me to put on this old shirt and baseball cap? Do you really think I’ll gain access to the Citadel with that on?”

“It’s better than that leather coat you’re always wearing. They can spot you coming a mile away.”

“Here’s what we do,” Parks continued as he put the shirt and hat on. “We’ll drop by Aaron’s apartment, and see if he can get us through in his car. I just hope he has enough authority to push past the guards.”

Parks took the route past the community playground and into Aaron’s cul-de-sac. The old station wagon seemed a bit out of place in the upscale neighborhood, but fortunately, people paid little attention as they walked their dogs, or jogged down the street. Parks pulled up in front of Aaron’s garage door, and turned off the car.

The large old plaid shirt Kirsten had found for him fit loosely over his leather coat as they approached the set of stairs leading to Aaron’s door. Like many of the tall, narrow buildings lining both sides of the street, there was a small open porch with an arch across the top that provided some protection from the elements. Kirsten and Parks waited patiently as they rang the doorbell several times, but Aaron didn’t come. Parks quickly became uncomfortable, realizing it was mid-afternoon, and he

212

was probably still at work.

"We can't stand out here all day," he said. "People will get suspicious."

He slid one of his crystal blades through the locks on the door, and pushed it open.

"Are you crazy?" Kirsten hissed as she followed him inside. "Someone may have seen you."

"No choice," he replied as he shut the door. "We need somewhere to be until he gets home."

Parks knew the layout of the apartment, and went straight for the kitchen. He searched the fridge for food, and came up with enough to make some sandwiches. They were hungry, and knew Aaron wouldn't mind sharing.

"Do you really think he can get us inside?" Kirsten asked as she settled into the couch in the small living room.

"I know he can get us to the gate and the guard," Parks replied. "I'll get us the rest of the way from there."

Parks grabbed a chair, and flipped on the television to kill some time while they waited. A news reporter was interviewing General Allison regarding a failed plot to blow up the city's fresh water supply.

"A group of resisters intended to destroy the main pump station," the general said. "Fortunately, security discovered their plan before they could pull it off. Let this be a warning to all similar terrorists who think they can disrupt our fine city, and hurt those responsible for the care of its good citizens. We'll find you. We'll stop you."

"Thank you, General," the reporter said as the camera faded back to the reporter. "Four people are in custody at this hour, and it's believed they are part of a larger group. We'll be following up with more information as it becomes available. In the meantime, here are the suspects, but we have yet to find out their names. If you have any information on these or others like them, please call the number on your screen."

They cut to pictures of Kenzie, Troy, Isaac, and Aaron.

"No way," Parks exclaimed as he jumped out of his seat. "I told Aaron to wait for me. Now it looks like he took matters into his own hands. This is a disaster."

"What are we going to do?" Kirsten asked anxiously as she grabbed him by the arm.

"I don't know," Parks replied grimly, "but I know they're in real trouble. We need to get them as quickly as we can."

"But where are they?" Kirsten asked as she followed Parks to the car.

"The Citadel is still a mess, so I know they won't take them there," Parks replied as he backed out, and turned down the street. "Management has a high-security facility on the east side where they processed everyone after the takeover. Aaron told me he saw reports indicating it was being prepared for something, which was part of the reason he became suspicious. Why spend money on something you don't need? My best guess is they're being taken there for interrogation, and then elimination after they have what they want from them."

Kirsten slid her hand around the handle of the crystal blade strapped to her waist as she looked over at Parks's hardened face. His knuckles were white, and his teeth were clenched as he gripped the steering wheel. Any thought of a clandestine attack was gone now. They were going in, and going in hard.

CHAPTER 29

Jim led the way through the back roads to the elementary school. There, he addressed the group as they formulated their plan.

"Rich, you, Philip, and James take as many firearms and as much ammunition as you need from the back of the truck. I'll handle the explosives. Once the broadcast is made, destroy the station so Management can't use it to send out any more lies. Then we call Tim, and move to the next phase."

"What exactly is the next phase?" David asked.

"Good question," Rich said. "If Jim can pull off what he intends, we'll begin hitting a series of Control centers. Here's what I worked out with Tim, and what he and the city fathers have planned."

He spread a map on the hood of the car.

"The broadcast station is near the heart of the city," he said, pointing. "Once it's destroyed, we work outward, hitting each center as we go. The city fathers will be coming in from JJ's Grace Mountain stronghold, and they'll work towards us, rallying city resistance leaders as they come. The end of the matter is when we join together, and turn full-force to the remaining members of Management at the Citadel. It's my guess they'll be ready to surrender by then anyway."

"What about Testers?" Philip asked. "All indications are they're here in the city somewhere."

"Leave them to us!" Normand exclaimed boldly as he pulled a crystal blade from his waist. "We have all we need right here to handle those red clowns. But we must locate the rest of the gang."

"I've been trying," David replied, "but, for some reason, the crystals aren't working. No one is responding. Kirsten thinks there's some kind of interference. We'll have to trust they'll find us without them."

"Ok, then," Jim said as he looked at Rita. "This is going

to be dangerous, so if anyone wants to wait this out, I'm good with that."

Rita reached into the open trunk, and pulled out a semi-automatic pistol. He just shrugged his shoulders, and hopped into the car he had gotten from Dr. Flint. Rita joined him in the front seat, and David and Normand took the back. The plan was for Philip, James, and Rich to stay far enough back in case someone targeted either one of them. Then the free vehicle would innocently approach, and overpower the cadets.

Jim drove across town, and was relieved there were no encounters or incidents along the way. He pulled into a large parking lot and drove around behind the broadcast station, where an unguarded rear entrance stood in the center of the building.

Rita stayed in the rig to watch for a Management response, and to warn them if anything went wrong. She was heavily armed, and could hold off a small army by herself if called upon. There were a few employees exiting and entering the rear entrance as James, Philip, and Rich parked in the front, and moved nonchalantly towards the front entrance, their firearms hidden under their coats.

The heavy wooden doors swung open as Jim entered. Normand stayed outside the building, leaning against the wall, pretending to be uninterested in everything. The building was built like a wheel, with spokes extending out to each of the studios from the central office hub. This way, the director could oversee every broadcast, whether they were live or being taped. It also was the one weakness Jim intended to exploit.

David walked a few paces behind Jim, avoiding eye contact with people they passed in the hall. Before long, before they arrived at the central control office, and pushed through the heavy glass doors to the reception area.

"Can I help you?" said a young man seated behind a large semi-circle counter. Several chairs were occupied by people apparently waiting for an appointment. They didn't bother to look up from the magazines they were reading as David pretended to examine a large painting hanging on the wall.

"Is the director in?" Jim asked calmly.

"I believe Mr. Peters is in," the receptionist replied. "Do you have an appointment?"

"I do!" Jim said firmly.

He opened his coat slightly to reveal the large firearm strapped to his waist.

"We can do this the hard way or the easy way. It's up to you."

The young man's face turned white as the blood drained out.

"Don't bother to call," he said softly as the young man reached for the phone. "Just lead the way, and everything will be fine."

The young man shot a worried look at David, who joined Jim at the counter. Jim was careful to keep his back to the others sitting behind him since he didn't know how well-known his face had become.

The receptionist got reluctantly out of his seat, and led the way through the large set of doors separating the reception area from the main offices. The hall cut in two directions, dividing the offices, but keeping the director's office central. It could be accessed from either hallway, and the young man chose to take the right hall, turning left into the director's office.

Inside was another reception area with an older, stately woman seated behind a large, ornate desk. Pictures of Management reporters and actors were sprinkled about the room, and behind her seat was a large oil painting of Mr. Peters. Jim pushed the barrel of his gun into the back of the man as they approached the woman's desk.

"Do you need something, Cody?" the woman asked the young man.

"Yes, these gentlemen need to see Mr. Peters," the young man replied. "I know they're not on the schedule, but they have some important information. Could you ring us through? I would like to accompany them, if that's ok?"

The woman looked Jim and David over, and her eyes narrowed slightly.

"He has a very busy schedule today," she said bluntly.

"Maybe if you want to try back later, I'll see if I can get you in for a few minutes around four, but I can't make any promises."

"We'll see him now!" Jim said, pulling a second gun from his right pocket.

"What do you want?" the woman stammered.

The whites of her eyes got large as saucers at the sight of the barrel of Jim's gun.

"Just keep calm, and lead the way," he ordered as he came around her desk. "Nobody's going to get hurt if you don't try anything foolish."

David locked the main doors to the reception area before following Jim to make sure they weren't disturbed.

The final set of doors opened to a large octagonal room. Jim saw a lone man sitting with his back to them. He had headphones on, and was watching through sound-proof glass as a news segment was being taped in one of the four studios he had direct access to. He was making some comments into a microphone as Jim approached. Satisfied with the results, the man took off his headphones, and spun around to make some notes on his desk.

"Mr. Peters," the tall woman said quietly.

The director jumped out of his seat.

"What?" I told you to buzz me before coming in."

"Sorry, sir, but these men are quite insistent," she said.

Jim stepped out from behind her where Mr. Peters could see him.

"Jim Banner!" the man said, stepping forward. "You're the last person I would have ever thought to see."

"Hi, Clint," Jim responded. "I see you're doing quite well for yourself since leaving HOT News."

"Well, I couldn't turn down the opportunity, you know," Mr. Peters replied. "They pay well, and I have complete control of all content. Not like at your old place, where I had to compete with you. Too bad Frank isn't here to see you. I know he always thought you were better."

"Frank's dead," Jim replied flatly. "Now, I haven't come here to reminisce about old times," he continued, raising his gun where Mr. Peters could see it. "I'm here about that content you were just referring to. You were once a decent reporter, but I see you've sold your soul to the highest bidder."

"Now just a minute," Mr. Peters protested. "You have no right to come in here and threaten me."

"That's where you're wrong."

Jim came behind Mr. Peters's desk.

"You're going to broadcast a truthful story for once, or so help me, you'll never broadcast anything ever again."

Mr. Peters looked at Jim's hardened face, and then at his two employees, standing helplessly under David's watchful eye.

"What do you want?" he said.

He plopped down into his chair, and pushed away from Jim.

"A little cooperation is all," Jim answered. "I'm going to use one of your live studios to broadcast a message to the city, and I just need you to keep your people out of the way, and keep your mind off reporting me until I am done. If you even try to bring in any Management thugs, you'll be the first one I shoot."

"We'll cooperate," Mr. Peters said, nodding to his two receptionists. "I suggest you allow them to return to their duties so as not to draw suspicion, but they'll do nothing."

"That's all I'm asking," Jim replied. "I have twenty five heavily-armed men outside who are under orders to storm this building at the slightest hint of resistance, or any sign of Management. They are under orders to kill everyone inside, so don't play with me," Jim lied.

"I want private access to a live broadcast studio where I can set up. It'll take me a few minutes to get ready, and I want you to cut into whatever is on the air at that time. My assistant here," Jim continued as he glanced at David, "will remain with you during the event to make sure everything goes smoothly."

Mr. Peters nodded reluctantly as Jim followed the two receptionists out of his office. He returned to the vehicle where Harry was bound and gagged. Rita was watching nervously, and drew a large sigh of relief when she saw him approaching.

"Mr. Allison," Jim said quietly as he removed Harry's

restraints, "We are going to walk into the building, and you're not going to say anything, or make any sudden moves. This gun will be firmly planted in your side, so don't try to test me. I've been through too much already to not blow your sorry butt away just because."

Jim held the door as Harry climbed out. Rita was to stay put and keep watch in case anything happened, but Jim was feeling confident. Harry walked beside Jim, and they picked up Normand at the door as they entered the building. Rich, Philip, and James had come in the front entrance, and stationed themselves at intervals where they could see each other, and watch Jim as he went through the heavy, sound-proof doors with Harry in tow. Normand came with them.

"Testing, testing," Jim said as he settled behind a mike and camera.

"Loud and clear," Mr. Peters affirmed from his office. "You'll be hot in five, four, three, two one!"

"This is Jim Banner, reporting to you from an undisclosed location," he began as he addressed the camera. "I come to you today with a message. Management has been filling the airways with outright lies and fake news, accusing me and others like me who would dare challenge them, of being enemies and traitors. But they're the true enemies, not the resisters.

This man seated beside me is Harry Allison, the former head of the Citadel, and city security. Approximately one week ago, you watched as a band of so-called resisters killed him on a live broadcast. You can see with your own eyes that he's alive and well, and I'm here to show you what is true. This is clear evidence they have been lying to us from the beginning, and it's time for us to retake our city.

I ask all able-bodied, good citizens to come together. Grab your guns and supplies, but be warned. This is war, and the Testers have once again been injected into our city. We have at least three confirmed sightings. If you have access to a safe zone, take your children there. If you can get out of the city somehow, do it.

To those of you that hesitate: evil is knocking on your

door. Fight if you can. Hide if you must. Leave if you will. Tonight is the night. Good luck to you all. This is Jim Banner, signing off."

"Everything looks good in here," David said over Mr. Peters's shoulder.

"Ok, time for phase two," Jim replied as he left the sound booth. "You know what to do."

"What does he mean?" Mr. Peters asked bleakly. "Phase two?"

"Instruct all your people to leave the building now," David said firmly. "Tell them you have received a bomb threat, and they need to gather at their rally points, and wait for further instructions. Do it now!"

Mr. Peters glanced at David's hard face before picking up the receiver, and giving the order. In a matter of seconds, alarm bells began ringing, and lights flashed throughout the facility, followed by instructions over the loud speaker system. Philip and James exited with the crowd in order to grab the explosives they had in the back of their vehicle.

They returned, and began placing them in strategic locations where they would do the most damage to the electronics and sending equipment. Meanwhile, Jim escorted Harry back to where Rita was waiting. This time, she injected Harry with a sedative, making the rest of the job easier. Jim returned inside, and helped lay out the remaining explosives, while Normand connected the detonators.   David kept an eye on Mr. Peters, as it was Jim's plan to keep him hostage, just in case anything went wrong.

"All set," Normand said as he met the group outside.

"Let's do this from the road," Jim said as he got in with Rita.

He had his hand on the detonator as they prepared to leave the parking area.

The employees were huddled together in marked areas where they could be accounted for as per protocol, and were far enough from the building to not be hurt by the explosions.

"I'm sorry," Mr. Peters said as Rita was about to pull

away from the curb.

"You're sorry?" Jim said. "Sorry for what?"

Just then, several large SUVs appeared from behind a grove of trees across the street, blocking their escape route.

"They told me you would likely try something like this," Mr. Peters explained. "But I didn't believe them until I saw you this morning. They had me rig a broadcast studio that looked real, but it wasn't. That's the one I put you in. You haven't broadcast anything anywhere. When I hit the alarm, it was a signal to Management, and there's more on the way. I'm really sorry, Jim."

"What!" Jim exclaimed in confusion. "This was all a trick? I can't believe it."

"You had better believe it," Mr. Peters said firmly. "Those are Nullifiers they're holding, and they mean business."

A new flood of black SUVs arrived off the main road, and fanned out in the large parking area, facing Philip's pickup. The passenger door to the one in the front opened, and out stepped a tall, thin woman with a bullhorn.

It was General Ivy Allison.

CHAPTER 30

"We're going to have to split up," Parks said.

They were back at the gravel pit where they had left the large transport truck.

"You take Joel's station wagon, I'll fire this thing up."

"I can't exactly storm the gate in this," Kirsten stated.

"No, but you could have a breakdown by the main gate. If they run that place like they did the Citadel, the guard will be all over himself trying to help a pretty girl. I think you know what to do from there."

"A flimsy plan, if you ask me. You expect me to overpower the guard with my charm, and then what, take over the place with my perfume? We can do better than that."

"Kirsten!" he snapped back, "You get control of the main gate, so I don't have to drive this thing through the wall. Once I get in, I'll disrupt as much of their security as I can, and be generally destructive.

"While I'm drawing their attention, you can search for everyone. Once you've located them, signal me with your crystal, and let me know where you are. Then be ready to jump on board, and we'll get the heck out. Doesn't that make sense?"

Kirsten looked at her brother for a moment, and nodded in agreement. It was a crazy plan, and they both knew it, but they had little choice. They had to rescue their friends, and quickly. Kirsten led the way to a rendezvous spot about a half mile short of the facility. Parks pulled the large truck off the road, behind a grove of trees just big enough to keep it out of sight.

"Ok, I'm going in," Kirsten said as she hopped off the running board. "I'll contact you as soon as the gate is secure."

"Wait a second," Parks said suddenly.

He opened the door, and craned his head around the exhaust pipe.

"Do you hear that?"

"Yeah, it sounds like an alarm. Maybe there's a fire or

something."

"No, that's not a fire alarm; that's an evacuation signal. I know because I used to test those for the television stations when I was at the Citadel."

"Hey, check that out!" Kirsten said.

A stream of black SUVs whizzed by, headed in the direction of the alarm. "Whatever it is, it really got their attention. Maybe this is a fortuitous sign, and they've left the hen house unguarded. That could make our job a lot easier."

Kirsten hopped into the old station wagon, and took off for the facility. As Parks had predicted, there was a singular guard, and he looked none too bright. She pulled to a stop not more than fifty feet from the gate.

She popped the hood, got out, and pulled a couple wires off the distributor to make sure it wouldn't start. It didn't take long for the guard to make his way over, especially since Kirsten kept her head under the hood, and her tight-fitting jeans in full view.

"Are you having engine trouble?" the young man asked as he walked up.

"Yes," Kirsten replied helplessly, swiping the hair out of her face. "I don't know a thing about cars, and my boyfriend is going to be so angry if I don't get this back to him right away."

"Now don't you worry," the guard said warmly. "I'll have one of our maintenance guys come out, and take a look at it for you."

"You would do that for me?" Kirsten asked innocently with a smile.

"Not a problem," the guard replied. "Why don't you come on over to the shack, and wait inside while I make a few calls."

Kirsten walked meekly alongside the guard, who was definitely feeling big in spite of the fact he was barely five foot six. He opened the door, and ushered her into the glass-lined guard shack.

The facility was built like a concentration camp, with tall wire fences capped with electrified razor wire. Inside were several large steel buildings of unknown purpose, except that at least one probably held their friends.

The guard reached to pick up his phone, and Kirsten hit him with the handle of her blade, right at the base of the skull. He dropped instantly.

She caught him before he hit the floor, and guided him into his chair. She propped him against the wall, and put his feet up on his desk, making it look like he was at duty. Then she pulled out the crystal, and focused on Parks.

She felt nothing. She couldn't contact him.

To her relief, Parks came lumbering down the road anyway, headed in her direction. She quickly hit the button, and opened the gate as Parks downshifted. He gave her a long look as he drove past, And she shrugged her shoulders in response. Obviously, he had tired of waiting for her signal.

His first order of business was to destroy as much as possible before anyone could respond. One two story building stood directly in line with the gate, and a second, larger building nestled behind, and off to the right. He guessed the two story building belonged to Management control and security, so he drove around behind, and quickly discovered a parking lot full of black SUVs and other security vehicles.

That's when Parks became a 'Monster Truck' driver, and began smashing everything in sight.

The giant transport carrier was quite able to run up and onto the line of vehicles and Parks had quite the time crushing them.

It was only a matter of seconds before a stream of cadets and other Management personnel came pouring out of the building. His hopes were confirmed, however, as there were not nearly as many as he had anticipated.

Meanwhile, Kirsten made her way around to the rear building, where she hoped to find their captured friends. She arrived at a heavily-built concrete building. It was long and low, with the main entrance consisting of a set of double doors. There were a few windows along each side, probably for the offices.

She watched from behind a delivery van parked near the concrete wall with a heavy steel roll up door with a walk door next to it as two armed cadets exited the building, headed towards her brother. When they were out of sight, she pulled a crystal blade.

The blade sliced easily through the lock, and she slipped inside.

She was greeted by pallets covered with a variety of items, stacked neatly on heavy steel storage racks. There was a single forklift sitting in the center, but nobody seemed to be around.

She made her way cautiously down several alleys, and arrived at another heavy steel door. A sign above it said, 'receiving station'. Next to the door she saw a buzzer, and a plaque with detailed instructions.

She ignored them, and slid her blade through the lock. The door led into a short hall with more heavy steel doors. The one on the end was open, and light spilled out as she crept along. She could hear voices, and paused for a moment, wondering if she had been discovered. A moment later, she relaxed. From what she could tell, it was the delivery driver with someone else, and they were just talking about an order.

Her door of interest stood at the end of the hall. It also had a buzzer, and a small window where someone on the inside could confirm the identity of the person who wanted in. She peeked around the corner, and saw the two men inside, engrossed in paperwork.

Her best bet was to slip by while they were busy, and through the final door to whatever lay inside. She waited until she was sure it was safe, and then moved quickly past. The window was outfitted with one-way glass, so there was no way to know if someone had already spotted her, but she had to chance it.

She ran into a problem immediately. The door was especially fortified, with locks that not only engaged the jamb, but also went into the floor and the header, and she was not tall enough to cut the steel off at the top.

She needed a new plan.

"I need your immediate and full cooperation."

She stepped boldly around the corner into the receiving

office, and pulled a second blade from her belt.

"What? Who are you?" the warehouse supervisor said.

He jerked his head out of the papers he was checking. The delivery driver wheeled about, and stumbled back against the wall.

"I know what you're thinking," she said calmly. "We can take her. She's just a girl. But you have to ask yourself some quick questions. How did I get in here, and where's everybody else? Now you're getting the idea," she continued as the men's eyes got big.

"First, we need to get rid of this," she said, and sliced through the cord on his phone. "I'm going to need you to stay in here," she said to the driver. "I trust you will not be so foolish as to make a fuss. You, on the other hand," she said to the warehouse supervisor, "will need to buzz me in to the other side of that door."

"Are you crazy?" the man said. "You know they'll kill you for this."

"Yes, I know. Now you come into the hall, and you stay right where you are."

The supervisor and driver did as instructed. Once the supervisor was in the hall, she closed the door and slid a blade through the handle, making it impossible to open from the inside.

"You're going to push the buzzer," Kirsten said as she got low behind him, "and say whatever is right for them to open the door for you."

She pushed her blade into the middle of his back to reinforce the point.

The man took a deep breath, and rang the bell.

"What do you want?" came the gruff reply over a small intercom next to the buzzer.

"I have the daily reports for Mr. Blankers," the man said.

"We have a lock down situation here," the guard snapped. "You'll have to wait."

Kirsten pushed the blade harder.

"Well, I think I heard a strange noise coming from the warehouse," the supervisor said nervously. "I think maybe someone broke in."

"Why didn't you say that in the first place?" the man snapped.

"I didn't think it was a big deal until right now," the supervisor responded. "I think someone may be in there."

"Just a moment."

There was a sound of electronic whirring,, and the door locks released.

"Head on down to the…"

The guard's words were cut short. Kirsten shot up from behind the supervisor, landing the handle of her blade squarely in his forehead. He crumpled to the floor. The supervisor joined him a moment later.

A long, narrow corridor stood before her, with a single set of lights hung down the middle. On each side were heavy steel doors with a slider near the floor, and one set about half-way up. The one near the floor appeared to be for food, and the other for the guard to check inside.

She made her way along, checking as she went. Unfortunately, each cell was filled with people of all ages. She had to control her desire to release them. Her first goal was to find Kenzie, and the rest of the guys. Once they were free, they could assist the remaining ones, and get everyone out.

She was nearly to the end of the hall when a feeling of familiarity washed over her as she looked into a cell.

"Please be Troy!" she exclaimed.

She opened the door with the keys she had taken off the guard.

The man was lying on the floor, and barely raised his head at Kirsten's voice.

"Kirsten?" Troy said slowly. "Is that really you?"

"It is you," she said, grabbing his hand. "Are you ok?"

"I'm not sure."

He did his best to sit up.

"Where's everyone else?"

"I haven't seen anyone in a while," he said, leaning against the concrete wall. "They took Aaron away when we first got here, but Isaac was being kept with me until this morning when they came for him. I don't know about Kenzie either."

"Let's find the others," she said encouragingly, and helped him to his feet.

"They took our crystal blades."

"I've got one you can use," she said, handing him a blade.

The expression on his face instantly brightened as his hand wrapped around the handle. "Which way do we go?"

"This way," he said.

He was becoming stronger with each passing moment. He led the way down the hall, and to a door leading to the miserable section of the building he had been taken to. Kirsten sliced the locked door, and pushed it open to reveal a complex resembling a hospital, with polished marble floors, and rooms lined with glass windows.

A woman screamed in agony from just a few doors down the hall.

He knew that voice.

Troy kicked open the door, choking with anger.

Kenzie was strapped to a hard wooden board, and Mr. Grey was holding a small red crystal over her forehead. It was glowing brightly, and seemed able to pass through her skull, into her brain, and then out again.

Her entire body was straining against the strong leather bonds, and her eyes nearly popped out of her head. Mr. Grey whirled around in surprise at the sound of the breaking door, but it was already too late. Troy had buried the long crystal blade up to the hilt in his chest.

Mr. Grey looked down at the handle, and then into Troy's eyes before dissolving into a dark gray mist, and dissipating as he had so many times before.

"Kenzie," he exclaimed in horror as he sliced off the leather straps. "Can you hear me?"

Her eyes were fixed on a spot on the ceiling, and she didn't respond.

Kirsten felt the crystal around her neck becoming warm. Without knowing why, she took it off, and held it above Kenzie's forehead.

Instantly, a red vapor streamed from Kenzie's head and into the blue crystal. It seemed like an eternity as they watched in amazement. Then she coughed, and blinked twice.

"Where am I?" she asked as she sat up. "What are you guys doing here?"

"We'll talk about that later," Troy said. "Are you going to be ok?"

"No one should feel the pain I felt," Kenzie replied as she slid off the board. "He made me see unimaginable things. I never knew there could be that much evil."

"We need to get out of here," Kirsten said as she helped steady Kenzie. "We're all in grave danger."

"I know," Kenzie replied. "I was in another place when he had me, and I saw our fate. It's not good."

"What about Isaac?" Troy asked. "Do you know where he is?"

"Isaac!" Kenzie exclaimed with a horrified look on her face. "We may already be too late. I heard that awful General Allison say they were taking him to the board. She laughed, and said he escaped before, but would never escape again. She said they would know what to do with the likes of him, and it wasn't going to be pretty."

Kirsten shot a worried glance at Troy as they helped Kenzie out of the room. She didn't know how Parks was making out, but was fairly certain a battle was waging outside.

But they weren't through yet. Kirsten was determined to find them, no matter where they might be. She had come to free her friends, and was not about to stop until they were all safe.

CHAPTER 31

"Get out, and lay down your weapons," the shrill female voice came over the bullhorn.

Jim looked over at Rita, whose tanned face was now white. He instantly knew they had no choice but surrender. He got out, and walked around the front of the vehicle, where he was quickly joined by everyone else.

"There's no point in resisting," a voice behind them declared.

It was Harry. He pushed his way through their line, and started walking towards the wall of vehicles at the entrance to the parking lot.

"Hey, you were sedated!" Jim exclaimed.

"Your stupid girlfriend put the needle in the arm that doctor at the Island repaired," he said, smirking. "It's mechanical. I was just playing until I had an opportunity to jump you. I guess I don't have to worry about that now."

"Wait, don't go out there, Harry," Jim insisted.

"You forget I'm still the manager of the Citadel," Harry snapped back. "They take orders from me. You just wait here, and I'll be right back to settle things properly with you and your friends."

"You don't get it," Jim protested. "They believe you're dead. You can't come back to life."

Harry just chuckled, and walked boldly towards the cadets and his daughter, General Allison.

"Stop right there," the general commanded over the bullhorn.

"It's me, your father!" Harry shouted.

"Dad?" the general said in confusion as she held the bullhorn down.

She froze for a moment as she realized her plan to be rid of her father, and take over his position at the Citadel was unraveling. She had to think fast.

"Imposter, don't come any closer!"

"No, it's really me," Harry said as he continued approaching the line of Management vehicles.

"It's a trick. Shoot him!" she shouted.

Nobody moved.

She turned to the cadet on her right who was holding a Nullifier, and ripped it out of his hands. She leveled the weapon, and Harry stopped cold in his tracks.

"Hold on there," Harry protested. "I'm your father, and your boss."

"My father's dead," the general growled.

The distinctive hum of the Nullifier gave way to a bright light that flashed across the parking lot to where Harry was standing. He raised his arm in defense the instant before he vaporized into a puff of white smoke. His bionic arm bounced across the blacktop. It was the only thing the Nullifier hadn't destroyed.

"I tried to tell him," Jim said under his breath with half a smile.

The general's attention returned to the line of people standing on the other side of the parking lot.

"Lie down flat, and spread your arms as if we're surrendering," Jim said quietly before the general could choose one of them for an equal fate. "But we aren't done yet. Cover your ears when they start moving towards us."

He flashed the detonator he was holding to everyone, and they instantly knew what he was planning.

"Go get them," the general ordered to her squad of cadets, "and bring them to the compound. I'll deal with them there."

She walked over, and picked up her father's bionic arm, and threw it into the back of her SUV. Her crew drove across the parking lot to take the resisters into custody. She was about to pull onto the road when the blast from the explosives planted inside the building knocked her truck sideways, and into the far ditch.

Jim had waited until the cadets had exited their vehicles,

and were approaching on foot before he detonated. Their group was protected, for the most part, as the majority of the blast went over their heads, but it still left them momentarily disoriented.

They had packed more explosives into the building than he realized.

All the windows and doors were blown out, and part of the building collapsed, while other sections looked like they would soon. Rich looked through the rising cloud of dust just in time to see the large broadcast antenna buckle, and begin to topple towards them.

"Come on," he shouted, helping Philip to his feet, "we've got to go now."

Everyone was already running for cover as the massive steel structure came crashing across the building. Rich and Philip barely escaped being crushed as twisted steel beams smashed into the parking lot. A couple of cadets farther away who had been partially shielded by their vehicles came staggering into the open, but they were in no condition to stop anyone.

One lone surviving SUV was still idling, and everyone piled in.

David was behind the wheel, and had it spinning onto the main road. He drove past a bewildered General Allison, who was standing at the edge of the ditch with an angry look on her face.

"Now what?" James asked from the rear seat.

"I'm out of ideas," Jim replied. "That was my best attempt to gather resistance and take out Management, but they already had that figured out."

"We better come up with something quick!" Rich shouted. "They're behind us already."

Sure enough, several black SUVs had pulled in behind them from off a side road. The general must have gotten the word out. Now there was no other choice but to run, since their weapons had been left behind at the station.

"Hey look what I found," Normand said from the rear seat.

The SUV was equipped with two rows of bench seating behind the driver's seat, and Normand was in the far back. He and Philip were hanging over the seat, checking the back storage compartment.

"That's a Nullifier," Rich exclaimed as Normand passed it forward.

"There are three more back here!" Normand exclaimed as he continued pulling them out.

"This should even the score some," Jim said as he grabbed one.

"They're older models," Rich commented as he looked it over. "The newer ones have a dissipation button that allows the energy to release if you accidentally pull the trigger."

Just then the one Normand had begun to hum distinctively.

"You didn't just pull the trigger!" David said incredulously.

"Don't let go!" Rich shouted. "You pull the trigger to activate the system, and release it to discharge."

"What do you want me to do with it?" Normand asked in a panic.

"Well, don't aim it at me!" David exclaimed as Normand spun around.

"Open a window!" James shouted.

"Too late," Rich replied as the hum became more and more intense. "It's going to blow if he doesn't let it go."

Normand did the only logical thing, and aimed the Nullifier at the rear of the SUV. The flash momentarily blinded them as the energy ripped all but the bumper off the back of the truck. David hit the brakes and fought to keep on the road, but swerved onto the shoulder before skidding to a stop just inches shy of a deep ditch.

Rich threw open the door, and wheeled around to face the approaching Management vehicles when he saw the pile of twisted steel in the distance.

The blast had done its work.

"You did GOOD!" James said encouragingly as he slapped Normand's shoulder.

They gathered in the middle of the road, and for a

moment, admired Normand's work. Apparently, the blast had not only destroyed half of their vehicle, but also hit the lead truck head on. The rest of the SUVs had slammed into it, making quite a mess.

"We'd better be going," Jim said quickly. "There could be more of them coming."

Wind whipped in through the open rear end as they drove along. They had only gone a few more miles when they noticed the prison-looking structure appearing on their right.

"What's that?" Rita asked as they approached.

"It used to be a holding center for resisters when the city was first taken," Philip answered, "but I thought it was abandoned. It looks like someone has rebuilt it."

"Yeah they have," David said as he slowed down. "Hey, it's Parks! He's in trouble."

Parks had just come running from behind the building where he had ditched the transporter after it got high centered on a large truck. He was being pursued by a group of cadets carrying swords-like weapons, bent on taking him down.

"Here we go again!" Normand shouted.

"The gate is open, but what about the guard?" David said.

"I got this," Normand asserted.

He dove out of the truck, and took off on a dead run towards the guard shack.

He pulled his crystal blade, and was prepared to attack, when he realized the guard was not moving. He was still unconscious from Kirsten's hit. He waved David through, and raced after the truck. They drove towards Parks, who saw them coming, and immediately recognized David at the wheel.

Parks was headed toward a rock formation along the rear of the compound where he could make his defense. He leaped onto a large rock, and scrambled up. David hit the brakes, and slid sideways between him and the rushing cadets. Jim jumped out with a Nullifier, followed by Rich and James, who each had one.

David got out, crystal blade in hand, and was quickly joined by Normand. The cadets coasted to a stop, and formed a line around the small group of resisters.

"Lay down your weapons, and you won't get hurt!" David shouted to the cadets. "I don't need to tell you the damage we can do with these things."

The cadets stood in formation as they considered their options. Each cadet had two unique swords, one in each hand, with a bright red crystal set in the handle. Then, in unison, they raised them over their heads, and began pounding them together in a rhythmic beat.

From across the yard, a familiar figure came out of the main entrance to the two-story building, and slowly walked towards the unfolding scene.

It was Barron. The cadets opened their ranks to allow him to walk through their line.

"Mr. Henry Jacob Parks," Barron said.

"Finally, we meet again," Parks answered, standing defiantly on a rocky ledge about ten feet above. "It's me you want. Let these others go."

"Let them go?" Barron sneered. "Why would I want to let them go?"

"You're the ones who need to lay down your weapons, and back off," David said.

He stepped in front of Barron with his crystal blade.

"Do you want to tell them, or do you want me to?" Barron asked.

He drew a red crystal blade from a leather sheath.

"Give me a second," Parks said.

He jumped down from the ledge with his back to Barron.

"This is not your fight," he said firmly and quietly. "Just be ready to make a break for it once I have everyone's attention on me."

David reluctantly stepped to the side.

"How about we make a deal, Barron," Parks said as he spun around. "Just you and me. If I win, these go free. If you win, I'll come peacefully."

"No deal, and you need to get used to calling me President," Barron replied coldly. "You really don't get it, do you? Yeah, I'm in charge now. All those years of watching you play the good guy, trying to be the hero."

He spat on the ground.

"Really, you're no better than me. In fact, we're more like brothers."

"Brothers?" Parks replied, confused. "We're not brothers. You're a murderer, and I'm nothing like you."

"Oh no?" Barron growled as he circled around. "Then what's with that big secret you've been keeping? You know, the one that's eating you up inside, controlling your thoughts, and keeping you up at night. It's time to be honest with yourself, Parks. You like those feelings, don't you? You like the power you feel. I know, because I saw what you did to my dogs."

"You're crazy," Parks protested. "No, No, NO! They were about to hurt Della. You've got it all wrong."

"Come on, Parks. I can see the conflict raging in you. Quit fighting it, man. Just give in like I did."

"Like you did? What are you saying?"

"Remember that day on Grace Mountain?"

"Yeah, what about it?"

"You faced the Zender, and thought you killed it. Well you didn't."

Barron moved in closer.

"You're so dense, Parks. The Zender can't be killed. It's not physical. It's an energy source that has more power than you can even imagine."

"That's where you're wrong. You weren't there. You don't know what happened."

"Do you think this is the only city that's ever been taken?" Barron's eyes narrowed as he continued. "I was like you once, caring about others, but I was smarter. I made the exchange, and live because of it. If you do the same, we can take our place together with the Dark Matter on the throne. I'll be the head, but you can serve with me."

"What throne? There's no throne. Are you crazy, Barron? There's no glory for us."

Barron looked long and hard at Parks for a moment.

"You have no idea what you're giving up," he said, stepping menacingly towards Parks. "I could have saved you, but now you'll learn the truth. Remember the first time we fought in the wilderness, and you got lucky."

"You mean when I beat you, and embedded one of my crystals in your chest?" Parks snapped.

"Yeah, that time," Baron answered bitterly as he rubbed his chest. "Well you weren't the only one with crystals," Barron continued as he reached up at Parks heavy leather coat.

Parks instinctively drew back, but Barron just smiled, calmly lifted Parks lapel, and pulled out a small red crystal.

"I put this under there that day when you weren't looking."

Barron laughed as he tossed it in the air, and caught it again.

"I've been tracking you ever since. I have to admit there were times I couldn't see you. Your crystals seemed to block its signal once in a while, but I saw enough. I have quite the extensive list of people to focus on, like your Island of misfits which we've already visited, that group of range rebels in the mountains, family and friends here in the city."

Parks could contain the anger no longer. His eyes rolled back in his head, and it felt like fire as the red light burned through his sockets. He leapt at Barron, catching him in the chin with his forearm. Barron sprawled onto the ground, and Parks pulled his blue crystal blade.

But Barron was on his feet again in an instant, holding his blade with both hands. He swung at Parks, barely missing his neck as Parks drew back. Barron continued swinging wildly. Parks deflected the blows, but one slipped through, slicing through his forearm.

"You should have made a deal with me," Barron said proudly.

He circled around, waving his blade high over his head.

"We could have been kings, you and I."

"I would never make a deal with you," Parks replied.

His arm dropped to his side, and a trickle of blood ran

down his fingers.

"There's no throne I would want to share with you."

Barron attacked again, this time cutting him on his left shoulder, and pinned him against the rock face wall with his forearm under Parks's chin.

David reached for his blade fearing Parks was losing but Parks glanced at David and shook his head no.

"You know, I wouldn't want to miss anybody when I'm done with you," Barron continued mockingly as he stared into Parks's glowing red eyes.

"I'm going to enjoy killing Della and your unborn child. No more 'Parks' left to bother me."

Parks screamed as he shoved Barron off. His eyes were blazing red, and he swung again and again with his crystal blade, driving him back. Barron did his best to deflect the powerful blows, but Parks kept coming and coming. He cut Barron again and again, until with his last blow, he sliced Barron's hand off.

It fell to the ground, still gripping the red crystal blade. It bounced twice before his dismembered hand popped open, and the blade rolled onto the cold rocky surface.

"Come on, Parks, do it," Barron laughed as he grabbed his arm, and stared into Parks's flaming eyes. "You're twice the killer I ever was. Kill me now, and stroke the beast raging inside you."

Parks stood there, trembling.

He could taste the blood in his mouth, and his heart was pounding through his chest. His eyes burned fiery red. Suddenly, he stiffened, looked up at the sky, and released his grip on his blade.

"I will not kill this man!" he shouted.

The cadets and the others watching the epic battle were frozen as Parks dropped to his knees in apparent agony. Barron stumbled back, not sure what to do next.

Suddenly, Parks convulsed, and fell onto his back. As he did, a dark gaseous cloud poured from his chest, and rose into the air. It took shape before their astonished eyes.

The crowd gasped as the broad head and thick neck of a

strange-looking animal began to form. It was heavy and muscular, with thick, silvery hair. The bright sunlight glistened off the beast's long claws, three on each paw, as it emerged from the gaseous fog and stood on its hind legs, looking around at those before it. Opening its lips in what resembled a wicked smile, it revealed rows of razor-sharp teeth.

Its focus turned to a distraught Barron.

Barron screamed in agony as the beast leapt on him, ripping his flesh to shreds. Parks raised his head as his mind slowly returned. Seeing what was happening, he instinctively jumped on the back of the Zender. It had Barron pinned to the ground, and was sinking its teeth deep into his neck and shoulder.

The beast shook Parks off, but when he fell to the ground, he reached for his blade, which had landed next to Barron's red crystal blade. They were so close to each other that Parks inadvertently grabbed both handles at once.

When he did, something incredible happened.

The two crystal blades began glowing brightly as he lifted them as one. He couldn't let go, even as they got hotter and hotter. He held them over his head, and their light became brighter than the sun.

In a few seconds, the two blades, one blue and one red, merged into deep purple light.

Energy flowed into Parks like he had never felt before. With one swift thrust of the newly-formed blade, he sank it deep into the heart of the Zender.

The beast rose from Barron's body, blood dripping from its lips, and made a noise so evil it sounded like death itself. It turned towards Parks as if to make one more attempt on his life. Suddenly, it fell onto the ground, dead. This time, the Zender didn't dissipate, or change into gas. It remained a large, scary, but dead beast.

"We'll get you to the hospital," Parks said.

He knelt beside Barron, and lifted his head.

"Just hang in there."

"You were a better friend to me than I ever was to you," Barron gasped.

A trickle of blood ran from his lips.

"I'm done. There's no saving me."

Barron coughed, and spat out more blood.

"They have all the information about everything. I told the board everything when they made me President. You have to stop them, Parks. They'll kill everybody you care about if you don't."

Barron's eyes rolled back in his head, and his body fell limp.

Parks stood up over the torn figure of a man he had once loved as a partner, but had to fight as an enemy. His attention was quickly turned as the roar of a beat-up line of SUVs full of cadets came tearing into the compound.

"You're all under arrest!" General Allison yelled as she slammed the door behind her. "I'll see to it that you're all hung for this."

Cadets armed with Nullifiers came running past her, and set up a perimeter with their weapons trained on Parks and his group.

CHAPTER 32

"Wait a minute," Troy said as they headed for an exit. "I heard a lot of people go past my cell, and even if I couldn't count them or see who they were, it sounded like only a few returned. Where do you think they took them?"

"I don't know," Kirsten replied tersely, "but we have to get out of here before we're spotted. We'll go back where you were being held, and then out through the storage area. I think we can commandeer the delivery van."

Suddenly, a bright light flashed, and caught his eye. It came from a small window at the top of a door as they moved down the hall. Troy stopped, and looked inside while the girls continued on, checking for the exit.

He watched as a man in a white coat directed an older man with no clothes on into a clear, cylindrical tube. The older man had a blank look on his face, and folded his arms across his chest. The attendant closed the door. Lights came on, even from the hallway, Troy could hear a distinctive humming. The chamber began rotating.

"Come on, Troy." Kirsten urgently whispered as she tugged on his arm. "We've got to go."

But he was frozen.

The humming increased as the chamber rotated faster and faster. A bright light flashed, momentarily blinding Troy. When his vision returned, the chamber had stopped rotating, but the man inside was gone.

Troy took a step back, and kicked the door open.

"What are you doing?" the startled attendant demanded. "This is off limits to all unauthorized personnel."

"Where did that guy go?" Troy demanded, grabbing the man by the collar. "What did you do to him?"

"Nothing," the man protested.

"What do you mean nothing?" Kirsten asked.

She pulled out her crystal blade, and slid it under his chin.

"What is this place?"

"It's the processing center," the man replied nervously as he felt the cold blade against his throat.

"Processing? Processing what?" Troy asked.

"Look, all I do is run the machine," the man replied.

He started to shake uncontrollably.

"What does it do?" Troy pressed.

"I don't know what it does," the man answered honestly, his face white. "Management has been testing people for a long time, and those who pass are sent here after they've been tested. The ones who passed the test are put inside, and processed. That's all I know."

"What are people tested for?" Kirsten asked.

"It's some kind of physiological exam. I took the test myself and passed, but was needed to run the machine because of my technical background. I was never asked to go into the tube."

"What does the test determine?" Kirsten insisted.

"Well, what they tell me is there are two kinds of people; those who are inclined to be followers, and those who lead. The test determines which one is which.

"Followers, those who believe most everything Management says without question, are then processed. I give them a shot of this serum," he said, pointing to a bottle of red liquid and a needle sitting on a nearby tray, "and then put them inside and turn it on, but I never see them again. The chamber always comes back empty."

"What do you think happens to them?" Troy asked, examining the tube.

"Like I said," the technician replied, "I never see them again, and no one has ever told me where they go. I thought maybe they were being processed for some great position, like they become cadets or something. I really don't know and try not to think about it too much."

"Hmm," Troy said thoughtfully, "maybe I should go for a ride in it."

"You can't do that," Kenzie protested. "You don't know what this thing does. It could hurt you, or worse, grind you up into plant food or something."

"These crystal blades we have are good for a lot of things," Troy replied. "If I keep mine out, the chances of any energy getting to me are slim, right Kirsten?"

"I can't say I know that for sure," Kirsten replied, "but we do need to understand what's happening here. If you're willing to go in, I say we all go. Maybe we'll find everyone else we're looking for in there. They don't appear to be in this part of the building."

"It'll be a tight fit," Kenzie said, looking inside, "and who's going to operate it once we get in?"

"Oh, I don't think that's a problem, do you?" Kirsten said to the lab technician. "If you don't do this exactly the way you're supposed to, I'm going to cut my way out of that thing and slice you into tiny pieces. Do you understand me?"

The man nodded his head, and judging by the fearful look on his face, was in no mood to challenge her. They stepped in, and the door shut with a hissing sound as he started the process.

The three friends looked nervously at each other as they heard the humming begin. It rotated away from the room, and continued turning at an ever-increasing speed.

At first, they hadn't noticed the openings. The tube was lined with holes, and suddenly, flashes of red lighting shot out. Fortunately, they were absorbed by the crystal blades they were holding tightly to their chests. The room spun for a moment longer, and then began to slow. It opened into a vast room, dimly-lit by lights hung from a very tall ceiling.

They stepped out, a little dizzy, but otherwise no worse for wear.

"Where are we?" Kenzie whispered as her balance returned.

"Good question," Troy replied. "Wait, I hear something coming."

In the distance, an odd-looking machine came rolling down the corridor. In its two large claws, it held a mold of some sort. It rolled to where its circuits said the occupant of the chamber would be, and closed the mold. It drove to the end of the hall, and put the empty mold onto a conveyor belt, which took it slowly towards another section of the building.

The three hustled after the mold, following the conveyor until it went through an opening in the wall, where it was received by a similar machine that stacked it among thousands of other molds.

"What is this place?" Kirsten marveled.

"Some kind of automated something or rather," Troy replied, equally amazed by the strange machines. "What do you think is in those things? It can't be people. That guy I saw go in would never fit in one of those."

"What if they compressed him?" Kenzie gulped. "There could be smashed people in these."

"Hmm, that seems like a lot of work just to mush people up," Troy said thoughtfully. "Why don't we open one up, and see for ourselves."

Kenzie gave Kirsten a horrified look, but Troy's curiosity couldn't be stopped. They were stacked to the ceiling but he found a row the machine was just starting on, and began to look for a release handle or catch.

"This thing's like an egg," Troy said as he felt around the smooth side of the mold, "and it's warm. Wait, this feels like something."

He pushed a small button, and air shot from inside as the mold cracked open. He pulled on the shell, opening it the rest of the way.

"Testers," he exclaimed.

He jumped backwards, nearly tripping over Kenzie.

Inside was a neatly-packed Tester in red armor, with an ax-like weapon strapped to its chest. Its eyes were firmly shut, and it didn't appear to be breathing.

"This is where the Testers come from," Troy said in horror. "They make them from people? They make them out of us?"

"How can this be?" Kirsten said. "People become these horrible killing creatures. It all seems so insane."

"Oh man!" Troy groaned.

He dropped to his knees, and stared at the red creature.

"What is it, Troy?" Kenzie asked.

"Don't you see? Testers are people, maybe people we know. Testers could be my mother, my father, anybody, and I killed some of them. What if I killed my parents?"

They looked at each other in disbelief.

"You couldn't have known," Kirsten said quietly, putting her hand on his shoulder. "No one could have known. Besides, they're not your parents anymore. Management made them into these things."

"But there must be something we can do," Troy said as he stood up. "Maybe there's a way to return them to who they once were."

"Someone's coming," Kenzie interrupted as she heard a door open. "Now what?"

"We'll see how many there are first," Kirsten whispered as she pulled her crystal blade. "Our next goal has to be to join up with Parks, and get the heck out of here."

The noise was coming from the other side of the wall, and sounded like someone starting a piece of equipment. They hid themselves behind the molds where they could see who it was, and waited. The noise became louder as a large forklift roared around the corner.

There were rows and rows of molds full of Testers, stacked nearly to the ceiling, and the machine was designed to pick up half a stack and haul it through a tall overhead door that opened as he pushed a control button in his cab.

The three escapees followed the driver at a distance as he exited the building, and began loading a huge trailer attached to a semi truck. It was clear they were taking the Testers somewhere to either store them or activate them, and they were certain they would be activated.

The driver disappeared for a moment as he entered the container to set his first load, but that was all the time they needed to duck outside around back. The vehicle returned into the building as Troy led the way off the loading dock, and around the corner where they could see the yard.

"We may already be spotted," Kenzie observed as she pointed to cameras set around the facility on towers, and one above their heads on the building.

"No point in hiding, then," Kirsten replied. "I say we make a break for the front gate."

"Without transportation," Troy said, "we won't make it. Come on; follow me."

The driver had just put the second load in the container when they crept around the building, and raced for the cab. The door was unlocked, with the keys in the ignition. Kirsten knew how to drive a big rig, and hopped into the driver's seat. Troy and Kenzie shared the passenger seat.

Kirsten fired up the truck, and released the air brakes just as the forklift driver arrived with another load. She threw it into gear, and pulled away from the loading dock, leaving the unsuspecting driver with nowhere to go.

The new stack of sealed Testers, forklift, and the driver fell five feet onto the hard concrete. The molds scattered across the loading area.

"Here they come!" Kenzie exclaimed as they rounded the building.

Three cadets came running from a side door, and fired at the truck. One bullet blew through the back of Kirsten's seat, nearly hitting her in the head. Two more came through the front windshield.

Kirsten swerved away as she picked up speed, knocking a pickup truck out of the way. It went spinning into another parked car, and flipped over. The trailer she was pulling skidded into a line of parked vehicles. It nearly tipped over, but she dragged it a good distance on one set of wheels, and it righted itself.

Meanwhile, Kirsten was up-shifting, and gaining momentum as she came around the two story building next to the gate. They passed Parks's handiwork, consisting of countless smashed and smoldering cars with the transporter sitting on top.

"Just have to make the gate," Kirsten shouted above the roar of the engine.

"Look up there," Troy said excitedly. "That's Parks. I see

Jim and Rita. Hey, there's David and Normand too."

"Yeah, but that's somebody we don't want to see," Kenzie said as she saw several cadets standing with General Allison.

"Nullifiers, they're going to shoot. Swerve, Kirsten!" Kenzie screamed.

Kirsten cranked the wheel and hit the brakes, sending the trailer whipping around. They felt the blast as half the rear of the trailer evaporated in a flash from the first shot. The second blast destroyed the other half.

She straightened the truck, pulling what was left of the trailer through the gate and onto the open road. The partial trailer followed in a shower of sparks with the wheels blown off. Smoke billowed from the dual stacks as Kirsten pulled the damaged trailer along. It came with them for a few hundred yards before it broke off, skidded to a stop, and partially blocked the road.

Kirsten continued shifting, and soon had the semi racing down the road, putting distance between them and their assailants.

"We can't leave them like that!" Kenzie exclaimed. "We have to go back and try to help them."

"I know, I know!" Kirsten replied as she made a sharp turn onto a back road. "And we still don't know where Aaron and Isaac are. But we have to be smart, or we're all sunk."

Just then the truck's communication device came on, and they instantly recognized the voice as a gravely screech echoed through the cab.

"Turn that truck around now, Ms. Parks," General Allison commanded, "or you can say goodbye to your brother and his band of misfits. Your precious ROD has lost. Do you hear me? You've lost!"

The radio clicked off as the three of them looked at each other in horror.

"We have to go back," Troy said glumly.

"I get that," Kirsten replied as she pounded the wheel.

"They're going to kill us all anyway, right?" Kenzie said as Kirsten turned the truck around.

"Maybe, but we can't be sure," Kirsten replied. "We have to believe there will be a trial. Either way, we have no choice."

"I didn't get the impression they're interested in trials," Troy said honestly, but he softened as he looked at Kenzie. "But maybe with Parks back it'll be different. He always seems to know what to do, especially when things look the worst."

"I can't go through what they did to me again," Kenzie said.

Her breath was coming in short little gasps.

"I was losing my grip on reality. You feel pain and grief, unbelievable feelings of regret, hatred, and sadness. The darkness settles over you like a thick, dark fog. Then you see death, and killing, only you are the one doing the killing."

"Killing! Killing who?" Troy asked.

"Killing you. Killing Kirsten. Killing everyone you love," Kenzie said with pain in her voice.

"Why don't we let her out?" Troy said as he put his arm around her. "We can say she jumped out of the truck, and ran off before we got the message."

"We have to go back," Kirsten said, ignoring Troy's statement as she looked into Kenzie's eyes. "You know we have to face this."

Kenzie turned for a moment, and stared out the window before replying.

"I know," she said finally as Troy squeezed her hand. "I'm ready."

Kirsten shifted up, and the truck roared on. They knew the real battle still lay before them, but they had to face it together. Yet deep down, Kirsten somehow felt this was supposed to happen. She had no idea why.

CHAPTER 33

"What was that?!" General Allison exclaimed as she whirled around.

The loud crash of the forklift hitting the ground, coupled with a large semi barreling around from behind the security building drew everyone's attention.

"It's the prisoners!" one of the cadets yelled. "They're getting away."

"Shoot them!" General Allison commanded.

Two cadets who had returned with the general pulled their Nullifiers, and took aim at the truck. The first blast missed the truck and hit the trailer instead. So did the second blast. They were quickly joined by three other cadets who were about to fire on the truck when Parks came flying into them. He knocked them into a pile, allowing Kirsten, Kenzie, and Troy to escape.

"Stop him!" the general barked to the large group of cadets who had first encountered Parks. "What's wrong with you people? Why aren't you attacking?" she screamed again.

But they just stood there, silently staring.

Meanwhile, Parks was making quick work of the five cadets. They brandished their new sword-like weapons Management had developed, which were powered by a red crystal embedded in the handle, but Parks's purple blade destroyed them easily. He did his best to subdue them without seriously injuring or killing any of them, and so far, he was succeeding. It didn't seem they had much fight in them.

It was quickly becoming apparent that whatever had happened with Barron had had some profound effect on the general's troops, because they refused to engage Parks.

While everyone's attention was on Parks and his battle with the cadets, she drifted around behind the others, and grabbed Philip by the throat.

"Stop," she shouted, and fired a shot into the air.

She put the pistol to his head.

Parks froze as he saw his father in danger. He lowered his blade, and dropped his arms to his side.

"Don't stop, son," Mr. Parks pleaded. "This woman is insane. She'll kill us all anyway."

"Shut up, old man!" the general growled. "He'll never stop me in time. I can kill you, and at least three more before he moves an inch."

"You won't have to do that," Parks replied as he released the handle and dropped the blade to the ground. "I surrender."

A cadet picked it up while others grabbed his arms, and began applying restraints.

"You're one difficult man," the general said as she released Philip, "but you've done me a favor today. Barron won't be in my way for the presidency any more than Harry was. What kind of animal this is?" she continued, steering clear of the Zender. "That thing looks nasty."

She walked to her truck, and placed a call to the escaped truck and its driver before returning to the scene.

"You," she said, pointing at a cadet.

"Yes, General," the cadet replied as he stood at attention.

"You're in charge here now. I'm making you Master Sergeant, and I expect this place to be put back in order ASAP. I want the names of all cadets who didn't respond to my order brought to processing immediately. Do you understand me, Sergeant?"

"Yes, Ma'am," the cadet replied, hesitating.

"Ok, now get all but Mr. Parks here under lock and key. I'll deal with them when I return. That truck you saw leave will also be returning soon, so make sure they're confined as well. And get these dead things out of here; I'm sick of looking at them. Why aren't you moving?"

At that, the cadet jumped into action, taking the group into custody. David and Normand had stepped alongside Parks when he went for the cadets, but they too had laid down their blades when Philip was threatened.

The general waved Parks over to one of the last remaining fully operational SUVs, and held the door as he got in. Parks's hands were shackled behind his back with heavy metal restraints as the general slid in behind the wheel.

"I think things are finally coming around," she crowed as she pulled onto the main road and headed towards the Citadel. "You've been quite the thorn in my side, but now you're like a sheep to the slaughter. All your vaunted skills and fighting abilities are nothing when it comes to real power."

"You may have me," Parks replied calmly, "but it's not over yet."

"Always the optimist, eh, Parks. You don't really believe you're getting out of this, do you?" the General sneered. "I'm taking you directly to the board. I should mention that any attempt to escape will result in the death of everyone we just captured, including your father. I'm tightening a noose around your neck so tight, your feet will be swinging free before you even know it."

She chuckled at the thought as she turned into the Citadel, passed through security, and parked at Management's main building.

The two cadets she had brought along shadowed Parks, one on each side with Nullifiers at the ready as they walked briskly towards the elevator. The general was tingling with excitement as the door opened on the top floor, and she came out, leading a bound Parks.

"Let the board know I'm here, and I have the city's main fugitive with me," she said to the receptionist.

The woman took one look at Parks, and dialed.

"They'll be waiting for you," the woman said.

She offered directions to the board room, but Allison scoffed.

"I can find it," she said confidently.

Her high heels clicked loudly against the marbled floor.

Her head was held high as she led the way through the expansive building past the President's office, and down a long hall to a room guarded by a solid oak door. The small brass plaque with the words "BOARD ROOM" engraved on it welcomed her as she pushed open the door, and entered the modest room outfitted with a large wooden table surrounded by seven plush chairs. A row of small chandeliers ran down the center, and the outside walls were windowless. Another door stood at the far end of the room.

General Allison took the open seat at the end of the table, and Parks, with the two cadets watching him closely, stood behind her. Six average-looking older men in dark suits sat around the far end of the table, heatedly discussing among themselves in hushed voices. They each had a brass name plate in front of them, with only a number from one to six set in front of them.

"Ahhum," General Allison said, clearingd her throat. "Sorry to interrupt your discussion, gentlemen, but I believe you will be interested in this."

"Ms. Allison," Number Six spoke as he pushed away from the table, and folded his hands across his belly. "We want to thank you for bringing Mr. Parks here for our review. You and your two assistants may leave now. We'll take it from here."

"What?" she said in surprise. "Sir, you don't understand. This man is a dangerous criminal. He just killed one of our key men, Barron. There's no telling what he might attempt next."

"We appreciate your concern," Number Three said quietly, "but your services are no longer required."

She began to sweat as she struggled to believe what she was hearing. This was her moment. She had to get the credit for doing what no one had ever done before.

She shot Parks a disgusted look, and started towards the door. Suddenly, she froze.

"No offense, sirs," she said, turning around, "but we have a situation here. The president is dead, or at least the co-president is. The citadel is without a Manager, and several of the facilities we run have been damaged, not to mention the Central Broadcasting Station, which is completely destroyed.

"If I could be so bold," she continued, walking back to the table, "you need me. I can do much more than my father or Dave, or anyone else for that matter. I'll get this city whipped into shape."

"You make an interesting proposition," Number One replied, "but I would strongly advise you to come back after we've completed our business with this man."

General Allison waved the two cadets from the room, and shut the door behind them.

"If it's all the same to you," she said, "I'll stay for Parks's judgment. I deserve that, since I'm the one who caught him."

"As you wish," Number Four said as they returned their attention to Parks.

"You've been on our thoughts for quite some time, but we've just come to the realization you're something more than ordinary. We felt the death of the Zender, and no one ever managed to solve that riddle before.

"The Zender's purpose is to encourage wild emotions, and stir up uncontrollable feelings. Some give in right away, while others resist as long as they're able, but eventually they all obey. Yet you have actually killed it. That's something we must understand."

"As you said, brother," Number Five chimed in, "he's different, but does he do these things because he has the gifts, or for some other reason?"

"What do you know about this?" Number Four asked the general.

"I haven't seen anything special," she replied. "I have his backpack here, but it's just full of junk, and then there's this blade he was carrying."

General Allison dumped out the contents of Parks's bag onto the table, and laid the purple sword next to them.

The board stood in unison, and leaned across the table to examine the items; the blade, a silver cord, the Magnifier, the old book, the parchment, and the medallion were there on the table.

"See?" the General continued. "Hardly things as mighty as the Gifts."

"Why do you keep these?" Number Six asked, ignoring her remarks.

"I like them," Parks replied coyly.

"Obviously, they're nothing," Allison insisted. "He's a

strange man, so who knows why he really carries things like this. Look, he has a coat and bag that was made from animal skins. The guy is just a wild man, nothing more."

There was a long pause as the board members huddled at the end of the table, and spoke quietly among themselves.

"We've heard the rhyme," Number One said finally in a mocking tone. "Six Gifts there are, and yet one more. The seventh stands before the door. He enters through to times before, and then emerges the eighth, who knows. All that was is no more, and then the generation, four."

"Do you know what that means?' Number Six asked Parks. "Do you know the answer to the riddle?"

"No one knows," Parks snapped, "and why do you care? They're just a bunch of words that sound good together, a rhyme like so many others I learned when I was a child."

"It means nothing to you, then?" Number Three asked, sounding slightly perplexed.

"Why should it? Does it mean something to you?"

"We sense you have a question," Number Four replied, changing the subject. "You've wondered about the Dark Matter, and you've come to the right place. We can answer that question for you. Will you join us inside the next room, and find the answers you seek?"

"I was brought here in bonds," Parks replied. "If you're asking me to cooperate, I'll not do so if my hands are tied."

"Release him," Number Six said to the general.

"But sir," she protested, "he's a dangerous man, and can't be trusted. There's no telling what he might do."

The six looked as one at her, and she reluctantly took out the key, and released the heavy chains holding his arms behind his back.

Parks rubbed his wrists as the six men rose from the table, and opened the rear door.

"Come this way, and bring those with you," Number Five said as they began filing through one by one.

Parks followed, with the general close, still holding a gun at his back as she scooped up the items from the table. They entered a dark, long, windowless room, with a dimly-glowing object set on a table in the center providing the only illumination. There were no chairs, just seven octagon raised platforms surrounding the table.

"This is our meeting room," Number Six said as they each took a platform. "Please take the remaining one while the general watches from over there against the wall."

"Then what happens?" Parks asked suspiciously.

"If you want answers to the questions swirling around in your head," Number Five replied, "you'll have to stand on the platform."

"Please lay out the items he was carrying on the table, general." Number Three said.

General Allison did as instructed while Parks eyed the six-average looking men for a moment.

He had no idea what they were up to, but he needed answers, so he took a deep breath and stepped onto the platform.

The six men turned their attention to the globe sitting before them. Suddenly, as they were staring into it, it brightened, and glowed a dark red. It rose slowly from the table, and started spinning.

CHAPTER 34

Kirsten was trying to come up with a way to help those she loved as she approached the facility, but nothing was coming to her. Surrender meant suffering and possibly death, but she had to think of a way out. She couldn't let her friends and family be summarily executed. She hoped that maybe, if she took full responsibility for the breakout, she would bear the brunt of the stiff judgment likely to be meted out by Management.

She shifted down as the entrance to the facility approached.

"No matter what happens," she said as they pulled in, "I want you two to know that we did our best. I'm sorry it has come down to this, but you must know Parks and I are proud of you, and always have been."

Kenzie and Troy reached out their hands as the truck coasted to a stop, and Kirsten put hers on top of theirs as a final sign of solidarity. Together, they shouted, 'R. O. D. forever!'

Kirsten popped the airbrakes, and the truck was quickly surrounded by a horde of heavily-armed cadets. One of them reached up, and opened her door.

"Follow me," he said evenly as they climbed out.

They did as instructed, and the cadet led them to a rear door behind the two-story building. He opened the door, and began climbing a flight of stairs to the second floor. Two flanking cadets remained behind, one on each side of the exit door.

No one said a word as they were led down a long hall to a set of double doors. He opened one of the doors, and signaled for them to enter. They steeled themselves against whatever was coming next as they followed his instructions.

"Kirsten!" a familiar shout came from the crowded room.

The large room was packed with people milling about, drinking, eating, and talking. Everyone suddenly went quiet as a man worked his way through the crowd.

"Dad," Kirsten asked incredulously as Philip Parks gave his daughter a warm hug. "What's going on?"

"Maybe we should let the young man behind you explain," Philip said as he made room for the cadet who had escorted them in.

"Ms. Parks," he said in the most respectful tone.

The room went silent as he explained.

"All my life, I dreamed of joining the Citadel, and eventually, becoming a member of the fabulous BOJ Order. My friends felt just the same, and we did everything we could to rise to that level. We thought it was great when General Olliver announced the Order was being opened to all. But they also told us Parks had become a traitor to the cause. He became our enemy, and someone not to be trusted. We believed what we were told."

The young man stopped for a moment, and looked down at his hands as if ashamed of what he was saying.

"But we met the real Parks today, most of us for the first time," he finally continued. "He attacked the facility with such power, it was shocking. Then he was cornered against the side hill when Barron came for him. No one expected what came next. First, he defeated Barron, and then a strange creature emerged from his body, and he killed that too. .."

"Did you say a beast came out of Parks?" Kirsten gasped.

"Yes. It was the most fearsome creature imaginable."

She instantly remembered Grace Mountain.

"Poor Henry," she thought, "all those years with that thing inside him. How did he ever survive it?"

"Finally," the young cadet continued, "Parks did his best to save the very man who had wanted him dead. If there is such a thing as the Band Of Justice Order," he said solemnly, "we aren't it. Parks once led the Order, and we all witnessed today what that really means.

There are a few of our members who still believe Management's right, but we locked them up until we get a chance to explain things to them."

"Well, what do we do next?" Jim interjected.

"Broadcasting is out, but there must be some way to alert the city."

"There isn't much left of the city to alert," the cadet replied. "We've been trucking people in here for weeks now, and have emptied all but the Northeast quadrant."

"What happened to all those people?" Rich asked. "There's not room enough for all of them here."

"I'm not sure," the cadet said. "Our job was to bring them in for 'processing', but where they go after that I can't say. I know some who fail processing are taken from here to the Citadel, but the rest just disappear. We never see them again."

"I know where they are," Troy said, "and we found out what processing means. They turn them into Testers, and are storing them in that cursed building."

"Turn them into Testers?" Rich was stunned. "That's impossible. You can't change people into those things."

"I would never have believed it either," Kirsten replied, "but I've seen it. They inject them with a red solution, and put them into a tube that changes them. Then they're packed inside a mold, and stored until Management ships them out. That's what the truck we stole was for. It was being loaded with Testers."

"They've been hauling at least six of those trucks out a day," the cadet said, "but they don't tell us where they're taking them."

"Yeesh!" Rich exclaimed. "Just what kind of technology are we dealing with here? I would like to have a look at that machine, and see if I can figure out how it works."

The young cadet named Jeff led Rich and Troy out of the building and across the yard to the internment building. All but a few of the cells were open, and those that weren't held cadets who had yet to convert. Amazingly, the technician was still inside the room waiting for his next 'victim' when Rich walked in.

"Are you here to be processed?" the man asked.

"There will be no more processing," Rich replied.

He began asking pointed questions. In a few moments, it was clear the tech knew little about the actual working of the device. His job was to inject each person slated for processing with the red liquid, and place them inside. After that, he simply started the machine, and then prepared the next.

Rich started with the liquid, noting it had a sweet smell, and glistened in the light. He poured some on the palm of his hand, and worked it between his thumb and forefinger. It was apparent the liquid had a substance in it that resembled ground up glass. He found a magnifying glass, and examined the liquid more closely. It was then he realized the ground up glass was actually minute particles of red crystals.

"What do you think it is?" Troy asked.

"I'm not sure yet," Rich replied, examining the cylindrical tube people were placed in. "They have large red crystals connected to power cables. It appears they release energy, energy that's attracted to the crystals in the person's blood stream. It must be this interaction between the two that creates a metamorphosis, changing the physical structure of the victim. It breaks every law, but it's the only explanation I can come up with."

"Can we change them back?" Troy asked excitedly.

"I'm totally guessing on how they changed them in the first place. This is technology I've never seen before, and I have no idea how to reverse the process. It's in no books I've ever seen. Take me to where the Testers are kept."

The cadet led the way this time, and it wasn't through the machine as before. They passed several heavily-secured doors, and the last opened into a vast warehouse. The only noise was the sound of their shoes as they passed row after row of dark red rectangular containers stacked to the ceiling. Finally, they arrived at the loading dock where Kirsten, Kenzie, and Troy had made their earlier escape. Troy led the way from there to where he had opened the Tester's container.

"It's over here. This is the one I opened before. There's a latch on the side that releases the seal."

Rich began examining the case before letting Troy open it. It was hard and didn't have breathing holes. In fact, it seemed to be completely sealed. He nodded to Troy as he stepped back to see what was next. Air released as the cover swung away.

"It is hard to imagine this was once a human being," Rich said as he carefully examined the Tester nestled tightly in the center of the case. "I have to admit, I've never been this close to one of these before. It seems to have some type of organic armor protecting it, but, I really don't like the weapons someone put in here with it. This thing has a battle axe laid across its chest."

"What do we do about all these things?" Jeff asked as he looked around. "Should we blow up the building?"

"We can't do that. I know this sounds crazy," Troy interjected, "but they're still people. We can't just kill them. We have to find a way to get them back."

"I'll do what I can," Rich said as they began the trek out of the building, "but I'll need one of these taken to my old building downtown. I have a laboratory there that would enable me to perform some tests. Maybe I can figure a way to get them back, or at least preserve them in their current state."

Troy was relieved to hear Rich say he would at least try. Rich was the smartest man he knew, and if anyone could do something, it would be him. They made their way through the building, and were nearly to the exit when a sharp sound echoed through the building.

"What was that?" Jeff asked, glancing around.

"Must be a rat or something," Troy answered as they turned back towards the exit.

They heard another similar sound.

"That was no rat," Rich said, "someone's down there. We should check."

"Right," Troy replied. "I forgot about the forklift operator we dumped outside. Maybe he's hurt. He might need help."

They turned, and headed towards the sound of the noise. Suddenly, the cases holding the Testers began to pop open. Just a few at first, but then more and more as Testers began to emerge from all over the building. Those stacked high either jumped, or climbed down into the cool warehouse. All the cases were opening and the place was quickly filling up as the Testers began to move into tight formations.

"We've got to go," the cadet said, running for the exit.

Rich and Troy were tight on his heels.

They broke out into the warm afternoon sun, and Jeff began shouting to his companions, while Rich and Troy went for the building, where everyone was still gathered. They heard the sounds of axes and sharp instruments striking against the walls and doors as the Testers began to break out.

"Everyone, we've got to go, NOW!" Troy shouted, bursting into the room. "The Testers are waking up."

Everyone froze for a moment before making a collective break for the door.

Kirsten and Kenzie helped keep people moving safely as they headed down the stairs, and out the door. The cadets were busy setting up a line of defense as the Testers broke free of the warehouse in ever-increasing numbers, and the parking lot quickly became a sea of red.

The smashed vehicles from Parks's earlier attack provided cover for cadets, who took up defensive positions. They had conventional weapons as well as Nullifiers trained on the Testers, which, for the moment, were only assembling in triangular formations. They had not yet indicated they would attack.

"We need to get people to safety," David said. "Let's see how many vehicles are still operational, and get moving."

David and Normand began frantically searching for operational vehicles while Philip, James, Kenzie, Kirsten, and Rich evaluated the status of the remaining people. Some were older and disabled, but others were well enough to fight, and they volunteered.

"I found four drivable SUVs," Normand reported as he came racing back.

"The transporter is operational too," David interjected, arriving just behind Normand. "We can get at least forty people in there. I also spotted a few cars and trucks that survived Parks's attack but we'll have to find the keys."

"I estimate there are two hundred people here, including the cadets." Philip said. "There's no way we can get them all out."

"We'll help defend the rear," Kirsten said. "Everyone else that can should get into something, and start moving. We have no idea when the Testers will begin their attack, but when they do, it won't not be pretty."

"You can't stay behind," Philip said to his daughter. "I'll stay in your place. You get yourself on one of those rigs, and go."

"I love you, Dad, and I miss Mom," Kirsten said, looking deeply into his worried eyes, "but you have to understand. This is what we trained for. This is why Henry and I spent all that time making these crystal blades. It was for today."

"But I can't lose you too," Philip said as he hugged his daughter tight. "With your mother gone, you and your brother are all I have left."

"Dad," Kirsten said gently. "Mom would understand. It has to be me. I'm the fourth generation daughter. And I'm sure Henry is ok. He must be battling his way back here by now."

Mr. Parks slowly pulled away from his daughter, knowing it could be the last time he ever saw her. As he turned to join those who were leaving, an eerie silence settled over the grounds. It was as if time and motion suddenly slowed, making movement difficult. It was like in those strange dreams when you're being chased and try to run, but you can't because your feet are caught in a gooey bog.

It was a heavy feeling, cold and dark.

Philip slid in behind the wheel beside his brother James, and closed the door. He watched his daughter for what could very well be the last time as they moved out of the facility, and headed towards the East river. Their next stop was to pick up Lori and the motor home, and then make a break for the wilderness or the mountains where the Ancients were. They had little idea what was really in store for them.

CHAPTER 35

Darkness flowed from the globe through the Six, and swirled like coal dust around them, filling the room. Their appearance changed from sharply dressed men to dark, vague figures. The air felt thick, choking. Parks watched in amazement as the room began to glow a brilliant dark red. A beam shot from the globe into the foreheads of the six men, Parks, and the general. The globe continued spinning faster and faster, spewing out blackness before it suddenly stopped.

"You can hear us," the six said in unison without opening their mouths or speaking. "We're connected now."

The general, who was standing against the wall by the door, was frozen stiff, her eyes bulging, and her mouth hanging open. Her mind was filled with thoughts of death and vile evil. She saw the helpless crushed beneath the feet of those with power. They reached out from the darkness, grabbing at her limbs, and trying to pull her down into the black darkness. She started screaming and looking around frantically for someone to save her, but the six just watched as her mind sank into black darkness.

In one last moment of lucid thought, she threw open the door, ran through the board room and out into the hall, screaming manically. The two cadets stationed outside took off behind her, but before they could catch her, she ran past the secretary, who watched in stunned horror as she leapt through a heavy glass window, and plunged forty feet to the concrete below.

"What are you?" Parks asked.

"We're what you've been seeking," they replied.

"I've never sought for things such as you."

"Oh, but you have," they continued. "We, on the other hand, didn't know you fully until today. You see, we come to all at certain times. Do you not remember the first time we met?"

Parks was confused at first, but suddenly his mind was drawn to a night many years before when he was fifteen. A night he bolted upright in bed, drenched in cold sweat. He remembered sitting alone fighting against feelings of dread as the people he loved were torn apart by some invisible force. He remembered the darkness closing in upon him, and the shadowy gray figures approaching from the corners of his bedroom.

"Those were you!" Parks exclaimed. "You were the things that haunted my youth."

"We come to everyone. Our purpose was to find that certain one we knew would want to understand the feelings, and find the answer. But in all our searching, we've never found one who could resist the creature. They all fell to the beast. The others before you couldn't find the gifts, but here they are, and here you are."

"How can you know these things are the gifts?" Parks asked, grappling with his thoughts.

"We can never be completely sure. You see, when we were here before, we found a being similar to you who had found the old book, and the parchment that lies here on this table before us now. We learned he had these things, and sought to locate him and destroy them, but he hid them from us, so we took the city and destroyed it instead as we harvested the darkness of those within."

"But, why are those things so important?" Parks pressed.

"They hold the secret of time. Whoever possesses them can move to places unknown, and from those places we can be destroyed."

"Well, I've had that book for quite a while now, and it hasn't done me any good. If what you say is true, we wouldn't be having this conversation, would we? You would be destroyed already."

"Nothing is ever that simple," they continued. "These things are ancient, and have powers you may never understand. We only protect the order of things. We keep things as they should be. Your kind will continue to destroy, and be destroyed. It's the will of who you are, and we profit from your weakness."

"You said you have the answers I want," Parks said to stay focused. "What questions do you think I might have?"

"You want to know about the Dark Matter."

"That not a question; it's a legend that's been told from generation to generation. You can explain that to me?"

They seemed to laugh at his response, and began to converse between themselves in a language he didn't understand. While they were seemingly distracted, Parks focused on the items lying on the table. His attention was drawn towards the folded parchment set next to the book. A light was emanating from it. He stepped off the platform, picked it up, and unfolded it.

A crude drawing of a man holding a candle in front of a door began to appear. The door was dull in appearance, with no handle on the outside, just hinges and a key hole. Parks had seen this once before, the day he opened the parchment in his apartment, but he hadn't touched it since. Now the inscription above the door was pulling him in.

"YOU MUST SEEK THE SIX TO FIND THE TRUTH."

"What truth do you hold?" he shouted to the six figures.

Their attention returned to Parks.

"What are you doing with that?" they demanded. "Put it down, and get back onto the platform."

"Not until you tell me everything," Parks snapped. "What's this secret truth you hold, and don't want anyone to know?"

"So you truly want to know," they replied, "then know you shall."

The red crystal began spinning faster, and the room increased its brilliant dark red color. The beam shooting from the globe became more intense as it bored into Parks.

Sights and sounds rushed into his mind, and he closed his eyes in pain. He saw all the times he had failed, or did something wrong. Waves of regret washed over him as he became increasingly aware of the lost lives. Haunting faces of those he had hurt came to him. He saw himself stepping over people, friends, even family, to achieve his own goals.

He was sweating profusely as he opened his eyes.

The spinning globe slowed, and then stopped as real-time events of people he loved began to unfold before his eyes. He became merely a spectator and could do nothing to stop the horror.

"We can jog to the Citadel," Kirsten said as the last vehicle pulled out. "That's where Parks, Aaron, and Isaac were taken. With the help of the cadets, maybe we can take it over, and make a stand there."

"And the Testers," David said. "Shouldn't we try and destroy them before we leave. You know what damage they can do."

"We can't destroy them," Troy insisted.

"Sure we can," David responded. "I know there are a lot of them, but we have our crystal blades, and have been trained for just such a battle. We also have the cadets, and they seem quite able to fight."

"No!" Troy exclaimed, grabbing David by the arm. "We can't destroy them because they're people. My parents may even be among them."

They all looked at Troy in disbelief, but suddenly realized the truth of what he had said. Testers were weak-minded people, changed though some hideous process into the dark red creatures assembled in front of them.

"Troy," Kenzie said, holding his gaze, "they were our friends, neighbors, and maybe even our parents, but they aren't anymore. Whatever happened changed them, and we can't think of them the same way. We must be willing to fight, or they'll kill us all. Would you sacrifice me and your friends for them?"

Troy looked around at the faces of the people he loved, and glanced at the gleaming red horde before answering.

"You're right," he sighed. "It's Management's fault. They made this happen, and they're responsible. If the Citadel holds the key, then I say we start running."

Before they could move, the Testers began advancing, holding their weapons in front, and quickly picking up speed as they approached the defensive line of smashed vehicles. Three cadets let off bursts from their Nullifiers, but instead of the Testers being blown apart, the blasts deflected off their breastplates, and dissipated harmlessly into the air.

"That's impossible!" one of the cadets exclaimed.

They opened fire with the conventional weapons they had. Machine guns, rifles, and shoulder-fired missiles ripped into the advancing Testers, but the effect was minimal. Just a few of the Testers fell, but the majority kept advancing. It seemed their formation, like the teeth on a saw blade, meant the ones at the points took the hit, but were immediately replaced by another Tester. This protected the main body as they advanced.

"We've got to go!" Normand shouted as he began running for the gate.

His admonition wasn't required though. The cadets abandoned their positions as the Testers began to climb over and through the twisted steel, slashing with their weapons. Fortunately, they were not known for their speed, and it wasn't long before the escaping group was putting distance between them.

"It's only a three mile run to the Citadel," Kenzie said encouragingly to David, who was running alongside her on the blacktopped road. "We'll be there well ahead of those things, and see what we can do then. There must be weapons there we can use to stop them."

"Oh no," David exclaimed as they arrived at the top of a small hill.

In the depression below, not more than a quarter mile away, lay a dark red gleaming sea of even more Testers. They bunched to a stop as the realization swept over them. They were cut off.

"They were waiting for us," Kirsten said, drawing her blade.

"What do you say now, Henry Jacob Parks?" the Six asked in a cold, even voice. "This is but the beginning, but you can stop it by agreeing to our terms."

"My sister will never give up," Parks said through clenched teeth as the sweat rolled off his forehead. "She trained those kids, and they'll destroy your Testers."

"So you say," the Six responded, "but we have far more to show you."

Parks mind was pulled back inside the red crystal, only now he was with the Ancients.

"Those red cubes we told you about," Julie said to Sterling, "that were being dropped off by those huge trucks have started hatching or something. Fred and I thought at first they were coming out here to dump garbage but now all we see are these short red armored things with sharp knives and axes."

"Testers," Sterling replied as he scanned the red mass with his binoculars. "We've got to get everyone to safety. I don't know how they found us, but they have."

"Do you think Parks told them where we were hiding?" Fred asked.

"Parks, not a chance," Sterling replied sharply. "But it doesn't matter how they got here. We've got to go."

"We can take the secret passageways to the other side of the mountain," Fred answered. "But I'm afraid we won't have time to get everyone in there, and the old and sick among us won't be able to travel at all. The best we can do is to get everyone inside the vault in the heart of the mountain."

"I'll gather those who can fight," Sterling said. "They'll have to pass through the narrow passage to reach us, and maybe we can hold them off long enough for you to move."

"You know that's not going to work," The Six said to Parks. "The Testers will find a way inside, even if they have to pile themselves up, and crawl over each other to get in. We designed them to never stop until they've fulfilled their mission. All your friends will die inside that mountain."

"I don't believe you," Parks shouted back. "They've survived for thousands of years, escaping your evil. You won't get them now."

"Do you really want to take that chance? What happens if you're wrong? One more thing to see, and then you will decide."

"My cameras are picking up thousands of Testers coming this way," the colonel said as he rushed into the hall.

"They can't get us down here, can they?" Della asked.

Just then the facility began to echo with the sounds of thousands of axes and swords, pounding against the heavy steel doors and hatches that sealed the Island from the rest of the world.

"They can," Greg answered as he joined the colonel. "My sensors already show damage, and one of the outer doors has been breached."

Greg was as calm as Della had ever seen, and he wasn't stuttering this time.

"We must move everyone below!" the colonel exclaimed. "They'll never be able to reach us there."

Greg didn't say another word as he led the way to the elevators. What they were doing, in effect, was trapping themselves, but there was no other choice. The Colonel knew it, but they could at least find some protection, and the Island had some powerful weapons which he was willing to use.

"Your friends, your family, your wife, and even your unborn son," The Six continued, "will all perish. It's up to you, Parks. Do you agree, or do we let the Testers continue?"

Parks screamed. He tried to leap at them, but couldn't. It was as if his feet were fastened to the floor.

"If any escape this time," The Six warned, "we'll comb over this city again and again until we find the very last one. We won't stop until you're extinct.

Parks's mind was racing and his heart crushed with pain as he stared at the six dark figures before him. But somehow, in the middle of the most painful moment of his life, a calming presence flooded over him, and his mind begin to clear. He began to understand the decision was his, and the power of the Dark Matter was simply a choice. His choice.

Suddenly, he knew what to do.

CHAPTER 36

Parks felt the full weight of what was at stake from the mountains, to the deepest part of the Island, to the core of the city. Everything he loved was about to be destroyed. But he was beginning to understand this strange adversary.

"One last chance for you to change the inevitable," The Six said. "You can submit and join us, or stand and watch as your world collapses around you."

"The Dark Matter," he replied as he fought to buy time. "I still don't understand. What is it really?"

The six looked at each other, and laughed cynically before returning their attention to him.

"The Dark Matter," they answered in one voice, "you fool, you still don't see. We're the Dark Matter. We challenge your innocence until your thoughts become corrupted, then we feed you your life circumstances and losses, and take peace from you. We take what you know to be right and real until you're ready, ready to give in to us. You're out of options, Henry Jacob Parks. Time has run out, so CHOOSE NOW!"

"No!" he exclaimed.

He placed his hands flat on the table, and looked into their glowing red eyes.

"I will not serve you."

There was a momentary pause as they looked him over intently. Then they spoke again in one voice.

"That is very unfortunate for YOU. We had clearly expected more."

The glow from the red crystal faded, and the room went black.

At first, Parks could only hear the sound of his heart pounding against his chest as he grappled with the feelings flooding his being, feelings of doom. A faint sneering echoed through his mind, growing louder and louder by the second, until he felt like his head would explode.

"Do we stand and fight?" David asked as the Testers behind them began to catch up.

More blocked their way to the Citadel, and started advancing towards them. They were being squeezed from two sides.

"I say we make a break for it towards the woods," Normand replied. "We can lose them there, and then circle around and regroup where we make our final break for the Citadel."

"Hey!" Kirsten said suddenly, "is that black smoke rising behind those Testers?"

"Not good!" the cadet leader replied as he pulled out his binoculars. "Those are the vehicles that just left. They're on fire."

"Let me see!" Kirsten said as she nearly ripped the binoculars from his hands. "The Testers are attacking!"

Kirsten threw the binoculars down, pulled out her crystal blades, and started running towards the approaching line. David and Normand hesitated for only a second before taking off behind her. They were quickly joined by Troy and Kenzie.

The Testers sensed their approach, and moved into a defensive posture, with their sharp instruments waist high. Kirsten didn't hesitate as she jumped over the front line, and into the midst of them, her crystal blades slicing through Tester after Tester.

David and Normand were next, but they took the direct approach, blocking the Tester's weapons with one blade as they cut their way through with the other. It was a vicious fight as Troy and Kenzie joined the fray.

For a moment, it looked like they would break through to the back side unscathed, but then a sharp curved blade cut into Normand's leg. He limped forward for a moment, still dealing blow after blow, when a second pointed spear slid under his arm, and into his chest.

David felt Normand drop, and turned to protect him just as a fresh wave of Testers poured in. All he could do was stand with Normand at his feet, and try to keep them from finishing him off, but he could feel himself weakening. Even though he had yet to receive a fatal blow, blood flowed from numerous shallow cuts and puncture wounds. He knew it would be only a matter of time now as he bravely fought on.

But then two buzz saws appeared through the mass of red, and drove the Testers back.

It was Troy and Kenzie, moving with precision and power as their crystal blades flashed in the bright sun. David picked Normand up, and carried him as the two warriors made a way for them through the blood-red sea. In a few moments, they emerged at the rear of the Testers line, and began running after Kirsten, who was just about to the horrific crash site.

Testers were attacking the transportation vehicles filled with refugees. James had found a heavy sledge hammer behind one of the seats, and was making any Tester approaching him pay. Rich and Philip fired their weapons continuously, even though they weren't very effective.

Philip's back was to the SUV. He ran out of ammunition just as a Tester came around the side. He turned to escape, but as he did, he ran straight into the sword of a second one.

"No!" Kirsten cried.

She leaped into the fray, cutting the two Testers in half. "Dad!" she cried over the sound of the battle raging around them. "Don't leave me, Dad. I'll get you out."

"No, not this time, Kirsten," Mr. Parks replied as he looked into his daughter's eyes. "I love you and your brother, but it's time for me to be with Pearl…"

Philip's eyes glazed over, and his body went limp. Kirsten buried her face in his chest, but then heard the distinctive sound of even more Testers approaching. There was no time for mourning as the shrinking group of resisters were surrounded on every side.

Suddenly, the ground around them erupted. Testers were tossed into the air as the distinctive shape of a Zyklone burst from the ground. Zyklones were huge creatures covered with reptilian scales and sharp knife-like protrusions covering their bodies. They spun like giant drills, allowing them to burrow deep underground, even through rock.

Its wide head with a hooked beak snapped several Testers in half as it rose above the earth, then dove back into the ground. Several more burst to the surface, and slithered across the ground, tearing into the ranks of the Testers before diving down again. The chanting and vibrations created by the Testers penetrated through the ground and drew them to the surface.

It was a miracle, and they were not about to waste it.

"Come on!" David said as he grabbed Kirsten by the arm. "We can't help your dad now, but we've got to go before they regroup."

"They've broken through the bulkhead, and are coming this way," Greg shouted.

"How long before they get down here?" the colonel asked.

"Well, I've shut off the elevators, but they are getting into the ventilator shafts," "Greg answered.

"It is only a matter of time now," the Six said as Parks sank to his knees. "Your father is dead, your sister is running, and your wife and unborn son will be found, and killed."

Parks could see it all.

The Testers came through the narrow opening in the rock wall leading up the mountainside towards the Ancients, but were immediately met by a large, powerful animal. The three sharp horns on either side of the Lawmule's forehead impaled some Testers as it flipped them high into the air. Others it trampled underfoot as it snorted and pounded the ground. It charged into the horde of advancing Testers as hot bursts of light flashed from the clear crystals set in the ends of Fred's and Julie's Whiterods. Together, they blasted into them as they worked to hold the line until Sterling could get everyone to safety.

But the Testers were too much. Their sharp instruments of death sliced the Lawmule, who went down with a deep groan.

"They killed him!" Julie anguished.

"We've got to go," Fred said as he grabbed his wife by the arm. "They'll be on us any second."

The Testers swarmed like ants over the body of the Lawmule as they chased Fred and Julie up the mountain. Several other Ancients provided cover from rocky outcrops with their Whiterods as Julie and Fred ran past to momentary safety. But there was no real safety with hordes of Testers battling their way up the mountain side.

"It will all be over soon," The Six said as Parks sank deeper into himself. "We'll even clean up those other two the general delivered. Mr. Grey will see to it right now."

Parks was beyond his breaking point as he watched Mr. Grey exit the building, and walk towards what was left of the Citadel. Parks had destroyed all but the basement of the building when he attacked, meaning the cells below were still operational. Aaron and Isaac were chained together in a dingy cell as Mr. Grey opened the steel door, and entered.

"What do you want with us now?" Aaron asked. "We don't know anything."

Both men had already endured Mr. Grey's interrogation, which was clearly evident by their blood-soaked clothes and broken ribs.

"Time for talking is over," Mr. Grey declared. "There's nothing you have to say that I'm interested in."

He walked over, and faced the two shackled men before addressing Isaac.

"You escaped me once," he said as a sickening smile crossed his face, "but not this time."

Mr. Grey slid his hands around Isaac's throat, and started choking him.

The visions swirled like a tornado over Parks's head as he felt the agony and pain. He slowly sank deeper and deeper into a hole blacker than darkness itself.

In the midst of his suffering, a subtle voice entered his mind. It settled into his thoughts like a small white feather, blowing on a gentle breeze.

"You shall seek the six to know the truth," the voice said gently.

Parks groaned.

"Six," the voice said again. "The SIX."

Then Parks realized there were TWO sixes as he looked at

the strange assortment of things laid on the table before him. The silver cord they had found in the greenhouse that saved him in the cave, the Magnifier found by Kevin Knobbs at the cost of his life, the Medallion he got from Kirsten, the purple crystal blade formed from the blue and red crystals, the ancient book and parchment given him by Sterling.

There were six objects before him, and six dark figures who were distracted as they focused their energy through the large red crystal against those he cared for. Parks begin picking up each item. He put the Medallion over his neck, and wrapped the silver cord around his waist. He unfolded the parchment, spreading it on the table.

He did these things without thinking, as if he were being directed by some unseen hand. Then he remembered the golden key, the one he had gotten from the strange teenager in the lost city. He had placed it inside the book for safe-keeping.

He opened the book, took out the key, and then put the book into the vest pocket of his coat next to his heart. Next, he popped open the Magnifier, and placed it beside the parchment. Finally, he picked up the purple crystal blade.

He stood there, staring at the parchment with the crude drawing of a man holding a candle in front of the door. This time, there was a key hole. He couldn't look away as the Magnifier began glowing, throwing an eerie light onto the parchment.

Somehow, the door was no longer just an image on an old parchment; it was before him. He reached out, put the key in the lock, and turned. It opened towards him, as if being pushed from the inside.

"What are you doing?" The Six said in unison. "Those items cannot help you."

A beam of red energy shot from the large crystal, and into his mind. Hot shards of pain shot though his being, and his body began to glow. The Six were now completely focused on him.

He could feel an evil so dark, he couldn't have imagined it even existed. He was the evil. He saw the pain of his mother when she died. The countless mistakes he had made in life. Every error, every wrong move or hurtful decision ripped into his consciousness. He felt responsible for everything bad that had happened, and now the looming death of everyone he cared about, especially Della.

Parks sank to his knees in agony. The end was only moments away. Then he looked again at the Magnifier, which stood balanced on the table, and the parchment with the door still standing open behind it. Without knowing why, he tied the silver cord to the leg of the table. With everything he had left inside him, he allowed his thoughts to flow through the Magnifier, and into the ancient parchment.

He felt the room swirling, and he began moving in a manner he had never experienced before. It was as if he was lifted above his body, and he watched as the energy from the red crystal grew brighter and brighter till he could no longer see himself. He dove towards the open door, and saw the silver cord, the one that had stretched without breaking, that had pulled him and countless others to safety, snap in two.

And then he was gone.

Parks could have been in there seconds, or it could have been thousands of years, he couldn't tell. Time suddenly meant nothing. He just knew something had happened, something he couldn't fully explain. He just knew he was somewhere else. Somewhere where there was no evil or darkness. Somewhere where there was life and power.

Slowly his thoughts returned to the darkened room, and the six. His body was still smoldering from the power of the red crystal as his eyes opened, and he stood up, But he felt no fear or dread. Instead, he felt new confidence, and a peace beyond words. He glanced down at the ancient parchment and the door. It was closed again, only now in place of the keyhole, was a wax seal with the initials, his initials, **HJP** pressed into it.

"I know your names," he said calmly as his faculties fully returned.

"Our names," The Six said in shock. "What do you know of us? You know nothing, nothing at all."

"Far from it," he replied as he turned, and stepped back onto the platform.

"Number One," Parks said, "your name is Hatred. You stir up deep feelings of resentment in people, and encourage them to use those feelings against others.

Number Two, your name is Lying. You put deception in people's minds, and take away the safety and comfort of truth.

Number Three, your name is Pride. You entice people to think of themselves more highly than they should so that they become jealous, and hurt others.

Number Four, your name is Anger. You work with your brother Hatred. Hatred creates the resentment, but you bring the pain.

Number Five, your name is Lust. You trick people into believing that what someone else has should be taken from them. You make them justify their actions, and provide excuses with thoughts of 'why should they have that, and not me.' You are sickening and vile.

Number Six, your name is the worst of all. Your name is Death. I don't mean the end of life. No, you're the ultimate thief of people's dreams, hopes and desires. You kill their true purpose in life, and bury it under despair and discouragement. You are truly the worst of all."

He stepped off the pedestal, and looked into the faces of each being, only this time without fear or anger. He felt nothing but disgust for energies whose sole purpose was the worst for people. He lifted the purple crystal blade over his head, and with one mighty blow, smashed the red crystal globe to pieces.

The room around him began to spin as the six dark figures rose with a scream so vile, it almost hurt to hear. They began to swirl, blending together as one for a moment as the broken pieces of red crystal joined them in a dark red cloud. Then, as suddenly as they had come that one warm summer afternoon to destroy a city and a people, Management was gone.

CHAPTER 37

Aaron was horrified as Mr. Grey lifted Isaac off his feet by his throat. He struggled as the little man in the neat dark suit and sunglasses slowly squeezed his windpipe shut.

Isaac's eyes were bulging as Aaron pulled against the chains holding his hands over his head. He coiled himself against the wall, and jumped with all his might. The chains snapped tight, but Aaron stretched his body midair, and kicked Mr. Grey in the head.

The impact knocked the little man against the side of the cell, and he dropped Isaac. Aaron struggled to his feet as Mr. Grey calmly turned to face them again. His twisted smile was still firmly in place, but then he froze for a moment with a puzzled look. His expression changed to one they had never seen before. Mr. Grey looked afraid, even terrified, before he changed to vapor, and disappeared into a dark mist.

They were stunned.

"If I had known all I needed to do was kick him in the head," Aaron quipped, "I would have done that a long time ago."

"Yeah, no kidding," Isaac responded. "I don't know what just happened, but hey, he dropped the key."

Isaac freed himself and then Aaron. Cautiously, they opened their cell door, and proceeded up the winding, broken stairs to daylight.

Moments before, Parks had watched as the six dark beings swirled around the broken red crystal before dissipating into blackness. He stepped back into the adjacent room. The meeting room of the six dissolved away, revealing the rear parking lot behind the building for just a moment before the door disappeared, and the wall returned. He turned, and walked back to the reception area.

Parks just smiled as he passed the receptionist on the way to the elevators. She stared at him with her mouth half open, not sure what to do, but then shook her head in disbelief, and picked up the phone. She frantically dialed number after number, and looked up in despair as the doors shut behind him.

Parks walked from the building up the slight incline, and across the yard to where Aaron and Isaac were just emerging from the Citadel, covering their eyes as they adjusted to the bright sunlight.

"You fellas ok?" Parks yelled. "You look like you were run over by a transporter."

"That's no joke," Aaron answered in his blood-soaked shirt as he rubbed the welts on his wrists. "But something's different. It feels like a new day."

"Even the air is fresher," Isaac agreed as he took a deep breath. "Are you ok, Parks?"

"Couldn't be better. And you're right, it is a new day."

"What happened?" Aaron asked.

"Management has fallen. It's over, for real this time."

"Over? How?" Isaac asked. "We were about to be killed, and then our little friend, Mr. Grey, just vanished."

"I know," Parks answered. "I saw what he was doing to you, but he's gone for good. But why didn't you tell him what he wanted to know?"

"Why?" Aaron replied. "Because we're the ROD. Resist Or Die."

Parks took a long look at the two young men. Kirsten had trained them well, and he couldn't have been more proud.

"You're both heroes, and I have a feeling there are a lot more like you. Anyway, I need you two to get patched up. There's still work to do."

"We're ok, Parks." Aaron replied. "What do you need us to do?"

"I'd say start in that building up there where you used to work. There are people inside who need your help."

Isaac and Aaron started off in that direction, not sure how Parks could have seen them in that dark cell under the Citadel, but they weren't about to question anything at this point. They were just glad to be alive.

The building was dark as they approached, and the door was unlocked.

"Strange that Parks would think there are people here," Isaac said as they entered. "This place doesn't feel like anyone's been here for a while."

The long front entrance was still set up with the tables and booths Aaron had used when he processed people from the county. It gave him an uneasy feeling realizing these simple things were once used to send people to their deaths, and he had been part of it.

"What about in here?" Isaac asked, snapping Aaron's attention back to the two double doors guarding the main auditorium. "These doors are chained shut with a combination lock."

"I'll see if there's a pry bar someplace," Aaron replied as he remembered the last time he had looked in there with Parks.

It was not a memory he enjoyed.

"Don't bother," Isaac said as he grabbed the chain with each hand. "It's not that heavy, and I think my ribs can take it."

Isaac held the chain tightly about chest level, and took a deep breath. He closed his eyes, tensed his muscles, and relaxed. Instantly, the chain snapped. It broke in two, and several links went bouncing across the floor.

"I wish I could have done that when we were held in that blasted cell," Isaac said as he unwound the chain from his hands.

"You did just fine," Aaron replied.

He slowly opened the door, not sure what they were going to find.

Immediately he was grabbed by several sets of hands, and shoved to the floor. A flood of bodies attacked, and began tearing at him.

"Stop," Isaac shouted.

He jumped to Aaron's defense, pushing a mass of people back. "We're not here to hurt you; we're here to let you go."

"You are?" a man said as he stepped forward. "We never thought we would ever hear someone say that."

The room was jammed with people of all ages, children,

adults, and older people who were obviously in great fear.

"They put us in here," the man continued.

He stood next to Aaron and Isaac as people thanked them while they flooded by.

"They said the board would be by to pass sentence on us. Well, we decided there was no way we were going down without a fight, so that's why we grabbed you."

"You don't need to explain," Aaron replied as they followed the last of the survivors out of the building. "Management is no longer a threat."

"What do you mean?" the man asked as the people huddled around.

"We don't have all the answers, but Management has left the city."

"No more Management?" one older woman said in disbelief as she looked at her husband. "What are we going to do?"

"Start over," her husband said with a smile.

There was a momentary pause before the crowd went wild. People were hugging, crying and laughing all at once as feelings of freedom rushed through.

"We've really won," Aaron said in amazement.

"I feel that," Isaac said as the realization swept over him too.

Meanwhile, Parks was on his own mission, and had jogged onto the main road when he saw Kirsten running his way.

"Parks! You're alive!" she exclaimed.

She wrapped her arms around him.

"I was so afraid I had lost you too," she sobbed into his shoulder. "They took Dad, Henry. I couldn't get to him in time."

Parks held her tightly as she wept.

"I know, Kirsten," Parks replied gently. "You did everything you could. You saved so many people, but there was nothing more you could have done to save Dad."

"How could you know that?"

"I saw everything from the Tower."

"You were in the Tower?"

"Yes, General Allison took me there to meet the board, The Six."

"Why? How did you get out?"

"It's a long story, and I'm happy to say I'll have plenty of time later to tell it."

Kirsten knew her brother well, but she could tell there was something different. He was the same, and yet not. She could feel it.

"Dad loved us," Kirsten said as they walked along.

"I know, Kirsten. Mom and Dad loved us, and they're very proud of both of us."

"I'm proud of us!" Kirsten replied. "Can you even believe what just happened here? We have our city back."

"Yes I can," Parks replied with a smile, and a peace he had never imagined.

"Hey, you two," Jim shouted as he and Rita pulled up in a barely-running SUV.

Jim jumped out, and rushed over to Parks.

"You won't believe what's going on. The Testers are gone, all of them, but there are some seriously naked people out there. We need clothing, blankets, anything we can find."

"The cadet quarter's still intact," Parks replied. "You should be able to find something there."

"What's your next plan?" Kirsten asked.

"I need to get to the Island. Do you know what happened to my bike?"

"It's over at Darla's," Kirsten answered.

"Don't you think we should figure out what's going on here first?" Jim asked. "What about Management? How can we be sure it's safe?"

"I'm sure," Parks said confidently. "I'm sure."

Jim looked at Rita in disbelief, and then she smiled. Jim grabbed her, lifted her off her feet, and they spun around several times, like two long lost lovers who just found each other again.

They came over a slight rise to where Kirsten had left everyone to find Parks. There were crowds of naked people moving about in a daze like they were waking up from a long sleep. Some had regained their senses, and were doing their best to find something, anything, to cover up with.

"Mr. Parks!" shouted an excited voice.

It was Troy, and he was leading an older woman wrapped in a blanket. "I found my mom!"

"Will wonders never cease?" Parks said, smiling.

She still appeared to be in a cloud of confusion and couldn't speak yet, but it was definitely Troy's mom.

"Once I get her somewhere safe," Troy said, "I'm going to look for Dad. He must be here somewhere too."

"We can hope, Troy," Parks said comfortingly.

"Philip was a good brother, and a good father," James said as he walked up and put his arms around Parks and Kirsten. "We're going to miss him."

"I've found more transportation," Jim said as he rolled up next to them with the window down. "Aaron said there's a parking garage just down from the Citadel with some large transporters, and more SUVs. He, Isaac, and a bunch of cadets are heading that way right now. They should be down here in less than a half hour."

Rita was already pulling stacks of clothing and blankets from the back of the truck, and Normand, David, and Rich began distributing them throughout the crowd. It wasn't long before people were covered ,and beginning to ask scores of questions,

Mostly, "What happened?" and "Where am I?"

"You go ahead," Kirsten said as she grabbed Parks by the arm. "We'll take care of these folks, but you need to get to Della."

Without hesitation, he jumped into the SUV Jim had left, and took off for Darla's, where he picked up his bike. In a few minutes, he was heading across the city, and into the wilderness. He didn't waste a second, jumping dry creek beds, and catching air over ridges with his powerful cycle.   Before long, the Island came into view. It was frightening to see shards of bent steel rising from the wilderness floor, and his heart sank as he saw the heavy steel covering that had been chopped through and torn back as the Testers broke inside. He hardly slowed as he followed their tracks, and dropped into the underground cavern.

He slid to a stop next to the elevators, and hit the button.

The door opened to a sight beyond belief. Just like where he came from, naked people were milling around in confusion as others were helping them with clothing and other coverings. He pushed his way through the crowd, searching for a familiar face.

"Iris!" Parks shouted as he spotted the young woman tending to an older man with a deep gash on his arm. "Where's Della?"

She pointed in the direction of the kitchen area, which had been set up for surgery. A heavy lump stuck in his throat as he opened the door.

"Parks," the colonel exclaimed, almost jumping with joy. "Are we ever glad to see you!"

"Yes, we are," Della said as she looked up from the wounded person she was caring for.

"Are you ok?" Parks asked tenderly.

"Yes," she replied as she hugged him tight. "But what about you? You look different, Henry."

Parks just smiled as he squeezed her affectionately.

"I've got to admit that's quite a trick," the colonel interrupted. "One minute we're fighting short red tin cans, and the next we're surrounded by naked people. What do you say to that?"

"It's a lot to understand," Parks said as he gently set Della down. "But for now, let's just say Management is through, and there's a lot of work to do."

"You're absolutely right there," the colonel replied. "We were just discussing the best way to treat some of the injured. We have folks with serious wounds, and I'm not sure how we can care for them. This place has good stuff but not that good."

"Can they travel?" Parks asked.

"Yes, if we prep them first. Why, what are you thinking?"

"Why not haul them to the hospital? I can have some large transporters out here in less than four hours, and some aid cars with them."

"The hospital in the city?" Della asked. "Are you sure it's

safe to return?"

"It's more than safe," he said, "and they'll need you. In fact, it's time everyone returned to the city, including you, Colonel. This is a great place, but I'm sure you're tired of living underground. What do you say we get you all out of here?"

The colonel looked at Parks in disbelief for a moment, and then realized he wasn't kidding. The city had been returned to its rightful owners, and there was no need to hide out anymore.

This same scenario was repeated one more time as Sterling came to the city, and sought out Parks. He described a similar situation, and how the Ancients had gone from defending their stronghold to helping a large number of people. Parks dispatched a fleet of transporters returning with people who had once been Testers, and many Ancients as well.

Dr. Larson set up large triage areas to treat the wounded, and the whole city gathered to provide clothing and temporary housing. People were alive again, and willing to do whatever it took to restore their city, but it would be a long time before things settled into a daily routine.

In the months that followed, the city underwent a serious rebuild. Not just with wood and brick, but with understanding. Their spiritual and emotional conditions had been devastated, but now it too was being rebuilt. Honor for those who were elderly, respect for those who deserved it, love for their fellow citizens, and a commitment to never allow someone to take those basic rights from them again.

Together, they wrote the Ten Principles of Freedom, and put them in their new capital building where all could see.

Jim and Rita led the effort to help people who were once Testers. They found it quite astounding that some of them came from places they had never heard of.

Jim was working late one afternoon when he heard a familiar voice.

"Hi, Mr. Banner," Greg said as he tapped him on the shoulder.

"Greg!" Jim exclaimed excitedly. "You're looking really great. How are things going?"

"Better than I could ever have imagined," Greg replied. "It's amazing what this city is becoming."

"Hey," Jim observed, "you aren't stuttering."

"I know, and I owe that to someone very special," Greg replied as he waved to a young woman who was helping Rita. "You remember Iris, don't you?"

"Well, you dog, you," Jim said, lightly punching Greg in the shoulder.

Jim and Rita and Greg and Iris had a joint wedding, attended by nearly everyone in the city. There were guests from the Island, and many Ancients. The colonel gave away Iris, and Parks gave Rita away. It was a special moment.

Jim returned to rebuild HOT News, and became director, with Greg as the city's new Weatherman. Normand, Isaac, Troy, and Burke went in together and started a new delivery service that became the most popular service in the city. It extended into the county and beyond, even to the Ancients, and the city of Abigail.

David took an apprenticeship under Rich, and became the city engineer. Kirsten married, and settled down on a large horse ranch. Kenzie started a successful law firm, and Aaron became president of the city's largest bank.

The colonel revised the Island, and created a new military protective force. He continued investigating tunnels, and found cities they had never seen before. He helped many people, once Testers, find the homes they had lost, and was instrumental in connecting cities together.

Della returned to manage the city's hospital, and built several more throughout the city. She even brought medical services to the Ancients. Parks built a new home on his father's property where he and Della raised their four children, two boys and two girls.

Late one night, Parks lay on his bed with his fourth child, his twelve month old son, laying on his chest sound asleep as Della snuggled in close.

"We wrote a new story to pass down through the ages, didn't we?" Parks asked, as he looked over at his loving wife.

"Not just a story," she replied gently, "we changed history. These are the things real legends are made of, and now we have a life with a promise attached."

She looked up at him, and smiled. They both realized there was no place they would rather be than where they were, that very moment.

Parks squeezed her tightly, and rubbed the angel-soft skin on his son's back. It was getting late, and he would be up before long to put his son in the crib, and check on the rest of the children before returning. He finally understood the price of feeling like this, and realized this was the life intended for all people. Any who were willing to face the darkest evil, and never give in. He fell gently to sleep, knowing the best was yet to come.

Meanwhile, far, far away, a young teenager bolted upright in bed, drenched in a cold sweat. Sitting there, frozen for a moment, she fought to get the thoughts out of her head as feelings of dread flooded her mind. Images of death, and the people she loved being torn apart rammed into her mind. The darkness closed in on her, and shadowy dark figures approached from the corners of the room.

She quickly turned on her desk lamp, and curled up, with the blankets clutched tight to her chest. Her courage returned, and she got out of bed. She walked across the room, pushing open the large heavy glass doors, and stood on the balcony overlooking the spacious beach below.

The warm ocean breeze felt good on her face as she listened to the waves washing in. Suddenly, she felt a white-hot heat as a blinding fireball shot across the night sky, illuminating the palm trees before crashing onto the sandy shoreline below.